NEVER DOUBT
I LOVE

PREVIOUS NOVELS BY PATRICIA VERYAN

NEVER DOUBT
I LOVE

Patricia Veryan

ST. MARTIN'S PRESS • NEW YORK

NEVER DOUBT I LOVE. Copyright © 1995 by Patricia Veryan. All rights reserved. Printed in the United States of America. No part of this book may be
used or reproduced in any manner whatsoever without written permission
except in the case of brief quotations embodied in critical articles or reviews.
For information, address St. Martin's Press, 175 Fifth Avenue, New York,
N.Y. 10010.

Design by Judith A. Stagnitto

Library of Congress Cataloging-in-Publication Data

Veryan, Patricia.
    Never doubt I love / Patricia Veryan.
        p.   cm.
    ISBN 0-312-11864-3
    I. Title
  PS3572.E766N48   1995
  813'.54—dc20   94-42079
                                                             CIP

First Edition: March 1995
10 9 8 7 6 5 4 3 2 1

Doubt thou the stars are fire;
Doubt that the sun doth move;
Doubt truth to be a liar;
But never doubt I love.
                    —William Shakespeare
                              Hamlet

PROLOGUE

he late afternoon sky was crowded with parading clouds, some wearing grey petticoats that promised rain before nightfall. A chill wind pranced along Pall Mall, tossing trees whose gowns were now more golden and russet than green. Ladies were obliged to restrain flying skirts, gentlemen to clutch at displaced tricornes, and chairmen swore as they threaded their way amongst carriages, waggons, horsemen, darting messenger boys and footmen, street vendors, and a scattering of scarlet-clad dragoons.

The Cocoa Tree coffee house was not crowded at this hour. If the company was thin, it was congenial, and talk and laughter hung pleasantly on the spiced air. Although daylight came but dimly through the mullioned windows, and as yet no candles had been lit, logs blazed and crackled on the deep hearth sending out a mellow glow that flickered on pewter mugs and immaculate china, and illumined the playbills, sketches, and caricatures that hung on the walls. The outer fringes of the large room were shadowed, and against that dimness some occupants, touched by the firelight, stood out in sharp relief; the earnest faces of three gentlemen locked in a political debate; the merriment of a group of young exquisites gleefully exchanging choice items of scandal; the tense expressions of a silent group seated about a gaming table.

The wall hangings fluttered wildly as a tall middle-aged man entered. He shut the door quickly and glanced about, then made his way to a quiet inglenook, where a somewhat portly gentleman a decade his senior was seated alone.

"Hello, Talbot," said the newcomer, a smile on his distinguished features. "You look to be pondering weighty matters. Should you prefer that I take myself off?"

Ramsey Talbot was a former Member of Parliament who had of late turned to the pen and was creating a small stir with his newspaper articles. He gave an inviting gesture and said heartily, "Not at all, Jonas. Pray join me. I'll be glad of your company. Heard you'd been reprieved from sailing off to Canton."

"Complications. Always complications. The Chinese do not want us, you know." Sir Jonas Holmesby handed his cloak to the serving maid who hurried to them, and ordered a tankard of ale for himself, and another glass of Madeira for Mr. Talbot.

Sharing the settle, he stretched his long legs to the fire and said with a grateful sigh, " 'Tis good to be out of the wind." After a closer scan of the company, he qualified his remark, saying regretfully that he might have to withdraw his patronage. "The house fairly swarms with Jacobite sympathizers."

Talbot nodded. "And gossip. 'Tis one of the best places I know to pick up snippets of information I'd never hear at White's or Brookse's."

"Aha! Nose to the grindstone once more, are you? And have your snippets been satisfactory?"

"After a fashion, perhaps." Talbot paused as the serving maid returned with their drinks, then went on, "There's some odd rumours going about, Jonas. You've likely heard them yourself. These street disturbances, for instance, and the growing public unrest."

Sir Jonas sampled his ale and shrugged. "There are always malcontents. I fancy 'twill all die down now the hot weather is past."

"Ah, but will it?" Bending a little closer, Talbot lowered his voice. "I heard a fantastical tale last week, holding that the riots are part of a seditious plot that involves shipping also. You find that amusing, I see. Then cast your mind back to all the fine ships that have been lost this past year alone. There's never been such a string of disasters."

Holmesby's smile faded, and he pointed out with a touch of acerbity, "Nor such heavy loss of life. There have been literally hundreds of innocent victims! 'Tis monstrous to suggest that civilized men would concoct so barbarous a plot! And for what possible purpose?"

Briefly, Talbot was silent. At length, as if reaching a decision, he responded, "The purpose, perhaps, of a malignant secret society; aristocrats all, intent on the eventual overthrow of our so much disliked Hanoverian monarch." He glanced up from under his brows, and said, "Now what d'ye think of that snippet?"

Sitting straighter, Sir Jonas answered with some force, "I think I would be extreme careful of accusing any well-born gentleman of treason!"

"Guy Fawkes was well born! Oliver Cromwell was well born! Derwentwater, and the Stuarts, and—"

"The *Stuarts*? Zounds! Have we not had enough of bloodshed and misery thanks to their vaunting ambitions? Must irresponsible gabblemongers stir up more tragedy?"

Mr. Talbot stiffened. "If you name me an irresponsible—"

"No, no! You know I do not, Ramsey! I know you for a fine patriot. But it distresses me that you listen to nonsense which contains, I'll wager, not a vestige of truth!"

"Mayhap. I don't yet have all the details. I do know there's a blasted lot of smoke. And where there's smoke . . ."

Dismayed, Sir Jonas half-whispered, *"Details?* You really *believe* it?"

"I think I did not say that. The thing is, there's a deal of it makes sense. The very fact that Whitehall pooh-poohs it causes my ears to perk up."

"But—surely you never mean to publish such stuff? 'Twould be purest folly! I beg you will not even consider it till you have proof."

"By which time it might be too late! No, listen another moment, Jonas. The tale goes that a group of blue-bloods is at work collecting great estates. If the estate is entailed and can-not be bought, they set about to disgrace and ruin the owner to the extent that the property is confiscated by the Crown and sold for debt. Whereupon, they acquire it."

"What stuff! 'Twould take a long-planned and elaborate scheme to achieve such a result! If for some reason a group of investors wants to buy large properties, there are plenty to be had without resorting to such lengths. And as for the shipping disasters, what would the loss of many great ships and their cargoes avail any sane man? Unless, of course, the passengers were all carefully selected enemies, which is even more fantas-tical!" Exasperated, Sir Jonas demanded, "Who has been fill-ing your ears with such rubbish?"

"I'll not tell you my source. But I understand there are some fine young fellows fighting this secret group, which is known, by the way, as the League of Jewelled Men."

Holmesby's lip curled. "Very melodramatic! Who are they?"

Frowning, Talbot said, "I've not such proof as enables me to toss names about. Suffice it to say they're rich and powerful. And deadly."

Suppressing a snort of derision with difficulty, Sir Jonas asked, "Then dare you name the 'fine young fellows' who oppose this—ah, deadly League?"

"In confidence, Jonas? I'll have your word."

Sir Jonas gestured impatiently. "Oh, as you wish. Lord knows, I'm not desirous of spreading such twaddle."

"Very well." Talbot glanced around, and leaned even closer. "Firstly, Gideon Rossiter. You'll mind he was sent home wounded from the Low Countries early this year?"

"Aye! And found his sire had brought financial ruin on half London by reason of his gross incompetence, and was for a time suspected of downright embezzlement!"

"Of which he was subsequently cleared! Pray keep your voice down, man! 'Twas young Rossiter first suspected the existence of the League. When the Horse Guards turned a deaf ear to his warnings, he gathered a small band of friends around him, and from all I hear they've engaged in some mighty desperate ploys to oppose the League."

"Have they! Rossiter, and . . . ?"

"Lieutenant James Morris, for one. He's related to Lord Kenneth Morris, of the Cornwall house. And there's Mr. Neville Falcon's son, August—"

"Zounds, what a combination to strike terror into the hearts of wrongdoers! The first, a cloth-headed ex-cavalryman who'd be easy to inveigle into any scheme, however ridiculous! The second, an acid-tongued half-breed who has publicly stated his loathing for the *haut ton*, well knowing that everyone in Town despises him! 'Fore God, Ramsey, you shall have to do better than that sorry trio!"

Flushed with irritation, Talbot snapped, "I make no doubt you will judge Viscount Horatio Glendenning, Captain Jonathan Armitage, and Gordon Chandler an equally worthless trio?"

Sir Jonas stared, then uttered a bark of laughter. "No doubt whatsoever! At worst Lord Glendenning offered his sword to Bonnie Prince Charlie in the late Rebellion, and at best is believed to have aided and abetted several fugitive Jacobite gentlemen to escape England! As for Captain Jonathan Armitage—why, the fellow is a damned scoundrel who was drunk in his cabin when his fine East Indiaman was wrecked with heavy loss of life, and—"

"Which he denies, and declares he was instead attacked and left for dead in a dastardly plot to scuttle his ship!"

"Yet he saw fit to disappear for two years, during which time he was involved in all kinds of skullduggery in Cornwall. His case has already been considered by two Boards of Enquiry, and may yet go to the High Court of the Admiralty. Certainly, 'tis far from settled, and though he walks free, many in Town favour a public hanging for the rogue! Who else was it? Ah, yes. Gordon Chandler. No, really, Talbot! The fellow's brother is a known Jacobite, and got out of England half a step ahead of a troop of dragoons! And was not Gordon Chandler himself recently suspected of involvement with a wrecking gang? Faugh! A pretty scoundrel!"

"If such were the case, yes. But the version I have is very different, and—Ah, never mind! I see 'tis hopeless, so we'll not argue further. Stay, though! What of Owen Furlong? As fine a fellow as ever I met, and with a splendid military record. D'you name him worthless, also?"

Sir Jonas' brows went up. "Is Furlong with 'em, then? I'll own, he's a good man. Although . . . Wasn't there something a few months after Culloden? Had to do with the escape of—cannot remember who, but some rebel or other. Another tarnished reputation, Ramsey."

Mr. Talbot shook his head ruefully. "The Lord protect me from government servants! I see why the efforts of Rossiter and his friends are ignored! You're a diplomat beyond question, Holmesby! Your mind is quite closed."

Affronted, Sir Jonas came to his feet. "I think I can see as far through a brick wall as the next man!" He turned to leave, hesitated, then turned back. "Ramsey, we've been friends too long to part in anger! Think, man! Your vaunted conspiracy is too far-fetched to be truth. No more than a vicious hoax, like as not; one of the dares silly young bucks get up to when they've nothing better to do with their time. They'll end by laughing at your gullibility, and you'll end in court on charges of slander that will ruin you! I *beg* you—have done with it!"

Talbot smiled and stood to take his friend's hand and grip it firmly. "You're a good fellow, Jonas, and I know you mean well. I'm sorry I couldn't convince you, but I thank you for your concern."

Holmesby sighed, and walked away.

Talbot called softly, "You'll not forget? You gave me your oath."

Without turning, Sir Jonas said, "I'll not forget."

A moment later a slight young man wearing the uniform of a Naval sub-lieutenant rose from a shadowed nearby table and strolled over to the inglenook.

Bowing, he said, "Have I the honour to address Mr. Ramsey Talbot? My name is Joel Skye, sir. I am presently an aide to Lord Hayes of the East India Company. I wonder if I might beg a moment of your time . . . ?"

CHAPTER I

rs. Garter is adventuring again." Zoe Grainger narrowed her clear green eyes and peered down the emerald sweep of hillside to where one sheep had drifted from the flock and was trotting purposefully down the slope and towards the River Windrush.

Aaron Bleckert glanced at the girl who sat on the stone wall beside him on this warm October afternoon, and his lined and leathery countenance twitched into what was almost a smile. "Now then, Miss Zoe," he said in his soft west country voice, "she be a fur piece off from we. How can ye be so assured 'tis Mrs. Garter? Ye'll never be saying as ye can see the band on her leg, or I'll know sure-ly as ye're at yer fancyings again."

Zoe's gaze sparkled at him briefly, then returned to the sheep. "You would be surprised by how far I can see, Aaron. But I do not have to see her garter to know 'tis her. She's the only one will go off alone like that. And how strange it is. Sheep always stay together. I wonder why she does it—and where she thinks she is going."

"Sheep doan't think, Miss. They got nothing in their heads but wool." Aaron knocked the tobacco from his clay pipe, then stuck it between his teeth again. "Most stupid creatures the Almighty ever made. Begging His pardon."

Miss Grainger's smooth brow puckered. "Then you had

best send Hops after her else she'll run right into the river."

The sheepdog lying beside them wagged his tail at the sound of his name, but did not turn his head.

"He's watching," said the old shepherd. "He'll go when he sees fit. Mayhap he knows how she likes to have her little escapes, and lets her go as fur as he allows."

The dog sprang up then, and, running with the swift but bouncing gait that had given him his name, was down the slope after the wanderer.

Zoe watched as the sheep was encircled and herded, protesting loudly, back to the safety of the flock.

"Poor thing," she said. "Thwarted again. I wonder if she longs to see far-away places, as my brother did."

"Aye." Aaron chuckled. "She be determined to get to The George in Burford, and take coach fer Lunon Town!"

"Silly creature! They'd never let her inside, and she'd fall off the roof, certainly." They laughed together at the picture this conjured up, then the girl went on, "But only think how narrow her world is, Aaron. There are so many lovely things to be seen. She knows nought of the rest of our countryside— Wychwood, for instance, and its great trees. Or the King's Men and the Whispering Knights—"

"She'd think them no more than old hunks of rock. As they do be," he put in prosaically.

"No, she wouldn't! I've told her all about the king who left his knights for a minute, and how they at once plotted treason and were turned to stone for their wickedness."

"And a waste of breath it were, Miss Zoe. Mrs. Garter bean't one for imaginings, like you do be, and she doan't listen. And if she did would know not a mite more at the end than at the start of it."

"Marplot," said Zoe merrily.

The old shepherd watched the sunlight awaken a shine on her tilted little nose, and strike coppery glints from her luxuriant auburn hair, and a sadness came into his rheumy eyes. "Ye love this west country," he observed.

"Of course I do." She threw her arms out, as if to embrace it. "I was born here. I hope 'twill never change. Do you think it will, Aaron?"

"Nay. Never. Allus were like this. Allus will be, I rackon. Ye'll be the one as changes, Miss Zoe. Ye'll be marrying soon, and going off wi' yer man, and having yer babes, and—"

"Pish! Who would marry me? Men want either a beautiful lady, or a rich one, and I have no fortune and a very ordinary face. And do not be telling raspers and saying I'm a beauty."

"I'll not." He said slowly, "But ye've beauty inside, Miss Zoe. A man with eyes can see it. Nor ye bean't plain, neither. Yer pa should've give ye a Season in Lunon Town so ye could—"

"And so he would have," she said, at once defensive of her father. "If—if Mama had lived." She pushed away the image of her new "Mama," with the tight little mouth, and the lovely eyes that darted malice, and said hurriedly, "The men are reaping the corn today. Do you smell it?" She put back her head and closed her eyes. "Delicious. I only wish . . ."

"What d'ye wish, Miss Zoe? To see Lunon Town, as ye should oughta?"

"No. I wish I were . . . a little more like one of the knights of old. Brave, and unfearing, even when facing mortal combat with great roaring dragons." She sighed. "I'm afraid I—"

"So this is where you vanished to! I might've known I'd find you here, instead of working at your 'broidery as you were told!"

Zoe jumped from the wall and turned a guilty face to the gentleman who came towards them.

Of no more than average height, Mr. Harvey Grainger was impressive in a superbly tailored blue velvet coat and a quilted blue and white waistcoat. There had been a time when he would have come across the meadows wearing a frieze riding coat, leathers, and top boots, instead of the satin knee breeches and high-heeled shoes that were so out of place in the country. And his thick hair would have been simply tied back, instead of having been cropped to accommodate the wig she knew he loathed. He was only one and fifty, and a handsome man still, but she thought, 'Poor darling. He looks so worn.'

"Oh, I could not stay indoors, Papa," she said, dancing over to seize his arm and beam up at him. " 'Tis such a perfect afternoon. And we'll not get many more, I doubt, now that autumn is busied at painting the trees, so I simply *had* to bring out my sketchbook! See there by the river—the poplars are gold already. And only mark how bronzed the beeches are, and that dear little maple looks so shy I vow 'tis blushing amid—"

"Yes, yes," said Mr. Grainger, whose patience was already strained. "Then you will have some sketches to show your mama, I trust?"

Zoe's lower lip jutted a trifle. She said in a very different voice, "My Mama is—" But she stopped short of saying "dead." The shepherd's wise eyes were on her and of what use to wound her father, who had sufficient reason to repent his folly?

"I'll be off, zur," said Aaron, rising and taking up his crook.

"What?" Mr. Grainger looked at the old man as if only now becoming aware of him, and he added with rather forced affability, "Oh. How do you go on, Bleckert?"

"So sharp and spry as ever was, thankee Mr. Grainger, sir. And sorry if I kept Miss Zoe from her drawings, grousing at her 'bout the hole in me thatch." He touched his brow with grave dignity and, having succeeded in turning his employer's thoughts, limped away, Hops at his side.

Looking after him, Grainger muttered, "Blast!" He found his daughter watching him, her little face unwontedly sober, and he flushed and said testily, "Well, there is no call to look at me as though I were an ogre! The old fellow's roof—er, slipped my mind, is all."

"Of course, Papa," she said loyally. " 'Faith, but I wonder you can order your thoughts any more with all Mrs. Mowbray's children clamouring and squabbling and racing about as they do!"

Grainger stifled a sigh. They did clamour. Indeed, they were the most noisy and quarrelsome brats he'd ever seen. The quiet old house was quiet no longer, and, as his bride said, not nearly large enough. If he'd but known— He blocked off such useless repining. "The lady's name is Mrs. *Grainger*," he reminded. "And you should show her more respect, Zoe. I know you loved your mama—as did I—but I was very—er, lonely after she went to her reward. And—and Mrs. Mow—I mean, Irene, is most solicitous and devoted."

He saw his daughter's mouth opening, and went on hastily, "But never mind that. You must come up to the house now. There is a lady arrived to offer you a great opportunity, and you will want to change your gown and—and do something with your hair. Really, child 'tis unseemly to be rushing about like any country wench, perching on walls, and with no cap on your head! You are a young lady now. Indeed, many girls have one or two children by the age of nineteen. Besides, 'tis past time for you to—to see some more of—er, the world . . ."

Gathering her sketchbook and crayons, Zoe was silent, and suddenly she was also cold, and very fearful.

Such a splendid thing for the gel, my lady," simpered Mrs. Irene Grainger, her most ingratiating smile pinned to her lips as she poured another cup of tea for her illustrious guest. "So good of you to even consider her. I would have taken her to

Town myself long since but," she fluttered her lashes coyly, "I am newly wed, you know, and 'tis hard to break away."

Lady Clara Buttershaw, tall, gaunt, and harsh featured, was perfectly aware that the second Mrs. Grainger had "broken away" to London several times since her marriage, always accompanied by her own two eldest daughters. It went against the grain not to give this silly upstart the set-down she deserved, but my lady controlled her natural impulses, and said, "To say truth, Mrs. Grainger, I have been unable to find a companion for my poor sister. Not a companion who—*suits*, if you take my meaning. We are, as all London knows, of most distinguished lineage. Indeed, I doubt it could be surpassed—or even equalled throughout the realm. When one is well born one is bred up to standards quite beyond the understanding of less-favoured persons. I insist that those standards be maintained in all our establishments. When we met in Bath last month, and you mentioned your rather cramped quarters here, and the fact that your step-daughter would benefit from some Town—er, polish, why it seemed to offer the ideal solution for both of us." She frowned as the sound of a male voice upraised in anger could be heard. "On the other hand," she added, a glint coming into her hard dark eyes, "if Miss Grainger is for some incomprehensible reason reluctant to accept of my generous offer . . ."

Mrs. Grainger practically gabbled assurances that Zoe was "fairly twittering" with eagerness. "She longs to visit the Metropolis, as all girls do, and she is besides, the very kindest creature," she went on, desperate not to lose this opportunity to be rid of the wretched girl. "She is not without accomplishments, ma'am, for she has been properly bred up. She knows her globes, plays the harpsichord adequately, sketches quite well, and has a rare eye for beauty. Though," she shook her pretty head sadly, "I must own it, she is far from being a beauty herself."

"We cannot all be Toasts," my lady allowed. "I well remember my dear Mama warning me in my salad days that I must have compassion for those to whom beauty was denied. For I do not scruple to tell you that I was quite the rage of London. As you will have heard, I am assured."

Transfixed by a challenging stare, Mrs. Grainger had to restrain the impulse to shriek with laughter. She thought, 'Why, you hatchet-faced old crow! The only rage associated with you was—and is—your horrid bad temper!' But she smiled admiringly, and lied, "I have indeed heard of how you took London, and Paris I believe, by storm. My step-daughter will have much to learn from you, dear ma'am. And she is very quick, I promise you, so—"

Lady Buttershaw looked displeased, and her bony hand shot up in an autocratic demand for silence. "You do not say that she is *clever*, I trust? I cannot abide clever gels!"

Mrs. Grainger laughed merrily, saw disapproval on the austere countenance of her guest, and at once strangled the laugh. Zoe was far from clever, she declared. Indeed, she was quite stupid, for she had rejected several unexceptionable suitors. "Still, she is amiable enough and will, I am very sure, be deeply appreciative of the honour you do her, *dear* Lady Buttershaw!"

This opinion was not shared by her spouse, who at that moment was on the verge of losing his temper with his far-from-appreciative daughter. "Of course I love you," he reiterated, pacing nervously about Zoe's bedchamber. "Have I not said it? 'Tis *because* I care so much for—for your well-being that I have accepted Lady Buttershaw's very kind offer."

"A very kind offer to obtain an unpaid servant," argued Zoe, trying desperately not to cry. "You know how much I love you, Papa, and—and my home. You never minded in days past that I had not found a gentleman I cared for. You used to say you needed me here after dearest Mama went to her reward. But now, because that—that woman wants me gone, you have let her six nasty children come and turn out your own—"

"That—will—do!" Scourged by these home truths, Harvey Grainger took refuge in anger. "You have resented Irene since first we met. I know you were deeply attached to your mama, and I have tried to make allowances for your jealousy and—er, and sullenness. But it cannot continue. Irene is my wife now, and—and no house can have two mistresses."

Zoe wrung her hands, and pleaded, "But it is not true, Papa! You know I never have interfered with her changes—no matter how silly they were! I never have been rude or said one word, even when her ill-behaved brats were—"

"You have usurped her authority at every turn! The servants resent her for your sake. And if 'tis true that you say nothing, your manner, your very silence is—is a criticism, and she feels it, for she is sensitive and highly strung."

"But—dearest Papa, I—"

The tears that trembled on her lashes, the pleading in her green eyes were upsetting Mr. Grainger. Besides which, he was finding it hard to remember all the other accusations Irene had listed with such martyred pathos. He interposed with the force of desperation, "No, never argue, Zoe. You do but make it more difficult for both of us. I have kept you cooped up here much too long, when you should have been in Town learning to behave as a young lady of quality. And only look at the result! All your friends are wed and setting up their nurseries, while you moon over silly novels, and likely believe such romantic adventures really happen. Which I can assure you they do not! And even if they do," he added, weakening his position, "you'll not find them while you hobnob with farm hands and village people, or go riding in the rain and come home, as you did last week, looking like a drowned rat!"

"I suppose Mrs. Mowbray said that!" inserted Zoe rebelliously. "I doubt she could mount a horse even were three strong men to lift—"

"When I found you with old Bleckert this afternoon," her father over-rode, raising his voice, "you looked more like a common dairymaid than Miss Grainger of Travisford! Irene says— I mean— Oh, I'll not wrap it in clean linen—if you are unwed 'tis because no gentleman worth the name wants a madcap and unbridled country bumpkin for a bride!"

That barb went home painfully, and it was all Zoe could do to plead, "Then if you must be—be rid of me, let me go to live with Aunt Minerva, Papa! I do not know Lady Buttershaw, nor her sister. At least let me stay with my own family, I beg you!"

This had, in fact, been Mr. Grainger's intention. His Irene had been quick to point out, however, that if Zoe moved into her aunt's country home so soon after her papa's remarriage, people were bound to think she had been made to feel unwanted, and would likely blame the new bride for that circumstance. On the other hand, to be invited to stay at the Town residence of so proud a pair as Lady Clara Buttershaw and Lady Julia Yerville, the daughters of an earl, would be judged a notable achievement.

"The decision has been made," he said with finality. "There is nothing more to be said, save Godspeed, and—and take care little . . . Zoe . . ."

She stretched out her arms. Tears streaked down, and her ruddy lips quivered pathetically.

Mr. Grainger really was very fond of her. He hugged her briefly, and fled, pausing in the passage to tear off his wig and mop his perspiring head.

The portmanteau, the band boxes, and the valises stood in a neat row beside the door. Sitting on the bed, staring at them numbly, Zoe heard wheels on the drivepath. She went to the window and looked down at the great coach and the four matched chestnuts who snorted and stamped and fidgeted, eager to be gone.

She was not eager to be gone. She felt lost and betrayed, and scarcely able to comprehend that her world had fallen apart so swiftly. Papa could not really be pushing her away from him, away from the only home she had ever known. Surely, he *could* not? But it was not his doing, of course.

"Oh, Travis," she whispered miserably. "If only you were here!"

If her brother had been at home, the pretty widow who had flung herself so blatantly at Harvey Grainger would never have succeeded in ousting his daughter from her home. Not for an instant would dearest Travis have stood by and let Papa be manoeuvred into such unkindness. But three years had passed since Travis had come down from Oxford, and within the month, full of pride and enthusiasm, had embarked on a promising career in the Diplomatic Service. Now, he was five and twenty, and in India, thousands of miles from Burford, wherefore Mrs. Mowbray had swept to victory, unchecked. There was little doubt that Lady Buttershaw's offer had come as a surprise to her. But a lovely surprise. Her unwanted step-daughter was to be packed off to her "glorious opportunity," and the new Mrs. Grainger would be able to rule Travisford without—

A knock at the door announced that the servants had come for her luggage.

Blinking away tears of despair, Zoe let them in, and followed them forlornly down the stairs.

Affection and respect for one's parents is commendable," acknowledged Lady Clara Buttershaw, her eyes fixed on the scene beyond the windows of the great carriage. "But I trust you do not mean to snivel all the way to London."

Since my lady's skirts took up the entire seat, Zoe had of necessity to sit facing her. She had hoped she was concealing her grief, but although those hard dark eyes had not once appeared to glance her way, a furtive dab at her tears had evidently been noted.

Lady Buttershaw's head, ridiculous with its high powdered wig and the wide-brimmed hat perched *á la bergere* atop it, turned to her. "I require a response when I address you," she declared awfully.

"I am t-trying not to be a watering pot, ma'am," responded Zoe, as steadily as she could manage. "But I had no notion this—this morning that I was to be ordered to leave my papa and—and Travisford, so—soon."

"In which case your step-mama has more brains than I had credited her with. Change is the more difficult when one has time to brood upon it. What is done, is done, and you will do better to stop such foolish repining and turn your mind to your great good fortune. The chances of a plain young female such as yourself achieving a respectable match while dwelling in the wilds of nowhere are, I may tell you, exceeding remote."

"I have no desire to—"

"Be—silent—miss!" Lady Buttershaw's harsh bray drowned the pounding of the horses' hooves and the creaking of the swaying coach. "You may speak when I have finished. And not before!"

Intimidated as always by a display of anger, Zoe shrank.

"That is better. Now, as I was about to say before I was so rudely interrupted—in coming to me, you will reside in one of the most admired mansions in London Town. It is, I must own, a new structure. Our family home was destroyed by fire twenty years ago. The Earl, my father, was an enlightened man. He saw the advantages of establishing a fashionable and select area away from the common herd. Others followed his example, of course, for Yervilles have ever led the way. I myself am a leader of *le haut ton*. I assume you know what that means. Whereby I shall select a suitable mate for you. With your lack of fortune, looks, height, and grace, 'twill tax my ingenuity, but I shall rise to the challenge. We will cross that bridge when we come to it, however. Our first task must be the matter of your unfortunate wardrobe. I refuse to have anyone dwelling in my house whose garments run the gamut of fashion—from bad to worse!" My lady folded her fan and rapped Zoe smartly across the knuckles. "You may now speak."

"Thank you, ma'am. But—"

"So I should think. Now—in return for the education you will receive in such vital areas as good taste, deportment, and social etiquette, you will act as a companion to my spinster sister. Let me tell you that you will not find your duties onerous. Lady Julia Yerville was severely burned in the fire I told you of, and has been a semi-invalid ever since. She is a gentle creature and will likely ask very little of you. Were I not so popular and in constant demand for Society events, I would provide all the companionship she requires." My lady pursed her lips and considered for a moment, while Zoe watched her in growing fascination. "No. I shall be honest," the *grande dame* continued. "For in all things I am honest. I myself possess a very high level of intelligence. You have doubtless already remarked it. On the other hand, my sister's powers of understanding are not anything out of the way. It is a strain upon me to converse with her for any length of time. Do not mistake me. Lady Julia is of superior stock, as are all the Yervilles, and before the fire she was considered exceeding beautiful. She was, in fact, about to make a splendid marriage, but— Well, that has nothing to say to the case. It is good that the poor creature has her interests. I myself find them childish, but you will likely be able to enter into them without too much difficulty. If you wish to comment, you may do so."

Zoe blinked, and decided that whatever else, life at Yerville

Hall would have its amusing side. "I was wondering, Lady Buttershaw, if the doctors cannot help your poor sister. Medicine has made great advances in this modern age, and—"

"Doctors," said my lady without equivocation, "are unscrupulous charlatans who charge outrageous fees for the privilege of practicing upon their unfortunate patients while they live, and have lately taken to cutting them up when they die from such practicing! It would surprise me not in the least to discover that in many cases they cut people up *before* they are deceased! I myself enjoy excellent health, doubtless because I have never permitted a physician to lay his hands upon my person. 'Faith, but I would as soon admit a wild boar to one of my musicales as to allow such a quack to cross the threshold! I see that your face bears an incredulous expression. Do you perhaps doubt the veracity of what I have said?"

Pierced by a militant glare, Zoe stammered, "No, no, 'Tis just that—well, I know Papa would become vexed with old Dr. Edgeware when he would insist that port wine was injurious, but he is such a gentle man. I cannot think he would cut people up."

"That is because your horizons are small and your thoughts ill-formed. You may believe *whatever* I tell you. All doctors are half-mad and will stop at nothing to exercise their knives. I have heard tales from sensible men that even I could scarce credit. Only last month a retired general of my acquaintance told me that he encountered a physician leaving the hospital late one night, with a long parcel under his arm. When the general enquired what the young fellow carried, he had the effrontery to admit that he had chanced to cut off the wrong leg of one of his patients, but that it was just as well because he could now take it home and use it to determine how toenails grow!"

"Good . . . heavens . . . !" gasped Zoe.

"Just so. Now, you will suppose, since you have no experience, that I mean to reach London tonight. Not so. I never undertake a journey that will leave me fatigued. We shall over-night at High Wycombe, which is in the valley of the Wye. It is a fairish town of great antiquity and is mentioned in the *Domesday Book*. I would not be surprised if some of my ances-tors stayed there at that time. In ancient days it was a Roman camp. I tell you these things to elevate your mind, for although it does not do for a lady to be *clever*, neither must she appear a stupid . . . In point of fact . . ."

On and on she went.

'Goodness me,' thought Zoe. 'I wonder whatever the sister will be like!'

The Three Horse Inn was a charming old Tudor establish-ment advantageously located on the Oxford-to-London road some distance northwest of High Wycombe. When the car-riage rumbled into the cobbled yard Zoe was surprised to find that they were expected. A footman hurried to escort them in-side. The host bowed himself double and assured Lady Butter-shaw that her own sheets were already upon the beds, and that Miss Grainger had been allocated the adjoining chamber. "Her woman," he added, "is waiting for her. If you will be so good as to come this way, my lady."

Astonished, Zoe accompanied Lady Buttershaw up the stairs. "How very kind in you, ma'am, to have re-hired Daisy for me. When my step-mama turned her off—"

"I am acquainted with no one called Daisy. These stairs are atrocious. You should have a more modern flight put in, host. I would not be surprised but that you are infested with wood-worms. I shall leave you the name of an excellent architect."

By the time the host, apparently acquainted with her lady-ship, had murmured his thanks, they had reached the first floor. Following him along the narrow passage, Zoe said, "But, ma'am, there is no need to impose upon your woman. I can manage my own toilette, and—"

" 'Tis painfully obvious that you can do no such thing," retorted my lady, her withering glance sweeping Zoe from head to toe. "Nor have I the slightest intention of requiring either my abigail or my dresser to assist you. There are far too many maids frippering away their time at Yerville Hall. I have promoted one to your service. She is not superior, but she has been well trained and knows what is expected of my servants. Here is my room. I shall rest now and do not require to see you again until a quarter to eight o'clock, at which time you may scratch upon my door."

The wide-brimmed hat nodded dismissal, and with a hushing of her satin skirts my lady sailed through the door the host threw open for her. Zoe heard a female voice enquiring solicitously after madam's venture into the wilds, and the host closed the door upon Lady Buttershaw's tersely uttered, "Just as I thought. Crude and primitive!"

The next door was flung open. As Zoe passed inside the host's eyes twinkled at her with amused understanding, and she smiled appreciatively. The chamber was small but cosy, immaculately clean, and with a fine four-poster bed.

A tall, severe-looking woman rose from the window seat where she'd been sewing, and came to make her curtsy. "Good evening, Miss Grainger," she said in frosty and affectedly precise accents. "Ay am Gorton."

Zoe's heart sank, but she said brightly, "Then you are my abigail. How nice that will be."

Eyes of a chill blue slid over her. A faintly aghast look dawned.

Zoe sighed. "Oh dear. Am I quite hopeless, Gorton? I am from the country, you know. This is my best travelling gown. I had thought it would be perfectly suitable for London."

"Never mind, Miss," said Gorton, repressing a shudder. "Ay feel sure we can—ah, improve matters."

An hour later, Zoe was forced to acknowledge the truth of that statement. Her gown had been removed and whisked away. Her hair had been brushed until her scalp tingled, then arranged into soft curls. Her corsets had been laced so tightly that for several seconds she had been unable to draw a breath. An excitingly fashionable gown of pale peach ribbed silk had been slipped over her hoops. The stomacher had looked so tiny that she'd been quite sure it would never encompass her, but under Gorton's ruthless assault it was secured at last. Surveying herself in the mirror while a dainty ruffled cap was placed on her shining hair, she could scarcely believe that the elegant young creature in the glass was Zoe Grainger, and when a simple gold chain and locket were added, she exclaimed an involuntary, "Oh, my! How nice I look! Thank you, Gorton!"

Meeting her abigail's glance in the mirror, she thought for a moment to glimpse a softening in the pale blue eyes, but the voice was as cool and detached as ever. "Ay tray to please, Miss."

It wanted fifteen minutes until seven o'clock, and Zoe was too restless to be confined to the small room for over an hour. She asked Gorton to find an appropriate shawl, and said she would take a stroll in the gardens.

The abigail turned a surprised countenance. "*Outside*, Miss?"

"Of course. The air will be cool now, I fancy."

"But—but 'tis getting *dark*, Miss Grainger! And we are in the wilds! It is not *seemly*!"

Zoe stared at her. "But that is silly! We are still in England and not lost in some snake-infested jungle. The shawl, if you please!"

There was a touch of hauteur in the young face, and authority in the firm tones. Elsie Gorton realized that her new lady might be the "poor little lass" she'd mentally dubbed her, but she was not entirely lacking in spirit. Which would, she thought, be interesting.

She opened the valise in which Zoe had packed the articles likely to be needed for the journey, and took out a white crocheted shawl exquisitely embroidered in pastel shades. Slipping it about Zoe's shoulders, she said admiringly that it was "Very nace. Was it you as done the 'broidery, Miss?"

'The accent slipped,' thought Zoe. "No. I am not clever with my needle. The shawl was a gift from my . . . Mama." The reminder of her beautiful and so terribly missed mother brought home all the ills of her present situation, and she hurried into the passage. It was remarkable that for a little while she should have almost forgotten that she had been banished from the home where she had lived all her life, and that Papa had carelessly fobbed her off on the odious Lady Clara Buttershaw.

She started down the winding staircase, and reflected that despite her odiousity it was extreme generous of Lady Buttershaw to provide her with new gowns. Pausing, she tapped her fan against her chin and her brows wrinkled. Odiousity. That didn't sound right. Odious-ness . . . ?

A discreet cough awoke her from her introspection. The stairs were narrow and her paniers wide. A gentleman waited at the foot, watching her enquiringly. She summed him up swiftly. Tall; lean; older—early thirties probably, but good-looking and well set-up with a fine pair of shoulders. His own hair, powdered; light complexion. Eyes: a warm blue holding a tentative smile, and with little lines at the corners, as though he had spent much time under a hot sun. 'Military' she thought. 'Or Navy, perchance.' And, liking him instinctively, she gave him her own sunny smile and hurried down.

"I do apologize, sir. I was lost in thought, you see."

Amused by this artless and most improper confidence, he

said in a lazy good-natured voice, "So you were. You appeared to be trying to recall something or other. Am I right, ma'am?"

"I was wondering," she replied, "which is correct. Is the word 'odiousness'? Or 'odiousity'?"

The smile spread from his eyes to his well-shaped mouth. He said gravely, "They both are charming. All things considered. But I rather suspect are not—ah, widely used. Might you perhaps substitute—'disagreeable'?"

Zoe pursed her lips and considered. "It has not quite the same force, do you think? And—what about the 'ness'?"

"Ah. Well, the 'ness' would make it into a noun, of course."

"Can one?"

"But with perfect propriety, ma'am."

"Then why can I not have 'odiousness'?"

The smile became a soft chuckle. "Heaven forbid I should deprive you of it. And you are quite correct. 'Odiousness' does indeed have more force."

"Miss!" Gorton hurried down the stairs, wrapped in a cloak and regarding Zoe in horror.

"Oh dear." The gentleman stood aside as Gorton passed, her outraged eyes accusing him. Bowing politely, he said to Zoe, "I am delighted to have met you again, ma'am. Pray remember me to your family."

Zoe promised to do so, and as she passed, he added *sotto voce*, "But—no odiousity, I beg."

She giggled.

Bustling along beside her, Gorton hissed, "Miss *Grainger*! To speak to a strange gentleman! And all alone! Most *improper*! May lady would think it—*fast*!"

"But—he was not strange. You heard him ask to be remembered to my family."

"We must tell may lady, Miss! And may lady will wish to have the gentleman's name, Ay am very sure!"

"Then my lady must be disappointed, for to say truth, I cannot recall it. I am dreadfully forgetful, you see. Are you going out?"

"Ay am accompanying you, Miss."

"Whatever for? I am unlikely to get lost in the gardens."

" 'Tis not *convenable* for a young lady to wander about without her footman, or a maid, Miss. Especially, a young and most attractive spinster lady of Quality!"

"Is it?" Zoe walked on again, then asked thoughtfully, "Do you say that whilst I am in London I must take you everywhere I go?"

"Unless Lady Clara or Lady Julia assigns a personal footman to you, Miss. Yes."

"How tiresome. But we are not in London now. And I particularly desire to be alone for a little while."

Gorton's shoulders rustled under her cloak, for all the world as though she had been a large bird ruffling her feathers. "In that case," she said with determination, "Ay shall follow at a discreet but proper distance, Miss Grainger."

Zoe sighed and, capitulating, passed through the open door and into the gardens.

Chapter 11

oe was pleased to find that the gardens behind the Three Horse Inn were quite extensive. In addition to a neatly scythed lawn there was a large flower garden with well-kept paths meandering among the various beds in which chrysanthemums were out-blooming some rather leggy late roses. An area for vegetables was separated from the main gardens by high hedges, and the rear of the property was taken up by a sizeable orchard.

Autumn was shortening the days; the sun had already gone down, and dusk was deepening to evening. The air was still fairly warm however, and carried upon it the smell of cooking and the tangy aroma of woodsmoke. Several other guests were enjoying a stroll before dinner. Zoe encountered a gentleman and two older ladies who nodded politely as they passed; a lady walked hand in hand with a small shy-eyed boy, and the bantering voices of several gentlemen could be heard beyond the hedges that screened the vegetable gardens.

Zoe wandered aimlessly, wondering what Papa might be thinking at this moment, if he was able to think at all. Mrs. Mowbray's children were wildly undisciplined, and although the two smaller ones would be in the nursery at this hour, the other four would be quarrelling and crashing about the house until eight o'clock. Poor Papa. How he would enjoy the peace and privacy of this quiet stroll instead of—

From the vegetable gardens there came a louder outburst of shouts and hilarity. Zoe drew back uneasily, which was fortunate, because something hurtled over the hedge, barely missing her before it thumped to the ground.

An indignant male voice was raised. "No, really, that is too bad of you, Templeby! You had no business to interfere with it!"

Glancing down at the object that had been "interfered with," Zoe uttered a shriek of horror. A human foot lay before her, the severed area above the ankle hideously gory and jagged. She felt faint, and heard again my lady's voice telling of evil surgeons and carelessly mistaken amputations. Sickened, she was grateful for the arm that steadied her as Gorton rushed to her aid, only to herself emit an even more piercing shriek.

There was a male chorus of muffled groans and exclamations.

"Oh—Egad! Women!"

"Now see what you've done!"

"I'm off! Go and make your excuses, Perry!"

"No you don't you villain! Hey! Come back! *You* threw it! *You* go and make things right! Blast the traitor—he's gone! Jamie—will you . . . ?"

Someone was pushing his way through a break in the hedge. Another man vaulted over a lower spot, almost colliding with Gorton, who informed him roundly that he was a callous viper and should be ashamed of himself.

The newcomer snatched up the foot and declared with shrinking nervousness that he and his friends were most sorry, and had no thought to have alarmed anyone. He was somewhere in the mid-twenties Zoe judged, with powdered hair, an open, boyish face, and freckles that were apparent even in the fading light. "I do promise you, ma'am," he stammered, "that we'd no idea ladies were—er, nearby, else—"

His agitated gesture had allowed her a brief but clearer view of the foot. Revolted, she thought, 'He has painted the *toenails!*' and she interrupted shrilly. "Oh! How *could* you be so grossly unfeeling?"

Gorton's view was also improved, and she let out a most ungenteel, "Fer shame! *Monsters* is what you is! Both on yer!"

The freckle-faced man gave a gasp of mortification and whipped the foot behind his back. A second individual emerged from the hedge, only to stumble and almost fall, so that his friend was obliged to steady him.

Zoe was sickened, but when inspired by a Cause, her usual timidity was forgotten, and she persisted, if rather unsteadily, "You are b-both intoxicated, is what it is! Disgraceful! I have heard t-tell of the atrocities perpetrated by your kind upon your hapless victims—"

"We are *not* intoxicated!" The defendant was about the same age as his freckled companion, but taller and more slenderly built, with dark, unpowdered hair, and a lean well-featured but stormy countenance. His brows had drawn down sharply at Zoe's words, and, still clinging to his companion, he protested indignantly, "And why you must gabble about atrocities, when all we did was—"

"Nothing, in your eyes, I collect," said Zoe. "I did not at first believe what I was told about you and your—your ilk! But I see that my informant was quite correct when she named you as heartless, depraved, and with not an ounce of feeling for the misery of those poor souls who come to you for help! I wonder—"

"I ain't surprised," the dark man interjected angrily. "I wonder too, don't you, Jamie? I wonder what the—I wonder what you have 'twixt your ears, madam, and would earnestly recommend that you change your ways! If you keep on rushing about the countryside accusing people of atrocities and—and ilks and what-have-you, some right-thinking citizens are going to have you clapped up! Were I you, I would get to bed with a calming powder!"

Throughout this inflamed monologue his companion had been plucking at his sleeve and mumbling nervously. Now, he begged in great agitation that "Terry" not raise his voice to the poor lady.

"Words will not harm me, sir," Zoe declared loftily. " 'Tis his knife that strikes terror in my heart. How many deluded innocents have you turned it on, I wonder, you—you black-hearted villain!"

At this, the dark gentleman's jaw dropped and he gawked at her.

Gorton pulled at her arm and entreated her to come away "before the evil creature turns his knife on *us*, ma'am!"

"God . . . bless . . . my . . . soul!" gasped the gentleman in powder.

"You're stark . . . raving mad," said his dark friend un-equivocally.

"Whatever I may be, sir," called Zoe as Gorton all but dragged her away, "at least I am not an intoxicated *physician!*"

He lurched forward, and with an alarmed squeal, Gorton tugged her into a trot.

"Did you see?" gasped Zoe. "Did you see the—the *toe-nails?*"

"I did fer—for sure, Miss," said Gorton, a shudder in her voice. "He had—he had *painted* em! And each one a different colour! It's downright *heathen!* I vow, Miss Grainger, we are lucky to have escaped with our very lives!"

They had by this time reached the rear door of the inn, and as Gorton swung it open a sudden outburst of masculine hilarity from the two "heathens" spurred them into a rush for indoors and safety.

Her heart thundering with fright and indignation, Zoe

said, "I shall call for a constable! Those wicked men must be taken in charge!"

Gorton was recovering her wits and her accent, and self-preservation asserted itself. She said shakily, "Ay beg you will not, Miss. May lady would be very cross and say 'tis may fault for allowing of you to venture into the poisonous night air."

Realizing that she herself would very likely incur my lady's wrath, Zoe reluctantly agreed not to report the criminals. She instead ordered that tea be sent to her room, and, dismissing Gorton's uneasy predictions that "may lady" would not be pleased, prevailed upon her new abigail to share it with her. Two considerably shaken women sipped tea and discussed the Savage Incident, and by the time Zoe went to scratch at my lady's door many of the constraints between her and her new abigail had disappeared.

Lady Buttershaw enjoyed her table, and the host knew better than to set anything but a most excellent supper before her. Zoe scarcely noticed what she ate, however. Her sadly changed circumstances, and my lady's loud and boring monologue concerning the *Domesday Book*, were overshadowed by the shiversome horrors of the amputated foot. As a result, her appetite was considerably impaired, which brought down upon her a severe reproof.

"Mine is a most amiable disposition," asserted Lady Clara with questionable accuracy, "and few things offered me. Even so, to peck at fine food when it is generously bestowed I judge both stupid and ungrateful. You would do well, Miss Grainger, to consider the many people in the world who are starving. Doubtless by reason of their own slothful ways, for there is work for all those willing to exert themselves." She paused, having momentarily lost her train of thought. Zoe started to respond, but was waved to silence, and her ladyship made a recover and swept on. "I will excuse your die-away airs this evening, on grounds of missing your family—though what there is to miss escapes me! However, when we reach Yerville Hall I shall expect you to mend your ways. You may now speak."

"I apologize," said Zoe, and deciding to confide in her "benefactor" added, "To say truth, I had a most upsetting experience while walking in the gardens, and—"

"There is much to be said for walking. I myself walk quite often in Hyde Park, which is situated conveniently close to my home. The neighborhood is of the first stare, though the other mansions do not compare to Yerville Hall, of course. Still, you will find yourself in the most fashionable of the new areas, and among the best people, for which you may be grateful. Not that I approve of new things, you understand. Indeed, my sister and I prize the things of antiquity. In especial, we are proud of our lineage. You are aware that our late Papa was a belted earl. I daresay you will be held spellbound for days together when you see the historical artifacts which Lady Julia Yerville has assembled. I will spare the time to give you some preliminary instruction on our family background." Lady Buttershaw cleared her throat, tucked in her chin, and was off again. "The first Yerville of whom we have certain knowledge was Montague de Yervillaunus, who came from Gaul with the Phoenicians to trade for tin in Cornwall; the time being about fifty years before Our Saviour was born. Montague was a great friend of Julius Caesar, and later became involved with the Druids. I should not be surprised if he was able to instruct the savages in the erection of Stonehenge. His eldest son . . ."

'I wonder,' thought Zoe, letting the "preliminary instruction" sweep past her ears, 'if there is a word of truth in all her nonsense.' The beady eyes were boring at her, and she smiled sweetly and nodded as though enraptured. It was a great pity she had not obtained the full names of the monsters in the garden. She could have reported them to the constable. There had been three of them, evidently. The one called Templeby she'd not seen, because he had run off like a coward. The gentleman in powder, whose name appeared to have been James, had referred to his foul-tempered friend as Terry—or might it have been Perry? Not much to go on, but if she ever saw either of the rogues again, she was quite sure she would know them.

After such a crowded and emotional day she was very tired, but she passed a restless night. As they tend to do, the hours of darkness deepened her grief and loneliness, and the future loomed grimly forbidding, so that her pillow was wet with tears when she at length fell into a deep sleep.

The morning dawned cold and overcast. A chill wind scattered the falling leaves, and the trees were beginning to acquire a threadbare look. Gorton's "refined" accent was not quite as pronounced when she assisted Miss Grainger with her toilette, but at a suggestion that she be called a less formal "Miss Zoe," the tall woman all but threw up her hands in horror. "May lady," said she, "would judge such a form of address to be an impertinent familiarity."

Zoe stifled a sigh. "Is Lady Julia Yerville of a—a similar disposition to her sister?"

Gorton hesitated, then answered carefully, "Lady Yerville does not enjoy robust health. She has a—er, very gentle manner."

"Oh." Brightening, Zoe smiled at her handmaiden.

Gorton's severe face relaxed into a grin. "Just so, Miss."

Fully prepared to be instructed as to the merits of porridge over bacon and eggs, Zoe went down to the dining room. My lady did not appear, however, and the host's wife, a stout and bright-eyed little person, conducted Zoe to a small table near to the window, "where Miss can look out at the gardens."

Zoe rather hoped that the charming gentleman she'd encountered on the stairs yesterday would come in, but the only other occupant of the room was an elderly clergyman who blinked near-sightedly in her direction, nodded his head, and retreated behind a copy of *The Spectator*. She did not want for company, however. The serving maid was of a friendly disposition, and Zoe's admiring remark about the gardens opened the floodgates. In no time both the maid and the host's lady were chatting with their guest. The minutes slipped away amid a flurry of talk and laughter and there was no time for pining or loneliness.

She felt quite cheerful as she climbed the stairs once more, but it soon became evident that Lady Buttershaw was vexed. Her stentorian tones reverberated along the upper hall, and Zoe paused, shrinking from an angry scene.

Gorton sounded tearful. "But, may lady, it was may understanding—"

"*Understanding?* It appears to me my good woman that your *understanding* is inferior! Which is quite contrary to what I was informed by my butler. Indeed, I shall have to advise him of my displeasure."

"Oh, may lady, never be cross with Mr. Arbour! Ay—"

"I shall be cross with whomsoever I please! Nor do I need instructions as to my dealings with servants! A pretty presumption, I declare! If you were so concerned for his position in my household I would think you might have followed my orders! I believe my voice is clear and my enunciation precise. Further, my instructions to you were couched in simple terms such as I felt not beyond your powers of comprehension. My nature is generous, however, and I will repeat them now and allow you to make one last effort to take them into your brain. Miss Grainger is *country bred* and does not know how to go on in Town. She is to be *never* out of your sight! If that is too complicated for your *understanding*, Gorton, you had best own to it at once, so that I can make other arrangements."

Quailing, Zoe tried to gather her courage. She had stood up to those two villains yesterday evening. Why must she be so much more afraid of this big, bullying woman? Because she was a coward, of course! And Lady Clara Buttershaw frightened everyone. But poor Gorton *needed* her! She took a deep breath, clenched her hands, and made her feet step forward. A maid carrying a pile of sheets scurried past, slanting a scared glance at her. Zoe opened the door.

Lady Buttershaw, her gaunt features flushed and her little eyes glaring, stood in the centre of the bedchamber. Wringing her hands, Gorton quailed before her.

Zoe's tongue seemed to freeze to the roof of her mouth. Travis always said she had an over-active imagination. She would use it, and fancy herself a warrior lady, like Queen Maud or Boadicea. She was surprised by the steadiness of her voice when she enquired, "Is something amiss, my lady?"

Lady Buttershaw spun around, but was for a moment rigidly still, as one battling conflicting emotions. She then said in a controlled but grating voice, "You are not to be blamed, Miss Grainger, for you have not as yet benefitted by my instruction. Gorton, however, knows very well that a young lady of refinement does not enter a public dining room unescorted."

'Queen Maud! Queen Maud!' thought Zoe, and responded, "As indeed she told me, ma'am. But—much as I like Gorton, you know, I had far rather go down with you, Lady Clara, for your stories I find prodigious fascinating. So I told Gorton I had rather meet you downstairs, and was most disappointed when you did not come. Was it wrong in me to hope for your company?" Even with the warrior queen's assistance, her nerves were fluttering. From the corner of her eye she could see Gorton's awed expression, but she smiled sunnily into Lady Buttershaw's suspicious countenance, and waited.

"Ahumph," said my lady gruffly. "Your motivation in this instance was commendable, and I shall not censure you. You will do well to remember, however, that you are in my care and I am responsible for your actions." She swept to the door. Zoe met Gorton's look of gratitude, smiled encouragingly, and barely managed to regain her saintly innocence before my lady turned back to advise that the coach would be ready to leave in a quarter hour and that she did not care to be kept waiting.

Gorton flew to close the door, this task evidently having been beneath Lady Buttershaw's dignity. "Oh, Miss," she said softly, "how brave you are! Mr. Arbour, the butler, is a kind gentleman, and his wife is in poor health. If he'd lost his situation because of me . . . !"

Zoe was feeling rather limp, which she concealed by crossing to the mirror above the hearth and straightening her cap. Travis, she thought, would be proud of Miss Timidity, as he'd been used to call her, for she dared to think she'd fought two battles rather well; first giving those horrid men with the foot the set-down they deserved, and then managing to turn Lady Buttershaw's wrath. With a mental heartfelt "thank you" to Queen Maud, she said, "Oh, I doubt her ladyship meant what she said. I fancy her heart is kind and she is not near so fierce as she pretends."

Gorton's lips tightened, but she said nothing and busied herself in gathering the last few items to be packed away.

Pausing, comb in hand, Zoe asked thoughtfully, "Is London an excessively dangerous place? I mean, is it safe for ladies to go about in the day time?"

"Oh, it is indeed, Miss. No one would dare interfere with a lady of Quality. There are special constables about, and lots of gentlemen besides, who would be quick to help if there was trouble." Gorton paused, and added with a frown, "Of course, there's been riots . . . Men who hate the aristocrats, and do most dreadful things. Malcontents, Mr. Arbour calls 'em."

"Ah. Then that may be why Lady Clara was so anxious I not go out alone. Is she as protective of her sister?"

Another hesitation, then Gorton said quietly, "In all my days, Miss Grainger, Ay never heard of Lady Buttershaw being protective. Of *nobody*! Not till now. She must've taken a real liking to you!"

Touched by sadness, Zoe thought that since she had been so unkindly thrust from home and family, it was as well that somebody had taken a liking to her. She stifled a sigh, then frowned at her reflection. To indulge in self-pity was disgraceful, she told herself sternly. She was young and healthy and had benefitted from a happy childhood with a loving family. Thus far her new life had not been too dreadful. Rather surprisingly un-dreadful, in fact. She had been given beautiful new clothes and was to live in a luxurious mansion in the greatest city of the civilized world. She would try to please Lady Julia Yerville, and perchance she could really be of help to the poor woman. Furthermore, with such an unfortunate disposition poor Lady Clara could not be a happy person. If she exerted herself, she might even win the *grande dame* to a more cheerful frame of mind.

This noble resolve was severely tested during the journey to London. When my lady was not criticizing the behaviour of coachmen, waggoners, postilions, and riders, she instructed Zoe on the history and industry of the various areas through which they passed. They were traversing the Thames basin, actually the London basin, which had been settled in the Iron Age. Fine furniture was being crafted in little Beaconsfield, "A fact that one would never guess from looking at the place." Miss Grainger was doubtless aware that Caesar's camp had been established hereabouts and that the great Roman emperor had much to do with the early development of the Metropolis, and had done "quite well, despite the fact that he was Italian." This last statement struck Zoe as so exquisitely humorous that she allowed a snort of mirth to escape her and was obliged to quickly convert it to a "hiccup."

My lady, unconvinced, fixed her with a cold stare. "I will tell you," she said repressively, "that foreigners are *not* to be trusted. Their personal habits are vulgar, their intellect inferior, and they have *no* manners. You should never associate with such people. Furthermore—"

The "furthermore" was cut off as a small group of horsemen came from behind, and with shouts and hoots of breathless laughter galloped past, two on either side of the cumbersome carriage. Zoe recognized one of those exuberant faces. It was the attractive gentleman she had met last evening on the stairs of the Three Horse Inn. She started to comment on that fact, but her words were drowned as a light carriage thundered alongside, the youthful coachman cracking his whip over the heads of his horses, egged on by a gentleman who hung half out of the open window shouting encouragement.

The road was not wide enough for both vehicles. Enraged, my lady rose from her seat and screamed orders for the "ill-bred young ruffian" to at once draw back.

A wheel went onto the grassy verge, the carriage lurched wildly, and my lady was bounced onto the squabs. The "ruffian" inside the other vehicle turned a dark and laughing countenance.

"Oh!" cried Zoe. " 'Tis that horrid *doctor!*"

Struggling to escape the hat and wig that had descended over her eyes, my lady uttered a strangled howl and elbowed her way up again. "STOP!" she commanded in a voice that should surely have caused strong men to tremble. "You . . . dastardly *villain!* Give way! *At once* I—say!" But the carriage rocked, and with an expletive that sounded suspiciously like a very naughty word, she was again tossed back.

Attempting to be of assistance, Zoe had as well have tried to restrain a tiger. Lady Buttershaw's long arms flailed, one skinny leg shot into the air, and, although muffled, there could be no doubt as to her *extremely* naughty words.

"My lady . . . ," gasped Zoe, also jolted about, but succumbing to the ridiculous aspects of the incident and fighting laughter. "Let me help—"

"*Doctor*, did you say?" screeched her ladyship. "Confound and—*curse* the wretch!" She heaved herself up, but the wig was her undoing and its might and majesty—and weightiness—bereft her of sight. All but incoherent with wrath, she struggled to her feet. The "wretch's" coach bade fair to skid into the ditch, and the occupant was lost to sight.

"Shameless . . . *animal!*" howled Lady Buttershaw. "How *dare* you?"

Muffled but defiant came the breathless response, "You've been—hogging the road for—miles, madam! Spring 'em, for Lord's sake, Florian, and pass this silly female!"

The light carriage all but leapt forward.

"*Silly—female?*" Gobbling with wrath, my lady's glittering eyes darted about, but found no suitable missile within reach. Her wig slid. She tore it from her head and hurled it, hat and all, at the man who'd dared defy her. He was in the act of picking himself up from the floor. A glimpse of tousled dark hair was blotted out by the flying wig, then his coach shot past, the wheels of the two vehicles all but scraping. Lady Buttershaw gave vent to a triumphant screech. "A hit, by the Lord Harry! It caught him full and fair! Did you see, gel?"

Zoe tried not to stare at the shorn aristocrat, and stammered, "I saw it—f-fly, ma'am. Did you recognize the gentleman?"

"*Gentleman?* Pah! A pox on him! I did not catch a clear look at his face, for the monstrous creature seemed more on the floor than on the seat. Intoxicated, I make no doubt! One of these young care-for-nobodies who call themselves Corinthians! I'd Corinthian him!" Lady Buttershaw leaned out of the open window to first howl abuse at her coachman for having allowed "that lawless viper" to best him, and then instruct him to turn off to Uxbridge. Breathing hard, she settled back on the seat. "My woman will procure me a new wig there," she said, seemingly unaware of the amused glances thrown their way by the occupants of the Portsmouth Machine as it rumbled past, westward bound.

Her ladyship's mousy brown hair was twisted into corkscrews and contained by hairpins. Bereft of the glory of her wig she looked oddly nude, but had lost not one whit of her arrogance and appeared not in the least embarrassed. Trying not to stare, Zoe mumbled, "I wonder you would—would bother with a wig, ma'am. Your own hair is so—abundant. Most ladies find it more comfortable nowadays to wear their hair short and—"

"Nonsense! I wear a wig, Miss Grainger, because I prefer to set fashion rather than follow it. Uxbridge is a very ancient town, and although it is not mentioned in the *Domesday Book*, there is sure to be a milliner there. Not of the first stare, naturally, but one most not expect the impossible."

Far from being overset by such a violence of temper, she was all but purring. Incredulous, Zoe thought, 'Why, I do believe she enjoyed herself!'

"Now," said Lady Buttershaw, "you may tell me the name of that young villain. I mean to lay an information 'gainst him at Bow Street."

She was displeased when Zoe confessed that she did not know the name of the miscreant, and demanded to hear what Miss Grainger did know of him. The tale was interrupted before it had properly begun however, because they came into Uxbridge and my lady forgot the matter during the search for a suitable milliner. The search was doomed to failure. Astounded when her footman returned from the tiny shop to report there was not a wig to be had, Lady Buttershaw's mood suffered an immediate reversal. It deteriorated even more drastically when it was discovered that the second coach with the servants and luggage had evidently failed to make the detour to

Uxbridge. My lady's resonance had already attracted a small but growing crowd, and the poor footman looked ready to faint. Zoe took pity on him, and leaving the carriage accompanied him into the little shop.

The proprietor was a large and amiable woman. She sent her daughter running to the church for the sexton, who was also the local hairdresser. With much bowing and scraping Lady Buttershaw was ushered from the coach. Her appearance was greeted by a sudden and complete silence. Never had Zoe seen so many jaws sag at the same instant. She had taken the precaution of warning the proprietor that they had suffered a small accident and that her companion, a great lady of rather uncertain temperament, had lost her wig. Wigless or not, Lady Buttershaw's haughty demeanour silenced any comments. She was safely inside the shop before the stunned onlookers recovered. The butcher snorted something having to do with being turned to stone, and Zoe closed the door on gales of laughter.

It was fortunate that the elderly hairdresser was a man of God, for his patience was sorely tried during the next hour, but at last my lady's locks had been arranged, pomaded, and powdered into what she termed "a faint semblance of style." Whatever her failings, she was not mean. Her generosity restored the good nature of her victims. She returned to the carriage, and as they drove off, favoured the crowd with a thin smile and a series of regal bows and waves. "Poor simple folk," she said condescendingly. " 'Tis rare for them to come into contact with the nobility. They will now have something to tell their children and grandchildren. Likely, 'twill become a legend."

She was to an extent correct. The locals had been vastly entertained. The story of the visit of the Medusa from London would be told and embellished for weeks to come, and was always good for a hearty laugh.

CHAPTER III

uncheon was taken at a fine posting house on a hilltop from which could be seen the distant spires of the City. Their departure was delayed while Lady Buttershaw instructed the host on the more efficient placement of the tables in his dining room, and it was late afternoon before their coach reached the outskirts of the Metropolis. The drizzle had by this time turned to rain, and the air was misty and chill, but, undaunted, Zoe was agog with excitement.

At the age of five, during a visit to the Richmond home of her favourite aunt, Lady Minerva Peckingham, she had been taken to London. Lady Minerva had not judged it sensible to show a young child the sites of history. Zoe was left with hazy recollections of endless narrow streets along which the houses were as if strung together; of countless people, an enormous noise and confusion, and grown-up luncheons and tea parties at which her aunt was very kind and talked to her gaily. That is to say, she was kind and chatty until, inevitably, one or more gentlemen would join them. Aunt Minerva thereupon appeared to forget her niece, and whispered and laughed with the gentleman despite the fact that they were evidently all "wicked" or "rogues."

Now, therefore, London was viewed as if for the first time,

and Zoe's eyes were wide indeed by the time the carriage was jolting through Hyde Park. Lady Buttershaw informed her that anything lying west of the park was "wilderness." She also observed that although King Henry VIII had been wise to appropriate the land, he should have had the foresightedness to ensure the proper upkeep of its roads. He would probably not have objected to the fact that today the park was much used as a duelling place, she added thoughtfully, for, whatever the century, honour must be upheld.

The coachman was instructed to detour so that Zoe might be shown the elegance of Kensington Palace, where her ladyship was "a frequent visitor." The history of the palace and its occupants was dwelt upon while the coach bumped and lurched off the atrocious park road, and after a smoother drive turned into a quiet square some half mile to the east.

A central garden for the use of the residents was enclosed by ornate iron railings, and the houses were scattered around it. Each was large enough to be counted a mansion, but her ladyship had not exaggerated; Yerville Hall was enormous. It was also, thought Zoe, extremely ugly. Two storeys in height, its wide stone front was broken by rows of small square windows. At the centre a recessed entrance portico was dignified by four tall stone columns supporting a large pediment. This structure partially blocked several of the windows, so that they appeared to Zoe to be hostile eyes peering suspiciously from under a frowning brow.

The carriage had evidently been anxiously awaited, for the front doors were flung open and a large and agitated butler came out onto the steps followed by three equally agitated liveried footmen. Lady Buttershaw was handed down and surrounded by a small crowd of solicitous and elegant ladies and gentlemen who swept out of the house and swept her inside again, all talking at the top of their lungs.

Zoe was assisted by a tall footman with a pair of pale and

protuberant blue eyes which scrutinized her curiously. He conducted her up the steps and into a large entrance hall, then with a terse nod took himself off. Awed, Zoe gazed at Gothic stone rib-vaulting that soared to the roof, and at the arched openings to the first-floor gallery that ran around the hall on three sides. The noisy crowd had vanished, but Zoe was too interested to feel abandoned. She wandered through more Gothic arches into another hall containing a magnificent wood-panelled staircase with the statue of a Grecian lady on the first landing, and a life-size portrait of a proud gentleman in a flowing periwig who sneered down at the stone lady from the facing wall. Beyond the stairs was a spacious wainscoted chamber wherein small tables were set among groups of chairs. Zoe peeped in.

"The morning room," said a soft voice at her ear, and she jumped guiltily, and jerked around.

The lady who stood there appeared to be somewhere between thirty-five and forty. Her features were delicate, and her eyes large and a very light blue. She wore a gown of white taffeta over modified hoops, the high neck buttoned to the throat and the full sleeves worn longer than the present style and gathered in at the wrists to falls of snowy lace that drooped over her hands. The unrelieved white of her attire, the powdered hair, the white cap, and the pallor of her face added to an impression of extreme fragility, and there was a wistful quality to her smile as she fondled the large black cat she held.

"Oh, I do beg your pardon," stammered Zoe, dropping a curtsy. "I am—"

"Miss Zoe Grainger, I think," said that gentle voice. "And 'tis I should apologize, my dear, that you were so rudely abandoned. I am sure you know who I am, for my sister will have told you of me. But I will introduce my friend." She held the black cat higher and its big green eyes scanned Zoe dispassionately. "This is Attila."

"He is very handsome. May I stroke him, Lady Yerville, or does he live up to his name?"

"You must call me Lady Julia; everyone does. And—no, he is very well-behaved. Until he goes berserk. But—"

"But since he frequently does so, he is *not* allowed in this part of the house!" Lady Buttershaw had come up unnoticed and her loud voice caused both ladies to jump. "Furthermore," she went on, frowning at Zoe, " 'twas impolite in you to go off on your own without waiting for proper introductions. One wonders if your mama ever taught you anything of etiquette!"

Lady Julia protested bravely, "But Clara, Miss Grainger had been abandoned and—"

"Nonsense! 'Twould not have harmed her to wait a minute or two whilst my friends greeted me. She has much to learn. I shall say no more on that head for the present, however." Lady Buttershaw's basilisk gaze was on Attila. "One might think that I could return to my home without being obliged to scold within the first five minutes, but as usual my wishes are ignored. You know very well, Julia, that my friends are distressed by creatures. Dare I hope that no more members of your menagerie are lurking about?"

Lady Julia sighed. "I know of only one of your friends who is distressed by my pets, Clara, and he is not here today."

"Were he able to be more comfortable in this house, I might more often have the pleasure of his company. Oh, I know what you are thinking, and I will admit that August is not good *ton*. But while I would not endanger our reputation by inviting him to a formal occasion, I hope I am not so proud as to deny him when out of the public eye."

"But of course you would not, Clara."

It seemed to Zoe that there was a touch of irony in Lady Julia's quiet words, but her sister inclined her head in the manner of one accepting her just due, then said, "One of your tasks, Miss Grainger, will be to keep Lady Julia's beasts confined to her quarters. Meanwhile," she gestured to a hovering footman, "you shall be shown to your own chamber so that you may prepare yourself for dinner. A word with you, Julia . . ."

Lady Julia went off with her, saying meekly, "How nice your hair looks, Clara. I am so glad you have discarded that silly wig . . ."

Grateful to have escaped, Zoe followed the footman upstairs.

My apologies." Sir Owen Furlong restored the valet's feet to the floor and kicked the front door shut behind him. "The fact is," he explained with a gleam of his disarming smile, "I've spent long enough in the rain this afternoon without being kept standing in it on my own doorstep."

The valet, a small fussy individual, was not appeased. Ignoring his spluttering incoherencies, Sir Owen upended his tricorne and poured a stream of rainwater from the brim into the large milk can that served as an umbrella stand. "My name is Furlong," he went on, thrusting his wet cloak and tricorne into the valet's unwilling hands. "I suppose you will be Captain Rossiter's new man." He started to the stairs, adding over his shoulder, "No need to announce me, but be a good fellow and send someone round to the stables with my mare, will you?"

Quivering with outrage, Ephraim Lewis glared after him. So this was the owner of the residence. His lip curled. In the short time he had served Captain Gideon Rossiter he'd formed some firm and inflammatory opinions regarding the gentlemen who frequented this house. They were, he'd informed his sister, as wild and radical a group of aristocratic young lunatics as he'd ever had the misfortune to encounter. The house itself, tall and narrow, was cursed with three flights of stairs and had been intended as a bachelor establishment. It was entirely unsuitable for a young married couple whose circle of friends was as wide as it was unconventional. Especially since those friends had the habit of dropping in at all hours and both expecting and being expected to make themselves completely at home. Poor Cook never knew whether to prepare dinner for two or twelve, and one was no longer surprised to come down in the morning and find some left-over guest asleep on the sofa or under the table.

Mr. Lewis had known when he applied for the position that, despite its agreeable location on Bond Street, this house would not suit him. He'd stayed only because Captain Gideon Rossiter and his bride had borrowed the house intending their occupation to be temporary. Very soon now they would be dividing their time between the large property in the Weald known as Emerald Farm, and the apartment now being readied for them in Rossiter Court, the splendid family mansion on Curzon Street. Neither residence could fail to add to the consequence of a London valet. The prospect of spending part of the year in the country did not appeal, however, and he was not displeased that such a threat may now have been removed.

He watched Sir Owen Furlong's athletic sprint up the stairs, then announced with smug malice, "Captain and Mrs. Rossiter are from home, sir."

"The deuce!" Furlong checked and turned back, one hand on the stair-railing and dismay in his eyes. "When do you expect them?"

"I really could not say, sir."

Furlong's rare frown dawned. Gideon had most assuredly been waiting for his report. He said, "You certainly know if they have left town. What is their destination?"

The good-natural drawl had vanished. There was command in the voice and it seemed to Lewis that the tall man stood even taller. He was aware that the Furlongs were among the most ancient and respected of England's great families, and remembered hearing that Captain Sir Owen Furlong had served with distinction in India. With the instinctive hostility of the small-souled toward any figure of authority, he thought, 'Much good his rank will do him here!' He knew very well where his employer had gone, and why, but, enjoying his moment of power, he repeated blandly, "I could not say, sir."

Furlong contemplated him, wondering whether to shake the information from the idiot. His gaze shifted to the coat rack and the second cloak that hung there. A wet garment. He turned with a grin and went on to the landing.

Irritated, Lewis called, "Sir, I told you—"

"I'll wait," said Furlong brusquely, and threw open the door to the withdrawing room.

A fire blazed merrily on the tiled hearth. A broad-shouldered young man with powdered hair, a whimsical mouth and strong nose reclined in a deep chair, a wineglass in one hand, and his feet propped on the brass fender. He turned a pair of irked green eyes to the new arrival, then sprang up to wring his hand and say with enthusiasm, "Furlong! I thought you were Morris! He was to meet me here an hour since."

"Likely run off by that stewed prune of a new man Gideon has found." Furlong clapped Viscount Horatio Glendenning on the back. "Where the devil has Gideon taken himself? I made sure he'd be here."

"They just left. He and Naomi have gone down to Emerald Farm." Glendenning hesitated for a split second, then asked, "Are you come to take your house back?"

"I hope I'm not such a villain." Furlong went over to the mahogany credenza that stood against one wall and took up a decanter. Pouring himself a glass of Madeira, he said, "I told Gideon he might borrow the house till his own is ready." Lost in thought, he stared down at the decanter and murmured absently, "I'll rack up at my club."

Curious, Glendenning asked, "Nothing amiss at your

brother's place, I trust? We expected you back last week."

"All's well at Keynsham." Furlong snapped back to the present and settled himself into a chair across the hearth. "My apologies, Tio. I fear I was wool gathering." He waved his glass in a silent toast and sampled the wine. "Since I was in the west country anyway I made a small detour to Admiral Albertson's estate. I go up and look things over from time to time. He likes me to tell him of it when I'm able to visit him, poor fellow."

"I fancy he does." Glendenning said soberly, "Who'd ever have thought that a man with his record of service and all those awards for heroism would be disgraced and ruined and end up in 'The Gatehouse'? Faith, I wonder they let him keep even that little piece of property."

"You may be sure 'twould have been seized with the rest, save that Albertson had put it into his son's name." Furlong gazed into the fire broodingly, thinking of gentle Hetty Albertson, to whom he had been betrothed, and who had been lost at sea two years ago. It had been an arranged marriage between two people who had seen each other seldom, but he had been fond of his prospective bride, and he muttered, "I'm more than ever convinced that Gideon's right, and that damnable League of Jewelled Men was directly responsible for the Admiral's disgrace and for Hetty's death. She'd not have been on that ship save that worry had undermined her health and her brother thought a stay in Italy would be good for her."

"Not much doubt of that," said Glendenning. "They were victims of the League."

"As are we all, one way or another. Lord, but I wonder those merciless demons can sleep o'nights!"

"I rather doubt that fanatics of that type are ever plagued by conscience. They've likely convinced themselves that in toppling the government and seizing power they're the saviours of Britain."

"Hmm. And if that bunch of pompous do-nothings in

Whitehall don't soon wake up and heed our warnings, the League will win, Tio! We can't hope to prevail against 'em all alone."

"Sad, but true. Is that what you want to discuss with Ross?"

"No, as a matter of fact. I've had a letter from Derek."

The Furlong brothers were deeply attached, and Derek's letters home were as lengthy as they were regular. The commander of an East Indiaman, he always had something of interest to relate, and his descriptive powers were such that his brother's friends looked forward to the letters almost as much as did Sir Owen. The arrival of these communiqués had become Occasions warranting a dinner party at the home of one or other of the small group, during which Sir Owen read from Derek's long letter. It was always the high point of the evening, the ladies being especially fascinated by the glimpses offered of life aboard ship and of mystical and romantic India.

Glendenning said with a grin, "Small wonder you're late, then. How many pages did you have to pay for?"

"Five, confound the fellow! And each page crossed! Well you may laugh, but I'm the one shall have to wade through it all over again for your benefit, and you know his hand is atrocious!"

"I can't deny that. But he writes a dashed fine letter just the same. Are you come to arrange one of our dinners?"

"Not entirely, though I suppose you'll all badger me to do so. The fact is . . ." Furlong shrugged and said deprecatingly, "Likely there's nothing to it, but something he writ struck me as rather odd."

"You'll be able to ask him about it soon. Don't you expect him home before winter?"

"I expected him home last month. Certainly, he'll have sailed with the north-east monsoon, so he must have left by February— March, at the latest."

"But you allow eight months for the voyage, no?"

"With luck, and Derek in command, less. Gad, but I'll be glad to see the rascal! We last met when I was selling out of the regiment in forty-five, and his ship put in to Bombay."

"What does he carry this time?"

"He says he's got a hold full of muslin and that Coromandel chintz the ladies like so well; and tons of pepper and spices, besides. He was delayed at Madras, waiting for some influential passengers, so he sent my letter ahead with a fleet ready to sail." Furlong looked troubled, and muttered, "Which probably means he'll be making a solitary voyage. I only hope he don't run up against one of those damned great Portuguese pirate frigates."

"Armed, ain't he?"

"Well, of course he's armed! Much chance he'd have of getting home without his cannon. He carries twenty-two nine-pounders, and four four-pounders."

"There you are, then. No need to be a gloom merchant, Owen. And if he's taking on passengers, they'll stand with the crew 'gainst pirates. Though I've heard that some of the merchants hide in the hold if there's an action."

Furlong smiled, but said thoughtfully, "It was Derek's account of one of his passengers that intrigued me."

"Aha! A young and lovely female, coming home, eh?"

"No, you lecher! A young diplomatist named Grant who had the misfortune to fall victim to the cholera, and has been ordered home. He goes in fear of his life."

"Oh, bad luck. It's not always fatal though, is it?"

"That's the odd part, Tio. Evidently, his fears are not because of his weakened health, but have to do with his conviction that somebody wants him dead. He was feverish one night, and told Derek that from the moment he sets foot in England his life won't be worth a button."

"Poor fellow. It sounds like delirium. What does your brother think?"

"Derek tried to calm him and thought he'd succeeded, but the following night Grant told him he'd writ out his Last Will and Testament, and asked that if he should expire, it be delivered to a friend in . . . Leadenhall Street."

"East India Company?" The viscount searched his friend's face and muttered frowningly, "Well, I suppose he could very well have a friend who works there."

"Just so. Failing that, he wants it sent to a man he admired at school and trusts implicitly."

"That's odd. Has the fellow no family?"

"Apparently he has, but he won't tell them he's coming home, for fear they should be distracted with worry for him. He is even sailing under an assumed name. It all sounds extreme melodramatic and peculiar, eh?"

"Extreme. But on the other hand, the same has been said of our own battles. Does Derek say anything more?"

"Only that he looked in on Grant one night, and the man leapt up in bed and started screaming that Derek was a murderous traitor!"

"The devil he did!"

Furlong nodded. "As you said, 'twas likely delirium. Still, I'll be interested to know the outcome. Thought Gideon would be interested also. How long will he be away, do you know?"

"I do not. No more does Gideon. I'd have told you at once, but I didn't want to greet you with such news. The farmhouse was set afire two nights since."

"Oh, what foul luck! Gideon loves that old place! No one harmed, I trust?"

"The caretaker was burned, but not badly. Ross is in a fury. They were almost ready to move in, you know."

They looked at each other.

Furlong said, "Arson, of course."

"The words *châtiment trois* were painted on the wall of the barn," said Glendenning soberly.

"Fiend seize those bastards! The League is punishing us again!"

There came a thumping of feet coming hurriedly up the stairs. The door was flung open and Lieutenant James Morris burst in bringing with him a breath of cold air and the smell of rain.

"Hey!" protested the viscount. "Shut the door, Jamie!"

Instead of complying, Morris looked from one to the other in a distracted fashion.

Furlong stood. "What's wrong?"

Morris panted, "August has taken Katrina down to Sussex. Their father was thrown yesterday."

Coming to his feet also, the viscount exclaimed, "Oh, Egad! Is it bad?"

Morris shook his head.

"Well, I'm glad of that." Furlong went over to pour a glass of brandy for the new arrival. "Can't say I'm surprised. August really should stop his sire from riding. Neville Falcon's a nice gentleman, but he must have the worst seat in the three kingdoms! D'you know any more of it, Jamie?"

Sinking into a chair, Morris took a pull at his brandy before answering. "He's lucky to be alive, by what I can gather. His head groom thinks the saddle girth was cut. I'd go down there myself, but I met my man outside. Been searching for me. M'sister's coach was crowded off the road and overturned. Niece and nephew inside. Nothing worse than cuts and bruises, thank the Lord, but I'm going into Surrey as soon as my fellow brings the coach around. What a beast of a week! Emerald Farm; Mr. Falcon; now, m'sister! It's a damned disaster epidemic!"

Glendenning said grimly, "It's that damned League, rather! They're chastising us again, Jamie."

His jaw dropping, Morris gaped at him.

Furlong nodded. " 'Tis to be expected, I suppose. We've set

ourselves up in opposition to a murderous group of aristocratic traitors, and although they're much more powerful than we are, we've managed to upset their plans several times."

"So now," said Glendenning, "they're coming after us."

Furlong muttered, "Or after our loved ones, heaven help us!"

Shocked, Morris exclaimed, "If ever I heard of such a thing! I mean, 'a lion don't roar at a butterfly!' "

Furlong stared. Familiar with Morris' maxims, Glendenning said, "I think he means that in a war the soldiers fight *one another*. They don't go after the enemy's innocent families. Is that it, Jamie?"

"Well, of course it is," said Morris. "Deuce take it, whatever else they may be, they *are* gentlemen, and they must know that sort of thing simply ain't *done!* I mean—it's not *fair play!* I mean—is it?"

Furlong said slowly, "Do you think the League of Jewelled Men observes the rules of fair play? I do not. Unless I mistake it, we're under siege!"

Those ominous words came clearly through the open door to the ears of Peregrine Cranford. It was three years since the Battle of Prestonpans had claimed his right foot, but there had been major setbacks, and stairs were still difficult for him. His friends knew better than to offer assistance, that privilege being reserved solely to his twin, Piers, wherefore James Morris, beset by his own anxieties, had paused only to mutter an incoherent apology before galloping up the steep flight. Following slowly, hating his clumsiness, refusing to acknowledge that he would do so much better with the peg-leg that Florian had carved for him, Cranford had fumed and struggled and, when he at last reached the upper landing, had leaned against the wall for a moment to catch his breath.

Now, his dark brows twitching together, he pushed himself clear of the wall, and walked more or less evenly into the room.

Horatio Glendenning was saying, "We must really have hurt them in the Cornish business, but if our families are at—"

Furlong interrupted heartily, "Hello, Cranford! You didn't say Perry was with you, Jamie."

There was no criticism in the voice, but Morris flushed scarlet and with a look of schoolboy guilt stammered, "Oh—so I didn't! Forgot! I do beg pardon."

Assuming the apology to be directed to himself, Cranford advanced to shake hands. "Never scold the clunch, Owen. I forgive him for not announcing my regal presence." He limped over to the chair Furlong drew forward and asked easily, "What's all this about jewels and a siege?"

He anticipated a light-hearted response and was astonished to see stark consternation in Morris' honest eyes. Furlong, who had started to the credenza, checked for a hair's-breadth, and Glendenning shot a taut glance at his back.

Morris gulped, "Oh—that. Just a—er, joke y'know, dear boy."

In the same instant, Glendenning said, "Cricket!"

Cranford stiffened. "A match you played in Cornwall?" he asked sweetly.

"Right!" said Morris, relieved.

"No!" said Glendenning simultaneously.

Furlong swore softly, and carried a glass of wine to Cranford. " 'Twas something of—of a comedy of errors, Perry," he said, his brain racing.

"Is what you get for wagering jewels," purred Cranford. "It *was* jewels you spoke of, no?"

Furlong saw the glint in the blue eyes and tightened his lips.

Morris said brightly, "Fools, dear boy! League of *Fooled* Men, we called 'em."

Cranford set his untouched wine aside. With a determined effort he managed to stand in a swift, smooth movement, and not to wince when his weight came down awkwardly on the abominable new foot. His head high and his voice chill, he said, "I'll be off, gentlemen. My apologies for having intruded upon a private conversation. Gad, where ever are my manners gone to?"

"Now don't be a gudgeon, Perry," urged Glendenning, slanting an unhappy look at Furlong. " 'Tis only—"

"A personal matter between you." Cranford bowed. "And none of my bread and butter. I spoke out of turn. I'll leave you—friends—in peace."

Furlong groaned.

Glendenning said, "We'll have to tell him, Owen!"

Aghast, Morris protested, "Tio, you've known him forever! I'd think you wouldn't want—"

It was the last straw. "Good day," said Cranford, starting to the door.

Furlong leapt in front of him. "Oh, go and sit down, you uppity fire-eater! I vow you're as hot-at-hand as August Falcon!"

"Oh, no he ain't," argued Morris. "Perry may be quick to take umbrage—"

"The devil!" exclaimed Cranford, trying to detach Furlong's hand from his arm.

"—but he don't go around challenging half the men in England to duels," finished Morris.

"I *may*," said Cranford furiously. "If you don't stand aside, Sir Owen—"

"Heaven help us," moaned Furlong. "He's flinging my title in my face."

Glendenning sighed. "Next he'll be 'my lord-ing' me, which I simply will not bear. If Ross cuts up stiff, I'll take the responsibility. Perry, you recall when Sir Mark Rossiter's banks and shipyards failed, and he swore 'twas a conspiracy?"

Resisting Furlong's efforts to restore him to his chair, Cranford said frigidly, "I believe Sir Mark cleared his name, my lord. Sir Owen, if you will be so kind as to—"

"Yes, but he was *right*," Furlong persisted. "It *was* a conspiracy, Perry. And part of a much larger plot."

Cranford's eyes widened. He ceased to resist, and sat down.

"Gideon Rossiter uncovered the ugly mess when he come home from the Low Countries," put in Morris, abandoning his attempt to protect Cranford. "We were both sent back to England on medical grounds, you'll remember, and I got into it with him."

In a typically rapid change of mood, Cranford asked eagerly, "What 'ugly mess'?"

Glendenning picked up the wineglass and thrust it at him. "Sit there like a good boy, and we'll tell you. As briefly as possible. Some wealthy gentlemen have banded together in what we call the League of Jewelled Men. An extreme secret society, that has set about to ruin and disgrace many of our most highly respected and influential citizens."

"And to acquire their estates," said Morris.

Cranford took a sip of his wine and argued, "But most such estates would be entailed and unable to be— Oh! I see! You said 'disgraced.' Do you mean by major crimes? 'Gainst the State?" His eyes gleamed with excitement as Glendenning nodded. "Zounds! In which case I believe the estates could be confiscated and sold for debt! Is that how they go about it?"

"In such instances, exactly so," said Furlong. "We've discovered that they've also purchased estates that were not entailed. If the owners don't want to sell, they resort to such charming persuasions as blackmail or intimidation, or even murder. We don't know how many unfortunately. We do know they've been responsible for some terrible tragedies."

Glendenning said, "They're also stirring up public unrest. You'll have noted all the little street flurries of late."

"Now there's a masterpiece of understatement," said Cranford. "I was nigh embroiled in a couple of 'flurries' I'd be more inclined to name full-fledged riots! But, what makes you think your—er, League can be blamed for 'em?"

"We don't think. We know," Furlong answered gravely. "They're well organized and well funded. They've sent out trained agitators whose task it is to spread discontent. They're expert at whipping the people into a frenzy. As prime examples of the degeneracy and corruption of those in high places, they point to the once-powerful gentlemen they themselves have deliberately disgraced and ruined."

"Be damned," muttered Cranford.

"Another of their jolly hobbies is wrecking," said the viscount. "You've read of all the recent shipping losses?"

Appalled, Cranford exclaimed, "But—that would be wholesale murder! Women, and little children! No, surely, you must be mistaken? What would they have to gain?"

"The cargoes," said Morris.

"But the cargoes were lost with the ships."

Furlong shook his head. "Not so, Perry. Morris and Falcon are recently come from Cornwall. They found Johnny Armitage there, and—"

"Armitage? Is he still alive? I thought he went down with his ship about two years ago."

"And in darkest disgrace, eh? Not so. 'Twas more of the League's brutal work, and succeeded to a point. Armitage had a very ugly two years, poor devil. But—"

Morris put in, "But August and I were able to give him a helping hand." He grinned at the memory. " 'Twas a merry brawl, I can tell you! We caught the League red-handed at their tricks, and found out that the ships' cargoes are stolen *before* sailing! Sooner or later during the voyage, the vessels are scuttled so that the thefts go unsuspected."

Stunned by the enormity of it, Cranford said haltingly, "And the passengers and crew are sacrificed to greed? No, you never mean it! 'Tis past belief that men could plan so dreadful a thing only for—"

"For a great deal of money," put in Glendenning. "Which is used to finance their plot to bring down the government!"

Cranford's jaw dropped. He half-whispered, "Bring down . . . the . . . You never mean . . . Is it Bonnie Prince Charlie again? Another Jacobite Uprising? Now—may God in His mercy forbid!"

"Amen," said Morris solemnly.

Through a long silent moment Cranford scanned one after another of their earnest faces. A frown crept into his eyes, and his fingers tightened around the glass. He demanded, "Do you say that you've set yourselves up alone 'gainst a large organization of insane traitors? Are you all gone demented? Whitehall must be told and—"

Furlong gave a gesture of impatience. "They've been told. Whitehall, and Bow Street, and the Admiralty Board, and the East India Company. But the League's been there before us. They've managed to convince the authorities that we're an irresponsible lot, bored and seeking diversion."

"Besides being of questionable loyalty," said Glendenning. "True in my case, as you know, Perry, having helped me out of a few tight corners."

Remembering some of those "tight corners," Cranford smiled, but his smile was brief. He murmured, "I wonder so ruthless a lot haven't simply put an end to the lot of you."

"They've given it a good try," said Furlong. "Rossiter, Gordon Chandler, Johnny Armitage, all have had narrow escapes."

Morris nodded solemnly. "And they properly trapped old Tio. Came within a whisker of having his head lopped. And his whole family with him!"

Cranford stiffened, and drawled a chill, "Really? How close you kept it, my good friend."

Glendenning said hurriedly, "Now pray do not go up in the boughs again. 'Twas beastly sudden. And at all events there was no call to drag you into my latest disaster."

"Very true." Cranford limped to the window and gazed unseeingly at the rain-swept streets. "What have jewels to do with it?"

Furlong said, "I fancy their ranks number in the hundreds now, but the identities of the six masterminds are kept secret, even from each other. With their heads at stake, they take no risks. We've learned they wear masks at their meetings, and each of them carries a small jewelled token by way of identification. The leader, or the Squire as he is called, may be the only man to know who they all are."

Cranford made no comment, but his lips tightened.

The afternoon was drawing in. Through a brief silence, Furlong took a taper to the fire and went about lighting candles.

Cranford said, "I'm with you, of course." Reflected in the glass, he saw the swift and apprehensive glance exchanged by the other three men, and his hand gripped tight on the handle of the casement. "And now that I'm one of you," he drawled, turning to face them, "I think you must play fair and tell me the rest."

Morris blinked at him. "The—rest?"

"Who they are. Who is their leader."

"Oh," said Morris, avoiding everyone's eyes. "That 'rest.' Er—well, the truth is—"

"That—alas, we don't yet know," interposed Glendenning.

"Is that so?" Cranford said silkily, "I'd have thought by this time you must have some suspicions at least."

Furlong hesitated. "The charges are too deadly to be—er, made without any real proof, but—"

Cranford's cool poise vanished. Flushed with rage, he

snarled, "Have done with your lies! A jolly time you've had with me, and I so gullible as to believe you for a while! You fabricated the whole nonsensical tale just for my benefit, did you? Very amusing! Ha, ha!"

Glendenning drew a hand across his eyes. "He's off again! I warn you, Owen—"

"Oh, by all means, warn him." Cranford stamped recklessly to the door. "Poor fellows—what lengths you were obliged to resort to only to shut me out of whatever you're really about! I'll give you all credit for lurid imaginations!"

At his most judicial, Furlong drawled, "If your temper's this uncontrollable, perhaps—"

Cranford cut him off savagely. "It ain't my *temper* you're concerned with. I saw you all taking your—your blasted silent vote and deciding a feeble cripple wasn't up to snuff! Well, never fret, gentlemen! Your private club will not be burdened by—by such an encumbrance as my useless self! I wash my hands of the lot of you!" Flinging the door open, he stalked through it, and tossed a furious and somewhat muddled farewell over his shoulder. "I give you good day. And you may go to the devil!"

The room he left was silent for several moments.

The front door slammed hard.

Morris jumped, and said unhappily, "Oh, Lord! Poor old Perry. I suppose 'tis logical he would think that."

"If he hadn't lost his silly foot, I'd have punched his head for him," growled Glendenning.

Furlong said slowly, "To an extent, he was right. He's had more than his share of misery, so we wanted to keep him clear. Now, he is. But I doubt he'll ever speak to any of us again."

"He didn't believe a word of it," sighed Morris.

"Not a word," agreed Furlong. "Jupiter! If one of our closest friends don't believe us, how can we wonder nobody else does?"

CHAPTER IV

oe awoke to find the bed curtains drawn back and sunlight flooding in at the windows. Delicious breakfast smells filled the room, and a tall maid-servant had spread a snowy tablecloth over the little round table and was setting out plates and cutlery, and some covered dishes.

Zoe blinked at her sleepily for an uncomprehending moment, then sprang up in alarm. "Gorton! Oh, my! Whatever o'clock is it? Should I be downstairs?"

" 'Tis half-past eight, Miss. Both of their la'ships take breakfast in bed, so you wasn't expected in the breakfast room. Since 'tis such a nace day, Ay thought you might like to sit here, where you can see the garden." Gorton poured hot water into the washbowl and added politely, "Ay trust you slept well?"

Hurrying through her toilette Zoe declared she had slept very well. "Which I did not expect to do, since London is so very noisy."

Gorton helped her into her dressing gown and assured her she would soon get used to city sounds, and that this was actually a very quiet neighbourhood. Pulling out a chair at the table, she waited until Zoe was seated, then said, "Perhaps you could tell me which morning dress you wish to wear."

Beyond noting that the two presses were full of garments, Zoe had been too downcast last evening to pay much heed to them. Now, beaming at two eggs, some succulent-looking slices of ham, and three steaming hot scones, she discovered another treasure—a little covered pot full of strawberry jam. With a squeak of delight, she took up her knife and answered, "I shall leave that decision to you."

Gorton opened the press and selected a gown of pale green taffeta. "May Ay enquire if you find the bedchamber to your liking?"

"Oh, very much so," said Zoe, spreading jam on a scone. "In fact, I am rather surprised, Elsie—yes, I shall call you that whilst we are private, for Gorton sounds so . . . unfriendly."

Slanting a quick glance at her, Gorton saw wistfulness in the expressive features, and felt a pang of sympathy. But Zoe's shoulders pulled back almost immediately and she went on brightly, "What I had expected, you see, was quite a small room, since I am really here only to serve as companion to Lady Julia." She threw a quick glance around the large and comfortably furnished chamber. "This room is much bigger than my own at Travisford. Is it, perhaps, a temporary arrangement?"

"Not that Ay am aware of, Miss. There is a plain white chemise, if you prefer, but Ay think this one with the green frill about the sleeves is nace."

"Yes. Lovely. From what I could tell last evening, the ladies' suites are at opposite ends of this floor—no?"

"Yes, Miss. Lady Clara not much caring for Lady Julia's creatures, if Ay am not too bold."

Zoe, who had dined with Lady Buttershaw in a large breakfast parlour, and gone early to bed, had not yet set foot in Lady Julia's apartments. She said, "Not at all bold. But here I am, in this fine big room, miles from either of their ladyships. Does that not seem odd to you?"

Gorton hesitated, then lied, "Nothing their la'ships do—er, does . . . seems—er, odd to me, Miss Grainger."

"Oh dear,' thought Zoe. 'She likely dares not say, poor thing. And 'tis naughty of me to question the servants. But—who else am I to talk to? And I am, after all, no more than a servant myself.'

Starting on the second egg, she asked, "How many—er, creatures, does Lady Julia keep?"

"Six, Miss."

Zoe blinked, and asked uneasily, "All—small animals . . . ?"

"Ay reelly would not say so. Caesar is a *good* size. Nor Ay wouldn't call Cromwell . . . small exactly. And Viking is a *giant!*" Closing the chest of drawers, Gorton added reassuringly, "Charlemagne is quite tiny. But a terrible troublemaker. When you are ready, Miss, Ay will brush out your hair. Lady Julia wishes you to go to her at ten o'clock."

By the time Gorton was conducting her along the wide passage, the loneliness that had assailed Zoe during the hours of darkness was forgotten, and her usually sunny outlook was restored. She inspected her new surroundings with ever-increasing curiosity. For such a modern structure, Yerville Hall had a pronounced air of antiquity. She thought, 'It even smells old!' The furnishings, while beautifully preserved, were ponderous and more of the thirteenth than the eighteenth century. Many of the portraits adorning the walls appeared to be very old indeed, the coiffures and apparel being those worn in medieval times. There were faded tapestries here also, and some large oil paintings, most depicting great castles or battle scenes.

Smiling at a maid who bobbed a curtsy as they passed, Zoe exclaimed, "Goodness me! I wonder why they did not simply move into a castle."

"May ladies were most fond of their ancestral home," murmured Gorton, "which was burnt. Although they could not do so on the outside, they tried to make the inside of this house as like it as possible. Even, so they say, to the secret passages and priest's hole. Here are Lady Yerville's quarters."

The passage ended at a pair of closed doors beside which a cadaverously thin lackey with a mournful expression waited.

Gorton said, "Miss Grainger is expected, Phipps."

His sad blue eyes scanned Zoe curiously, then he rested his ear against one of the doors for a moment before opening it with slow caution. He peered inside, then stood back.

"Go on, Miss!" urged Gorton on a note of urgency. "Quick!"

Zoe slipped past.

The door clicked shut behind her.

She whipped around and was dismayed to find that Gorton and Phipps had remained outside. It was foolish, but her heart began to pound faster and she found herself tiptoeing as she walked on.

Only the chiming of a clock sounding the quarter hour broke the stillness. The passage stretched out before her, seeming at first much the same as the one she'd just left. She came to realize, however, that this area was even more museum-like, and there was a decidedly musty smell on the air. Probably, she decided, from the tapestries, for there were many of those, some faded and curling with age, alternating with great banners and more paintings. A suit of armour was set in a shallow alcove; a war axe hung above a fine Italian dagger complete with furnishings. Looking at all the curiosities, Zoe heard six chimes in a deeper tone than the clock that had sounded the quarter-hour. Neither had been right. Even the clocks, she thought, were behind the times. A moment later yet another peal announced the half-hour. Zoe's amusement vanished and she gave a squeak of fright as she trod on a small ball, skidded, and almost fell. She was relieved when a footman hurried from an open doorway to offer his hand and murmur apologies.

"They should have seen fit to let me know you was here, Miss," he grumbled. "My lady is wai—"

A small ginger and white cat shot from another open door and raced past at frenzied speed. There came a sudden pounding, scrambling noise, and a deep, terrifying growling. The footman gave a shout and leapt aside. Her heart in her mouth, Zoe shrank against the wall as an enormous black and white hound thundered straight at her. Its claws slipped on the polished boards, and the powerful back legs slid from under it. The floor shook. A narrow table was slammed against the wall and a marble urn toppled. With a bark that rattled the suit of armour, the hound recovered itself, and tore in pursuit of the cat.

"Oh, my heavens!" cried Zoe, distressed. "The poor little moggy will be killed!"

Muttering something under his breath about "reducing the livestock," the footman straightened the urn, then said blandly, "That was Charlemagne, Miss. It'll be all right. It's his cat. This way."

He stalked off, and Zoe followed, wondering who "he" might be, and why it had never occurred to her that there might be a Lord Yerville.

Such speculation ended when she was ushered into a spacious parlour.

"Miss Grainger, milady," announced the footman, and withdrew, closing the door softly.

Fine rugs were spread on the polished floors; mauve and white hangings tied back with gold ropes were at the windows. A curio cabinet, two bookcases, and a fine escritoire were white. Two graceful white chairs covered in mauve velvet were set to one side of the Italian marble fireplace, on the mantelpiece of which stood a splendid gilt tower clock. There were more clocks in the curio cabinet and on the escritoire, each one ticking away busily. All this Zoe noted in fragmentary fashion as she approached the gold brocade chaise lounge set before the windows. Lady Julia Yerville reclined there, book in hand. She wore a white satin negligee trimmed with blonde lace. A dainty matching cap was tied over her neat wig. A tabby cat sprawled on her lap, and a big liver and white spaniel lying at the foot of the chaise lifted its head and looked at Zoe, its tail thumping a welcome. The large black cat she had met yesterday was perched, Sphinx-like, on the window seat, and a small white terrier that had been lying nearby jumped up emitting shrill barks and expressing its mistrust of the new arrival by a series of hysterical charges and retreats.

"Boadicea, hush!" cried my lady, lowering her book.

Boadicea instead became more strident, so that Lady Julia clapped her hands and said a sharp, "Bo! That will do!"

Annoyed, the tabby abandoned her lap to resettle itself in a sunny spot on the rug. Boadicea cowered and fled to the window seat where she crouched, growling, behind the black cat, who ignored her and continued to watch the proceedings with aloof boredom.

"My apologies," said Lady Julia with a rueful smile. "Pray do not be alarmed, Miss Grainger. My friends will soon get to know you."

A beam of sunlight touched the white satin negligee so that the frail lady seemed almost to glow. Zoe thought her ethereally lovely, and she came forward shyly to make her curtsy and clasp the fine-boned hand that was extended to her.

Her ladyship indicated a nearby chair and said in her gentle voice, "Do sit down, my dear. How very pretty you look this morning. I am so glad to see that Hermione's garments fit you. My sister was sure they would. Ah, you look mystified. The fact is that my cousin's youngest child was to have come as companion to me, but she was reluctant, so Lady Clara ordered a complete new wardrobe sewn to entice her. Alas, the prospect of waiting upon an invalid dimmed the lure of new fashions. I do not blame Hermione at all for refusing such a glorious opportunity." Patting Zoe's hand, she said with a twinkle, "Are you offended to be offered garments intended for another lady?"

Zoe was relieved rather than offended. "Not at all, ma'am. In fact, I had wondered that Lady Buttershaw should have ordered so many garments for me. As if, you know, she had been sure for some time that I would come. It seemed . . ."

"A presumption? Or perhaps that she could see into the future? Fie upon me, for dispelling so lovely a mystery!"

As she spoke a clock chimed four times. For the first time Zoe realized that there were actually six clocks in the room, only one of which displayed the correct time.

Lady Julia said, "Ah, you have noted my clocks. 'Tis one of my hobbies. I shall tell you all about it later. We have plenty of time. If you will forgive the play on words."

They laughed together, and the spaniel pulled himself up and came over, tail wriggling, to sniff at Zoe's shoes and permit himself to be stroked.

"There," said Lady Julia. "Cromwell has accepted you already. But I must introduce you to the rest of them. The cat Boadicea hides behind is Attila—you will remember him from yesterday. The tabby is called Caesar. My little ginger pussycat, Charlemagne, and the largest of my pets, Viking, are somewhere about."

"They—er, passed me in the passage," said Zoe. "I see that I must have misunderstood. I thought your footman said that the ginger cat belongs to a gentleman."

"A *gentleman*, is it?" Amused, my lady shook her head. "I doubt he rates so dignified an appellation! 'Ruffian' would be more apropos, and he can upon occasion be very rough indeed! But I am being naughty and confusing you again, poor child. The thing is, you see, that the three dogs were all gifts as puppies, whereas the cats, as cats will, adopted me from time to time. I was fearful for their safety at first, but the strange thing is that as each cat came into my life, it chose a dog for itself as one might choose a friend and protector. I know that sounds unlikely, but 'tis really so. Little Boadicea is Attila's dog, and Cromwell here, my most amiable spaniel, belongs to Caesar, the tabby."

Zoe asked in awe, "Then do you say, ma'am, that the tiny little ginger cat chose that enormous black and white hound?"

"Viking." Lady Julia nodded. "Just so. Is it not quaint? Charley—or Charlemagne, to be precise, teases Viking constantly. Truly, I marvel that the mischievous creature has not been savaged. But although Viking chases him ferociously, he has never yet done more than make a great deal of noise, and they are actually inseparable. If Charley wanders off, sooner or later Viking will go in search of him. 'Tis most amusing to see their antics, I promise you. But enough of my pets. We must learn about each other. My life, alas, is dull, for I never married and have no children to fill my days. My uncle, the present earl, allows me to live in this house for my lifetime. Lady Clara had a large home, but she is childless, and when her husband went to his reward she moved back here." She smiled and said confidingly, "She worries about me, you know, although I am not nearly so frail as she chooses to believe. Even so, my health does not permit that I go about very much. Fortunately, I have friends who are faithful, bless them, and call upon me, so that I am not altogether out of the world. Have you friends, Miss Grainger?"

"Oh, yes, my lady. My best friend married last year, and went out to the Americas with her husband." Zoe stifled a sigh. "I miss her. But that is the way for young ladies." Here, recollecting Lady Julia's single state, she blushed hotly, and stammered, "N-not always, of course. Some ladies are not inclined towards—towards matrimony. Indeed, Papa says that I am well on the way to becoming—" She had done it again! Biting her lip with mortification, she choked the words off.

Lady Julia chuckled. "Becoming what? An old maid? Nonsense! You were born to be loved by some lucky man. And do not be thinking that the single state is mine by choice. I was betrothed to a gentleman I adored, and who loved me as deeply. We were about to be wed, in fact, when . . ." The brilliant light blue eyes became closed and remote suddenly. She finished in a far-away voice, "There was a—a terrible . . . accident."

Acutely embarrassed, Zoe said, "Yes, ma'am. Lady Buttershaw told me of the fire. I am so sorry, but you were spared any— I mean, there is no sign of—" She floundered, and gulped, "You are very pretty, ma'am."

"How kind." The wistful eyes saw her again. "I will tell you about it, though, so that you do not have to wonder, or feel sad for my sake. He was young and very handsome, you see. A vital, healthy man from a noble house. He had to have heirs; sons to follow him and carry on the name. And my life was despaired of, so . . ." She shrugged and gave a wry smile.

Aghast, Zoe exclaimed, "Do you say he drew back? No, surely not? If ever I heard of such a thing!"

Lady Julia unbuttoned her cuff and rolled up her left sleeve. Zoe could not restrain a gasp. The arm was red and shiny, the skin puckered and cruelly scarred. "My face and hands were not marked," said my lady, "but much of me is—as you see. How could I blame him?"

Zoe exclaimed fiercely, "I could blame him! If you love someone you do not abandon them only because they are ill, or—or hurt, through no fault of their own! Had he been burned or crippled or something of the sort, I am very sure you would have stood by him! I vow, you are well rid of—of such a fair-weather friend, ma'am, and will find another suitor who is far more worthy of such a sweet and pretty lady! Not all gentlemen are so lacking in character. I know my brother would never behave in such a way!"

Lady Julia, who had listened to this impassioned speech with increasing amusement, now gave a little trill of laughter and held out her arms. "You dear, warm-hearted girl! What a fine champion I have found. Come, and let me hug you! Oh, we are going to go along splendidly, I know it. Now, sit here beside me, and tell me all about this gallant brother of yours. Is he at school? Shall I have the pleasure of meeting him soon?"

Returning that scented embrace, Zoe sat where her ladyship indicated, and with very little coaxing was soon telling her all about Travisford and Papa, and her beloved Travis.

The moments slipped away. Lady Julia watched the bright, animated young face, and inserted a question from time to time. And, listening, she could envision the rambling old house, the silver ribbon of the river, the kind but foolish father, the beloved brother. After a while, the big black cat, Attila, jumped up and appropriated my lady's lap. The little white terrier, Boadicea, at once came over to fuss and fidget about Zoe resentfully, but settled down when Lady Julia extended a quieting hand.

The door opened softly. A tall elegantly attired gentleman looked in and raised an enquiring eyebrow. Over Zoe's shoulder, my lady met his glance, and shook her head slightly. The gentleman withdrew, and the door was closed as softly as it had been opened. The spaniel, who had started to the door, barked. A frown flickered across my lady's face, and Zoe glanced around.

"Oh, how I have run on," she said. "You should not let me waste your time, ma'am."

"But you did no such thing. I have thoroughly enjoyed our chat. Cromwell likely heard someone arriving, and they will wait, never fear. Tell me now, do you think you will like to stay here? I promise not to burden you with many duties, for my hobbies keep me very occupied, and my friends are always coming and going. Sometimes, I will want you to read to me, but mostly, I will ask that you take care of my pets; groom them, and take them for walks, and keep them from bothering Lady Clara, for she is not fond of animals. You will have plenty of time for rides in the park, and shopping, and if there is some special entertainment I wish to go to, you shall accompany me. What do you think? Will it suit?"

It would, said Zoe fervently, suit very well indeed.

And so, for a while, it did. The sisters had not exaggerated when they'd said there would be few demands on her time. Lady Julia told her kindly to spend the first few days exploring the great house and identifying the servants. At some time each day, she was summoned to brush the cats or take one or other of the dogs for a walk, or to talk to Lady Julia while she rested in the afternoon. The frail lady was unfailingly kind and gentle. She betrayed a flattering interest in Zoe's childhood and in her life at Travisford which sounded, she said wistfully, so jolly compared to her own rigidly controlled youth. "I have never climbed a tree in all my days," she sighed. "Never played rounders with other girls and boys; never galloped a pony over country meadows, or gone for long walks with a beloved brother and his friends. Mama and Papa were very strict, you see, and they moved in such select circles that Clara and I were always obliged to be models of propriety."

The picture of such a restricted way of life appalled Zoe, although she could not but wonder that anyone would judge Lady Buttershaw to be a "model of propriety." She saw that formidable *grande dame* seldom during these early days, for Lady Buttershaw seemed always to be rushing off to some function or other, usually with Hackham, her personal footman, in attendance. On the few occasions that they met, Lady Buttershaw would have many suggestions for the improvement of Zoe's dress and deportment. She also showed an interest in life at Travisford, but her remarks were invariably disparaging, and she lost no opportunity to criticize Mr. Grainger and his son, both of whom she felt had been remiss in failing to ensure that Zoe be properly instructed and given a London Season. Zoe found herself constantly obliged to defend her father and to regale the lady with accounts of Travis' scholarly achievements and of her sure belief that honours must attend his diplomatic career. This became rather tiresome. Fortunately, however, her ladyship's voice was exercised the instant she crossed the threshold. Zoe noticed that when those piercing tones were heard, the passages would quickly empty of all the servants who dared escape, and she lost no time in following their example.

The promised rides with Lady Julia had not as yet materialized, but Zoe kept busily occupied. The house was a regular museum of artifacts, all having to do with England's history, and the large part the family Yerville appeared to have played in it. She spent her free time in wandering about the mansion, and wrote long letters home and to her brother, telling of her discoveries.

After the first excruciating evening spent dining with and being "educated" by Lady Buttershaw, she was not sorry to be left to take her meals alone. But the breakfast parlour was large and silent, the butler waited on her with quiet efficiency, and she found solitude to be, after all, not much of an improvement over Lady Buttershaw's trumpeted monologues.

Following an excellent meal on her fourth evening at Yerville Hall, she wandered into the book room. It was vast and chilly, with no fire on the hearth. The room was not pitch dark, for the moon was up and painting the rug with its silver rays, but there was no sign of the lackey who should have come to light candles for her.

She crossed to the window and looked out. The street was bright with the glow of the flambeaux that blazed on each side of the entrance. The square was deserted, and the little garden at the centre looked dark and mysterious. A coach came rattling up the street, and stopped outside. The footman sprang down and threw open the door, and three gentlemen alighted. They were laughing and talking cheerily, and Zoe watched them, envying their good-fellowship as they started up the steps. She could tell when the front doors were opened, for the increased light shone across the pavement and cobblestones, and deepened the shadows in the central garden. How differently things appeared at night time; one of those shadows might almost be the figure of a man . . . Curious, she moved closer to the window. It *was* someone, for the figure had drawn back quickly, as if fearing to be seen. The light faded as the front doors were closed. The coach rolled away, and the street was quiet again. There was no sign of anyone in the central garden now, and although she stood there for at least five minutes, she could detect no more movement.

Perhaps she had imagined it, after all. Perhaps it had just been a trick of light and shadow. Or it might simply have been a servant from one of the great houses, walking his master's pet, even as she had done earlier. But surely by this time he would have opened the gate and left, or at least have moved about? And why would a servant, who had every right to be there, have behaved in so furtive a way? If it was a tramp, seeking a place to spend the night, the unfortunate creature would have good cause to hide, for he would not have had the key to the gate and must have climbed the fence, and it was a crime for unauthorized persons to go into the private garden. She thought with a chill of fear, 'Perhaps 'twas a Jacobite, making his way to the Thames to take ship for France! They say there are many desperate fugitives, still in hiding!'

And there she went again, romanticizing, just as she and Travis had loved to do; taking a trivial incident and endowing it with mystery, each of them layering one dramatic possibility on top of another, until he would laugh and say he could not compete with her "overblown imagination." She smiled nostalgically, and, half-convinced she must have been mistaken once again, heard something there was no mistaking: an urgent whispering and a half-smothered giggle.

At the open door two figures were briefly outlined against the glow from the corridor; a man and a girl, both tall, who slipped inside but made no attempt to light candles.

"Cecil! You must be fair addled!" This said in a breathless female voice that continued urgently, "No! Stop that! What a dreadful chance to take! If we should be caught may lady would—"

A deep male voice, kept low, and with a hint of cockney, interrupted, "Be green with envy is what she'd be! The old harpy likely don't recollect how it feels to have a man's arm round that skinny waist of hers! I haven't had a word with you for days, love. Give us another kiss, do!"

"All right . . . Now *go!* For mercy's sake!"

"But I just came. And I can slip out quick, if—"

Zoe, who had been much titillated by this conversation, awoke to the fact that she was eavesdropping, and said quietly, "I think you had best stop."

A faint scream.

The man groaned, "Oh, Lor'!"

" 'Tis no use to run away," said Zoe, as the woman jerked back. "I know who you are. Close the door and light some candles, if you please."

The woman began to cry. Zoe heard the scrape of flint on steel and in another moment the flame of a candle revealed two terrified faces.

Forgetting her accent, Elsie Gorton sobbed, "Oh, Miss! Oh, Miss—don't tell! I beg you! Don't tell her la'ship! We'd both be turned off without characters, sure as sure, and—and we'd starve! Oh . . . *Miss!*"

The man was Stone, Lady Buttershaw's coachman, a brawny individual of about five and thirty, with narrow dark eyes and heavy weather-beaten features. He was pale, but he put one arm protectively about Gorton's shoulders and said with hoarse desperation, "It's my fault, Miss. Not Elsie's. She told me not to come to this part of the house, but their la'ships is usually not about at this hour, and we don't get much chance to—to meet, Miss."

"Why?" asked Zoe, interested. "Are not your intentions honourable, Stone?"

"That they is, Miss! But Lady Buttershaw don't allow no— what she calls 'flirty-fying' among her servants."

"She says 'twould turn our thoughts to—to sinful behaviours," put in Gorton tearfully. "When we'd oughta be thinking of her."

Incredulous, Zoe said, "But surely you wouldn't think of that *all* the time?" She saw Stone's eyes widen, and her face flamed as she amended hurriedly, "What I mean is—are you obliged to think of my lady every minute of the day and night?"

Gorton tore at her handkerchief and nodded. "May lady says that them as works for her pay belongs to her, and she don't want her servants having no indecent distractions."

'Good gracious,' thought Zoe. She said, "But you are able to meet on your days off, no?"

"I only get a afternoon, Miss," said Stone. "And that has to be fit in when I'm not wanted. And Elsie gets one day a month. It's"—he gulped and his face became red, but he persisted doggedly—"it's awful hard, Miss, when a man's found the— the One And Only Woman, and she's give up her—her heart in return, as you might say."

Zoe looked from one to the other. Who would have dreamed that the rigid and prim Gorton should be concealing a passionate attachment? Or that behind Cecil Stone's stolid and commonplace exterior beat the heart of an ardent lover?

Misinterpreting the astonishment in the young face, Gorton blurted out, "Oh, Miss, I know you must think 'tis shocking, but—I do so love my Cecil! And to not even be able to say a word to him hardly, for weeks on end, is very sad. I—I don't even dare smile at him, for fear Mr. Whipley should see! He wanted his sister to be your abigail, and he'd like nothing better than to tell Lady Julia I'm a evil woman!"

"He's a toadying sneak, he is," growled Stone.

Improper as it was, Zoe could not judge his observation to be unfounded. Lady Julia's personal footman was soft-spoken, fastidious in the matter of his appearance, and the soul of devotion to his mistress. But there was a trace of sly amusement in Whipley's dark eyes when they rested on Zoe Grainger, causing her to feel uneasily that she was being laughed at. No, it was not hard to believe the man would carry tales.

She asked thoughtfully, "Why do you not seek work elsewhere? Surely you could go to some post as man and wife, and not be obliged to be separated?"

They looked at each other.

Gorton sniffed, and dabbed at her eyes.

Stone said reluctantly, "I got mustered out of the army after Culloden, Miss. I couldn't find a situation. So many men was looking for work. I come nigh to starving. I—I snabbled a coney down at Sundial Abbey, and got caught. I could've been transported, or hanged, but her la'ship's steward is a kind man and give me a chance as a groom. Last winter I was made Lady Buttershaw's coachman. Then someone give me away. Her la'ship was proper vexed and I'd have been sent packing to say the least of it, if Lady Julia hadn't of spoke up for me. The end of it was that Lady Buttershaw says so long as I please her, she won't turn me off. But—if I was to try and leave, Miss . . ." He shrugged helplessly.

Absorbed by their discussion, none of them had heard the arrival of another carriage, but now a bell rang stridently. Above a flurry of chatter, Lady Buttershaw's voice was upraised. "Miss Grainger? Where on earth are you got to?

Botheration! Hackham! Go and fetch Miss Grainger."

Gorton cringed and clasped both hands to her mouth. Stone paled again.

Snatching up a book, Zoe hissed, "Blow out the candle!" and went into the corridor.

Hackham was sprinting in the direction of the stair hall. A swirl of green velvet was vanishing into the withdrawing room. Zoe followed the green velvet.

The withdrawing room was a blaze of candlelight, the air redolent of costly scents, and ringing with the loud voices and shrill laughter of an elegant company. The chatter died away when Zoe entered, and about two dozen faces turned to her.

A tall young exquisite in ivory satin with knots of red ribbon at his knees, put up his quizzing glass and drawled with a toothy smile, "Pray, who is this new blossom, Lady Clara?"

Beside him, a slender gentleman in a splendid purple and silver coat uttered a high-pitched giggle and said in a nasal voice that dear Gilbert's vision was failing him. " 'Tis not a blossom, but a wood nymph," he declared, waving a little fan as he circled daintily around Zoe. "Look you, my lords, ladies, and gentlemen. A new face has burst upon the London scene. A pretty face, stap me if it ain't! Dewy with youth and a bright-eyed innocence. Name her, dear hostess, ere we die of curiosity!"

Lady Buttershaw boomed, "Now you have made her blush! Behave, Reggie! This lady is in my charge, and being new come from the country is unaccustomed to your Town sauce."

"Aha," exclaimed the gentleman in ivory. "A rustic goddess! Did I not guess it by the roses in those pretty cheeks?"

A horsey-looking young woman in a Watteau gown of peach brocade with diamonds spread across a great deal of snowy bosom, murmured something behind her fan, and the lady beside her gave a squeal of laughter, and said in mock scolding, "Samantha! 'Pon rep, but you are a naughty thing!"

Acutely embarrassed and feeling very much the country bumpkin, Zoe longed to be elsewhere.

"My dear friends," brayed Lady Buttershaw, "I present to your notice Miss Zoe Grainger, of Travisford in the Cotswolds. Make your curtsy, Miss!"

Zoe curtsied obediently, but hit her chin on the large book she held, evoking more subdued titters.

Lady Buttershaw looked irked, but proceeded to introduce her all around. The gentlemen's bows were elaborate; the ladies' curtsies barely polite. Trying to fix their names in memory, Zoe was later able to recall very few: Lord Gardiner Coombs, a very stout middle-aged man who was half-asleep and half-intoxicated; Lady Melissa Coombs, at least fifteen years her husband's junior, the heavy application of paint on her face failing to disguise many spots; Mrs. Samantha Golightly, the toothy young woman with the large bosom, whose snapping black eyes held amused disdain; Mr. Reginald Smythe, the dandy with the high-pitched giggle and the purple and silver coat; and Sir Gilbert Fowles, of the ivory satin, who had named her a "rustic goddess." There was a very tall thin young man whom everyone called "Purr." He was shy and appeared never to complete a sentence, and was so undistinguished that she could not afterwards remember his full name. There were only a few ladies, the gentlemen predominated, most being, she gathered, unmarried.

During the course of the introductions, several conversations ensued, and by the time Zoe had met all the guests the room was a babble of talk.

Lady Buttershaw's voice sliced through the noise like a knife through butter. They were to enjoy refreshments, and then the treat she had promised. "Sir Gilbert Fowles, having recently returned from Paris, has a vastly important piece of news for you. I will tell you it is *not* news to me, for I am well informed, and having been for some time aware of the development, have acted accordingly. But the rest of you will find it fascinating, I make no doubt."

Amid the immediate flutter of excited speculation, Mr. Smythe made a great to-do over ushering Zoe to a chair and drawing another close beside her. The rest of the company disposed themselves about the room, and Arbour appeared, followed by two footmen who handed around trays of little cakes and sweetmeats and glasses of wine and punch.

There was more of the shrill laughter, and a lot of chatter, most of which revolved around society gossip.

Lady Coombs glanced at Zoe and murmured something in the ear of her somnolent husband, who roused himself sufficiently to peer in Zoe's direction and utter a snort. This reduced his lady to helpless laughter, and she trilled that dear Gardiner was "a wit of the first stare."

"A half-wit," sniggered Mr. Smythe in Zoe's ear. "But poor Melissa has to pretend she admires him, you know, lest everyone think she married him out of desperation." He selected a cake and a sweetmeat from the tray the footman offered, and passed the small crystal plate to Zoe, who was rendered speechless by his unkind comment. Accepting a glass of wine, he added with a broad grin, "Which she did, you know." Zoe said nothing, and in a hissing change to the dramatic he added: "You have made an enemy, pretty creature. Be warned."

"Good gracious! I have scarce spoken. What have I done to offend you?"

"In scarce speaking, you grieve me, but I am not easily crushed. Your offence, sweet maid, is that clear and lovely complexion. 'Tis sure to be admired. Melissa will never forgive you, and she has a nasty tongue."

Zoe thought his own tongue was far from nice. She replied lightly that he had an odd way of offering a compliment, and was relieved when a young woman with a giggle, whose name she could not recall, tapped him with her fan and engaged him in whispered gossip interspersed with muffled squeaks and observations that he was "a naughty rogue."

Sir Gilbert Fowles responded to a question by announcing that he was the richer by "a monkey" and that "old Neville" would be a sight more cautious in challenging him in the future.

Lord Coombs roused himself and remarked that it was unkind to add to "poor old Neville's" woes. This led into a discussion of the "Mandarin," who was, Zoe gathered, poor old Neville's son. She listened in astonishment to some extremely caustic criticisms of this unknown individual, which Lady Buttershaw cut short by clapping her hands and announcing that it was past time for Sir Gilbert to honour his promise.

His "important piece of news" was delivered with much drama, and consisted of the warning that wigs for the ladies were all the thing in Paris. "It grieves me to tell you, fair creatures," he said with a grin that contained little of grief. "Your pretty locks are doomed! Paris is agog, believe me. They say that by the turn of the decade every female will be obliged to follow fashion's whim, as are we gentlemen. Wigs or powder, m'dears. Wigs or powder!"

Consternation reigned. Anyone watching and unable to hear the words might well have imagined that some great disaster had wiped out half England's population. Although she took no part in their lamentations, Zoe responded politely when she was spoken to. She could not fail to be impressed by the beautiful materials and styles worn by the ladies; the back pleats of Watteau gowns, many of which extended into sweeping trains, the great skirts with the new flattened French paniers. She was less impressed by the jewels displayed, some of which she thought so opulent as to be vulgar, and that were rivalled by the gems that glittered from the cravats and shoe buckles of the gentlemen. The bag-wigs worn by two younger dandies, which were the very latest style, she thought utterly ridiculous. The hours dragged past, and she could not have been more pleased than when Lady Buttershaw rose, and announced abruptly that it was time for her to go to bed.

The guests lost no time in saying their farewells and departing.

Arbour and a lackey began to make the rounds, locking doors and closing windows. Hackham waited at the foot of the stairs to hand candles to Lady Buttershaw and Zoe, and my lady paused only long enough to say she hoped her protégé had learned something of the Top Ten Thousand and how to "go on," before stalking up the stairs.

'I have indeed,' thought Zoe, following the *grande dame*. 'They are very silly!'

Over her shoulder, her ladyship said ominously, "I shall expect your report tomorrow at luncheon, Miss Grainger."

CHAPTER V

church bell was striking the hour of eleven, and the Strand was bustling under a bright morning sun. It was a pale sun, and there was a nip of frost to the air that warned of the fading of autumn and of colder weather to come.

"Hey! Perry! Hold up!"

Peregrine Cranford, who had been trying not to use his fine amber cane for anything more than show, recognized the voice and turned to the coach that pulled into the kennel beside him. His eyes widened and his determination to be cuttingly polite was forgotten.

"By Jove!" he exclaimed admiringly. "What a fine turnout! Had to tool it yourself, did you? Is it as light as it looks?"

Very dashing in a caped riding coat, with a whip in one gloved hand, Sir Owen Furlong smiled down at him from the box. "Jump inside and see."

"Inside be damned! I'm coming up!"

"Oh, I say, dear old Peregrine," shouted a gentleman from the window of a passing carriage. "Do take care! 'Twould be *such* a pity if you were to fall!" A fading howl of laughter followed the caustic remark.

Heads turned.

'Fowles!' thought Cranford, gritting his teeth with rage.

Furlong held his team steady, and prayed, but Cranford negotiated the climb successfully, and sat on the box beside him. Noting the blaze in the blue eyes, Furlong enquired, "Why does that wart hate you so? Did you steal his bird of paradise or something of the sort?"

"I thwarted his ambitions, I'm happy to say! Fancied himself an athlete at school." Cranford grinned suddenly. "Wasn't."

"And you were. Typical of Fowles to be so mean-spirited. You may have to do something about him, my pippin."

"Very true. But never mind that. Deuce take it if ever I saw such a spanking coach. Did you find it in Longacre?"

"I did not!" Furlong eased the leathers, chirruped to his team, and the coach, a rich mahogany brown with gold trim, moved neatly into the traffic. "Designed it myself," he said proudly. "And the coach builder did splendidly, for I must say it handles like a feather. Thought I'd take it for a maiden run through Hyde Park. Care to come?"

"Jove, but I would! Provided you let me have a turn at the reins. And if you mean to say I am too enfeebled to—"

"For mercy's sake, have done, Perry!" Claiming the right-of-way over a ponderous Berliner whose four fat horses were proceeding at a snail's pace into the Haymarket, Furlong protested. "You know we all think highly of you." He waved his whip jauntily at the elderly gentleman who roared at him from the window of the Berliner, and added, "You really must try not to be so hot-at-hand. Your friends have a right to—"

"To coddle me?" snapped Cranford. "To invent nonsensical stories if I dare ask what they're up to? I know damned well there's something havy-cavey afoot and that you want to keep me out of all the fun. But I'll have you know— 'Ware that blockhead! *Idiot!*" he shouted as a muffin man made a suicidal dart under the noses of the team. "I'll have you know that I get about remarkably well, Furlong, and would not be a liability to you!"

"No. If you would condescend to wear your peg-leg instead of that fancy new appendage of yours." Darting a quick glance at his friend's aloof countenance, Furlong said, "You know that an artificial foot has never worked for you. I'll be bound your pretty lady would by far rather have you comfortable than—"

"My pretty lady," said Cranford, in this much interrupted conversation, "is mine no longer. What, hadn't you heard? Gave me the go-by, dear boy." His lips tightened, and bitterness came into his eyes at the thought of the lovely girl who had charmingly accepted his adoration and his gifts, but had dropped him without an instant's hesitation when a wealthy peer began to throw out lures. He added brightly, "Contrary to what you suppose, it seems she found my—ah, peg-leg an embarrassment."

'Blast the woman,' thought Furlong. 'So Jamie was right! That's why he had that stupid new foot made!' He said, "Then you're well rid of her. There are plenty of other ladies in the world, Perry."

"Perhaps. But I do not care to be looked upon with pity or teary-eyed compassion, thank you! And furthermore—" Cranford gave a gasp as they turned onto Piccadilly and Furlong had to pull up sharply to avoid a sedan chair.

"I vow this traffic gets worse by the day," grumbled Furlong. "I'm going to turn off." A moment later, he did so, only to swear furiously as a black carriage that had followed them for some distance, suddenly swung out to pass. With a fine display of skill, Furlong kept his vehicle from being crowded up the steps of a house. "Only look at that Bedlamite!" he raged, glaring after the fast-disappearing carriage. "He should be kept under restraint! A fellow don't spring his horses in Town!"

"Likely making a dash for St. George's," said Cranford, un-clenching his fists.

"Then may his bride prove to be a harpy!"

"I second the motion. But meanwhile, this is a nice quiet area, and a good place to rest your mangled nerves. So you may prove you're a sportsman by allowing me to take the ribbons for a space."

It was lightly said, but Furlong knew that the least sign of hesitation on his part must turn the knife in the wound Cranford's admired lady had dealt him. "Oh, very well," he grumbled, halting the team and climbing down from the box. "But since you are determined to play coachman, I shall try the squabs and let you freeze as you deserve." He paused, looking up as he swung the door open. "One scratch, Perry, and it's pistols at dawn!"

Cranford's appealingly boyish grin flashed. "Aye, aye, you ruffian, but I can't hang about here all day!" He raised his whip warningly. "Get in, or I'll give 'em the office!"

The team was nervous and moved faster than he'd intended, and Furlong was obliged to dive in and slam the door while the coach was moving off. Picking himself up, he opened the window, leaned out and howled a wrathful, "Devil take you, Perry! And slow down, you madcap, the street's not traffic free!"

Exhilarated, Cranford made no move to slow their spanking pace. "Jove, but she moves well," he shouted. "How is it inside?"

"You'll find out as soon as we reach the park, for that's as far as you're allowed to tool it!" But sinking back against the velvet squabs, Sir Owen was so gratified by the comfort of the ride that after a few minutes he jumped up to lean out of the window again. "Smooth as silk, Perry! You must— Hey!"

Cranford, who had glanced down at him, jerked his head up and was aghast to see a very large blue carriage bearing down on him from the opposite direction, while the black coach that had all but forced them off the road earlier must have had to make a detour, for it was again close behind, and coming up much too fast.

"Stay back, you fool!" roared Furlong furiously, but the black coach, the horses at a full gallop, swung level with them as Cranford pulled on the reins, fighting desperately to avoid a collision.

There was no choice for the oncoming blue carriage; with a shouted curse the man on the box drove his hacks up onto the flagway.

A young lady who'd been strolling alone had no choice either, and flung herself down the areaway steps of the nearest house.

The black coach shot past.

From nowhere, horrifyingly, a man appeared in front of Furlong's terrified horses.

Blanching, Cranford whispered, "My dear God!" and strove mightily.

The black carriage raced away, free and clear.

Furlong's animals reared and whinnied shrilly, trying to avoid the man before them. The coach rocked and jolted.

But it was hopeless.

Cranford felt the sickening bump. For an instant of pure horror he was on that ravening battlefield again, fighting to keep his men from deserting . . . falling . . . quite unable to escape the heavy iron wheel of the gun carriage as it smashed onto his foot . . .

Dangerously near to overturning, Furlong's beautiful new equipage slammed against the side of the big blue coach and came to a rocking halt, with Cranford hanging on for dear life.

The coachman was raving; all the horses were neighing and prancing in panic; several pedestrians were running to the aid of the poor creature who had gone down under those iron-shod hooves; doors and windows were being flung open, and more people were gathering around.

There had been not a sound from Furlong, who was not the man to draw back at such a moment, which brought the additional fear that he might have been thrown down when the coach lurched so crazily.

"Poor cove's stone dead!" An organ-grinder, his scared monkey chattering and clinging about his neck, straightened from the pathetic figure under the coach, and shook his fist at Cranford. "That there young gentry cove playing coachman done it! Murder's what it is! I see it all! Going like the wind he were! Much his kind care fer the likes of us! Our lives don't mean no more'n a dog's!"

From beyond the blue coach came a feminine scream, followed by an outraged if fading demand that the Watch be summoned.

Cranford knew that voice. Making his awkward descent from the box, he thought grimly that there was no end to the evils of this terrible morning.

Shortly before Peregrine Cranford first glimpsed Furlong's new coach, Elsie Gorton was exclaiming uneasily, "But, Miss! Ay have been give strict orders you are never to be out of may sayt!"

"Oh, I do wish you would stop talking in that foolish fashion." Zoe slid her hands into her muff. "Why can you not speak in your natural way?"

Gorton sighed. "Because Ay mayt forget, Miss. Ay do sometimes. And her la'ship likes it. She thinks Ay tray to copy her talk, and that pleases her."

"Oh, very well. As for your not letting me out of your sight, pish! I'll not be far away." She glanced out of the carriage windows. "Are we almost there? Faith, but I'd forgot how crowded the city is! All these people and houses and shops! And so much noise and confusion."

Scanning her anxiously, Gorton said, "Are you sure you'll be all right, Miss?"

Zoe realized she was behaving like a very green girl, and gathered herself together. "I am not straight from the schoolroom, you know. I will have a lovely time in the emporium, and you and Stone can go off to a quiet place where you can chat for a little while in peace. Is what you would like—no?"

Gorton clasped her hands and emitted an ecstatic moan.

"Very well," said Zoe. "But now you must help me, Elsie."

With a worshipful and tremulous smile, Gorton mumbled that she would be ever so proud to think she could help Miss in *any* way.

"Well, you can," Zoe confirmed, "by telling me about this report Lady Buttershaw seems to expect from me this afternoon. Do you think I am to answer questions about the fashions the ladies wore last evening?"

Thinking very much, Gorton said carefully, "Likely so, Miss. And—er, the gents, Ay expect."

"Hmm. I collect I had better not say that those little black bags they stuff their wigs into at the back look stupid!"

Gorton grinned and agreed that would be best left unsaid. She glanced out as the carriage pulled to a halt on busy Bond Street. "This is the New Emporium. Oh, Miss! I'm all a'twitter! It is so good, so very kind in you, but—if anyone should recognize you . . . !"

"If anyone should recognize me, which I doubt, I shall tell them I sent you off to purchase something for me." Zoe paused, listening to the tolling of a church bell. "There! 'Tis eleven o'clock. Now you must pick me up again in no more than thirty minutes, for I do so want to see some of the famous places in the city. Is agreed?"

It was, said Gorton huskily, agreed.

A porter hurried from the emporium to open the carriage door and hand Zoe down the steps. He waited for Gorton, but Zoe shook her head, the door was slammed shut, and the carriage rolled away. Her heart beating rather fast, and well aware that the porter eyed her curiously as he opened the door to the shop, Zoe smiled her thanks and went inside.

She entered a large crowded room, warm and fragrant, where many long tables were piled with ells of cloth, pattern cards, embroidery silks, ribands and braids, silk flowers, zephyr shawls, dainty mittens and gloves, and lacy fichus. Ladies wandered about with friends, or were followed by servants. Clerks hovered and made deferential and carefully pronounced suggestions. And throughout was a hum of conversation and an air of elegant prosperity.

Fascinated, Zoe moved from counter to counter until, overhearing a matron say without bothering to lower her voice that there was a most exceptional milliners "just around the corner," she abandoned this house of treasures and ventured outside once more.

She had evidently not left by the same door through which she'd arrived, for this street was unfamiliar and less travelled. She hesitated, but the porter was watching, the corner was only a short distance away, and pride forbade that she admit she was lost in the big city. Hurrying on, her hands in her muff and her steps betraying a confidence she could not feel, she went around the corner only to find herself on a residential street of large and prosperous-looking mansions. It was, she thought, a charming street, and she liked the fact that there were trees here and there. It was a great pity that there were not very many trees on London's streets. Houses and shops and churches were all well and good, but—

She gave a gasp of fright as a large blue coach that had been proceeding towards her swerved sharply. From the opposite direction came two more carriages, one black, one brown, racing abreast and taking up the entire street. She had a split-second awareness that there was not enough room for three vehicles. There followed a rapid and nightmarish series of events. The team of the blue carriage was forced onto the flagway and ran straight at her. In a frantic dive for life she flung herself down the area steps of the nearest house. From the corner of her eye she saw the black carriage thunder away, even as, the ultimate horror, a pedestrian was struck by the team of the rival brown coach.

All then was pandemonium, the snorts and whinnies of frightened horses mingling with shouts and cries of shock and angry accusation. With blackened mittens, a torn gown, her cap hanging down, and her knees shaking, Zoe struggled back up the steps. Some men were peering under the brown carriage. A scream escaped her as she caught a glimpse of a pathetically twisted figure lying under the wheels. There was blood . . . Faint and sick, she looked up at a familiar face that seemed to float high above her. A handsome face, white and strained now, and with a tight-lipped look of desperation. Revolted, she cried out something, but the scene was fading. She was trembling so violently that she could not stand . . . Someone was supporting her, but she could not see who it was . . . In fact, she could not see anything . . . at all . . .

I must protest, officer," said the motherly housekeeper indignantly. "The young lady has suffered a severe shock and should be conveyed to her home at once. I am very sure my employers would insist upon it."

The officer from Bow Street, a slender man with a thin intelligent face and a hawk nose, bowed slightly, but pushed past her and said in a chill and authoritative voice that in his experience, the sooner statements could be taken down, the better. Producing a pencil and notebook, he walked across the tastefully furnished withdrawing room and drew a chair close to the chaise longue where Zoe lay. "If Miss Grainger is feeling better . . . ?" he said with a hint of a smile.

Much embarrassed, Zoe set aside the brandy that tasted horrid, but had to an extent restored her. She was still trembling, and her knees felt weak, but she said apologetically, "I am indeed sorry to have caused such a fuss. I promise you I have never in my life swooned, before this."

"Small wonder," said the housekeeper, coming to stand militantly beside her and fix the officer with a challenging stare. "The shock of being almost trampled and run over by a coach and four is enough to cause any lady to swoon; much less seeing a poor creature as good as murdered before her very eyes!"

Zoe shuddered, and took up the horrid brandy again.

The Bow Street Runner watched her narrowly, and with pencil poised, asked, "Is that your view of it, Miss? Was it deliberate murder?"

Blinking, she coughed and said hoarsely, "I—wouldn't say . . . deliberate, exactly. But had he not been going much too fast, 'twould not have happened."

The officer wrote busily. "I know that as this lady said, you've suffered a great shock, Miss. But I'd be much obliged if you could describe exactly what took place."

The housekeeper's chin drew in, and her ample bosom thrust out. She said, "I think it would be best, Miss Grainger, if we was to send for your people—they'll likely be worrying for you."

The Runner slanted an irked frown at her, but Zoe said at once, "Oh, yes, if you please. My maid was running an errand for me and left me at that lovely emporium just around the corner. She will be beside herself." She looked at the housekeeper imploringly. "If someone could be sent? Her name is Gorton."

The housekeeper patted her shoulder kindly. "Never you fret, Miss. I'll send the fireboy round at once."

Watching her bustle out, the Runner stifled a sigh of relief. "You were saying, Miss Grainger . . . ?"

"Oh . . . yes. Well, I saw the big chariot, the blue one, you know, coming down the street towards me, and then two more carriages came along, racing side by side. The blue chariot had no room and was crowded onto the flagway! It was making straight for me! So—I threw myself down the area steps, and the brown coach knocked that poor man down!" She closed her eyes a moment. "Oh, 'twas . . . dreadful!"

"Yes, indeed, Miss. Is a mercy you were not killed also! Then the brown coach struck the victim as he crossed the street?"

She nodded.

"By which time the black coach had gone past?"

"Yes."

"So the black coach was not actually involved when the gentleman was knocked down?"

"No. As I said, it had already passed by when . . . it happened."

She was shaking visibly. The Runner said gently, "I will be as quick as I can, but I must beg that you are very clear on these points, Miss Grainger. The victim *walked* across the street?"

Zoe stared at him. "He may have run, I suppose."

He gave a small tight smile, and persisted, "The black coach was in the *lead*, and appeared to have been racing with the brown coach?"

"That was all I could think, yes."

An acid voice said from the open doorway, "Then your thoughts were scrambled, madam!"

She jerked her head around, and was surprised by the shrill

note to her own voice as she cried, "How can you *dare* say such a thing? Were you at your collecting again, doctor?"

"I am *not* a doctor! If you want to know—" Peregrine Cranford started forward, but a constable put an arm across the doorway, restraining him. He snarled fiercely, "I don't mean to attack the silly chit, you fool! The fellow *jumped*, I tell you! He jumped from that damnable black coach right under my team's—"

"I'll thank you not to use strong language in front of this lady," scolded the Runner.

"And it is besides so much stuff and nonsense," said Zoe angrily. "Why would anyone do so mad a thing?"

The Runner nodded. "Your point is well taken, ma'am."

"Her point is poppycock!" From under dark and frowning brows a blue glare scorched at Zoe. "There could be any number of reasons why the poor fellow jumped out. I doubt this lady was in any state—or in a proper position—to see clearly what transpired."

"I am not in the habit of telling falsehoods," declared Zoe.

"Indeed?" Cranford said hotly, "In my experience, that is precisely your habit!" He turned to the Runner, and added, "I'd not be surprised was this poor creature deranged!"

"Oh!" Incensed, Zoe gasped. "How *dare* you say such a wicked thing, only because I am not accustomed to seeing people ch-chopped up every day—as you are!" And fighting a sudden need to weep, she counter-attacked, "You are a bad man, sir. I do not scruple to say so!"

"No, you don't, madam! I can vouch for that sorry fact! If you *had* any scruples you might stop and think before you jumped to your erroneous conclusions!"

"Constable," interposed the Runner, standing. "Please remove this gentleman. I will talk to you later, sir."

"You will talk to me sooner, or 'twill have to be at my house, for I've to get my friend home. In case it has slipped your mind, he was injured and I must call in a physician."

"What a pity," said the Runner scornfully, "that you did not have more concern for your friend than to race another coach on a city—"

"Curse you for a blockhead! I was *not* racing! I have told you—"

"You have told me, sir, an extreme doubtful tale, which I cannot but question. *Beyond* question is the fact that Mr. Burton Farrier, a highly placed civil servant, lies dead. And that several witnesses, including this lady, are willing to swear that your grossly improper and reckless speed brought the tragedy about."

Struggling against the constable's efforts to drag him away, Cranford raged, "That is a lie! I tell you, this woman is addle-brained at best and wouldn't know what she saw *if* she saw it! The fellow *jumped*—or was—"

The Runner raised his voice, "If I have your statement properly written down, and brought round to your home, will you sign it, Miss Grainger?"

Meeting the murderous glare of the amateur coachman with unyielding defiance, Zoe said, "I most certainly will!"

An hour had slipped away by the time the hackney stopped in front of the large and pleasant house on Henrietta Street where Peregrine Cranford lived when in London. His rooms were on the ground floor, and he called to his servant as he limped into the small entrance hall.

Florian came running. Of slender build, he moved with fluid grace and with anxiety clearly written on his delicate features. Olive skinned and dark-haired, his birth and background were unknown, but he was soft-spoken, with a precision to his words that Cranford believed was due to English not being his native tongue. He had been sold into a gypsy tribe as a small boy and escaped a life of cruelty and servitude by running away in his teen years. Cranford had rescued him from a hand-to-mouth existence and, against the advice of all his friends, had taken the youth into his service. He had never regretted it. Florian was faithful and utterly devoted.

Cranford asked in a distraught fashion, "Has he come round? Has a doctor seen him? Is it bad?"

"Yes, and yes, and—no, sir. 'Tis a concussion that the physician says is not serious. Save that—er, it has brought on an attack of that fever he suffered in India."

"Oh, Gad!" groaned Cranford, allowing Florian to take his cloak, and thrusting tricorne and cane into his hands. "Is he abed?"

"In the spare room, sir. Are you—"

Cranford was already limping rapidly along the passage. "I'm well," he called over his shoulder. "Lunch, if you please. I'm also starved!" And he thought bitterly, 'Even if I have just murdered someone and put a good friend into a sickbed!'

Florian ran ahead to open the guest room door. His attempt to say more was cut off as Cranford brushed past, and with a resigned sigh, he closed his lips and retreated to the kitchen.

The draperies were drawn over the bedchamber windows and the sparsely furnished room was dim. Tiptoeing to the four-poster, Cranford peered anxiously at the long still shape of the man who lay there.

Sir Owen's eyes were closed, his powdered hair was dishevelled and he was frowningly pale except for two ominous spots of colour high on his cheekbones. Cranford, who had dreaded to see bandages, was relieved by the lack of them and hoped prayerfully that the physician was correct and the concussion not dangerous. Poor Furlong was shivering though. Cautiously, he pulled up the eiderdown.

"If you think to turn me up sweet, you waste your efforts," growled Sir Owen, not opening his eyes.

Cranford groaned and pulled a chair closer to the bed. Sitting down, he said, "I am so *very* sorry! It's all my fault!"

Furlong scowled at him. "Well, it certainly ain't mine! I was in-in-ssside my once-beautiful new carriage!"

"I know you were. Dear old boy, your teeth are chattering. Is there anything— What can I do?"

"You can bl-blasted well tell me what the d-devil you were about! Much against my better judgment I let you tool my new coach, and what must you do but st-start to run a race with some d-down-the-road cloth-head! I w-wonder you didn't slaughter half-a-dozen ladies, to s-say nothing—"

"Lord knows I didn't mean to kill the silly— I mean, the poor fellow. Owen, I swear he—"

At this, Furlong lurched up and demanded in an aghast voice, "What are you saying? Perry . . . ? You didn't *r-really . . . ?*"

"Deuce take it, I thought you knew! No, *please* do not go into the boughs! I'd not have mentioned a word about it if I'd even suspected you weren't told!"

"I wasn't!" Furlong was paler than ever, and there was an alarming glitter in his eyes. "Am I to t-take it that you *struck* someone?"

Pulling himself together, Cranford ordered, "Lie down and calm yourself or I'm leaving."

Furlong glared at him, then lay back and pointed out, "Can't leave. This is-is your house, not mine."

"Oh, so 'tis. If you stay quiet, I'll tell you, though I probably should not. It was that same maniac in the black coach who nigh ran us off the road earlier. You'll recall you shouted at him not to pass?"

Furlong answered uncertainly, "Vaguely. But I did not mean you to kill the poor devil."

"No more did I! He came on at the gallop. At the *gallop*, Owen! There was not the time or the room to overtake. I was sure he would slow his team. But he didn't. Passed like the wind and right under the noses of the hacks of that antiquated chariot on t'other side of the road. I had all I could do to keep your cattle from bolting. And then . . . Oh God, 'twas awful! A poor fellow jumped out in front of us!"

"*Jumped?* The devil you say!"

Cranford searched his friend's horrified face and pleaded hoarsely, "He must have, for he appeared as from thin air! There was the most fearful bobbery, with people shouting that I was a murderer, and that repulsive young woman screeching that I was driving too fast!" Cranford dabbed his handkerchief at his pallid and perspiring brow. "But that was not the way of it Owen! I *swear!* I *had* slowed, but there was no least chance to avoid him. He was in front of the team and under the wheels in a trice!"

"But—but why should the poor m-man have jumped in front of you? Was he a suicide d'you think?"

"That—or mayhap he was running to help the screecher and misjudged his distance from our team."

"Why should he help the scr— er, the lady?"

Cranford pressed a hand to his head distractedly. "What? Oh, well she was almost run down by the blue coach, for it was forced up onto the flagway. She started screeching, and then swooned, and the Bow Street Runner came, and— 'Fore God, Owen, I never saw the poor fellow in time! It is so ghastly to think I . . . killed an innocent—"

He looked devastated, and Sir Owen intervened comfortingly, "No, no. I am very sure it wasn't your fault, Perry. Do not bl-blame yourself, old lad. We must talk with your screeching lady and convince her to see reason."

"Reason! I doubt she's had a rational thought in her entire life! She took me in violent aversion in High Wycombe last week, only because Tio Glendenning's madcap brother hove my new foot over the hedge."

Sir Owen lay back against his pillows. "What, Michael Templeby? Never say he threw your foot at the lady?"

"Well, he didn't. But you know what a scatter-wit he is. He had made off with the foot just after I'd collected it from that fellow in Oxford who carves 'em for me. Templeby stole it away and painted it so that it looked just like a real foot." Momentarily diverted, Cranford sighed reminiscently. "It really did, Owen. Deuced clever the way he did it. Toes, and even toenails, each one a different colour. And at the top—Jove! It was pretty ghastly. Jamie Morris thought it hilarious, but I was ready to strangle Templeby. He ran off with the foot, and Jamie almost had him, so he tossed it over the hedge."

"And—and hit the poor lady?" asked Furlong, awed.

"I don't think so. But she's a very silly female. Swoons at the slightest thing . . . She set up her screeching and started accusing me of being a *doctor*, of all things! And now she's at it again!" Cranford groaned and said distractedly, "Heaven above, how quickly one's life can be ruined! Yesterday, my greatest annoyance was that I'm obliged to call on some distant relative I've never even met. And today, I'm a—a murderer, with Bow Street preparing the chains for my feet, and the screecher fairly slavering with eagerness to bear witness 'gainst me, and Whitehall levelling their guns, and—"

Furlong's head had not been helped by this erratic tale and was pounding miserably. Confused, but trying to make sense of it all, he now stiffened, and intervened sharply, "Whitehall? How are they concerned?"

"It seems my unfortunate victim was some highly placed and much admired public official. Of all—"

Struggling to one elbow, Furlong demanded, "What is—was his name?"

"Dash it all, I don't know." Cranford drove a hand through

· 103 ·

his hair. "I can scarce recall my own at this moment. Bernard—somebody. Or—no, 'twas a family name I think . . . Bentley, or Barton— Burton! That was it! As for the surname, though— Oh, egad! What's the matter? Are you—"

His voice quivering with tension, Furlong said, "Not— *Burton Farrier*, surely?"

"Yes. That's it. What are you about? You can't get up!"

"I *must* . . . get up," argued Furlong, pushing back the bed-clothes doggedly.

Restraining him as best he might, Cranford gave a cry of relief when the door opened and Florian came in with a laden tray. "Thank heaven! Put that down and come and help. Sir Owen has suffered a spasm, I think! There, that's better. Lie back, poor fellow. Only see how you've exhausted yourself." And as Furlong sank down, weak and panting from his efforts, Cranford added in a very gentle voice, "Whatever is it, Owen? Never say that to add to all else, I've contrived to murder a friend of yours?"

"You've contrived to . . . to despatch a . . . a very great . . . snake," gasped Furlong. " 'Terrier' Farrier's dead, Florian!"

"Aieee!" exclaimed the gypsy youth, his dark eyes very bright. "Justice, sometimes it really does prevail!"

" 'Terrier'?" echoed Cranford, frowning. "I've heard something of a man called that. A sort of bounty hunter, wasn't he?"

Furlong closed his eyes wearily. "He was. A murdering villain who snuffed out . . . many fine lives."

Cranford bent over him, then beckoned to Florian, and tiptoed to the door. In the passageway he whispered, "I've to go and see my solicitor about this wretched business. Keep a close eye on him, lad. He must rest."

The gypsy youth nodded, but after the front door had closed on Cranford, he returned at once to the quiet bedchamber.

Sir Owen said, "I'm awake. I didn't want you to say too much."

Florian sat in the chair Cranford had vacated. "Burton Farrier!" he exclaimed. "Why should such an unfeeling creature commit suicide?"

"Exactly so. You know he was a tool of the League of Jewelled Men?"

"Yes. Ah, then you think it was an execution!"

"He made mistakes. The Squire d-don't permit mistakes. I think they gave him more latitude than-than most, but they decided to punish him, and to do so in such a way that one of us would be blamed."

"You, Sir Owen! Praise God, it did not work."

"It came blasted close to working! Their fiendish coach passed us the first time to make sure I was driving. On their second p-pass, they must not have realized that Lieutenant Cranford had taken the ribbons!"

Florian said gravely, "A neat trap, sir. Meant to kill two birds with one stone."

"But sprung on the wrong man. You-you must f-find Lieutenant Morris and t-tell him all this."

"Not now, sir. Forgive, but you are shivering again. When Mr. Peregrine comes back, I'll slip away. Please, try to rest now." He stood and walked to the door, then turned back. Sir Owen was watching him. He said, "One last question, if I may, sir. Shall you be able to keep my master clear of the League? Is it possible, now?"

Sir Owen sighed. "I don't know, Florian. We can sure as the devil try!"

Chapter VI

y the time a pale and fearful Gorton had been restored to her and a very scared Cecil Stone had driven them home, Zoe felt quite wrung out, and ready to follow Gorton's suggestion that she lie down and rest in her quiet bedchamber. In some mysterious fashion, however, news of the tragedy had preceded them. They reached Yerville Hall to find Lady Buttershaw's great coach drawn up outside, with her coachman and personal footman on the box, two lackeys standing up behind, and three mounted gentlemen apparently ready to serve as outriders.

Lady Buttershaw herself emerged onto the front steps, wearing an awesomely high wig, wrapped in a sable cloak, and clutching a furled umbrella much as if it had been a military baton. She waved the umbrella on high and howled, "Forward to . . . Bond . . ." Catching sight of Stone and the small coach at that point, her call to arms faded. The rescue mission was disbanded, and, looking somewhat thwarted, my lady led the way into the house. Lady Julia hurried to Zoe's side, and one glance at her pale and anxious face was sufficient for Zoe to declare that she had suffered no injuries beyond a few bruises, and would be quite all right if she might just rest for a little while.

Comfortably settled on a sofa in the withdrawing room,

with a hot cup of tea in her hand, she gave a very brief account of the incident. Lady Julia uttered occasional murmurs of shock or sympathy. Lady Buttershaw was attentively silent, her thin lips tightly compressed and her eyes glittering.

"It was truly dreadful," said Zoe, her voice tremulous. "That poor gentleman! I never saw anyone k-killed before."

Lady Julia squeezed her hand and said understandingly, "Of course you did not, poor child! I wonder you were in a condition to be driven home, I am sure such a sight would have left me quite prostrated!"

"I have not a doubt of it," Lady Buttershaw agreed, with a scornful glance which reduced her sister to silence.

Zoe said quickly, "I knew you would be worried for my sake, so I asked to be allowed to come home at once, instead of making a statement at the scene."

From Lady Buttershaw came an explosive snort. "If there is one thing I cannot and *will* not countenance, Miss Grainger, it is that any least breath of—*scandal*—should touch this house!

Taken aback, Zoe protested, "Surely, 'tis not scandalous, ma'am, that I chanced to witness an accident?"

"Accident? I understood you to call it by quite another name. Did not you, Julia? Was this debacle not described to us as a foul murder?"

Lady Yerville said hesitantly, "Well, er, yes. But if—"

"Exactly so. And murder, I advise you, will be reported in the newspapers. Vulgarity in its most depraved form." Lady Buttershaw shuddered, and closed her eyes. "I never *dreamed* the day would dawn when anyone under my roof would consort with such low people!"

Beginning to feel like a criminal, Zoe said, "But I did not consort with anyone, my lady! I promise you I would have nothing to do with that horrid—"

"Had you not been wandering about the back streets *unes-*

corted, you would have been spared such a tawdry encounter! Indeed, why Gorton was not at your side is something I shall be pleased to have explained to me!"

"Yes, but the poor child must be quite worn out, Clara," interposed Lady Julia valiantly. "Surely we need not—"

"One gathers," Lady Buttershaw swept on, overriding her sister's gentle tones, "that we must be grateful Miss Grainger escaped the indignity of being hauled off to Bow Street!"

"The Runner wanted me to go there," admitted Zoe. "But fortunately, he agreed to bring the papers here inst—"

"What? What papers?"

"Why, I—I promised the Runner I will sign a statement that I saw the way that disgusting creature was driving, and—"

Lady Buttershaw thundered, "You—will—do—no—such—thing!"

Zoe had never heard even her step-mother shout so, and she shrank. But although her voice shook, she persisted bravely, "My apologies an that dis-distresses you, ma'am, but I consider it my duty to testify—"

"Consider again, gel! While you are under my roof—"

Surprisingly Lady Julia put in with quiet but rare firmness, "Now Clara, we must not be hasty."

"I cannot stand idly by," persisted Zoe, "and let that evil doctor—"

"Doctor? 'Twas my understanding that the person driving—" Lady Buttershaw's teeth snapped shut, as if she'd said more than she intended.

Lady Julia stroked Zoe's hand soothingly. "Are you acquainted with the gentleman, my dear?"

"Not acquainted, ma'am. But I had—er, encountered him before, as I tried to tell Lady Buttershaw, when he drove past us on the way to London."

Lady Buttershaw stared, then, comprehension dawning,

she demanded, "Do you say your murderous driver was that same insolent *ruffian* who made off with my wig when we came up from High Wycombe?"

It was one way of putting it, thought Zoe. "The very same, ma'am. And at the Three Horse Inn I had seen him playing with—with a severed limb!"

"God bless my soul," gasped Lady Julia. "The man must be a monster *veritable*!"

Lady Buttershaw, who had been struck to momentary silence, now bellowed, "Why was I never *informed* of this? I will tell you, Miss Grainger, that it does no *good* to go through life with your tongue in your pocket. You are duty bound to supply whatever details Bow Street may require of you. Especially since you were an actual witness to the crime. Collect your thoughts and tell them exactly what you saw. Pon rep, but I fail to see the difficulty!"

Zoe's head was aching and she was beginning to feel very tired indeed. She said, "I will, ma'am. Though . . . if you please, I do not want to think of it any more today! It was so horrid!"

Lady Julia stood. "It must have been, indeed. Clara, the child must not—"

"Dwell upon it?" her sister interrupted. "I agree, and we shall change the subject, for I've a more important matter to discuss."

Zoe's heart sank, and Lady Julia exclaimed with real indignation, "*Now?* Surely this is not the time!"

"Why ever not? My dear sister, pray do not indulge your foolish habit of making every molehill into a mountain! It was a sad occurrence, and the perpetrator must be punished. But the unfortunate victim was, after all, unknown to Miss Grainger, and while it would be proper for her, in Christian charity, to include him in her prayers tonight, his passing has nothing to say to us, and there is no cause for her to be weeping and wailing and gnashing her teeth!"

A little flushed, Lady Julia ventured, "Nor is she doing so, but I scarcely think—"

"That is all too apparent! If you did so, Julia, you would realize that I have gone to considerable pains in behalf of Miss Grainger, and I am entitled to hear what she has to say!"

"Yes, but not—"

"You may leave us, sister. I am very sure your creatures are pining for you!"

Pierced by a blazing glare, Lady Julia stood her ground for a moment, then wilted, murmured something incoherent, and drifted away.

"There," said Lady Buttershaw as the door closed behind her sister. "Now we may be comfortable. I should warn you, Miss Grainger, not to be unduly influenced by Lady Julia Yerville. She is good hearted, but hers is not—er, in the general way of things—a strong spirit. You will do much better to model yourself after me. But we will say no more on that head, for I require to have your opinions."

Zoe, who would have thought her opinions were of not the slightest interest to this formidable matron, stammered, "My—opinions . . . ? On—on what, ma'am?"

"Great heavens, gel! What would you suppose? The *prospects*, of course! Heaven knows, I gathered the pick of the current crop for your approval. All scions of the finest families and with the best of connections. Charming young gentlemen, of most excellent address. And, last, but by no means least, not one having less than fifteen thousand a year!" A crocodilian smile was levelled at Zoe's astounded countenance. My lady prompted coyly, "Well, my dear?"

Zoe gulped, "Do you—do you refer to the gentlemen who attended your party l-last evening, ma'am?"

"To whom else would I refer, pray? Hackham? Or my coachman? Do try not to be such a widgeon! I promised to find you a husband, did I not? Be so good as to tell me which one you favour."

Conjuring up Sir Gilbert Fowles' leering grin; the vapid incoherencies of the man called "Purr"; Mr. Reginald Smythe, with his malicious tongue and high-pitched giggle; Zoe thought numbly, 'And those were the best of a very silly lot! My heavens!'

I cannot properly express my admiration of you, my dear boy." Lady Buttershaw fluttered fan and eyelashes at her morning caller, and purred disastrously, "To venture out on a rainy morning, only to see me! And especially when it must be monstrous difficult for you to get about."

A muscle rippled in Peregrine Cranford's jaw. Yesterday's appalling tragedy and his subsequent battle with the Bow Street blockheads had been nightmarish. He'd hoped today would be better, but he had not dreamed when Great Uncle Nugent desired him to call upon a distant relation that he would become the victim of so tiresome a lady. The "tour" of the innumerable historical artifacts in this gloomy saloon had taken a full hour, during which time he'd made a really heroic effort to appear interested. He had thought then to escape, but had been thwarted at every turn, and was now trapped with a glass of sherry in his hand and a strong sense of ill usage in his heart. He declared that he found it not in the least difficult to "get about," and was further irritated to be the recipient of a sympathetic smile and a murmured, "So brave! So uncomplaining!"

"Furthermore, ma'am," he pointed out, "the rain stopped half an hour since, and the sun is shining. As I said, the general desired me to call and present his compliments, which I have been pleased to do."

"Thus so kindly granting me the pleasure of your company, *dear* cousin Peregrine," she trilled.

So far as he could unravel the family connection, the general's late wife, Great Aunt Eudora, had been second cousin to Lady Buttershaw's mama-in-law. To name him "cousin" in so proprietary a fashion was, he thought aggrievedly, taking advantage of the situation. Further appalled by her coy glance, he lied that the "pleasure" had been all his, and rather pointedly set down his glass.

"Ah, but you are eager to leave me," she said, pouting a little. "Alas, alas! And just as I was trying to summon the courage to avail myself of dear Nugent's generous offer."

He thought, 'Heaven help us all! Now what?' and lifted his brows in faint enquiry.

"How well you do it!" She gave his wrist a playful little rap with her fan. "Such a proud tilt to your handsome head; so haughty a droop of your lips. Every inch the proud aristocrat. Disdain conveyed, yet with not a word uttered that might give offence! I have seen it practised by *la fine fleur de la société* and I will tell you that—aside from August Falcon who is a master of the art—I never saw it done better! Which is remarkable in so young a man!"

His face flaming, he said, "Ma'am, I assure you I meant no disrespect, but—"

"But I bored you with our family history, and then irked you by referring to your affliction, and like all proud men you do not like your wounds touched, no?"

The glittering eyes that bored at him, and the smile that made her upper lip appear glued to her teeth held more of triumph than amusement. Almost one might have heard the ring of crossing swords; a duel she had won—thus far, at least. He met her regard steadily and evaded in a cool drawl, "I believe you referred to an offer the general had made?"

"And I am properly set down. Bravo!" Her laugh set his

teeth on edge. She said in that too-loud bray of a voice, "No, my fine gallant. *You* did. Never say you have forgot, naughty one. The general commanded you to be of service to me. That *was* what you told me, I think?"

"But, of course, ma'am." Dreading her answer, he enquired, "Have you a commission for me?"

"Just a very . . . *teensy* one. But— No! Not for the world would I interfere with the far more important demands on your valuable time! So you are free to go." She sighed. "Even though our visit has been sadly brief. "Or so it has seemed to me, at least."

It was neatly done and without a shred of sincerity, for she knew perfectly well he was bound to follow his great-uncle's wishes. He said, " 'Twould be my very great pleasure to serve you, ma'am. Indeed, the general would be vastly put out did I fail you. Providing, of course," he added as a last resort, " 'tis within my power."

"Ah! I *knew* breeding would prevail! Bless you, dear boy! I feel sure you will not be overset in granting my wish, and you will bestow a great favour upon an unhappy child, besides!"

That didn't sound too bad; he liked children. Brightening, he desired to know how he might be of assistance.

" 'Tis an all too common tale." She shook her head mournfully. "A second marriage; an unwanted child. Neglect. Unkindness. All cunningly concealed, of course, for the family is prominent in the county society. But *I* saw, for there is little escapes *me*, I promise you!"

He had no doubt of that fact, and began to wonder uneasily if he was expected to adopt some unfortunate waif.

"I rescued the poor little gel," my lady went on. "Brought her to Town and have provided for her. But she is lonely, and has lost all her friends, of course. I promised to take her for a drive this afternoon to see some of the city. And now, I am summoned by an ailing dependent and must disappoint her.

She will be heartbroken. I was wondering . . ." She fixed him with one of her arch smiles.

Ineffably relieved, Cranford said, "If I would conduct her about? Why, 'twould be a pleasure, ma'am." He stood. "Would half-past two o'clock be convenient?"

Zoe sat at the escritoire in her bedchamber and frowned over the notes she'd made. Lady Buttershaw's instructions that she must give a clear account of what she'd seen of yesterday's accident had begun to worry her, and she'd realized that some of her recollections were hazy at best. In an effort to organize her thoughts she'd written down her impressions, and now, reading over what she'd written, she was troubled.

Watching her, Gorton asked, "Is it that you are still too overset, Miss? Perhaps you should not go out driving this afternoon."

Zoe's brow cleared. "Oh, no. Thank you, Elsie, but truly I am feeling much better today, and besides, 'twill take my mind off . . . things. There is so much I long to see, and Lady Buttershaw promises to take me to St. Paul's, and the Tower, and Westminster Abbey, and Convent Garden, and—all the places I have so looked forward to seeing!"

Gorton laughed. "La, Miss! You'll never see the half of them in one afternoon! But Ay had best get you changed now. Her la'ship told me particular as you was to look your best. Likely you'll be meeting up with more of her friends on your way."

Zoe said nothing, but as her wrapper was replaced with an underdress of white embroidered in blue, and then a charming *robe à la Française* of powder blue silk was thrown over, she could only pray that she was not to be presented to more "prospects."

When she'd nervously admitted to having been unimpressed with any of her alleged suitors, Lady Buttershaw had tightened her lips to a thin line and taken a deep breath, as though girding herself for battle. Convinced that she was to be dealt a harsh scold, Zoe had been reprieved. She was, Lady Buttershaw advised, "an ungrateful gel, which might be expected of one with no knowledge of the *ton,* or of proper behaviour." She'd been packed off to bed then, and had fallen asleep almost at once, awakening briefly for a drowsy hour and a light supper, and then sleeping through the night.

She had been overjoyed this morning, when Lady Buttershaw had sent her footman with news of the afternoon sightseeing drive, "to make up to poor Miss Grainger for her terrible ordeal yesterday." She'd also felt a twinge of guilt. She had supposed when she'd been brought to Town that she was to enjoy the life of a cheap drudge. Instead, she had been given her own maid, provided with every luxury and comfort, asked very little of in return, and now, so astonishingly soon, it had been decided that a suitable husband must be found for her.

She experienced a stirring of unease. It was rather odd, she thought, that a comparative stranger should go to so much trouble in her behalf. Unless . . . perchance Lady Buttershaw and Papa's new wife were not such strangers as she'd supposed. Could this entire affair have been planned between them with a view to marrying her off so as to permanently remove her from Travisford? And, good gracious, there was her naughty imagination at work again! How uncharitable of her to entertain such suspicions. It was far more likely that Lady Buttershaw and her sister had decided that Miss Zoe Grainger was a hopeless country bumpkin who would not suit them, and sooner than send her packing were taking this means to provide for her. Behind her odd humours and that dreadful temper, Lady Buttershaw must hide a warm heart, for her intention had been kind, and she very likely considered that she had been repaid with rank ingratitude.

'But I wonder if any one of those gentlemen dreamed he had been chosen to wed a "country bumpkin," ' thought Zoe with faint amusement. True, several of the "Prospects" had been lavish with their compliments, but her innate common sense had told her these were rank insincerities and she'd paid them no heed. She was very sure none of them was in the slightest interested in her, so it was as well that she had found not one of my lady's friends to be either warm-hearted, witty, charming, or in the least degree attractive. Certainly not to be compared to her beloved brother, or to the gentleman she had encountered on the stairs of the Three Horse Inn. Even the murderous doctor might be judged comely by anyone unacquainted with his depraved nature, and he had a vital and manly way about him, which was more than could be said for Lady Buttershaw's collection of—

A knock at the door interrupted her musing. Hackham advised that a gentleman had called, and could Miss be so good as to come down now.

"It must be the man from Bow Street," said Zoe, glancing instinctively into the mirror. She was given pause by the sight of her reflection, and exclaimed, "Goodness me! I do look nice!"

Gorton said indignantly, "Well, of course you do, Miss Grainger! Except that in may opinion you look *lovely*!"

Zoe smiled, and collected her notes. "If I do, Elsie, 'tis all due to your skill, and to this beautiful gown."

She was reminded of her bruises when she went down the stairs, but she was not as stiff as she'd feared might be the case. A footman ushered her into the morning room. Lady Buttershaw was alone, and stood at the window, looking down into the street. She was clad in a gown of figured blue and green brocade worn over extremely wide paniers. Not a very wise choice, thought Zoe, for a long drive. Her wig was so high that Zoe could all but hear Travis' amused reaction that the lady was "a proper figure of fun." There was little of fun in the dark gaze that was turned upon her, however.

"I have brought you here," said her ladyship grimly, "so that I may have a private word before we go up to the green saloon where the gentleman awaits. I am glad to see that Gorton had the wit to dress you in something that becomes you. Although, you are too pale still." Advancing on Zoe, she pinched her cheeks hard. "There. That is some improvement. One can but hope he is not repulsed."

Indignant, Zoe exclaimed, "I must say, ma'am, I would think it the greatest presumption for a Bow Street Runner to comment on my appearance!"

Lady Buttershaw stared. "A Bow Street Runner . . . ? Ah, I see what it is! No, you are mistaken. The Runner has not yet arrived. I have instead a lovely surprise, which you do not at all deserve since you chose to turn up your nose at the peerless beaux I selected! Fate has smiled upon you, however. A distinguished and highly placed gentleman, whose wife was distant cousin to my mama-in-law, has sent a relation of his to call upon me. Is a prodigious charming and mannerly young man of insinuating address, splendid lineage, and—ah, comfortable expectations."

'Oh—*no!*' thought Zoe with an inward moan. 'Not another one!'

"I shall now make you known to him," said her ladyship, hurrying Zoe into the stair hall. "He lacks the polish of my own friends, and has a slight—I may say very *trite*—affliction. But he has been properly bred up and is a handsome fellow. If you take *him* in aversion, you have maggots in your head, and I do not scruple to say that I shall be *quite* provoked!"

She swept up the stairs, expanding as she went on the subject of her patient and even-tempered nature.

By the time a lackey was swinging open the door to the green saloon, Zoe's heart was heavy and her only hope lay in the fact that Lady Buttershaw believed this latest "Prospect" to lack the "polish" of the others. He might thus, she thought, be halfway human.

Her optimism was short-lived. A tall, dark-haired young man stood gazing up at a faded tapestry. He turned to reveal a rather drawn but well-featured face in which a pair of deep blue eyes held a smile that vanished abruptly.

"*You!*" growled Peregrine Cranford, his dark brows snapping together over the bridge of his nose.

Zoe exclaimed shrilly, " 'Tis the horrid *doctor!*"

"*What?*" roared my lady.

"I am *not* a doctor!" snarled Cranford.

"Of course he is not!" agreed Lady Buttershaw, glaring at Zoe. "You must be demented, gel!" She bit her lip, and, with a furtive glance at her "Prospect," mended her fences hurriedly. " '*Mistaken*,' is—er, what I mean to say. Now, if we may observe proper behaviour—Miss Zoe Grainger, I present Lieutenant Peregrine Cranford."

Cranford offered a stiff bow.

Bobbing an equally stiff curtsy, Zoe said, "How do you do? But, your pardon, ma'am, I am not mistaken! This is the man who was responsible for the death of that poor gentleman yesterday!"

Lady Buttershaw's jaw dropped and her eyes became glassy.

" 'Twas an *accident*," Cranford said between his teeth. "As would have been perfectly plain to any but an hysterical henwit!"

Zoe countered, "I suppose 'twas an *accident* at the Three Horse Inn when you threw some poor creature's severed limb at me!"

Incredulous, he gasped, "No! You *cannot* have supposed it to be—*real?*"

"I am not such a henwit as you hoped, sir! I saw that—that pitiful object all too clearly! And yesterday I *saw* you as good as murder that poor gentleman!" She flourished her papers under his nose. "As I shall testify for the authorities at—"

Lady Buttershaw fairly sprang forward and tore the pages from Zoe's hand. "Do—you—*dare?*" she hissed. "Do—you—*dare* to imply that any member of the Yerville family, however remote the connection, is a common *criminal?*" Her small eyes glittered; her features, never attractive, were now so flushed and contorted with rage that she looked almost maniacal.

Frightened, Zoe stammered, "N-no—I never meant to—But—but, ma'am! This evil person—"

"*Be—silent!*" raged her ladyship, only to countermand the order by demanding, "Make your apology—a most *humble* apology to Lieutenant Cranford at once! *At once*, I say!"

Almost as stunned as Zoe, Cranford saw all the colour drain from the young face. She was short of a sheet, but he could not like to be responsible for her being so severely reprimanded, and he started forward. "Pray do not scold her, ma'am. Miss Grainger is sadly in need of spectacles, is what it is."

"Who needs spectacles?" Holding the tabby cat, Caesar, in her arms, Lady Julia surveyed them from the doorway.

Lady Buttershaw's baleful gaze darted to her. "Julia, you know very well I do not like your creatures in—"

"Yes, and I am truly sorry, dear. Only I thought something really dreadful must have chanced. Whatever is amiss? I understood Mr. Cranford was come to take Miss Grainger out driving?"

Cranford was to take her driving? Still trembling, Zoe was caught offstride by this new horror and could not keep back a shocked gasp. She said falteringly, "To say truth, ma'am, I would prefer not to go out today."

Lady Buttershaw was rigidly still.

Cranford, who wanted nothing more than to be gone from

this horrid house, thought, 'And that dishes you, m'lady!' His voice icy, he said, "I think we must take into consideration the fact that Miss Grainger holds me to blame for a tragedy, ma'am. I cannot, under those circumstances, ask her to accompany—"

The door still stood wide. Through it came Cromwell, Caesar's springer spaniel, all ears and big pounding paws. Caesar yowled and struggled to be put down. Lady Julia let him go. Ears back, he tore around the room. Cromwell barked happily and gave chase. Cranford, who had been moving towards the two ladies, tried to avoid stepping on the dog, lost his own footing, and staggered awkwardly.

Lady Buttershaw leapt to his support. "Poor boy!" she exclaimed throwing both arms around him. "That you should have suffered such humiliation in my house is unforgivable!" She relinquished her hold on the scarlet-faced man, flailed her fan at the circling animals, and with cries of "Shoo! Go away! Begone!" chased them from the room.

Cranford flung out an arm to steady himself against a chair.

Zoe's shocked gaze dropped. Clearly, he found it difficult to regain his balance, and his right shoe was oddly twisted. She realized that although she had seen him standing upright, she'd never actually seen him walk. A dreadful suspicion came into her mind.

Mortified, infuriated, and very conscious of her fixed stare, Cranford snarled, "Quite correct, ma'am. The foot that was tossed over the hedge at the Three Horse Inn was mine own. Or at least, what nowadays passes for my own."

She lifted a repentant face. "Oh, my!"

Lady Julia said softly, "Lieutenant Cranford fought valiantly for his king and country and was wounded at the Battle of Prestonpans. He is entitled to all our respect." She sat down with Zoe beside her, and waved Cranford to a chair.

Gritting his teeth, he limped over to seat himself, resigned to endure an excruciating half hour with this wretched young female who would now be tongue-tied with remorse and would cast him the tearfully pitying glances that he found so hard to bear. He risked a quick look in her direction. There was more of interest than pity in her expression; in fact those clear green eyes were scrutinizing him with frank curiosity. Perversely outraged, he thought, 'She even lacks the sensibility to be properly ashamed of herself!'

Lady Julia said, "Now, pray tell me why you hold Mr. Cranford responsible for a tragedy, Miss Grainger. Has it to do with the sad accident you witnessed yesterday morning?"

Zoe's mind had been busied with the possible disposition of a certain wig, but she put that question aside. For the moment. "He was driving the coach that struck that poor man," she said.

Cranford put in, "Miss Grainger states that she saw me *racing*—which I was not, ma'am! She says that the poor fellow *walked* in front of my carriage—which he did not! I fear the lady is given to making hasty and unfounded judgments."

"Hasty judgments!" echoed Zoe, indignantly. "An you were *not* racing, how came it about that you and that black coach were abreast and travelling at a reckless rate of speed on a crowded city street when—"

" 'Twas *not* a crowded street! Not when I turned onto it, at all events. And the varmint came up behind me like a madman and all but forced us from the road! As I explained at the scene, if you recall."

"And perhaps you can also explain how the victim came to be struck if he was *not* crossing the street? I suppose you will say he fell from heaven!"

"Hush, hush," said Lady Julia, who had watched this

heated exchange with faint amusement. "My dear, you must own that you *were* in error when you assumed Mr. Cranford to be a doctor."

Zoe flushed. "Well, yes. I fear I was. And I do apologize for that, sir."

"My thanks, ma'am," said Cranford dryly.

"And is it not possible," Lady Julia persisted, "that you also mistook the events leading up to the accident? Might not this black coach really have tried to pass Mr. Cranford in an unsafe fashion, just as he says?"

"I—'tis *possible*, my lady, but that still does not explain—"

"Are you so very sure, Zoe, that the unfortunate gentleman was crossing the road *before* Mr. Cranford's coach came up? What if he was, for instance, intoxicated at the time? He might very well have wandered blindly from the flagway and into the horses, thus bringing the tragedy down upon himself."

This was the very detail that she had been unable to clearly recall, and Zoe frowned dubiously.

Impatient, Cranford said, "Miss Grainger is quite determined to paint me the deliberate villain of the piece, ma'am. If you think—"

Lady Julia lifted her hand, silencing him as Lady Buttershaw's shrill tones could be heard in the passage. "What I think, Mr. Cranford," she interposed hurriedly, "is that you and Miss Grainger should discuss the matter where you may be private and not—er, unduly influenced. Of course, if Miss Grainger has given you a distaste for her, I will say no more."

She had said enough, thought Cranford glumly, to thoroughly trap him. The small henwit was watching the door apprehensively. And—'fore heaven, anything would be preferable to again listening to the rantings of that dragon of a dowager. He rose and bowed. "An you will trust yourself to me for an hour, Miss Grainger, I promise to give my coachman the strictest instructions to drive sedately."

With far more reason than he to escape Lady Buttershaw's wrath, Zoe took the lesser of two evils and said she would be pleased to accept his kind invitation.

CHAPTER VII

he wind had risen and Zoe's skirts fluttered as
Cranford handed her into his light carriage. He
called directions to his youthful coachman, then
climbed inside, swung the door closed, and sat beside her.

Zoe shot him an uneasy glance.

At once irritated, he said curtly, "An you think this is the
murder carriage, be at ease. 'Tis my own. The other belonged
to a friend."

"I was thinking of something quite different," she said.
"Besides, I know what the other coach looked like, since I
saw . . ." Her words trailed off.

"Not what you think you saw," he finished grimly.

She said with a spark in her eyes, "If you brought me out
only to bully me—"

"Well, of course I did not! That is to say, I hope we can
discuss the affair civilly. You certainly cannot think Lady Yerville would let you drive out with me if she believed me to be as
guilty as you claim."

"Lady Julia was not there! I was!" said Zoe rebelliously.

"Well, if that don't beat the Dutch! In other words, you
willingly went out for a drive with a man you still believe to be
a brute of a murderer! I'faith, madam, you must indeed be desperate to see more of the city!"

He was flushed, his chin high, and his eyes alight with anger. It was a fine face, Zoe had to admit, with its high cheekbones, straight nose, and firm chin. There were lines between the thick dark brows that one did not usually find in someone of his age. He had known suffering, this proud man. The tilt of his head reminded her suddenly of her brother, and she stifled a sigh.

"No. I think I have changed my mind. I don't believe that of you any more. What *did* happen?"

"I thought you *saw* what happened!"

"Do not sulk."

"Sulk! Of all the—"

In an unaffectedly spontaneous way that startled him, she put her hand over his lips. "Sulk. If I am willing to reconsider, you must cooperate. Now do not scowl so."

Despite himself, he was won to a smile by that earnest little face hovering so close to his own.

Zoe drew back. "That's better. Now, you must admit you were driving much too fast."

"No such thing! I had my team well in hand until that Bedlamite in the black coach came up behind me like a streak of lightning, and da—er, dashed near ran me into somebody's cellar! I'll own that then I had all I could do to hold my cattle together!"

Zoe considered in silence.

He said, "If you were to cast your mind back—"

"Hush. I am."

He watched her for a moment, then prompted, "You didn't actually see him walk across the road, did you?"

She closed her eyes and answered slowly, "I had been obliged to jump down the area steps, and when I climbed up, I saw him . . . under—" She broke off, and ducked her head, shuddering.

Cranford took one of her hands. " 'Faith, but I'm a villain

to make you think of it again. It was horrid, I know."

"Yes. But . . . I have been thinking of it. And I suppose 'twas only logical to assume . . . After all, if he did not walk across the road, where *did* the poor soul come from?"

"Be dashed if I know. One minute there was no one there, and the next—" He freed her hand and looked down at it, noting absently how ridiculously small it was. "Lady Yerville could very well be right. Perhaps he *was* lushy— Er, I mean—"

"I have a brother, sir. I know what you mean, and I'll admit it does seem logical that the man was intoxicated."

He said eagerly, "Then you won't make that statement to Bow Street?"

"I shall have to amend it, certainly. In fact I had already writ out some notes, trying to set down what I really did see. You saw Lady Buttershaw take them from me. And I am very sure she means to forbid me speaking 'gainst one of her relatives."

"Pray acquit me of that! We are not blood relations. Indeed, if we are cousins, the connection is so many times removed as to be almost out of sight! Why my great uncle should have insisted I must call—" He checked that remark looking embarrassed, and said hurriedly, "I mean no disrespect, but there's no denying the lady is a Tartar. I could not credit how her demeanour changed when she was provoked with you. I had not thought it possible, for when first I arrived she was so kind and welcoming. Lord knows why."

"I know why." Watching the passing scene as the carriage threaded its way along streets bustling with traffic and lined with fine houses, Zoe giggled suddenly and turned to him, her eyes twinkling. "She wants you to offer for me."

Cranford paled, staring at her in horror. "Oh . . . Zounds!"

She threw her hands over her ears. "What an unkind reaction! I am scorned and rejected! And sworn at, besides! Cruel! Cruel!"

Appalled, he blurted out, "No, I never meant— I *do* beg your pardon! But—but you *cannot* be serious! We have but now met, and I said nothing to give her cause to think— Well, nor did you. *Did* you?" Not waiting for a reply, he rushed on, "Of course not! And I doubt you're even *out* yet, much less— The woman must be *mad*! Jupiter—there I go again!" He saw her laughing face then and said with a sigh of relief, "You quiz me, is that the case? The lady has no such scheme."

"Oh, yes she does!"

"Well then she is most definitely demented! No, be honest and admit you don't want me for a husband."

She said with a chuckle, "Goodness, no! Where are we going?"

"I guessed you would first want to see Westminster Abbey, and then the Tower and Mrs. Salmon's waxworks, and, if we have time, St. Paul's of course. Does that meet with your approval, ma'am?"

"No. Why are you cross again?"

"I am not cross," he said crossly. "Where do you wish to go, if my route does not gratify your whims?"

"I would like to see the Abbey, but my brother writ that the slums about it are the worst in the city. And I would adore to see the waxworks, but I am very sure Papa would say it was frivolous to visit such a place before I have seen the more historical buildings. So—St. Paul's first, if you please."

He rapped his cane on the roof and the trap was opened to reveal his coachman's smiling face. "St. Paul's, Florian," he ordered.

The trap closed, the carriage lurched and turned left into the Strand.

Sitting back, Cranford drawled, "You will want to keep your eyes closed when we pass the Temple, lest you see the Jacobite heads on Temple Bar."

She gripped her hands together. "Oh, how *awful*! Are they still there?"

"You had as well ask if there are still Jacobites. Of course they are there." A pause, and then he asked, "What *do* you desire in a husband, may I ask?" His lip curled. "A title, I suppose. And great wealth."

"Those would be lovely, of course. But they are not the most important thing. Nor," she added, "should I reject a prospective suitor had he lost a limb."

He caught his breath and shot a glance at her face. It was full of mischief, a dimple hovering at the corner of her mouth. He enquired coldly, "Do you feel better for having said that?"

"Do you feel better for having thought it?"

"An you can read minds, ma'am, you will make a fortune at theatres."

All innocence she said, "Is that *your* profession, sir?"

His eyes narrowed.

She laughed and patted his arm. "No, let us not fence so. You deserved it, you know, for having judged me so mercenary in my requirements for a spouse."

It was impossible to resist that merry sparkle, and the hard line of his mouth relaxed. He said, "*Touché!* And once more I must beg your pardon. Will you satisfy my curiosity? What *do* you look for in a gentleman?"

Without an instant's hesitation, she said, "Kindness."

"Kindness! Is that all? 'Pon my soul, you are easily pleased, Miss Grainger. Is that perchance why a humble fellow like myself was judged suitable?" His warm smile flashed as she looked at him thoughtfully, and he added, "No, you must have more requirements than mere kindness. Do you place no value on such attributes as birth, an informed mind, position in society? A comfortable fortune, at least?"

"Of course I do. But of what value would be a highly born

and learned husband if he never deigned to share a discussion, or laugh at a joke with his lady? Of what pleasure a proud position in the *ton* if she was treated with contempt in her home, or, worse, ignored? Could a wife enjoy a fortune if in private she was ill-treated or beaten?"

"Pshaw! You choose extremes and fantasy, ma'am. Or have you personal knowledge of such sorry unions?"

"Not personal knowledge, I grant you. But my brother used to bring all the latest London *on dits* when he came home from school. And our cook had worked in several great houses and loved to gossip. Unless they both fibbed to me, the examples I mentioned are not fantasy but fact for all too many unhappy ladies. And kindness, you know, is so little a thing; so cheap, and yet with such great power. A smile, for instance, given freely to a—a milliner's assistant, say, or a tired housemaid, may brighten that person's whole day and be passed on and multiplied endlessly. A kind word that costs nothing can warm a lonely heart. A little simple caring for others . . ." She checked, knowing she was talking too much, and added pertly, "Besides which, Mr. Cranford, you were not the only candidate chosen for me."

"Indeed? Am I to know who else was so favoured?"

"I probably should not say." She lowered her voice and peered around the carriage as though there were ears everywhere and whispered with high drama, "If I do, will you promise to keep it a secret?"

Again that irresistible sparkle was lighting her big green eyes, and he entered into her game saying with equal drama, "I promise. Name my rivals."

"All right. There were quite a number actually, but I am dreadful at remembering names. They all were very—fashionable, and Lady Buttershaw promised me they were not paupers. Let me see now—there was a gentleman named 'Purr,' though I did not quite hear his last name. Another called Reginald

Smythe, and—er, oh yes, Sir Gilbert somebody . . . And your chin is hanging down, Lieutenant."

Cranford gulped, and then succumbed to such gales of laughter that she drew back, regarding him with displeasure. "Those . . . simpering . . . dandies?" he gasped, between howls. "Purleigh Shale . . . ? And . . . that idiot Smythe . . . ? And—and—Gil *Fowles*? Oh, burn it! If ever I heard the like! Do you—do you say they all . . . *offered*, ma'am?"

"Not exactly," she said, frowning at him. "They were—ah, *offered*, you might say."

He was using his handkerchief to wipe tears from his eyes, but at this his head jerked up. "What's this . . . ? Do you say—they—they didn't even . . . *know?*"

"No more than did you. And I am very sure my lady would never have considered you had she recollected that you made off with her wig!"

It took a second or two for this to be comprehended, but when Cranford grasped it he was hopelessly overcome once more, his mirth so unrestrained that it caused passers-by to look at the carriage curiously.

On the box, Florian grinned his appreciation. His employer had been downcast when they'd set out this morning, and the last thing he'd expected was that they would soon be escorting a lady about London Town. Not a lady to draw all eyes wherever she went, perhaps. But she seemed a nice little thing, with a sort of brightness about her, and she'd made Mr. Peregrine laugh. He hadn't laughed since Loretta Laxton had thrown him over . . . With luck, they'd be seeing more of Miss Grainger!

The object of his thoughts uttered a squeal as Cranford sobered abruptly and whipped a hand across her eyes. It was removed before she could pull it away, and she looked out of the window, straining her neck to see what she had missed. "Whatever is wrong? Was there someone you did not want me to see? Oh, what a great gate! What was it? I do wish I had seen—"

"Temple Bar," he advised brusquely. "Most ladies do not care to look."

At once chastened, she half-whispered, "Oh. Were there . . . ?"

"Half a dozen. On pikes."

"How ghastly! Why ever must such things be? But I sup-pose, having fought the Jacobites, you think it justified."

Tio Glendenning's laughing face came to mind. He said, "I've a good friend who came precious near to being one of those poor devils." And he thought, 'Pray God he never comes any nearer!'

He looked very grim, and Zoe turned her attention to the window and was silent for a moment. Her excitement could not be dampened for long, however, and she remarked, "This is quite a different neighborhood, is it not! Oh! I saw a ship! Are we near to the Thames, then? Do but *look* at that lovely china cat in the shop window! Oh, sir, *pray* can we stop? 'Tis just what Lady Julia would like, I know, for she loves cats and it looks so much like Charlemagne!"

"But we are near the cathedral. You can see the dome up ahead."

"Yes, but 'twould take only a minute, and if we wait till later the dear little cat might be gone. Oh, *please*, Mr. Cranford!"

Amused by her excitement, he rapped on the roof again, and in a few minutes was limping along the narrow flagway be-side her, while Florian took the team down a side street with instructions to pick them up again in ten minutes.

The little shop was soon reached, and having warned Zoe to gather her skirts close as it looked none too clean inside, Cranford bent his head and followed her up the steps. He had to intervene when the shopkeeper demanded a price for the china cat that was exorbitant. The shopkeeper was indignant, Zoe was anxious, and Cranford was adamant. The bartering became heated. Vaguely, above it, Cranford heard some shouts outside, but not until they had left the shop and he was carrying the parcelled cat along Fleet Street did he realize that traffic had come to a standstill and there was a violent altercation nearby.

Zoe said, "What a commotion! Oh, there is Whipley!"

"Who is Whipley?" he asked, craning his neck to see what the uproar was about.

"He is Lady Julia's footman. I know he saw us, but he has gone slinking off. If that is not just like—"

She broke off with a gasp as a crowd burst from an alley behind them, and they were surrounded by pushing, shouting, angry men. Cranford whipped an arm about Zoe and dragged her into a doorway. A brick was thrown. Glass shattered. He pulled her close and rammed her face against his chest. Insults and epithets flew. So did fists. A big man wearing a baker's hat plunged into them and swore as Cranford warded him off. Zoe caught a glimpse of a very red face and reddened eyes full of hate. The bloated features contorted. He shouted, " 'Ere's one of 'em, mates! A damned nob what's left 'is bloody castle ter mix wiv us commoners! Let's—"

Cranford jerked Zoe behind him and struck out hard.

The belligerent baker howled and reeled back, his nose spurting crimson.

Cranford seized Zoe's arm. "I must get you out of this!" He limped rapidly into the alley from which the mob had come, and thence onto a narrow street.

The sounds of combat faded.

"Phew!" he said, with a grin. "Are you all right, ma'am?"

"Yes," she said breathlessly. "And I believe my brother would say you've a splendid left, Mr. Cranford! Does this sort of thing go on all the time in London? I should— Oh, do look!

Those horrid men have knocked over a poor flower seller's barrow!"

"So they have. We must be thankful they didn't knock us over! If we— Great heavens, ma'am! What are you about?"

Busily restoring bunches of flowers to toppled pots, Zoe said, "There is still some water in—"

He seized her by the elbow and said urgently, "No, do get up! You must not do that! Your gown is getting dirty. Egad, ma'am, will you listen? These are not your flowers, and—"

She resisted his agitated tugs. "No, but everyone seems to have gone to watch the fight. We cannot leave them, they'll wilt, poor dears. Now *stop* pulling me, sir! An you will help, 'twill only take a minute or two."

He groaned helplessly, and setting down his parcel, bent to restore a battered pot. "If the owner comes back, he'll likely think we're stealing the dratted things!" He thrust a bunch of chrysanthemums into the pot. "This is no neighbourhood for—"

" 'Ere! Wotcher a'doing of? Making orf wiv me stock in trade! 'Elp! Thieves!"

A wiry woman with a dirty face and straggly grey hair advanced, brandishing a cane and howling.

Zoe said earnestly, "No, really, ma'am. We are only trying to—"

"My dear God!" moaned Cranford, dodging a swipe of the cane. He tossed a crown to the flower seller. She snatched it up, but she had taken his measure, and, having deposited the coin in her bosom, redoubled her howls.

Cranford knew when he was beaten. He seized Zoe's arm and made a spirited attempt to run. *"Kindness!"* he exclaimed bitterly.

"She just . . . misunderstood . . . ," she panted as she was rushed along the alley.

Cranford gave a cry of relief. "Here's Florian, bless his

woolly stockings!" The carriage lurched to a halt beside them. He wrenched the door open, and all but threw Zoe inside.

Stepping up after her, he shouted. "Get on, Florian! Quick!" and slammed the door.

The carriage started to turn again.

Cranford pulled the window down and leaned out. "Where are you going?"

"We can't get through, sir," shouted Florian. " 'Tis a full-fledged riot. There's crowds fighting all the way down to the Fleet Ditch. I was lucky to get back to you!"

Cranford instructed him to go along to St. Clement's, then turn up Drury Lane. Closing the window, he said, "We'll drive past the theatre, and then you can see"—the coach rocked, and he was staggered—"Covent Garden," he finished unevenly, sitting down. "Unless you are too shaken."

He was pale suddenly, and she had noted the quick snatch of white teeth at his lower lip. She said, "No, but I think you are. Have you hurt your foot again?"

The straps had loosened and his full weight had come down on the edge of the artificial foot. His leg hurt so badly that he felt sick, but he managed to declare that he was "quite well. I thank you, madam."

She eyed him anxiously. Clearly, he was trying to keep his countenance, but his eyes were veiled and there was a tell-tale twitch to his lips. She said, "What I simply cannot understand, is why you had to make it so horridly real?"

Battling nausea, he said, "I cannot think . . . what you mean."

"Of course you can. Have you forgot I saw the—the *toe-nails*? All different colours! And the horrid—" She made a face.

In an attempt to hide his distress and shock her into silence, he said ghoulishly, "The gore, where it had been . . . hacked off?"

She was not so easily silenced. "I suppose 'tis commendable to accept your misfortune in so light-hearted a way, for I expect that to lose one's foot must be a great nuisance."

"But you think that to make the replacement look authentic was . . . vulgar."

"It seems so to me. But there is no telling what gentlemen will find amusing."

She was very earnest, and, whatever else, she did not appear to be revolted by his handicap. The pain was easing now and he felt less limp. He said, "I have a friend who is clever with his paints and quite fails to be embarrassed by my—er, loss. He delights to play such tricks. Some fellows can be very silly, you know."

A beaming smile dispelled Zoe's gravity. She clapped her hands and said merrily, "Was that the way of it, then? 'Tis just the sort of thing my brother would do! Have you been able to take your revenge upon the wretch?"

"I have to catch him first. And just now, unfortunately, he can outrun me."

"I'm not surprised." She peered at his foot. "It doesn't seem to fit very well."

He was beginning to find her candour refreshing rather than offensive, and countered with a grin, "Did no one ever tell you, ma'am, that 'tis impolite to comment upon an infirmity?"

"What stuff! How silly 'twould be if everybody looked the other way and pretended not to notice. Oh, if you had a wart on the end of your nose I should say nothing, of course. But to lose a limb in battle is no cause for diffidence, is it?"

At this, he burst out laughing.

She was pleased to have won him to a smile again. Laughter brought a sparkle to the very blue eyes, and drove the hauteur from his mouth. Indeed, this was a quite different gentleman to the monstrous image she had created. He didn't look in the least murderous. And then she thought, 'Oh, dear me!'

Cranford said, "Now you are angry again. Do you think I mock you?"

"I have just remembered my china cat!"

"Oh, Jupiter! I must have left it with your flower seller. I *am* sorry! I'll find another for you."

"Not only that," she added with deep tragedy, "we have been talking so much I have missed *everything!*"

The carriage had halted outside the famed old theatre. Cranford reached for the door. "Well, I can show you around the Bard's stamping ground, at least."

Her hand checked him. "No more stamping around for you, Mr. Cranford!"

Ignoring her, he started up, flinched, and sat back again.

She said sternly, "You see? Your foot may *look* the real thing, but it does not go the right way. 'Tis a silly vanity and you must be done with it. Find someone to carve you a peg-leg with a properly cushioned top. Yes, I know you would like to put a period to me for referring to it again, but 'tis the height of folly to allow pride to cause you so much discomfort."

For a moment he could almost hear his beautiful Loretta's husky voice: "But I like to *dance*, Perry! And besides— Oh, I have *tried* to be patient, but that hideous peg-leg quite makes me ill . . . !"

He said broodingly, "I know very well how a lady would view a man who—stumped about Town on a peg-leg."

"Had the lady a scrinch of common sense she'd want him to be comfortable, and not give a fig for a silly painted foot!"

"Easy said," he jeered. "Would *you* go about with a cripple?"

"Of course I would! However much I might want to shake him for indulging in such blatant self-pity!"

Scarlet again, he gasped, "Why, you—you little wretch! It just so happens that I *have* a peg-leg. 'Twould serve you right, my girl, did I wear it tomorrow and come calling! Then what would you do?"

Her eyes alight, she answered, "Demand that you take me to St. Paul's *and* Covent Garden!"

Reclining on the chaise longue in her private parlour, Lady Julia sipped a dish of tea and listened to Zoe, who knelt on the rug brushing Charlemagne and recounting the afternoon's events. "Bless my soul!" exclaimed her ladyship in dismay. "What a monstrous shocking experience! Faith, but I marvel that you can be so calm after such a string of disasters! Most ladies would be laid down upon their beds in high hysterics. Your papa will think we have plunged you into Bedlam!"

Zoe looked up with an arrested expression. "Why, I never thought of it in that way, but you are right, ma'am. It *has* been rather far from tranquil. My journey to Town with Lady Buttershaw was not exactly uneventful, and then there was that hideous accident, and today—" She restrained Viking, who had pushed in jealously and tried to seize the brush. "Your turn next, sir," she said firmly, "I am not yet done with your cat."

As if aware he was the lucky one, the little ginger Charlemagne rolled over and offered his white stomach for grooming.

Lady Julia murmured worriedly, "I can only be grateful to Mr. Cranford for bringing you off safely. My poor dear London . . . What a sorry pass she has come to!"

"I had no notion there was so much trouble," said Zoe. "Do you know what it is all about?"

"I fancy there are several causes. A great many people secretly resent our Hanoverian King. Indeed, I believe there was widespread sympathy for the Stuarts who, with all their faults, *are* British."

Zoe dismissed Charlemagne, and turned to Viking, who at

once sat down and panted at her expectantly.

"La, but he is bigger than you are," said Lady Julia, laughing. "You shall have to stand up to reach him, my dear."

Zoe stood and took off the hound's studded collar. "It sounded to me as if those people were full of hatred for all the Quality. The horrid man who attacked Mr. Cranford shouted that he was a 'nob,' which means aristocrat, does it not? And he said some very bad words. I was quite surprised, you know, that—stand *up*, Viking! No, I do not want your paw, sir!—I was quite surprised that Mr. Cranford was able to floor him so deedily. He is not a big brawny type of man, but he has a punishing left!"

Lady Julia gave a ripple of laughter and shook her head. "Zoe, Zoe! Where do you come by such terms? Is from growing up in the country with your brother, I suppose! I shall write and scold the young rascal! What does your papa say of him, by the way? You had a letter this morning, I believe?"

"Yes. But Papa has not heard from Travis. It seems a long while since he last wrote." Troubled, Zoe said with a sigh, "I pray all is well. I know I should be pleased that he has been given this wonderful opportunity, but I do wish he were not so far away. He is very dear to me, and it will be years, I dare swear, before I see him again."

"Try not to be sad, child. He will get a leave, you may be sure, and in the meantime you should picture him as being happy and contented in his new life. Now pray tell me more about the riot. You say that Mr. Cranford was able to knock down the lout who attacked him?"

"Yes, ma'am." Viking nudged Zoe's hand, which had stilled, and she smiled and resumed her task. "And he made me run, for there was fighting all around us. In fact— Oh, but I expect Whipley will have told you."

Her ladyship looked puzzled. "Whipley? How should he know of it?"

"Why, he was there, ma'am. I saw him across Fleet Street, just before the commotion."

"Are you sure? He ran some errands for me, but none that would have taken him so far east. I think perhaps, with all the uproar, you must have been mistaken."

"Oh dear. I do seem to be making a lot of mistakes of late. But, I was so sure . . ."

"Then I shall ask him about it, although 'tis of no real import. Perchance the naughty fellow has a light o'love in the district. I trust Mr. Cranford was not hurt in the encounter?"

"No, ma'am. Well, not exactly. His wound troubled him a little, I think, but only because he is foolishly proud and will not wear a peg-leg. As I told him."

"You never did! My goodness! Whatever did he say? Was he vexed with you?"

"Oh, yes." Zoe giggled. "I think he was ready to murder me. But he promised to wear his peg-leg when he takes me driving tomorrow." She added hastily, "By your leave, ma'am."

"Of course you have my leave. Did you suppose I meant to keep you locked up with an invalid four and twenty hours a day? Mr. Cranford is, I think, a most commendable young gentleman, and one who knows the Metropolis and will treat you with the utmost respect while showing you about."

"Respect! He told me I was a wretch! But I think I was wrong about the accident, just the same. I shall have to change the statement I promised to Bow Street."

"I trust he did not bully you into that decision, my dear."

"No, ma'am! He is not that type of man at all. His temper is quick and he can give a crushing set-down, but I cannot imagine him ever mis-using a female. Indeed, he was quite terrified when the flower seller struck him, and he made me run away from her."

Lady Julia said softly, "And you like him after all, do you not?"

Again, the brushing ceased while Zoe considered that question. "Yes," she said slowly. "I suppose I do. He is rather nice."

"I agree. Now, 'tis almost time to change for dinner, but first—*do* tell me, why did the flower seller strike the poor soul . . . ?"

Jolted from sleep, Zoe sat up in bed, her heart pounding madly. It was cold and pitch black in the room and she pulled the eiderdown up around her chin. Scarcely daring to breathe, she huddled there, straining her ears. Not a sound broke the stillness, but just as she decided she must have had a bad dream there came a stealthy movement, as though someone was opening her door. She gave a scared gasp, then slipped from her bed and threw back the window curtains. It was a windy night, and tattered clouds raced across a half-moon that gave sufficient light for her to distinguish that her door was tight shut. Relieved, she crept to it and leaned her ear against the panel. She gave a yelp and jumped back as the door rattled. Shivering, she called tremulously, "Who—who is it?"

The reply prompted her to groan with mingled relief and exasperation. She opened the door. Attila's dog, the little white terrier called Boadicea, charged past, leapt onto the bed and turned around three times, barking excitedly.

Zoe ran to the bed and threw the eiderdown over her unwanted visitor. "Be quiet, you silly creature! Whatever are you doing in this part of the house? Don't you know you will get your mistress into the greatest trouble?"

Boadicea made it clear that she thought this a great game and had no worries.

Desperate, Zoe ran to close the door, but the terrier was before her and scampered merrily into the corridor. Zoe's mad lunge failed. Boadicea raced triumphant to the stairs and plunged down them, her little legs flying. Zoe moaned and ran after her. She could hear the click of nails when she reached the ground floor, but in the darkness could not see which way the dog had gone. Her low calls and threats brought a sudden mad dash. Boadicea galloped around her and shot away again. Cold and vexed and fearing that at any minute someone would hear, Zoe tried another tactic. "Bo! Come!" she called softly. "Walkie!"

The bribe succeeded and the terrier rushed to throw herself at Zoe's feet, tail wagging trustingly. She was caught up at once. Zoe said, "I am sorry, little Bo. That was deceitful. Never mind. I'll scratch behind your ear; you like that."

The consolation prize was graciously accepted, and Zoe hurried back to the stairs, the terrier under her arm. With one very cold foot on the bottom step, she halted, breath held in check as she heard a man's voice, low pitched but angry.

". . . have been diverted, for a space, is all. I wish to God we might have written *finis* to the lot!"

Footsteps. A light began to move along the upper corridor. It dawned on Zoe's numbed mind that several gentlemen were coming towards the stairs. And that in her haste to prevent Boadicea from disturbing Lady Buttershaw she had not stayed to put on her dressing gown. At any second she would be discovered *en déshabillé!* She could well imagine the uproar. Beyond doubting, she would be sent packing at once; back to Travisford in deepest disgrace. And Mrs. Mowbray would rant and rave until she made poor Papa's life a misery!

She turned and fled across the entrance hall and into the red saloon. Boadicea wriggled and whined a protest. Zoe held the little dog close and scratched her ear, whispering commands that she be quiet.

She could see the glow of the candle brightening, and a second higher-pitched voice murmured warningly, ". . . would all too likely be believed, had we taken such a step. Which must not happen."

They appeared to have halted in the entrance hall. Zoe thought prayerfully, 'Oh, *why* do I do such silly things? Open the door! Hurry and go home, please!'

Instead, a third and even more agitated voice exclaimed: "No, it must *not*, by God! Not at this stage of the game. Zounds, but if the others got so much as a hint of what that confounded spy made off with—"

"You had best see to it they do not!" snapped the man who had spoken first. "I do not intend to be blocked now! She was clever, I grant you, to have secured the most likely contacts. But she's too confident by half!"

The high-pitched voice said, "We have left nothing to chance, Squire. Our people are in place. When our long-awaited Lady Aranmore makes—"

Boadicea whined, and struggled to be released.

"What the devil? Who's there?"

A flurry of running steps. Desperate, Zoe put the dog down and huddled behind the jut of the sideboard.

Boadicea raced out.

The light from the candle seemed blinding. Zoe threw her hands over her mouth to muffle her breathing.

" 'Tis only the little terrier," said the agitated man.

The one they had called Squire said dryly, "We shall hope the creature does not wake the house! Ah! I hear the coach."

Footstops, receding. The sounds of hooves and wheels outside. Murmurs Zoe could not catch. The front door was opened and quietly closed. She heard the carriage driving away. Then, silence.

Shivering with cold and fright, she breathed a little prayer of gratitude that she had not been discovered, started out of her hiding place, then shrank back again. Once more footsteps approached. Had she been seen after all? Was she about to be denounced? She could have wept with relief when there arose a sleepy grumbling, and the grating of bolts being shot. Bo yapped as she was caught and borne away, and the shuffling steps, the glow of the candle faded and were gone. One of the footmen or a lackey had been sent to lock up, of course.

How strange, she thought, were the ways of going on in London. Faith, but there were more differences between town and country customs than she ever could have imagined. 'Twould be downright scandalous for guests at Travisford, or any other home she knew of, to wander about the house in the middle of the night without the escort of their host or a servant; certainly, they would not depart without being politely ushered from the premises. She might be a country bumpkin, but she could not admire such careless hospitality!

There were no further sounds, but she waited for several minutes before daring to creep up to her bedchamber. Snuggled in the blankets, waiting for her icy feet to get warm again, she wondered what it had all been about, and who they were. Most probably, something to do with money . . . She yawned. Lots of money if the urgency of that discussion was any indication. Her last thought before she fell asleep was that the lady they were waiting for must be someone of great importance . . .

CHAPTER VIII

urlong's hand shook visibly as he offered the Madeira, and Ramsey Talbot sprang up to snatch the glass and guide the swaying man to an arm-chair.

"My dear fellow! You should be abed! I wonder Cranford let you get up!"

"He—he forbade it," faltered Sir Owen, mortified by this unexpected relapse. "Truth is, I thought I was-was over it this mor-morning."

"Well, you ain't. I'd best ring for his fellow." Mr. Talbot stretched a pudgy white hand towards the bell on a small and cluttered table.

"No!" Trying to enunciate clearly, Furlong said, "Be better in a minute. Pr-promise you. Tell me about—what was his name?"

"Skye." Taking a chair and dragging it closer to Furlong's, Mr. Talbot sipped his Madeira and, watching the younger man narrowly, asked when Gideon Rossiter was coming back to town.

"He sent a note yesterday. The damage to his farmhouse is ex-extensive, it seems. And Ross is detained by the local con-stable. They've a suspicion, you see, that 'twas arson. He hopes to be b-back in London by the end of the week."

Talbot grunted. "One trusts it won't be too late." Furlong looked startled, and Talbot went on, "Where's that madman August Falcon?"

"Down at Ashleigh. His sire took a nasty toss."

"Did he, though! Neville's a fool to buy those showy hacks. Only man I ever knew who could fall off a horse when 'twas standing still! What about Glendenning, or Morris? Either of 'em about?"

"Glendenning's off to Bristol to enquire after my brother's arrival. Jamie's in Guildford. His married sister's coach overturned."

"By thunder!" Talbot's shrewd brown eyes were suddenly very round. "Too many nasty coincidences here! The League's work?"

"So I think." Furlong nodded, and held out a tanned hand. "There. Much steadier now! And I'm afraid you shall have to make do with me at all events, sir, unless you can wait till Ross comes back. Is it about the accident on Tuesday? I assume you saw the account of it in *The Spectator*?"

"I did. A strange affair, and no charges brought as yet, I gather. Are you up to telling me about it?"

Furlong's account was concise. When he finished, Mr. Talbot was leaning back in his chair, frowning at the swordbelt that hung over the edge of the mantelpiece, and the holstered pistols propped against the fender. He said, "The article fell short of blaming Cranford, and the witnesses were not mentioned by name. Are you judging it to have been an execution?"

Furlong shrugged. "The Squire allows but one mistake, as you know. Farrier was a valuable tool, but he had f-failed on several counts. He let Horatio Glendenning wriggle out from under the axe; allowed a treacherous co-plotter to slip through his fingers; and then Gordon Chandler escaped the very neat web he'd woven. I think Farrier was-was killed and then tossed

· 146 ·

under the hooves of my team in an attempt to throw the blame on me."

"Ugly." Talbot pursed his lips. " 'Twould have given the League a glorious opportunity to name it deliberate murder."

"Exactly. I'd have been lucky to escape a public hanging, and our cause would have been badly damaged. Certainly, these confounded street agitators would have trumpeted all over London that 'twas yet another proof of the arrogance and inhumanity of the 'nobs' as they call us. And the dunderheads in Whitehall would be reinforced in their comfortable belief that Rossiter's Preservers are mischief-making young ne'er-do-wells, and our warnings so much silly twaddle!"

Talbot nodded. "This fellow Cranford," he said thoughtfully. "Isn't there a fine old family of that name in Hampshire? As I recollect, the parents were lost some years ago, on the way out to India. Tragic thing. Victims of that wretched James and Mary sandbank in the Hooghly River. Lucky they'd left their children here. Any connection?"

"Yes, indeed. Mitten, that is Miss Dimity Cranford, married Sir Anthony Farrar a couple of years back, and now lives near Romsey. Her twin brothers spend most of the year at the family home. Piers is the heir, but I think they both regard it as a sort of joint ownership. There's rather an astonishing bond between them."

"Often the way with twins, I've heard. Didn't one of them lose a leg in the Uprising? Not your fellow, I trust?"

"A foot. Yes."

Talbot's glance returned to the weapons by the fireplace. "Can he use those?"

"He's a crack shot. A bit of a fire-eater, in fact. He seconded August Falcon in a duel in April, and—"

"Lord! Who hasn't? Got into it with his principal, did he?"

"Not—exactly. His—er, his peg-leg got stuck in the mud. Falcon was—er, rather put out."

Talbot gave a hoot of laughter. "I can see it, be dashed if I can't! It sounds as if young Cranford's a good man. Is he a member of your small army?"

"No, sir. And we've no intention of enlisting him."

"But—he knows? You've told him? Jove, but you must! He'll be a marked man now!"

"I hope not, and I don't really think so. The League was after me, not Perry. I'm very sure they know he's not one of us. To say truth, sir, he's—er, well, he's had a very nasty time of it. We none of us expected him to survive after what he went through on the battlefield, but he did, and then it was touch and go again because the pneumonia set in. He's a fighter, and he pulled through, but later suffered a bad fall, and an infection resulted in more surgery. Came near to turning up his toes several times. To top things off, his *chere amie* just threw him over and made no bones of the fact that she could no longer put up with a—er, maimed man."

"Damme! What a heartless jade! Beautiful, I suppose?"

"Very. He was hit hard. You can see why I'd as soon steer him clear of this business. We'll keep an eye on him—as s-soon as we can keep an eye on anyone. We're rather pared down at the moment, unfortunately, but I think Cranford means to stay in Town for only a day or two. He's not likely to get into trouble in that short time. Is he connected with this fellow you spoke of earlier?"

"Joel Skye? No, I don't think they're acquainted. Skye's a Navy man, and I must say he seems like a decent sort. Just got promoted to sub-lieutenant and was so proud of it that I stood him a cognac and we toasted his prowess. He's on the staff of Lord Hayes of the East India Company. Who chances to be his uncle. Ah, I see you know him."

"Not personally, but I believe he was present when Johnny Armitage was hauled up before a Board of Enquiry. Wiry young fellow. Doesn't say much, but I think he doesn't miss much, either."

"Just so. He called on me—in a manner of speaking. I was at the Cocoa Tree, actually. Skye introduced himself, and dropped a few hints."

"About Armitage?"

"About your fabled League of Jewelled Men."

"Did he, by Jove!" Furlong leaned forward and asked intensely, "Never say he believes there is such a group?"

"He wanted to hear all that I know of it, certainly."

"And when you'd told him, he roared with laughter, no doubt!"

"He did not so much as crack a grin. What he did do was imply that a few men in high places are beginning to wonder if there may be something to what you've been saying this past year. And he wanted to know if you have *certain* knowledge of interference with East India Company cargoes."

Furlong frowned and was silent, and Talbot admitted with a nod, "Yes, it could be a trap, of course."

Furlong said slowly, "When Gideon Rossiter named several of the men we know to be members of the League, he was ridiculed, and told he should be ashamed of having attempted to malign such sterling pillars of the community. The rest of us have fared no better."

"Aye. Well, if you'd had some *proof* perchance . . ."

"Jonathan Armitage had proof. He was charged with dereliction of duty in the foundering of his East Indiaman, despite the sworn testimony of his ship's carpenter."

"Which I understand was in direct opposition to statements taken from the other survivors. *Including* the supercargo, whose word held more weight than that of the ship's carpenter, you may be sure. And even had Armitage been believed, he had nothing to link the scuttling of a fine ship to any member of the League of Jewelled Men. Nor, in fact, any proof that such an organization actually exists!"

Furlong said passionately, "Are the authorities blind? They have only to look around Town to see what's going forward. They've only to read the incredible lists of shipping losses. Don't they find it unlikely that so many impeccably honest gentlemen in high places should suddenly commit the most outrageous crimes, and wind up disgraced and imprisoned and their estates confiscated? Can they really believe 'tis all chance, or coincidence?"

"Can you prove beyond doubting that 'tis not?"

"No, dammitall! We have no such ironclad proof! And while we fight to obtain it, our time is running out! Rossiter believes—we all believe—that the League is almost ready. I've no need to tell you that rabble rousers are everywhere. The riots grow more frequent and more violent. And the fools in Whitehall yawn and chat over luncheon of the menace of France or Spain, and pay no heed to what is happening right under their stupid noses!"

Talbot gazed at his wineglass. "Not all, dear boy. Not quite all."

"Do you mean Hayes?" asked Furlong eagerly. "Has something happened in Town to shake his complacency?"

"Something has happened. But not in *this* town." Talbot set down his glass and leaned forward, linking his hands. "It seems that Hayes has a little network of spies scattered about the world—just sort of sniffing around, as you might say. Apparently, one of his best men got wind of a secret meeting between some powerful British gentlemen and some equally powerful gentlemen of France. All extremely treasonable, of course. Rumour has it that large sums of money changed hands, and an Agreement was signed. We have no details, but one of the Frenchmen was killed later that same evening in an apparent street brawl, whereupon, according to Hayes' man, there was an incredible flurry in Paris. The gates to the city were closed, hundreds of known thieves and criminals were seized, searched, and questioned with varying degrees of brutality."

"Does Hayes' spy know what was being sought?"

"*Allegedly*, a painting of great value was taken from Versailles." Talbot smiled thinly. "But 'twould be interesting to remove the back of that *objet d'art*!"

Furlong whistled softly. "And Lord Hayes believes that the secret meeting may have had to do with the League?"

Talbot nodded. "Just so. Hayes believes that the man who was slain may have been carrying the French copy of the Agreement."

Deep in thought, Furlong muttered, "I wonder . . ." He glanced up from under his brows. "Sir, what do you know of Marshal Jean-Jacques Barthélemy?"

Talbot's eyes opened wide. "What, France's national hero? I know he's a splendid soldier, a born leader, young, handsome, intelligent, and—so they say—threatened only by his own ambitions. And I hope to God you do not suspect he's got a finger in this pie!"

Furlong said slowly, "I don't know. We have information that would seem to point that way, but—nothing very definite, I'm afraid. I take it you do not have the identities or occupations of the Frenchies who signed the Agreement?"

"Not yet, more's the pity. They might simply have been merchants contracting to supply armaments and mercenaries."

"Or our ambitious French Marshal might fancy himself as President of a British republic! But, either way, sir, this could be the turning point for us! If only we had the copy of that Agreement! When was it lost?"

"Last year."

"Last *year*! Oh, deuce take it!"

"Never look so discouraged. The search has continued ever

since. A most deadly competition between British and French Intelligence agents, private spies, and soldiers of fortune, all slavering to be first to find the stolen copy. And with the lives of those who signed it hanging in the balance." He paused and said curiously, "Owen, you look like a cat with the choice of mouse or rat. What now?"

The suspicion that had crept into Furlong's mind was far-fetched, but his voice was tense with excitement as he answered, "Likely a piece of nonsense, sir. But have you *any* notion at all of the present location of that Agreement?"

Talbot hesitated, but it was clear that Furlong thought he had something. He said, "In the very strictest confidence, Owen! I've heard that a dying man in Mozambique passed it to the priest who administered the last rites, and that the priest in turn handed it to a British officer; a Major Rathdown."

Furlong let out his breath in a long sigh. "So much for my silly suspicion. Then this Major—er, Rathdown, has delivered it safely?"

"Not to my knowledge. So far as I'm aware, he is dodging about India, and damned hotly pursued, you may be sure!"

After a pause, Furlong muttered, "God help the major! I'd not trade places with him for any amount!"

"Nor I! But I'll tell you one thing, my boy. Even if that poor devil is never heard of again, the incident has done one thing for you. It has caused Lord Hayes to begin to believe there may indeed be a conspiracy afoot. And he is thinking far more seriously of the possible existence of your League of Jewelled Men!"

M iss, are you sure you can manage him?" Gorton eyed Viking uneasily as he alternately led the way along the street, or dragged Zoe to a halt while a promising scent was attended to.

"He is nigh as tall as you and has twice your strength. Pray allow me to take him." She reached courageously for the lead, but her hand shot back as Viking turned and showed her his teeth.

Zoe pushed back the curl that the wind would persist in blowing into her eyes on this blustery morning. "Thank you, Elsie. But he knows you fear him, you see. It would not do."

"Everyone fears him." Gorton eyed the rambunctious hound without affection. " 'Tis not may place to criticize, but Lady Julia should better require Phipps or Whipley to exercise the beast."

"I wish I may see it!" Zoe chuckled at the prospect of the thin and timid lackey taking the big dog for a walk. "Poor Phipps is terrified of Viking, and Whipley is far too grand. That is the difficulty, I think. Viking has not been taken out sufficiently often to learn how to go on. But he is really a good dog. He just—" She hung on desperately as the "good dog" hurled insults at two passing chairmen and strove to come at them.

Gorton gave a shriek and threw her arms supportively around Zoe's waist.

Abandoning his interest in the rapidly retreating chairmen, Viking showed a distinct inclination to devour a link boy, then turned his attention to a dandelion.

"He just likes to play the bully," Zoe finished breathlessly.

"*Play!*" Restoring her cap, which had slid during their efforts, Gorton panted, "Ay only hope—"

Her hopes went unrevealed as the wind whipped the cap from her fingers and danced it back the way they had come.

"Run!" urged Zoe, restraining Viking from doing so.

The cap was a fetching article, recently bestowed on her by Coachman Cecil, and Gorton threw constraint to the wind and galloped in pursuit.

Watching with interest, Zoe was suddenly jerked around.

There came an outburst of shrill barks, punctuated by Viking's deep growl. A tiny fluffy dog pranced up, and Viking plunged to the attack. Hanging on for dear life, Zoe found herself entangled with leads, quarreling canines, and a lady who scolded and darted in a spirited attempt to remove her pet from harm's way.

"Viking—*down!*" cried Zoe with all the fierceness she could muster.

The tiny victim, evidently deciding that attack is the best means of defence, reinforced Zoe's command by turning about and nipping Viking on the nose.

Viking howled and slunk behind Zoe, pawing at his hurt and giving every appearance of an innocent bystander cruelly persecuted.

"Oh, my goodness!" gasped Zoe, unwrapping herself. "I *am* so sorry, ma'am!"

"And considerably outweighed," said a laughing voice.

Zoe glanced up hopefully, and met a pair of brilliant dark eyes that held the friendliest smile imaginable. The lady's face was a perfect oval, the finely arched brows and high cheekbones, the delicately carved nose, beautifully shaped mouth and firm chin, framed by glossy dark curls, atop which was a most fetching lace-trimmed cap. Vaguely aware of a rich maroon velvet cloak and a dark pink gown, Zoe thought that she had never seen such exotic loveliness, and she exclaimed in her forthright way, "Oh! How very pretty you are!"

"Now that is unfair! How may I protest your naughty hound when you are so charming?"

There was only amusement in the rich, husky voice, but Zoe blushed. "Alas, I must learn not to be so bold, but—"

"But, 'faith, 'tis a delight! And I think my little Petite has defended the family honour admirably, so you are not to be embarrassed."

"You are too good, ma'am. But despite your kindness, I am ashamed of Viking's uncivilized behaviour."

The small Petite advanced upon the skulking hound, and Viking whimpered and retreated.

Petite was swept up and her mistress said affectionately, "Restrain yourself, my pet! We will not further alarm the large one, *che cosa dice?* Luigi! Kindly make me known to this lady."

A liveried footman, who had hung back during this lively exchange, now came forward, and announced in halting English, "La Signorina Maria Benevento say her compliments to Miss . . . ?"

"I am Zoe Grainger," supplied Zoe with a curtsy.

A slender hand was removed from its velvet muff, and Zoe took it gratefully.

"No, but I am in England now, and am *Miss*, not Signorina, if you please. Ah, here comes your woman. And I am sure she would judge this a most improper introduction, so I had best leave you. Do not fret yourself, Miss Grainger. There is no harm done, and my pleasure has been to meet you."

"And mine," said Zoe earnestly. "I do hope we shall meet again."

"Perchance we will. Until then, *arrivederla.*" With a smile and a nod she passed by, the footman following respectfully and the small Petite prancing along with the pride of the victor.

"Miss Zoe!" panted Gorton, hurrying up clutching her cap.

"No, pray do not pinch at me, Elsie. I know I must not speak to strangers. But truly, I could not escape it, and we were introduced most politely. I assign all the blame to Viking, who was very naughty. But I cannot be sorry. Did you see the lady? I never met anyone so lovely; so vital."

"She looked foreign," said Gorton disparagingly, making a hurried effort to replace her cap as they walked on together with an uncharacteristically well-behaved hound.

"Why, so she was. Italian, I think, though she had the very faintest of accents."

"Her complexion was dark, surely."

"A little sallow, perhaps. But so clear, Elsie! And with such a glow to her cheeks. What a fascinating creature!"

Gorton relented and said, "Ay vow, Miss Zoe, you have not a jealous bone in your body. The lady was likely envying you that lovely auburn hair and your pretty green eyes. But if Ay may make so bold, 'twould be best not to mention your meeting to Lady Buttershaw."

"Good gracious, no!" agreed Zoe. "Most *certainly* not!"

Cranford was frowning when Zoe walked into the library. He had to admit that she presented a charming picture in a blue cloak worn over a cream-coloured gown, with a blue-and-cream striped petticoat. Conducting her own appraisal, Zoe thought him quite dashing in shades of green, his cloak flung back carelessly from one shoulder, revealing a light dress sword. A tricorne was under one arm, and his hair was powdered and neatly tied back. Her gaze dropped. Aware of it, he stuck out his right leg and shook it defiantly. She suffered an odd little pang to see the short peg-leg; which was ridiculous, since she had teased him into wearing it, and had been fully prepared for such a change.

"Very good," she said matter-of-factly. "Had you supposed I might swoon at the sight?"

"I had thought you might be ashamed to come downstairs, since you took such an unconscionable time to gather your courage."

She twinkled at him. "I know. Isn't it silly? I came down twenty minutes ago, but was rushed back upstairs because 'tis expected that a lady will keep a gentleman waiting."

It was the last response he had anticipated, and his irritation vanished. "What next will you say?" he said with a broad grin. "I think I must carry you off before you commit any more indiscretions!"

He turned to the door and found that Lady Buttershaw stood there.

"Here you are, *dear* cousin Peregrine," she gushed, clasping his hand as though enraptured at the sight of him. "I will tell you that a parcel was delivered to me this morning. From 'An Admirer.' And inside was the very loveliest wig!" She giggled and tapping her fan on his knuckles said conspiratorially, "Sly rascal that you are! Well, I shall not delay you further. The weather looks a trifle uncertain this morning, but do not be anxious. We shall see no more rain today, I promise you."

She walked with them to the front doors, elaborating upon her skill at predicting the weather, which was so accurate that she would be of great assistance to a mariner. "If you are acquainted with any such persons, Cousin Peregrine," she said expansively, "you may advise them to consult with me."

She had turned to face him, her great skirts blocking the entrance so that he was unable to escape without brushing past her, which was, of course, not to be thought of.

"Alas, my acquaintanceship with mariners is extreme small, ma'am," he confessed. "I've a friend whose brother commands an East Indiaman, but—"

"Aha! Only think how he could benefit from my expertise. I shall insist upon your bringing him to call on me."

Heartily wishing that she would have done with this trite chatter, he smothered his impatience and said that he was very sure the gentleman would be delighted. "Unfortunately," he added smoothly, "his ship is at this moment somewhere between Calcutta and Bristol, so the poor fellow has lost his opportunity to consult you."

Lady Buttershaw declared that she had a fondness for nautical gentlemen, and that she would not dream of denying his friend her advice. Laughing heartily, she said that she would be "monstrous put out" was the captain not brought to see her as soon as he returned to England. "And I will tell you, sir, that 'tis considered a high honour to be invited to Yerville Hall!"

He murmured that he was very sure of it, and made a mental vow that he would have no hand in delivering Derek Furlong into the lady's clutches.

The coach standing at the kennel rocked as the team sidled impatiently, and my lady simpered that dear cousin Peregrine was an audacious flirt, but he must have a care for his horses and not stay here captivating her any longer.

Cranford hove a sigh of relief as she went back inside. Ushering Zoe into the coach, he threw a glance up at the box. Florian's face was lit by a sly grin, and Cranford winked an acknowledgment of the well-timed "touching up" of his team.

The footman slammed the door, Cranford sat beside Zoe, and the coach went bowling along towards Piccadilly. After a silent moment Zoe peeped at his scowl and said, "Lady Buttershaw seemed pleased with you for returning her wig. But I think your visits to Yerville Hall will not be frequent, sir."

He grunted. "The next time my great-uncle asks me to visit one of his relatives I shall have an ironclad excuse well-rehearsed, and if that fails I'll at once emigrate to the New World!"

"Alas, what a set-down," she said with a sigh. "And I had so counted upon your asking for my hand this morning."

He shot her a startled glance, saw the twinkle in her bright eyes, and laughed. "If ever I met such a tease! I hope you have advised her that I am a rejected suitor."

"Well, of course I have not!"

"Then you had best do so, my good girl, or the next time the lady tries to turn me up sweet I shall tell her to her face that

I am betrothed to—" He paused, and finished quietly, "To the most beautiful lady in all England."

"Oh, pray do not! *Pray* do not! 'Twould place me in the most dreadful position!"

Indignation replaced sadness, and he snapped, " 'Twould place *me* in the most dreadful position did I allow that match-making dowager to believe I am trying to fix my interest with you! Egad, but now I think on it, the fact she allows me to take you out unchaperoned may well mean she already thinks—"

"No, no!" Zoe seized his arm and said agitatedly, "We have but now met! How could she possibly be so silly as to think you have formed a *tendre* for me? Were I a ravishing beauty, per-haps, but—well, look at me. I am scarce the type of lady to ensnare a dashing young man about Town on so brief an ac-quaintanceship."

"No, but Lady Buttershaw is in my opinion *very* silly. She has made up that adamantine mind of hers to find you a hus-band, and—"

"But 'tis just one of her whims! It can be nothing more. I am not related to her. She has no real interest in whether I wed a cockroach or—"

"Well! Of all the— One instant I'm a dashing young man about Town, and the next—"

"Oh, you know what I mean. I was brought here only to be companion to her sister. Why she should have taken this silly maggot into her head less than a week after I arrived, I cannot think. But she will soon forget it, I know she will. I am very sorry to inconvenience you like this, when you have so many more entertaining things to do, but . . . *Please*, Mr. Cranford! If you tell her you don't want me, she'll start flinging more of her ridiculous 'Prospects' at me again! Could you not bear with me for just a little while? I will be very good, I promise."

She was clinging tightly to his arm, and looking down into her imploring eyes, he could not but sympathize with her.

"Poor mite," he said kindly. "Do not be so put about. She cannot force you to wed anyone you don't wish to."

"No, but she can send me home in disgrace, and then my step-mama will tell Papa what a hoyden I am and life will be horrid again."

"You are not a hoyden! You're young and full of—of fun and interest in everything, is all. Your step-mama is likely green with envy because you have such smiling eyes and your complexion is so clear and smooth. Why ever did your father wed such a shrew?"

Zoe sighed. "She is very pretty, and Aaron, he's our shepherd and a darling, says she's got a prime foc'sle and—"

Cranford's shout of laughter interrupted her and she beamed at him hopefully. "Is that funny? What's a foc'sle?"

"The forecastle of a ship, you little rascal! Only he was referring to her—that is to say, he meant she is—er, well endowed. Is she?"

"Rich? No, I don't think— Oh!" The light dawned, and she patted her bosom. "You mean *this*! Yes." She made an expansive gesture. "Vast! In fact—"

He choked back laughter this time, and threw up an arresting hand. "Never mind! 'Twas most improper in me to enquire. And do not *ever* let anyone hear you use such an expression, or you'll really be packed off home in disgrace!"

"I probably will at all events," said Zoe, despondent again. "For I seem always to be getting into trouble. I wish I could please Lady Buttershaw. I know she's a dragon, but she really has been good. She gave me all these lovely clothes, and I have a personal maid who is the dearest thing. And they really ask very little of me. All I do is take care of Lady Julia's pets, and read to her sometimes. And she likes me to tell her of my home and my family. Poor little creature, she's had such a sad life, and she is so gentle and kind."

"Then she will doubtless understand you're not used to

Town ways yet. You'll soon learn." Watching her poke an errant curl under her cap, he thought, 'Which will be a pity.' The trusting eyes lifted to meet his and he added hurriedly, "Besides, I don't see how they can blame you because you chanced to witness the—er, accident. You had nought to do with it."

"No, but I wouldn't have been nearby save that I sent Gorton off with her light o'love—which they would not at all have liked. And then I wandered out onto the street by myself, which is not done, they say. Though why it should not be done I cannot think. The streets were made to be walked upon, and London is a civilized city in a civilized country, after all. 'Tis not as though we were in the hills of Spain or Italy, surrounded by wicked bandits—which reminds me of something I *must* tell you, for I think she would be just what you would like—and only look how I caused you to be attacked by the flower seller yesterday. And there was that *awful* thing last night! If they found out about that . . . !"

In an attempt to untangle these intriguing threads, he asked with a grin, "What happened last night? Did you drop one of the cats in the soup?"

Zoe smiled ruefully. "I was asleep, and Boadicea—she belongs to Attila, you know—well, you don't know, but there it is. Bo came and scratched on my door . . ." She embarked on the tale of the gentlemen who had almost discovered her in her nightrail, and was relieved when Cranford seemed more amused than shocked. "You may laugh," she finished, "but I thought they would never leave. And they were extreme vexed, and I'm sure would have been even more so if they'd found me!"

" 'Tis very well they did not. Who were they? Your unwitting 'Prospects' again?"

"No. Not those kinds of voices at all. Much more manly. Firm and strong, the way you speak. Indeed, one of them was quite—frightening. I could tell the others were afraid of him.

I'd not want anyone to use that tone to me."

"Oh? It was a quarrel, then?"

"Not . . . exactly. I think it had to do with business, and someone who had made them very cross. And they are in the greatest impatience for a lady to arrive. Lady . . . Oh, I forget her name."

"So you should. You had no business listening to a private conversation."

"As if I would intentionally have done such a dishonourable thing!"

"All right, all right. Don't go flying up into the boughs again. To say truth, I'm the one being dishonourable by asking you about it. We must talk of something else."

She agreed readily and asked him about his home. They were soon in a deep discussion of the merits of country life as opposed to dwelling in Town, and pleased to find themselves in complete agreement.

Glancing out of the window, he exclaimed, "Only look, we've chattered away our time again and here's Ludgate Hill already. There's the cathedral."

"Ooh!" she squeaked, gripping her hands tightly as she peered out of the window. "How magnificent! 'Tis so much bigger than I'd imagined. But it does not look sixteen hundred years old."

"Of course it doesn't. It burned down in the Great Fire as did most of the city. They only finished rebuilding about thirty or so years ago. 'Faith, I thought everybody knew that!"

"Well, I did, but there are so very many interesting things in this world to try to remember, are there not? Little bits and pieces get tucked away in my head sometimes, and I cannot always fish them out when I need them. Oh, just *look* at all the people! May we go inside? Are we allowed to climb up to that little house atop the dome?"

Cranford, who was uneasily eyeing the double flight of

steps to the West Front, thought, 'Heaven forfend!' and said that it would be highly improper for a lady to attempt such a climb. "Besides, you couldn't do it!"

"Indeed I could! You should only see me climb our big oak tree! My—"

An elderly lady who chanced to be passing, emitted a horrified gasp, and the stout gentleman on whose arm she leaned, puffed out his cheeks several times and sent a shocked frown at Cranford.

Inwardly bubbling with laughter, he pulled the miscreant's hand through his arm and advised her that he would never be able to show his face in the cathedral again if she did not behave with more restraint.

"Oh, I *am* so sorry," she whispered penitently. "I will be meek as a lamb, I promise." Her chastened state lasted for thirty seconds. She began to giggle, leaned closer and hissed, "Did you see his whiskers vibrate? 'Twas like corn in a strong wind!"

Cranford whispered, "Lady Buttershaw could make 'em fly, did she only thunder at the poor old fellow!"

That picture made Zoe giggle so much she had to hide behind her muff and pretend to be sneezing, but when they reached the vestibule and could look down the length of the nave and crossing and choir towards the distant High Altar, she was struck dumb and stood motionless, her lower lip sagging and her wide eyes drinking it all in.

Cranford had only visited the cathedral once before, and was as awed by its magnificence as was Zoe. His murmured suggestion that they move on was ignored, and he had to tug at her hand to gain her attention. "Do come along," he urged. "People are staring. They think you're one of the statues."

She smiled at him blindingly, and walking on, murmured, " 'Tis even bigger inside than outside!"

He grinned. "Silly chit. That's not possible."

"Well, it *seems* bigger." She gave a sudden skip, and look-ing at the floor, yelped, "Oh, my goodness! Are we stepping on people?"

A small group of passers-by frowned at her.

A verger came up and said sternly that voices should be kept low in the cathedral.

"The lady meant no disrespect," responded Cranford, irked.

"If your lady has a question—" began the verger, with a quelling glance at Zoe.

"Oh, I am not Mr. Cranford's lady," she explained ear-nestly. "We have only just met."

Cranford moaned under his breath.

A large military gentleman put up his quizzing glass and subjected them to a piercing stare. The sour-looking lady he escorted snorted audibly, "Whatever next!"

Zoe said hurriedly, "But I do have a question, if you please. How was it built? I mean—did it go up one part at a time, so they would have a place for services while the rest was a'build-ing?"

The verger elevated his nose. "Sir Christopher Wren," he divulged loftily, "had the entire foundation laid at one time."

"Jolly sensible," said Cranford. "Some wooden-headed banker was sure to have come along and started penny-pinch-ing, otherwise."

"Just so, sir." The verger felt something heavier than a penny being slipped into his palm, whereupon he warmed to this unlikely pair and took them under his wing. "If you will step this way, sir, you will note that the dome is not as high as it appears from the outside . . . That is because . . ."

An hour later, as they walked back towards the vestibule, Cranford declared that never in his life had he heard anyone talk so much. "All that stuff about the Romans, and Inigo

Jones, and that fellow Dugdale! I thought he never would stop! And you had to egg him on with all your questions!"

"But only think, Mr. Cranford. How marvellous that 'twas all built in only five and thirty years, whereas it took a century and a half to build St. Peter's! And all directed by just one man. What a wonder he must have been! And—oh, wasn't his epitaph the loveliest thing? Especially the ending—'Reader, if you seek a monument, look about you.' Which is perfect truth." Glowing, and deeply moved, she flung out an arm. "All this—"

There came a startled exclamation. Appalled by the awareness that in her enthusiasm she had struck someone, she turned quickly. "I *do* beg your—" She broke off. "Oh! 'Tis *you!*"

Cranford jerked his head round apprehensively. 'By Jove!' he thought, and stared admiringly at a darkly bewitching female countenance with a pair of great dusky eyes that seemed to dance with laughter. Her taffeta gown was of vibrant orange, and tiny orange flowers banded her dashing ruffled cap. Her footman was restoring a dull rust velvet cloak that had slipped from one shoulder. Even as he gazed, the shapely red lips parted in a warm smile and a gloved hand was extended to Zoe.

"We meet again," she said in a husky and faintly accented voice.

"How lovely!" Clasping her hand, Zoe said, "Miss Benevento, may I present Lieutenant Cranford?" Formality deserted her and she said exuberantly, "He is not in uniform now, so I expect I should not use his military title, but I think it rather nice. This is the lady I was telling you about— Oh, but I didn't finish telling you, did I, Mr. Cranford? Well, you see, I was taking Viking for his walk this morning, when somehow—"

Cranford interposed laughingly, "Yes, and I must hear all about it, but I fear we block the way, ma'am."

Her face fell. "I should *so* like to talk with you, Miss Benevento. Are you leaving also? Perhaps we might walk together for a little way?"

The dark beauty said that she would be delighted to have another chat, but as they reached the portico, she looked about dubiously. "Alas, I fear 'tis coming on to rain, and the wind is chill. I am engaged to meet my old nurse at the Piazza at half past one o'clock. Perhaps another time?"

The prospect of going into the popular coffee house with Zoe Grainger on one arm and this vivacious lady on the other inspired Cranford to at once beg the honour of Miss Benevento's condescending to join them until her friends should arrive. "It wants an hour until half past one," he pointed out. "Plenty of time for us to enjoy a cup of chocolate together, while you two ladies tell me all about your meeting."

"Yes, yes," said Zoe, pressing Miss Benevento's hand. "Do say you will!"

The dark eyes turned dubiously from Zoe's eager face to Cranford's smiling one. It was an engaging smile, and her own dawned. "Very well," she said. "I expect my footman will think it quite shocking, but I accept. 'Faith, but I could not be more pleased, for I am new come to London and have few friends."

Not by the flicker of an eyelash had she betrayed any awareness of the peg-leg. She was, thought Cranford, as poised as she was beautiful, and he was quick to endorse Zoe's fervent declaration that Miss Maria Benevento had just found two new friends.

It was agreed that they would meet at the Piazza, and as they set out Zoe described her meeting with their new acquaintance. "She could very easily have been cross," she admitted, "but was instead so kind and friendly. And did ever you see anyone so beautiful? She would be just right for you." Before he could catch his breath, her brow wrinkled, and she added with a trace of anxiety, "Or is she too old?"

Amused, despite himself, he said, "What, trying to fob me off already, and our betrothal not yet published?" Zoe laughed, and he went on, "You are outrageous, which I am sure you have been told before, and I have no need of a matchmaker, I thank you! Furthermore, if the lady is past four and twenty I should be very much surprised, and although you likely judge that ancient, I assure you 'tis not. She is likely already betrothed. Indeed, with her looks and charm 'twould be astonishing if she was not."

Despite Lady Clara Buttershaw's assurances to the contrary, it was raining steadily by the time the two carriages reached the Piazza. The coffee house was crowded, and Cranford was far from displeased to see all eyes turn to them as they walked in, and to note that Gilbert Fowles, whom he loathed, was among those present, and watched him with envy. Since he was well known here, he was able to secure a comfortable table away from draughts, and a waiter hurried to welcome him and take his order.

By the time the steaming chocolate arrived they were chattering like old friends. Cranford marvelled at the fact that Miss Benevento, so vibrantly lovely, was apparently unattached. Her slight and charming accent was explained when she told them that she was of Italian birth, but had lived in Switzerland for some years with an elderly English aunt. She seemed completely unaware of her beauty, and listened attentively to whatever was said. Her interest was so warm and sincere that Cranford suddenly realized he had been talking for some minutes about his brother and sister and their happy childhood at dear old Muse Manor. He was not the man to rave of the stellar qualities of those he loved, and he broke off in no little embarrassment to apologize for boring on at such length.

"This is not the case," said Miss Benevento. "I miss my own family greatly, and am glad always to learn as much as I may of life in my new country. Besides, London is a great city, but"—she gave a rather wistful shrug—"one can easily be lonely here."

Cranford found it difficult to believe that she could be left alone for a moment. "We cannot have that," he declared. "Can we, Miss Grainger?"

"Certainly not," said Zoe, and asked with sudden shyness, "would you be so kind as to call on me, Miss Benevento? I am sure Lady Julia Yerville would be very pleased."

"Lady Yerville might," answered the beauty. "But, alas, Lady Clara Buttershaw she would not be pleased at all. I have met her you see, at—oh, I forget where, but I was properly snubbed, and rather obviously judged to be not good *ton*. No, my dear. I cannot call on you."

Zoe looked crestfallen, and Cranford said, "If you wish, Miss Grainger, I could take you driving in the park and we could meet Miss Benevento there. Or perhaps you can walk together when you exercise your dogs."

This suggestion was happily received by both ladies. They were planning their next meeting when a boy brought a note to say that the lady who had hoped to meet Miss Benevento was detained and regretfully would not be able to come today.

Cranford lost no time in persuading their new friend to join them for a light luncheon. It was a merry hour, and farewells were exchanged with the firm understanding they would all meet again very soon.

Zoe had thoroughly enjoyed her day, and thanked Cranford profusely, but he was uneasily aware that he'd kept her out much longer than had been his intention. When he returned her to the door of Yerville Hall, however, Arbour informed them that Lady Buttershaw was from home, and Lady Yerville had left instructions that she was not to be disturbed for the rest of the afternoon. Zoe gave a sigh of relief, and having received her permission to call the following day, Cranford was able to leave without fearing she would be taken to task.

erched on a stool in the laundry room, Zoe watched Gorton press the primrose silk robe *à la Française* she was to wear tonight, and argued, "What is so frightful about my being here?"

Gorton slanted a nervous glance at the door. "It is not fitting for you to be in this part of the house at all, Miss. Ay doubt their la'ships have ever in their lives seen a laundry room."

"Good," said Zoe blithely. "Then they're not likely to pop in and catch me! I could not wait to tell you about my day! I had the most wonderful time. I don't mind the rain a bit, and besides, we were in the cathedral most of the morning. It is so *beautiful*, Elsie! I had all I could do not to weep! And Mr. Cranford was prodigious kind to me, even when some people looked fussy because I told him how deedily I can climb trees."

Gorton wailed, "Oh, Miss! You never did!"

"Of course I did. My brother and I used to— Oh, I see what you mean. Well, I don't know that I'm grown up, of course." Zoe grew pensive and added, "I cannot but feel sorry for children who never are allowed such fun. Did you climb trees when you were little?"

"Wasn't any. Not down by the river."

Appalled by the vision of children growing up treeless, Zoe

exclaimed, "How dreadful! You poor dear! Do you know, London is grand and wonderful, but there's nothing like the country . . . But then again," she said, brightening, "we don't have places like the Piazza in Burford."

"Took you there did he, Miss? 'Tis a grand place to see and be seen."

"Oh, it is! And we were seen, I promise you! When we walked in *everybody* turned to look at us!"

"And whay not, Ay should lake to know? You was so pretty as any picture this morning!"

"Pish and posh, Elsie! They were not looking at me, but at Miss Benevento, the lady I met when we took Viking for his walk this morning. By a lucky chance she was at St. Paul's, and I vow looked lovelier than ever. She is so—oh, everything I would like to be. And she was not at all starched up, or critical of the silly things I say sometimes. Lieutenant Cranford could scarce take his eyes from her."

"Huh! Then, if Ay were you, Miss, Ay would not meet her when he is with you. He seems to me a very nice gentleman, if you did not mind about—about his—er . . ."

"You mean because he has lost his foot? I think it should be a point of pride that he fought so gallantly for his country! But if you are paying heed to Lady Clara's notion that he would ever offer for me, disabuse your mind of such stuff. He was horrified when I told him of it."

"*Ow!*" yelped Gorton, equally horrified. "You didn't!"

"I did. And he was. And if you do not move your iron 'twill scorch! Though I must say he wanted for tact, not to at least pretend . . . But I think he is—comfortable with me, Elsie, and does not feel the need to be tactful. Which is good. I expect . . . You should only see how the ladies watch him. He thinks 'tis just because he limps. But it isn't. I saw them. And he is very good-looking, do not you think?"

"Ay do. And Ay fancy Miss Benevento does."

"Yes. She was pleased with him, I am sure. She would be just right for him, as I told him."

"You *never*! Oh—Miss! Whatever must he *think*?"

"Poor Elsie. Have I disgraced you again? I suppose I have no Town polish, as they say. And I rather fancy I never shall have. Better for you had Miss Hermione come as Lady Yerville's companion, instead of me."

Gorton chuckled, and replaced her iron on the hob. "Ay think Miss Hermione would never suit her la'ship. She is very lazy, if Ay dare remark it." She picked up the other iron and licked her finger before testing it, then set it on its heel to cool for a minute. "Lady Clara says 'tis because she has too much flesh."

Intrigued, Zoe asked, "But she is very young, no?"

"And very *fat*, Miss! A kind young lady, but too fond of comfits for her own good. Lady Clara flies straight into the boughs when she comes here, and carries on alarming about the sin of gluttony. Miss Hermione, she just smiles and pays no heed. Proper drowsy she is. Nothing upsets her. Ay will bring the gown along in just a minute, and you wish to put on your wrapper, Miss. Lady Julia dines early, and you will not want to keep her waiting."

"No, indeed!" said Zoe, standing at once. " 'Tis kind in her to invite me. I expect she will like me to tell her all about the cathedral."

"And the lieutenant," murmured Gorton with a twinkle.

It was raining steadily when Florian guided the team on to Henrietta Street, but Cranford was more light-hearted than he had been for weeks, and as he left the carriage was mildly surprised to realize that he hadn't thought of his lost love for hours.

Florian waved, and drove off to the stables. Limping up the two shallow front steps, Cranford heard the postman's horn and waited at the door. How much more comfortable he felt having worn the peg-leg today. Little Zoe Grainger could be thanked for that, and for their merry luncheon at the Piazza. She was a good-hearted creature, and with not an ounce of affectation, which was as rare as it was refreshing. It was remarkable, he mused, that, in view of their unfortunate first encounter and the fact that he'd known her for such a short time, he now felt so completely at ease with her.

The postman came up, undaunted by the rain that dripped from his hat, and announced with his customary cheerful grin that there were two letters this afternoon. One was from Piers, for which Cranford paid gladly. The other, addressed in a poor hand he did not recognize, required a sixpenny fee, and he went, grumbling, into his apartments.

He tossed his wet cloak over a chair and broke the seal on the sixpenny letter, reading it as he wandered slowly to the hearth and the still-glowing remnants of the fire.

"What a damnable scrawl," he muttered, peering at the signature. It looked like 'Rohdean,' nobody he knew. He moved to the window, holding the much rumpled sheet to the gloomy light of this grey afternoon, and trying to decipher the ill-formed words.

"You will by this . . . heard from our mental fiend—(Gad! That can't be right!) Oh—*mutual friend*, and will be thinking me the . . . for passing my . . . to his shoulders. Pray believe . . . your . . . Father . . . save for this confounded illness, especially since he is in little better case. But . . . choice . . ." Cranford groaned with frustration as the following line was totally incomprehensible, and skipping to the next, struggled on with ever-increasing bafflement.

He heard a step behind him and muttered, "That was speedy, Florian!"

There was no response.

Glancing up, he had time to glimpse a tall cloaked figure and a low-drawn hood, before the downward flailing pistol butt brought a hideous shock and the end of awareness.

I tell you, I could not see his face!" Cranford sprawled in the fireside chair as Furlong dabbed cautiously at the cut on his head. "He was— Ow! Those are my brains you're playing about with!"

"Is that what it is?" muttered Furlong. "Thought 'twas a nest of woodworms! No, do be still, you maniac! This is a beast of a lump, but the cut's nothing to speak of, and your hair will hide it. Now, an you are not feeling too wretched, tell me more of your unexpected caller."

Cranford settled back again. He did feel wretched. Had Furlong said his head had been split open with an axe he would not have questioned it. He yearned to lie down upon his bed, but rage was the uppermost emotion, and he answered in short, furious bursts: "The swine was tall. A big fellow. No prigging cove. I think—"

Furlong interrupted sharply, "What d'ye mean—no prigging cove? He followed you in here, did he not, and broke your head! *Assurement*, he intended robbery."

"Perhaps, but he was too well dressed to have been—" Cranford swore and raised a trembling hand to his head.

Watching him with narrowed eyes, Furlong said, "Gently, my poor chap. Gently."

The door was flung open. His tricorne and cloak scattering raindrops Florian rushed to the sofa and dropped to one knee beside it, scanning Cranford with frantic anxiety. "Is he—?"

"I'm alive," said Cranford wearily. "One gathers the bastard got away?"

"There was a coach at the end of the street, sir. It drove off as I ran up. But 'tis almost dark and with the rain so heavy, I was not able to make out if there was a crest on the panel, or if anyone was inside."

"Can't be raining," muttered Cranford, his eyes closing. "She said . . . no rain." He chuckled to himself.

Sir Owen and Florian exchanged sober glances. Sir Owen said quietly, "Better go for an apothecary, lad."

"No!" Cranford opened his eyes again. "D'ye take me for a milquetoast? Just a bump on the head, is all. You must have—have found me right away, Owen."

"I was awake, luckily. I heard you go down. Florian came in while I was trying to lift you, and I sent him haring off after the varmint."

Cranford said with a quivering grin, "A fine quiet place for you to recuperate. My apologies. What did—did that miserable hound make off with?"

Florian lit a taper at the fire and hurried around the room lighting candles. "I do not see that he took anything, sir."

"Must have!" Cranford peered about painfully. "Even a prigging cove don't break into a man's house and—and beat his brains out for nothing. Hanging offence. Wouldn't be—Hey!" He flinched, but gasped out, "My . . . my letters! Where are my . . . letters?"

It was getting cold in the room. Furlong went over to throw a shovel-full of coal on the remnants of the fire, then sat on the chimney seat, watching frowningly as Florian searched about, to report at length, "No letters, sir."

"That worthless weasel!" groaned Cranford. "Of what possible use were my letters to him? I hadn't even read the one from my twin!"

Furlong asked, "Was the other letter of any special import?"

"Import! 'Twas 'a tale told by an idiot,' more like! And an idiot I've never met, if I deciphered the signature correctly. The writing was so bad I . . . could scarce read it. And when I did, be dashed if I could make sense of the silly thing." Cranford leaned his head back cautiously and sighed, "He could've had that, and welcome. But I could strangle the hound for—for making off with my brother's letter."

"Yes. But why would he? Perry, my dear fellow, I know you're properly wrung out, but—can you recall *none* of it?"

Cranford had a deep liking for Owen Furlong, who was not the man to lack sympathy or understanding. He knit his brows, therefore, and despite his throbbing head, made an effort to remember. "The handwriting was a disgrace," he said slowly. "Not the work of an educated gentleman—unless he is aged, or very ill."

"And the signature?"

"I think 'twas Rohdean. Nobody I ever heard of. Truly, 'twas just so much fustian, Owen. Something to do with . . . a mutual friend, and illness, and—and his shoulders, and . . . now what was it? . . . Oh, yes. My *father*, of all people!—who died, God rest him, fifteen years ago!" He gripped his head and sighed. "I'm—dashed sorry to be so stupid. There was more, I know. But I cannot seem to think—and to say truth, I'm inclining to the belief 'tis more of young Templeby's practical jokes."

"Then when Tio returns we'll put a flea in his ear about his rascally half-brother! My apologies for pestering you. Help the lieutenant to his bed, Florian. You rest, Perry old lad, and Florian will brew us a pot of tea. You'll feel good as new in the morning."

"And what of you?" asked Cranford, turning in the doorway as Florian guided his uncertain steps. "You're in little better case than am I."

Furlong grinned and declared that tomorrow he would run Cranford a race to London Bridge and back, to prove how much his health had improved.

But after the door had closed behind his friend, his smile died. "Rohdean," he muttered. "I wonder . . ." He carried a candle to the small desk beside the window, sat down and found some paper and a pen. "I wish to heaven you would come back to Town, Gideon," he wrote. "I fear I have properly let you down and am unable to keep watch on my assigned schemer, as I promised. I've the strongest notion that Perry Cranford is being dragged into this desperate business, which I know you will not like!" He was obliged to pause as a paroxysm of shivering wracked him, and from the corner of his eye, saw the outer door open slowly.

With a lithe spring he was at the hearth and had snatched up the poker. The rapid movement made his head swim, but he steadied himself against the mantelpiece and stood ready for combat.

"Bless me crumpet," exclaimed the huskily built man who entered. "It's only me, mate— I mean, Captin, sir!"

"Tummet!" cried Furlong, relieved.

"Shining-bright-but-I'm-a-sight," said Enoch Tummet, advancing with a broad grin to relieve Sir Owen of the poker. "Me guv—Mr. August, I mean—says as you might be in need of me services, like. So, slam-bang-'ere-I-am!"

"And welcome, indeed," said Furlong, gripping the muscular arm of August Falcon's unorthodox valet. "Your 'guv' could scarce be more in the right of it!"

Lady Julia was not alone when Zoe was shown into the gold saloon in her apartments. Her visitor was a slim gentleman of middle age and average height, with a lean intelligent face, a soft voice, and a twinkle in his grey eyes. His wig was neatly ironed, his dark blue coat rich with silver frogging, the work of a master tailor. He rose and bowed over Zoe's hand gallantly, but she was surprised when Lady Julia introduced him as Lord Eaglund. The viscount's fame had spread even to quiet Burford. He was known to be a fiery orator in the House of Lords, a tireless advocate for the poor, his generosity in the cause of children legendary. She thought, 'And he looks so mild and ordinary!'

As always, her face betrayed her, and Eaglund's mouth hovered on a smile. He murmured, "My son was in the right of it, I see. Miss Grainger is indeed out of the common way!"

Zoe blushed and thanked him, but cast an enquiring glance to Lady Julia, who reclined on a chaise longue, looking ethereal in a gown of white brocade threaded with gold. "His lordship refers to his eldest son," she explained, stroking the tabby, Caesar, who sat neatly Sphinx-like on her lap. "You have met the Honourable Purleigh Shale, I understand."

Mystified, Zoe murmured uncertainly, "Have I?" Then, comprehending, she added sunnily, "Oh! You mean the one they call Purr! I never did know what his last name was."

"I am scarce surprised," acknowledged the viscount, stepping over Caesar's dog, Cromwell, and ushering Zoe to a chair beside the fire. "My heir, alas, is not the most—ah, loquacious of men."

Trying to find an appropriate response, Zoe said, "No, but he is so—tall!"

Lady Julia's musical laugh rippled out.

The viscount said apologetically, "Very true. But for all my own lack of inches, I—ah, I really am his father, you know."

"Well, I cannot think you would claim him for your own, if you were not," said Zoe disastrously.

At this, his lordship could not restrain a hearty laugh. "A wit! And so young! My dear, that innocent face of yours gives you an unfair advantage."

"I warned you, Rupert," said Lady Julia ruefully.

Zoe sighed. "I am very sorry if I said something I did not mean."

"My dear," replied the viscount, "in a Society where most females spend so much time choosing their words for effect that they often say nothing at all, 'tis my delight to meet a lady who is so honestly outspoken."

She liked his kindly smile and gentle voice, and she said, beaming at him, "I believe that means you think I am not very wise, and you don't mind. But you should not restrict your criticism to females, my lord. I have listened to some of my Papa's friends telling him repeatedly how fortunate he is to have found my step-mama. Which is very silly, for I know they do not mean a word of it."

Lady Julia disappeared behind her fan.

Lord Eaglund chuckled. "I think the man who wins your hand will not lead a dull life, little Miss Grainger. Most certainly my criticism does not apply only to the ladies. In fact, an you will cry friends with me, I shall take you to the House of Lords, where you will hear many learned gentlemen taking great pains to say what they do not mean."

Lady Julia laughed and clapped her hands, and Zoe declared happily that she was making lots of lovely new friends. Two more guests were announced at this point. One was the Honourable Purleigh Shale, Lord Eaglund's tall and inarticulate heir, and the other, Lord Sommers, a big, bluff man of about forty, with a red face and an amiable manner.

The Honourable Purleigh bowed without grace and mumbled several half-completed sentences appearing to indicate his pleasure at meeting Miss—er, again; this less-than-scintillating performance earning him a pitying glance from his famous sire. Lord Sommers' bow was brisk, and, casting an unabashedly approving eye over Zoe, he said he had heard a good deal about Miss Grainger and was delighted to see he had not been misinformed.

"But you have only half the story, Ambrose," said Lord Eaglund. "You are in for a treat, I promise you."

Hackham appeared with wine for the gentlemen and ratafia for the ladies. The conversation swept along easily. Zoe's opinions of London in general and St. Paul's in particular were solicited, her frank replies often bringing laughter. The Honourable Purleigh let out some sudden and startling guffaws, and so far overcame his shyness as to stammer that he had met her brother "at school," and trusted the "rascal" was well. Zoe was thus enabled to boast of her beloved Travis' accomplishments and his promising entry into the world of diplomacy.

Dinner was a lengthy procedure, with much earnest discussion of the street riots and nostalgic references to the "good old days," and Lady Julia's father, who had, Zoe gathered, been an admired leader of the Tories as had his father before him.

"And before him, and before *him*," said the viscount, smilingly. "I fancy you have learned much of this family during your stay here, Miss Grainger. 'Tis one of the oldest and proudest in all England. I'faith, but one can scarce think of England without thinking also—Yerville!"

Zoe nodded. "Lady Buttershaw has told me of many of her ancestors. They seem to have had a great deal to do with our history."

"Till now," said Lady Julia with a sigh. "Poor Papa. He did so yearn for a son. He would turn in his grave did he know that neither Clara nor I have provided a male heir to carry on our traditions. Uncle Faulkner does his best, but he will not live here, as he should, and insists upon remaining always at the Abbey."

"Cannot blame the fellow for that, m'dear," said Lord Eaglund. "One of the loveliest old places in the realm. Have you visited Sundial Abbey, Miss Grainger?"

"Not as yet," Lady Julia put in. " 'Tis our country seat, Miss Grainger. Very ancient and as full of history as it is beautiful. But too far from London to be the permanent residence of the Earl of Yerville, or to enable him to take his seat in the House as he should do. Of course, one must not be harsh, and the present earl does not enjoy good health."

Lord Sommers asked, "Who will the title pass to, Julia? Not that ne'er-do-well boy of his, I trust?"

Lady Julia closed her eyes, and shuddered.

The viscount changed the subject hurriedly, and very soon afterwards Lady Julia and Zoe left the gentlemen to their port and nuts. They were alone for only a short while, and the tea tray was carried in at ten o'clock sharp. By half-past ten, as if by custom, the company departed. Zoe was sure Lady Julia would dismiss her, but instead the lady asked her to stay for a short while.

"At last, my dear," she said, when Whipley and Phipps had led all the dogs downstairs, the cats trailing after them. "Now, we may be at ease, and you can tell me *all* about your visit to St. Paul's today. Was Mr. Cranford kind to you? I am told his temper is rather unpredictable."

Zoe lost no time in coming to his defence, and launched into a spirited recounting of the day's events. Lady Julia listened with amused appreciation until Zoe mentioned Miss Benevento.

"Maria Benevento?" she asked with a lift of her brows.

"Yes. Do you know her, ma'am? I think she must be the most beautiful lady in London Town, and with such charm and liveliness."

"She is most attractive, I grant you. But I believe Miss Katrina Falcon is the acknowledged Toast, although quite ineligible, unfortunately. You say Lieutenant Cranford asked Miss Benevento to join you at the Piazza? That was not very wise. But he may not know . . ." The words trailed off and she stared rather blankly at the hearth.

Zoe asked curiously, "Is she not accepted, ma'am? Am I not permitted to know her? I was so hoping she would be my friend."

"Poor child." Lady Julia said kindly, "You are lonely, and small wonder. What does Cranford say of her?"

"Oh, I think he finds her fascinating. In fact, he was meaning to leave London, but now he says he will stay on a little longer."

"That is not surprising. From what you tell me, you have taken his mind off his—troubles. I rather suspect 'tis *you* he finds fascinating, my dear."

Zoe felt her cheeks burn, and stammered that she was sure Mr. Cranford had no least interest in her. "Not in *that* way. 'Tis just that we find the same things amusing, you know. And when I get him to talk about his home and his family, he looks younger and so happy."

"Even so, I cannot think why my sister sees him as a favoured applicant for your hand." Lady Julia looked dubious. "He is in some way related to her, of course. But Clara tends to become extreme enthused about people, and very often later finds to her sorrow that her confidence was misplaced. In truth, we know very little of him. I sincerely hope he does not mix with unsuitable companions. Have you met any of his friends? Are they of good *ton*?"

Zoe was bound to admit that she had small knowledge of Mr. Cranford's acquaintances, but said she would attempt to learn more of the young man, and pleaded to be allowed to accompany him if he should call to take her driving tomorrow.

"Very well," said Lady Julia. "But you must tell me whatever you learn of him, child. I do not want Lady Clara to fly into a pucker without due cause."

Zoe thought about their chat as she lay in bed that night watching the moonlight send pale fingers across the polished boards. So now Lady Julia was not quite so sure of Lieutenant Cranford. Faith, but her ladyship was quick to change her mind! Only yesterday she had said she judged Cranford to be "a most commendable young gentleman." Come to think of it, not until Miss Benevento's name had been mentioned had Lady Julia seemed to entertain doubts, and she had been evasive when asked if Miss Benevento was accepted by the *ton*. Was there something in the exotic beauty's background to put her on the outer fringe of Society, perchance? Her looks, certainly, would cause many ladies to take her in dislike. But Lady Julia was so kind and gentle; surely the last one to be jealous. Drifting towards sleep, Zoe yawned, and wondered which of her lovely new gowns to wear when she drove out with Lieutenant Cranford on the morrow . . .

Her eyes shot open, and suddenly she was wide awake. Almost, she could hear Lady Julia saying playfully, ". . . my cousin's youngest child was to have come as companion to me . . . I do not blame Hermione at all for refusing such a glorious opportunity . . ." But Gorton had said distinctly that Miss Hermione was *very fat*. If that was true, then the new gowns could not *possibly* have been intended for Miss Hermione! Modest as she was, Zoe could not help but know she had a pretty figure and an unusually tiny waist, and some of the new gowns fit so snugly that before the stomacher could be set in place Gorton had to lace her stays to the point she could scarce breathe.

Perplexed, she stared at the bright square of the moonlit window. Why on earth would Lady Julia have said that all those lovely gowns had been meant for her cousin's daughter?

And, more disquietingly, came the inevitable following thought: 'If they were really made for me, then my coming here must have been planned for some time. But—why? Why would they especially want *me*?'

That foolish Caesar's coming after us, Miss," said Gorton, clinging to the spaniel's lead and glancing back over her shoulder.

"Hold on tight," urged Zoe. "If Cromwell sees him, he'll very likely—"

Her warning came too late. As if sensing that his cat followed, Cromwell barked, swung around and tore back down the street, with Gorton hanging on for dear life and uttering shrill and ineffectual commands that he stop at once.

Zoe laughed and called that she would wait in the park. Viking showed no inclination to join the rout, and she unlocked the gate and took the big dog inside. It was a glorious morning, the sky darkly blue even at this early hour, the sun brilliant, the air cool and stirred by a brisk breeze. There was no one in the little park, and Zoe sat down on a bench, removed the lead, and allowed Viking to wander about freely for a while.

All was quiet and peaceful. In fact, she mused, were someone to be magically conveyed to this small oasis, they would never dream they were in the middle of a great city. How quickly she had become accustomed to living here. She could scarce believe that two weeks ago Peregrine Cranford had not entered her life. Or that their ladyships, Gorton, Maria Benevento, and the guests who visited Yerville Hall had been unknown to her. So many interesting people to have met, so many fascinating places to have seen, and so very much more to—

A shout and a deep bark broke her reverie, and she started up in alarm. It would appear she was not as alone as she'd supposed. A man knelt by the fence opposite Yerville Hall; a gardener, apparently. He was brandishing a trowel defensively at Viking, who crouched, clearly about to attack.

"No!" cried Zoe, hurrying to the rescue. "Viking! Bad dog! Down, sir!"

The hound curled his lip at the gardener, then pranced over to Zoe with wagging tail and his best playful-puppy grin.

Zoe attached dog to lead.

The gardener scrambled to his feet and snatched off his hat. He was a broad-shouldered, ruddy-complected individual, probably in the neighborhood of forty, whose features bore the evidence of some desperate encounters. In fact, she thought, he looked more like a pugilist than a gardener. "I am sorry if my dog annoyed you," she said kindly.

" 'E didn't annoy me, Miss," the gardener answered, his accent pure cockney. "I thought 'e was of a mind to 'ave me fer breakfast!"

Viking growled, and the hair on his back started to lift again.

Zoe suggested, "I think it might be well for you to stop pointing your trowel at him like that. He probably thinks you mean to attack him. Don't you like dogs?"

"Dogs, yus, Miss. Great 'ounds wot's 'alf-way to being a pony—them I can do without, thankee kindly! I knows another wot might be 'is bruvver, 'cept 'e's all black! Name of Apollo. Nasty? You wouldn't believe! Apollo—wotta name fer a dog! *I'm* more of a Apollo!" He grinned suddenly. "Which don't flatter the 'ound, do it, Miss?"

Smiling back, she said, "Your eyes are much too kind for me to think you would ever hurt an animal. Have you been working in this garden for very long?"

"On and orf."

"Do you ever work after dark? I mean, as late as nine o'-clock?"

"Not me, mate! Er, I mean, ma'am! Can't see no weeds at night, canyer now?"

Elsie called, "Are you in there, Miss Grainger?"

"Coming," answered Zoe, and with a smile to the gardener, walked back to the gate.

He was shorter than the man she'd seen watching the house the evening before the accident. And more craggily built. And besides, as he'd said, you cannot see weeds at night . . .

You look confounded green about the gills, Perry." Having offered this considered opinion, Mr. Cyril Crenshore scooped a pile of cards, bills, and letters from the windowseat in Cranford's parlour and occupied it himself. He was a large young man with a bronzed face that attested to his preference for the outdoor life. An ardent sportsman and much admired amateur boxer, he was well liked, and of a generally amiable disposition. "Burning the candle at both ends, eh, dear boy?" he murmured, settling his muscular legs across the cushioned seat, and balancing a tankard of ale on the window-sill. "I saw you going into the Piazza yesterday with that little beauty. Don't believe in letting the grass grow under your feet, do you?"

"If you spill that on my correspondence, I'll grass you!" said Cranford, feigning indignation though he was far from displeased by the latter remark.

"I'd think you would be grateful to have me wash out a few of these bills. Though I see you've some invitations among 'em." Crenshore took up a card addressed in a fine copperplate hand. "The *Eaglund* musicale!" He whistled, and his brows went up. "Wasn't aware you moved in such exalted circles! Be dashed if I received an invite. Not that I'd waste an afternoon listening to scraping fiddles and screeching sopranos. Do you mean to take the new Fair? Who is she, by the way?"

"If you refer to Miss Maria Benevento—" said Cranford loftily.

"Don't. She's a diamond of the first water, surely, but too fiery for my tastes. Type that makes a fellow nervous. No, 'tis the glowing little lass with the auburn locks and the big green eyes I speak of. You had the extremes there, Perry. Bewitching midnight on one side, and a ray of sunshine on the other. I rely on you for an introduction. Don't fob me off, my lad, or you'll rue the day!"

Cranford had enjoyed a long sleep, and although his head still ached, he felt a good deal more himself this morning. He'd had not the least intention to accept Lady Eaglund's invitation, and no less than Crenshore was he surprised to have been so honoured.

Relaying their conversation to Owen Furlong after Crenshore had gone off to Tattersall's, he said slowly, "I'll wager that was why the invitation came my way. My uncle's cousin, or whatever she is, hoped I'd take little Miss Grainger to that confounded musicale." He frowned, and muttered, "I fancy she'd like to go."

Cranford was not fond of the opera and had been heard to remark that he'd as soon have a case of the plague as suffer through a musicale. Aware of this, Sir Owen winked at Florian who was gathering up yesterday's newspapers, and asked innocently, "How is your head this morning, Perry? I fully expected to find you cleaning your duelling pistols before going off after Michael Templeby."

Puzzled, Cranford said, "What, because he painted my new foot?"

"No, you clunch. Because he sent you that ridiculous stolen letter."

"I did accuse him of that, didn't I! I must beg his pardon. I realized afterwards, Owen, that the letter could not have come from Templeby. Not unless he's found some magician to waft him off to Russia, or some such place. I had to pay sixpence for the silly thing. Must've come a distance. I wonder I didn't think of that at the time."

"I wonder you could think of anything at all, considering everything that was going on with your brainbox."

Cranford grinned. "It may have been dented, perhaps, but my brains aren't addled if that's what you mean."

"What I mean," said Furlong, "is that I begin to suspect you're acquiring a fondness for Miss Grainger's company. Which is not surprising. Don't you agree, Florian?"

"I do, sir," answered Florian. "And I think Mr. Crenshore was right. Miss Grainger is more than pretty, and when she smiles, she really is a ray of sunshine."

'By George, but she is!' thought Cranford.

Half an hour later, he was riding to Yerville Hall to ask if he might be allowed to escort Miss Zoe Grainger to the Eaglund musicale this afternoon.

His dashing appearance on horseback won many admiring glances from female eyes. His mood, however, was not quite as cheerful as it had been earlier. Owen Furlong, who was of course invited everywhere, had said thoughtfully that although as a rule he avoided such occasions, he just might attend this one. "If only to meet your little ray of sunshine."

Such a good fellow, was Owen. The best of men. But Cranford found himself wishing he'd not mentioned the invitation. Owen had such a confoundedly unfailing ability to set the ladies' hearts a'flutter!

CHAPTER X

hen asked if you would sign a statement specificating as the gent was racing of his carriage," said Mr. Young of Bow Street, consulting the papers he had brought to Yerville Hall, "your eggsack words was—'I—most—certinly—will!' "

He was short and sturdy, with a deeply lined face and a truculent chin. He had refused to sit down, and stood in the centre of the morning room with the air of a gladiator prepared to take on all comers. His eyes, deep-set under great bushy eyebrows that stood straight out from his face like miniature chevaux-de-frise, lifted, to dart accusation at Zoe.

"Yes, I know I did," she said apologetically. "But, you see, when I stopped to think about it—"

"You thought it best to change 'will' to 'will not'!" he growled.

Zoe frowned. "I can understand your feelings, Mr. Young, but kindly do not use that tone of voice to me. At the time of the accident I was upset and did not stop to think that—"

"You thought enough," he interrupted again, consulting the statement. "You thought enough to say as this here Mr. Perry-green Cranford was 'a—bad—man.' And when asked, specific, if the victim had *walked* crost the street, your very own words was: 'Of—course—what—would—you—think?' "

"Oh, dear. I did say that. But—"

"But now, you bin and changed your thoughts, ma'am. And what I would like to know is this: What brung about this sudden change? I bin round afore today, ma'am. And I were turned away every time. And now you tells me as this *good-looking* young *gentry* cove ain't a bad man after all, and that you was—"

"Be so kind as to tell me who this—person—is, Miss Grainger," commanded Lady Buttershaw, coming into the room with a rustle of satin and an expression of abhorrence. "And why you saw fit to interview him alone."

The Runner held up a short baton surmounted by a crown. "I am a officer o' the law," he announced. "Exercising of me right as such to—"

"I believe I asked you a question, Miss Grainger," barked Lady Buttershaw, ignoring him.

The face of the officer of the law became a darker red, his eyebrows more bristly than ever, and his jaw even more pugna-cious.

Zoe said, "This is Mr. Young, from Bow Street, my lady. He brought the statement that—"

"A fig for his statement! He was told yesterday, *and* the day before, that you had erred and had no clear recollection of the incident. I have no time to waste on silly nonsense. Arbour!" Her ladyship turned to the doorway where the butler hovered. "Show this person out!"

"If you please, ma'am," said Zoe firmly. "I feel I owe Mr. Young an explanation of why—"

"Once again your feelings are misplaced! You owe him nothing! Any Bow Street officer worth his salt should know better than try to force statements from a gently bred-up young lady who is clearly in a swooning condition!"

The Runner snapped, "The *law*, me lady, is *the law*! And not *no one's* got the right to—"

"Be still, you insolent creature!" Lady Buttershaw's volume made Zoe wince, and rattled the prisms on a lamp shade. "You do not browbeat some poor unfortunate commoner! Let me warn you that my late husband was well acquaint with Chancellor Hardwicke. As am I! And if you do not take yourself off at once, 'twill be my duty to apprise him of your disgraceful manners! Remove yourself, my good man!" She waved her long arm regally. "You offend my sight! Begone!"

The mention of the mighty Lord Chancellor had caused Mr. Young to shrink. He lost all his ruddy colour and it seemed to Zoe that even the chevaux-de-frise wilted. With abject bows and murmurings of "most sincere apologies" and "deepest regrets" he beat an ignominious retreat.

"If ever I heard the like!" snorted Lady Buttershaw. "You will, I trust, have learned something of how a person of Quality must deal with such presumptuous mushrooms! The creature, one hopes, is thoroughly ashamed of himself!"

'If *he* is not,' thought Zoe, mortified, '*I* most certainly am!'

When Gorton came into her bedchamber an hour later, she was writing a letter to advise Aunt Minerva of where she now resided, and to ask what that dear lady knew of the present family Yerville. She was still seething over the Turkish treatment that had been accorded Mr. Young who, although rather rude, had some excuse for being provoked and had simply been doing his duty. "Yes?" she asked, without her usual smile.

Gorton eyed her uncertainly. "Ay knew you would be cross, Miss Zoe. But as Ay told Chubb, he had only himself to blame."

"What? Who is Chubb? And what has he done?"

"One of the lackeys, Miss. Leastwise, he was. Ay beg your pardon. I thought you knew, and being so kind-hearted as you are . . . But he shouldn't have let in that Runner. Got turned off."

Dismayed, Zoe cried, "Oh, never say so! Whatever will become of him?"

"Says he'll take the King's shilling. Likely he will. Ay don't think he much enjoyed being a lackey. The Army will suit him better. Now never be upset, Miss. 'Tis not your fault. And only look! Ay have a letter for you! And Lady Buttershaw wants you to change into your prettiest gown. Mr. Cranford has asked permission to take you to Lord Eaglund's house this afternoon! Only think, Miss! A musicale at the home of a *viscount!*"

"And such a nice gentleman! How *lovely!*" Clapping her hands with excitement, Zoe jumped up and danced over to take the letter. "Oh, 'tis from my *Papa!*" She flew back to the desk and broke the thick seal with great care, but as she spread the closely written and crossed sheet another piece of sealing wax fell out.

Papa's news banished the joy from her eyes. Travis had been very ill and was coming home.

Gorton hummed merrily as she selected her personal favourite among Miss Zoe's new gowns, a *robe battante* of silvery blue damask, very décolleté, the neckline and stomacher trimmed with silver lace.

A shadow had fallen over Zoe's happiness, and she gazed in silence at Papa's ominous words. Absently, she took up the little fallen piece of wax and fitted it back into place. Or would have. But there was no splinter in the seal. She had opened the letter so carefully that the wax had broken cleanly. She saw then the broken piece seemed to have attached itself to the underside of the paper, and that it was a darker shade of red, almost as though . . . Stunned, she thought, 'Oh! My heavens! Almost as though it has been opened and re-sealed!' Shock was succeeded by incredulous anger, and she had to struggle to appear calm and to remind herself that she must not again jump to conclusions. It could be a simple case of Papa having forgotten something and being obliged to break his initial seal so as to add a note. Only—there was no note; nothing had been added after his signature. And surely he would have written a little postscript to explain why he had opened the letter, rather than going to such lengths to disguise the broken seal? But if Papa had not opened the letter, who had? Her suspicion turned at once to the logical culprit, but she had to abandon that unkind thought. Papa had mentioned at the end that he was a lonely bachelor again, as his "dear wife" and the children were at Hampstead, visiting her parents. So Mrs. Mowbray had not been at Travisford to pry into his letter. In which case . . .

When she could command her voice, she asked quietly, "What becomes of the post when it is brought in, Elsie?"

Inspecting the blue damask for creases, Gorton answered, " 'Tis all delivered to Lady Buttershaw, Miss, so her la'ship can sort it out. Then, she gives it to Mr. Arbour, or Chef, or the proper party."

"I see. And when did my letter come?"

Gorton turned to look at her curiously. "Why, today, Miss. Lady Buttershaw gave it me just a few minutes ago. Is something wrong?"

Zoe brought herself up short. To discuss her suspicions with a servant was unthinkable. To even harbour such suspicions must be the height of ingratitude. "Oh, no," she said lightly. "I just wondered. I had not heard the postman's horn."

"Likely not, Miss. In the morning he comes at eight o'-clock, and your room being at the back of the house, you'd not hear him."

Zoe nodded and returned to her letter. But she could not write. Her anxiety for Travis distracted her, and her thoughts kept turning also to the several things that worried at the edges of her mind. Foolish little worries by comparison, she told herself. But they were beginning to mount up; to form a pattern she could not understand. And that was starting to make her uneasy.

The home of Rupert Shale, Viscount Eaglund, was one of the Bloomsbury palaces. " 'Tis even bigger than Yerville Hall," Zoe confided to Cranford as they moved across the marble floor of the extremely large entrance hall, "only more cheery. Take that pretty painting over there, for instance. So much livelier than all those dusty old tapestries."

Since the "pretty painting" was of a voluptuous nude that the eyes of ladies usually avoided, Cranford was hard put to it not to laugh, and suggested piously that Miss Grainger might do better than to stare at it so obviously.

She glanced up at him and saw laughter glinting in the blue eyes. Her own bright beam dawned at once. "You are quizzing me again. But, do look, Mr. Cranford. Surely the artist has exaggerated. Even my step-mama does not have such enormous—"

"Very true, ma'am," he over-rode loudly, and hissed, "quiet, you little wretch, or you will cause the dowager behind us to swoon dead away! Lord Eaglund's art collection," he went on in his normal voice, "is believed to be one of the finest in Europe."

"I think you are very prim, for an Army man," she whispered mischievously. "My brother used to—" She stopped and her face clouded.

Cranford said, "What is it? I had no thought to hurt your feelings, Miss Zoe. 'Tis just that what can be said to one's brother in the country, is not always—er, *convenable* in London Town."

She sighed. "I know. I am hopeless."

He patted the small hand that rested on his arm. "You are a delight," he said, and realized with something of a shock that he meant it.

Zoe halted abruptly, and searching his face, said an astonished, "No, am I? Nobody ever said that to me before."

"Dare I ask what improprieties you have been voicing to this lovely creature?" enquired a deep, amused voice.

Cranford swung around. "You did come! Are you all about in your head, Owen? You know you should not be here!"

Far from endorsing these sentiments, Zoe said impulsively, "Oh! 'Tis my odiousity instructor! How nice to see you again, sir!"

"You've met?" asked Cranford, surprised.

"To my very great pleasure," Furlong answered. "Be so good as to present me."

Bemused, Cranford made the introduction, then said with a dark frown, "This all sounds very havey-cavey, Owen. You never told me you were acquainted with Miss Grainger. When did you meet? And what a'plague is an odiousity instructor?"

"Must I tell you all my secrets?" Sir Owen bowed, and offered his arm, smiling down at Zoe as she placed her free hand on it. "Have you been afflicted with this oaf for very long, ma'am? If so, I'll be more than glad to relieve you of his—"

"Oh, no, you don't," interrupted Cranford indignantly. "Go and find your own lady!"

They walked along together, and Zoe pleaded that Sir Owen not be sent away. "I like him."

Furlong chuckled. "There. That gives you back your own, Perry. You are the one to be dismissed. Miss Grainger has chosen wisely."

"If I had chosen at all, which I have not," said Zoe, clinging tightly to Cranford's arm. "I would not have chose you, sir."

Sir Owen looked taken aback. By now accustomed to Zoe's frankness, Cranford grinned.

Zoe patted Furlong's arm kindly. "You are very handsome, Sir Owen, although you look rather wan today. I so much like your smile, and the way you have of making me feel I am somebody. But I scarce know you, and Mr. Cranford is an old friend. Or," her brow wrinkled, "he *seems* an old friend. The thing is, though, that I should like to keep you both, if you please." Her artless gaze travelled from Cranford's dark, finely cut good looks, to Furlong, Saxon fair and equally, though differently good to look at, and she added, "It cannot fail to add to my consequence, you see."

They were all laughing merrily when Lord Eaglund came up. He bowed gallantly over Zoe's fingers, shook hands with Cranford and told him he was glad to see him in Town again, and scanned Furlong's pale features and shadowed eyes with some anxiety. "Not another bout with that miserable fever, Owen?"

"Just a slight brush with the beast, sir," admitted Furlong. "Nothing I can really grumble about."

"It don't look so slight to me. I wonder you came to this affair." The viscount leaned nearer and said with a wink, "Cannot stand musicales myself. Still, Lady Eaglund will be most pleased to see you. To which end, we should probably go upstairs. We're to have some poetry readings first, I regret to say. Afterwards, there will be refreshments downstairs in the ballroom before the music begins, so you may escape then."

Furlong laughed, and Cranford said with a grin, "You must take us for a graceless lot, my lord. I thank you for inviting me."

"You must come more often, Perry." Eaglund smiled at Zoe. "Especially if you mean to bring this lovely little creature."

The guests were starting to drift up the wide staircase, the viscount's attention was claimed by a small colonel with a big voice, and Zoe and her two escorts mingled with the brilliant throng.

The music room on the first floor was large and superbly Romanesque. Quite a number of people had already assembled here. Few had settled on the numerous chairs that had been grouped about, however, and were instead engaged in chatting merrily and greeting friends and acquaintances. Cranford guided Zoe to three chairs, as yet unclaimed. Furlong was buttonholed by a statuesque young woman wearing a magnificent gold silk gown, and Cranford leaned to Zoe's ear, and murmured with a grin, "Mrs. Pettifor. A widow. Striking, isn't she?"

"Sir Owen seems to think so."

"The poor fellow was born to be a diplomat. Truth is, the lady has pursued him relentlessly ever since his fiancée was lost at sea in forty-six, and—Now what have I said to throw you into gloom again?"

His use of the word "diplomat" had inevitably brought Travis to mind. Zoe said, "There is something I want so much to tell you, and—and to ask for your advice."

The worry in her face inspired him with an urgent need to dispel it. "I am not very wise, alas," he told her. "My brother has all the brains in the family. But 'twould be my pleasure an I could help. We will find a way to be private after the readings."

He stood as several military acquaintances and their ladies came towards them. It was the start of a steady stream. He struggled manfully with introductions, but the names swept into Zoe's head and out again. It seemed that half the people in the room wanted to shake Cranford by the hand, and tell him how pleased they were to see him. He responded gratefully, if rather shyly. Zoe sensed that to be the object of so much attention embarrassed him, for which quality she did not like him any the less.

Lord Eaglund rang a little bell for quiet; the crowd dispersed to their places, and Cranford sat down with a whispered, "Phew!"

Furlong eased into his chair, murmuring that he'd fancied he would never fight his way through the crush of Cranford's admirers.

A plump and jolly woman moved to the centre of the clear area before them, and extended a welcome to her "dear friends." She was a far cry from the proud viscountess Zoe had imagined, and with such a natural manner that her popularity was easily understood. She introduced the first reader, and a gaunt and grim gentleman clad all in black made his bow and offered an "Ode to the Damsel Dark." His intonation was sonorous, his ode a gloomy tale of unrequited love, and Zoe's thoughts wandered to her brother, and Papa's letter. She was startled when Cranford nudged her and she joined hurriedly in the applause.

A moment later, she was applauding in earnest. The second reader, breathtaking in a magnificent gown of dark pink velvet trimmed with swansdown, was Miss Maria Benevento. There were several admiring cries from the gentlemen, and so much applause that she held up her hands at last in an amused plea for quiet.

A hush fell. The beauty stood there, slender, poised, half-smiling, as she scanned the room. Her first selection was from A *Midsummer-Night's Dream*, and she began to read, the familiar words enhanced by her rich, faintly accented voice.

> "I know a bank whereon the wild thyme blows,
> Where oslips and the nodding violet grows
> Quite over-canopied with luscious woodbine,
> With sweet musk-roses, and with eglantine . . ."

Sudden tears stung Zoe's eyes. Almost she could see herself and Travis wandering among the great trees of Wychwood in the springtime, gathering the violets that dear mama had so loved . . . And now her brother had near died from the dread cholera and was coming home, never having writ a word to let them know— She gave a gasp of embarrassment, for Cranford was nudging her again. Preparing instinctively to clap her hands, she realized that Miss Benevento had gone on to another selection, this time from *Richard II:*

> " . . . *happy breed of men, this little world,*
> *This precious stone set in the silver sea,*
> *Which serves . . ."*

Another nudge. Indignant, she saw that Cranford's eyes were alight with mirth. He nodded very slightly towards Furlong. Curious, she turned to her left. Sir Owen was leaning forward, so still that he seemed scarcely to breathe, and his eyes had a dazed look as they held intently on the lovely reader. That husky voice was stilled. A brief hush, then the air rang with applause. But Sir Owen Furlong remained silent and motionless, as one bewitched.

Applauding heartily, Cranford bent to Zoe's ear. "I think your new friend has captured another heart, or else poor Furlong has turned to stone! We shall either have to wake him up, or have him hauled away!"

She turned to him, her eyes sparkling. "I do believe you are in the right of it! Oh, what a lovely couple they would make!"

"Cruel!" he exclaimed, with a hand clasped to his heart. "I am betrayed and tossed aside! You promised the lady was just right for *me!*"

Zoe's eyes fell. He was only funning, of course, but her cheeks were hot and she was seized by an unfamiliar confusion. "Oh," she said. "Well, I did. But I—er, I changed my mind." Peeping up at him, she met a brilliant grin that set her pulse galloping in the most foolish way. Thrown into deeper confusion, she stammered, "M-might we go downstairs now, do you think?"

"Miss Grainger! Oh, how glad I am that you came!"

Maria Benevento was hurrying to them. Zoe had not dreamed that the beauty would break away from her admirers only to renew their acquaintance, and she returned a hug gladly. "Lieutenant Cranford was so very good as to bring me," she said. "I so enjoyed to hear you read. 'Twas prodigious moving."

Watching Cranford as he endorsed those sentiments and bowed over her hand, Miss Benevento said shrewdly, "Something troubles you, I think, sir."

Zoe's gaze flashed to him. She had thought him a trifle heavy-eyed, but had supposed he'd stayed late at his club.

Furlong put in, "Perry will tell you 'tis nothing, ma'am. But the truth is—"

"The truth is that this presumptuous mushroom is desperate to be made known to you, ma'am," interrupted Cranford hurriedly. He performed that small service, but for a breathless instant neither Furlong nor Miss Benevento made the slightest response, standing there, facing one another, motionless and silent, as though in the grip of some powerful spell. Zoe found that she was holding her breath. Then, the beauty started and sank into a graceful curtsy. Furlong bowed over her hand and touched it to his lips, but again, rising, she made no attempt to reclaim her hand through another exchange of rapt glances.

Zoe sighed, and smiled mistily at the handsome tableau.

Catching sight of Cyril Crenshore waving eagerly from across the room, Cranford seized Zoe's elbow. "Come. Now is our chance to go downstairs."

"But we cannot leave Sir Owen," she protested as he hurried her away.

"My dear girl, are you blind? Poor Furlong has quite forgot

we exist! I fear," he added, as they went into the crowded corridor, "there will be no bearing him for months! Cupid just dealt him a thundering broadside."

"Yes indeed, and was it not the dearest thing? So *romantical*! As if they both were enchanted in the very instant they met. I never believed there was such a thing as love at first sight, did you?"

"No. And I still do not," he said, making his difficult way down the stairs. He added thoughtfully, "It has pierced my reluctant intellect that when one tumbles so quickly into love, one tumbles out of it even more quickly."

"You, sir, are a marplot," Zoe advised him.

"And you, madam," he countered in amusement, "are a frustrated matchmaker. I pity London's bachelors when your daughters are of marriageable age! Do you wish to find a place to talk, or shall I first acquire some of those deliciousnesses I see being carried about?"

The refreshments crowding the tables that had been set up in the ballroom did indeed look delicious. Despite her anxieties, Zoe could not resist, and Cranford went limping off, to return with a tray of little tarts, iced cakes, and pastries, and two glasses of champagne punch. He found a deserted anteroom, and they settled down together to enjoy their small hoard.

Zoe took up a cheese tart, then glanced at the door. "Is this proper, sir? I seem to make so many etiquettal errors."

He grinned. "I've not the reputation of a hardened rake, and the door is wide, so I fancy you're safe from your 'etiquettal' mis-steps. A good word, that! Now tell me what brings the worried look to your pretty face."

She sipped her champagne punch, and said hesitantly, "You will likely think me foolish, but—well, there have been several things that seem . . . odd."

"Such as Lady Buttershaw deciding I was the ideal mate?"

He thought she would smile at that, but instead she answered gravely, "Well, I had only been in Town a few days, and there had been no mention of a suitable marriage for me before I left Travisford."

"Is it not possible for her ladyship and your sire to have discussed that in private?"

She chose a lemon puff, and held it poised in the air while she considered, then acknowledged, " 'Tis possible. But even if they had, it seems a very sudden business. Especially since I was come to be companion to Lady Julia, and have scarce begun to be of use to her. And then," she nibbled daintily at the lemon puff and said, "there was the clothing, you see . . ."

Cranford listened with interest as the tale of the garments ostensibly sewn for the "very fat" Hermione, was followed by an account of the man Zoe had seen watching the house at night.

"Hum," he said, poking absently at his apple pasty. "Do you fancy he was one of those you heard when you were jauntering about in your nightrail?"

"I was not jauntering! And I could not tell—'twas too dark. But—why should he have been standing for so long across the road in the private garden? And now, there is this horrid business of my letter!" She looked at him with deep tragedy. "Oh, this is dreadful! I should not even entertain such suspicions! But—I simply must discuss it with *somebody*!"

"Of course you must. And there's no call to look so distressed. I am only flattered that you can feel comfortable in sharing a confidence with me. I won't betray it, I promise you. Say on, lady fair."

She smiled at him gratefully. "It is that my maid brought me a letter this morning. From my papa. It was not good news, alas, and I did not at first realize, but . . . Oh, Mr. Cranford! It had been *opened*! And then re-sealed!"

Taken aback by so damning a statement, he exclaimed, "The deuce! If ever I heard of such a thing! Are you quite sure? Was there a broken seal?"

She described the care she'd taken in opening her father's letter, and the evidences of it having been re-sealed, then regarded him anxiously.

For a long moment Cranford made no comment, then he said, "I must own you are in her care, and 'tis not considered proper for an unwed young lady to receive letters from admirers. I fancy her ladyship could claim she was exercising her rights."

"But 'twas *not* from an admirer! 'Twas from my own father!"

"Yes, but she would say she was not to know his writing. Still 'twould have been far more gracious to have asked you about it before taking such a step."

"Much more gracious," said Zoe. "And if she held such thoughts, why would she have gone to the trouble to re-seal the letter, to make it look unopened?"

He pursed his lips. "A good point . . . unless . . . You know, I have meant to ask you. When first we met, whatever gave you the notion I was a physician?"

It was not what she'd expected him to say, but she told him of Lady Buttershaw's conviction that doctors enjoyed to cut up living patients. A gleam of unholy joy crept into Cranford's eyes, and when she recounted my lady's tale of the evil physician who had cut off the wrong leg and taken it home to determine how toenails grow, he went into gales of laughter, his mirth so infectious that Zoe could not resist joining in.

" 'Pon my word," he gasped, wiping tears from his eyes. "There is your answer, m'dear. I do not mean to speak ill of a lady, but—your poor dowager dragon is short of a sheet! I beg pardon! What I mean is—"

"I know what you mean. She is eccentric, I own, and I must admit is tiresome at times, but I cannot think her intellect is disordered."

Still chuckling, he said, "Eccentric, is it! For a lady who holds the honour of her house so high, to pry into the correspondence of others is carrying eccentricity rather far. My apologies an I seem to make light of your fears. I do not. 'Faith, but I can well imagine how irksome it must be to have your letters read. Have you spoke of it to Lady Yerville?"

"No." Zoe sighed worriedly. "I thought of doing so, but she and her sister do not deal very well, and I should not care to cause more trouble between them."

"And you think Lady Yerville would spring to your defence?"

"I believe she would be outraged, yes. Do you think I should drop a hint to Lady Buttershaw? Tactfully, you know?"

"I think the lady don't know the meaning of the word, and would likely explode like any volcano. Can you not meet the postman and collect your own letters?"

"I doubt he would dare give them to me, even if I was there each time he came. All the mail is taken to Lady Buttershaw, and she distributes it."

"But you have a perfect right to follow the delivery to her study or whatever, and demand . . ." She looked terrified, and he said hastily, "No, I see you could not. Well, at least you received your letter. Mine was stolen."

Zoe gave a gasp. "Stolen? What a dreadful thing! Do you say a thief broke into your house?"

"Yes. I've rooms, actually, in Henrietta Street. The varmint got in whilst I was reading one letter, and—"

"While you were *reading* it? Could you not have prevented him?"

"I fear my unheroical failure must cause me to fall very far short of your beau ideal," he answered with a wry smile. "But the fact is he crept up behind me and bent his pistol over my head."

Her own troubles forgotten, she reached out to press his hand and said with ready sympathy, "How dreadful! Oh, but I am a selfish beast! I was so full of my own worries I did not notice, but you do look rather pulled. I am so very sorry! You only came here for my sake, no, never deny it. Likely your head is paining you dreadfully, yet you uttered not a word of complaint. We shall leave at once so that you may rest, my poor friend!"

Deeply touched by such kind concern, he said, "I'm glad you recognize my nobility. No, truly, Miss Zoe, you must not reproach yourself. I am perfectly fit, although I'll confess to being irked that the lamebrain made off with my letters."

"Was that all he took? But why would anyone do such a thing?" Her eyes brightened. She asked hopefully, "Was there news of great value?"

"I wish I could think there had been, but—no such thing. Not in the one I had time to read, at least. I'll own I'd not so much as broke the seal on the one from my twin."

At this point a lackey came in to take the tray, and murmur that the guests were assembling for the musicale.

Zoe had been using her fan for some minutes, and as the man left them Cranford suggested, "Shall we slither into the gardens instead of going upstairs again? I doubt Furlong would miss us."

She was only too willing to agree. A footman escorted them through some French doors opening onto a terrace with a wide flight of steps that led down to the lawns. A few other couples were strolling about. Cranford offered his arm, and they went down the steps and walked slowly along a flagged pathway.

Zoe took a deep breath of the cool afternoon air. "Thank goodness! I do dislike overheated rooms. I was thinking, Mr.

Cranford, about the letter from your— Why, you said 'twin'! I didn't know you had a twin."

"There are lots of things about me you don't know. All bad."

"Foolish man. Is he like you?"

His smile faded. He said musingly, "Very. In the days of our mis-spent youth, we took great pleasure in confusing people. You'd not believe the antics we got up to!"

"I can well imagine! My brother knew a boy at school who was one of a pair of twins. He was captain of the cricket team, and a great sportsman. Travis admired him enormously, and thought him the very model of what a young gentleman should be."

Cranford started, and looked down at her sharply.

"I don't remember his name," she went on, "but I should, for Travis was always talking of him. I recall his making Papa laugh very much with the story of a cricket match. It was a prodigious hot afternoon, and his idol seemed off his form that day, but not until the end of the game—"

"Did they discover the wrong twin had captained the team."

She laughed. "Yes. 'Twas all—"

" 'Twas a dare," he interposed again. "Which should never have been taken."

Her eyes grew very round. They stopped walking, staring at each other in astonishment. She gasped, *"You . . . ?"*

"Jupiter, it must be! But— My apologies, Miss Zoe, but be dashed if I can remember anyone named—Travis, did you say?"

"Yes. Travis Grainger. Oh my! How *exciting* this is! 'Tis quite understandable that you would not remember him. He was two years your junior, he said, and he went in such awe of you, he never plucked up enough courage to try and talk to you."

Cranford reddened, and began to walk on again. "Oh, come now. All I did was play a pretty fair game of cricket. If there was any young chub silly enough to—" He broke off, and halted again, then said an explosive, "*Hops!* I'll wager that's who it was! Used to follow me about, but when I tried to talk to him, he'd colour up and run like a rabbit." Turning to Zoe, he asked eagerly, "You never had a sheepdog?"

"Hops! Yes. But why would you call my brother after him?"

"Don't be cross, I beg you. Boys are merciless little savages, you know. The lad was so painfully shy. When he first came to school he'd the habit of sort of shifting from one foot to the other when he spoke to a senior. He was always talking of his home, and between his mannerism and the name of his sheepdog— Did he never tell you of his nickname?"

"Never." She gripped her hands with delight. "Oh, is it not famous? To think that you know my dear brother! And all this time we never guessed it!"

"Which makes us old friends," he said, restoring her hand to his arm and limping towards a bench. "So it will be perfectly convenable for you to call me Peregrine, instead of Lieutenant, or Mister. And I, with your permission, shall call you Zoe. When we are private, that is. Agreed?"

"Yes. Oh, yes!"

"Good. Now sit here beside me, and tell me about your brother. Does he live in Cotswold country? Or is he off somewhere, making a name for himself?"

She said agitatedly, "He is—or was in the diplomatic corps. In Calcutta. I have been worried because he usually writes regularly, but we've received no word for a long time. And now, Papa has writ that Travis has been terribly ill and has been sent home. And what is worse, or so I think, Travis said nothing. Papa only learned of it from a friend who came home last month and called to enquire if Travis had arrived as yet. 'Tis so unlike my brother. He must have guessed we would be anxious. Why he did not let us know he was recovering from the cholera, I just cannot understand."

Cranford could think of several reasons why a sensitive young fellow would fail to send letters home. He might have other difficulties besides the fearsome cholera. Got into some superior's black books, perhaps, or disgraced himself with one of the Indian girls who were, he'd heard, very beautiful. If the worst had happened and he'd been dismissed, he would likely be beside himself with worry, and dread to face his family. He said bracingly, "Now, never be so distressed, little Zoe. As I recollect, your Travis is the type of lad who would very likely hold back from sending home bad news. Besides, if he was very ill, he may not have been up to writing."

"Well, I thought of that, of course. But he must have friends. Or his superior could have notified us. Papa went to the East India Company, and could learn nothing, save that Travis is not on the passenger list of any homeward bound vessel that has arrived recently. Yet Papa's friend said my brother had secured a berth on a ship that was to sail from Calcutta with his own fleet. How can that be? Oh, Peregrine," she held out her hand, and he gripped it strongly, "ever since I came to London, strange things have been happening, and now—" Her voice shook. "I just do not . . . I simply *cannot* think what I should do. Must I go home at once, or—"

He put a finger over her lips and said soothingly, "Hush, now. You must not allow imagination to drive you into an attack of the vapours. Have a thought for my poor nerves. I'm a rank coward and should likely swoon away beside you." Her smile flickered at the picture this conjured up, and he went on, "That's better! There is likely a perfectly logical explanation for everything. You have asked for the benefit of my mighty brain, so let me see if I cannot dust off the cobwebs and put it to work."

He considered in silence for a few minutes, and said at

length, "I think I have not the right to advise you. But, as a friend, I can tell you what I would do in your situation."

"Oh yes," she said imploringly. "Pray do so."

"Very well. First: I think you should not speak to either of their ladyships regarding your violated letter. Not yet, at least. You really have very little proof, you know. Lady Buttershaw would probably advance the arguments I mentioned, and even if she did not, to make such an appalling accusation *without* proof must only cause a very great dust-up. Second: Your brother might have sailed on someone else's ticket—or he could be listed as a member of a party, or family, in which case only the leader of the group might be named. Third: Much of the shipping business is done at the Jerusalem Coffee House. The place is usually a maelstrom of activity, and without a connection your papa might have received short shrift. I've a friend who is a subscriber on one of the vessels and can often be found there, or at Lloyd's. I'll seek him out first thing tomorrow morning, and see if he can't help me learn something of your brother. Will that set your mind at ease, for today at least?"

"Indeed it will." She blinked up at him gratefully. "I can only thank heaven for sending you to be my friend. How good of you to take the time to go to Lloyd's tomorrow. Oh, but—what of your poor head?"

He looked grave. "I'm a merciless tyrant, I know, but I mean to bully it into going with me!"

He had his reward in her broken little laugh.

espite the cheerful optimism Cranford had shown to Zoe, he could not dismiss a sense of apprehension. After he returned her to Yerville Hall, he went straight to his rooms, intending to consult with Sir Owen, whose strong common sense he valued. En route, a rock was hurled at his coach, barely missing Florian, and there were hooted obscenities and loud laughter from a group of ruffians lounging at the mouth of an alley. Incensed, Cranford drew the pistol he carried in the coach in these troubled times, and shouted to Florian to turn about and give chase, but the ruffians ran for it when they saw the coach rushing upon them, and the alley was deserted by the time Florian drove past once more.

Sir Owen was out when Cranford arrived at Henrietta Street. He went into the parlour, poured himself a glass of Madeira, put some more coal on the fire, and sprawled in a deep chair. Watching the exploring tongues of flame, he mulled over what Zoe had told him. He'd said there was probably a logical explanation for the "strange things" that had befallen her, because she'd been so distressed, poor sweet, and he'd felt bound to try and ease her worries. But the more he thought of it, the more convinced he became that there was a decidedly sinister ring to some of those happenings.

The man she'd seen watching the Hall, for instance. A would-be burglar, perhaps? Yet there had been no subsequent thefts. The furtive midnight conversation she had innocently overheard could have been nothing more than a business discussion, but if that was the case, why so secretive? Why the angry reference to something a "confounded spy" had made off with? There were spies in the world of commerce, so one heard, and in a matter that might involve large sums of money, passions could well run high. But, if the romantically inclined Zoe had not embellished her tale, the discussion did sound to have been excessively grim.

The inconsistencies regarding new gowns ostensibly intended for a fat lady seemed trivial. Possibly Zoe's garments had been too countrified, and feeling it necessary to improve upon them, Lady Yerville, who was apparently of a very gentle nature, had not wanted the girl to feel under obligation. And yet . . . He frowned, staring into the strengthening dance of the flames unseeingly. And yet . . . if they'd actually been intended for Zoe, then she was perfectly right: her removal to Yerville Hall must have been planned in advance. And why in the world should that have required such hole-and-corner tactics? Her impression had been that Lady Buttershaw's offer had astonished her step-mama, and the little Zoe, despite her happy naïvete, was not all wool between the ears. Further, why in the name of old Nick should a slightly—er, faulted young man of no more than comfortable expectations have been so abruptly selected as a promising candidate for her hand? Lady Buttershaw scarce knew him. Unless she really thought of him as her "cousin" and wanted to keep Zoe in "the family."

"Horse feathers!" he snorted, jerking out of his chair and crossing to pour himself another glass of wine from the sideboard decanter. "Now *I'm* building fantasies out of trifles!"

But going back to the fireside, he had to admit that if Zoe was right about her letter having been tampered with, then either Lady Clara Buttershaw was without a sense of honour, or something decidedly havey-cavey was afoot. Given pause by another and even more startling thought, he frowned. It was stupid, of course. Ridiculous. But . . . could there be any connection between Lady Buttershaw's snooping and the theft of his own letters? Were little Zoe's affairs in some unknown fashion linked with—

He glanced up as the door opened.

Owen Furlong said blithely, "Hello, Perry! Why do you sit alone in a darkened room? Contemplating your misdeeds, old fellow?"

"Contemplating my dinner," said Cranford. "What is the hour?"

Furlong went about lighting candles. "Seven, pretty near. And my apologies if you were waiting for me. I've an engagement."

"So I guessed. If ever I saw such a transformation! You look not only a well man, but a man with not a care in the world. Now what, I wonder, could have brought about this small miracle?"

Furlong laughed, and straddled the end of the sofa. "I'll not dissemble, Perry. I was handed a leveller this afternoon. I know now what it means—to be struck by lightning." He flushed slightly, and said in a more serious voice, "Be honest now. Did ever you rest your eyes on a lovelier, a more vivacious creature? Small wonder she's the rage of London! I'd thought myself a pretty sober and settled old bachelor, but—Jove! One look into those magnificent eyes and I was—lost! Bowled out completely, and forever. Please—don't laugh."

Cranford said quietly, "I won't. I take it Miss Benevento is the lady who has conquered your impregnable heart at last. Do you think— I mean, does she . . . ?"

"Was it mutual? I have known the lady for such a short time. How presumptuous 'twould be for me to dare think her reaction matched my own. I can only pray it did. I know I shall never, ever, feel the same. Every fellow at the musicale was fascinated by her, Perry. They all crowded around, begging to be allowed to call on her, to take her riding, or driving, to carry her muff or her gloves, or to escort her to this or that function. But—she chose *me!* Me! I drove her through Hyde Park, and then we walked until we found a bench. And we talked and talked for hours and hours. She has the merriest sense of humour; the most informed mind. She has been about the world a good deal, and we discovered we share a liking for so many of the same places. I am allowed to take her to dinner this evening! Gad! Can I believe my good fortune?"

Cranford watched him in silence, marvelling that this gallant gentleman who had survived murderous battles, wounds, and deadly fevers should have succumbed so suddenly, so completely, to the charms of a beautiful woman. That, having seen thirty and more summers, he should stand here, his fine eyes aglow, blushing like any lovesick schoolboy.

As if reading his thoughts, Furlong stood, and added with a rather shy smile, "Pray forgive me. I'm new to this, you see. I promise I won't moon on forever and bore you with my ecstasies."

"Good," said Cranford. "For I want very much to talk with you about something, if you can spare—"

"I can't, old fellow. Not now. I must leave at once. My coach is waiting outside. I only came to thank you for all your kindnesses. I must rush to my club and change clothes." He clapped Cranford on the shoulder and strode to the door.

Cranford rose also. "Owen, wait! I really must—"

Furlong turned back. "I shall call tomorrow morning, I promise. Thank you again, Perry. And—my apologies if I sound a blithering idiot. 'Tis just . . . I think I have never been so happy . . . do you see?"

Florian came in as Sir Owen left, and bemoaned the fact

that not a single ostler had been present at the stables and he'd been obliged to care for the team himself. "Nor I didn't feel I should leave, sir. Not till the night man came."

"Certainly not! You did just right. I'll put a flea in old Gibson's ear tomorrow, 'pon my soul, but I shall! Never worry about dinner, I'll walk over to the Bedford."

Carrying out this plan, Cranford was pleased to encounter a group of friends at the popular coffee house and to enjoy both the cheery company and a hearty meal. He declined an offer to go on to White's, pleading an early morning appointment, and took a chair back to his rooms.

August Falcon's valet was talking with Florian in the kitchen.

"Hello, Tummet," said Cranford. "You're late abroad. Is Mr. Falcon back in Town?"

"Wisht 'e was, sir," said Tummet, who was not the model of a gentleman's gentleman, but possessed his own unique and much-valued qualities. "I 'opes as you don't 'ave no objections to me bangin'-the-spout." His broad grin dawned. "Wanta word wiv Sir Furlong."

"Banging-the-spout," repeated Cranford thoughtfully. "Ah! Hanging about! Right?"

"Right y'are, mate! Can't diddle you wiv me rhyming cant! Orl right if I waits, sir?"

"I fear you'd be wasting your time," said Cranford, yawning. "Sir Owen has moved back to his club. I doubt he'll be there till the wee hours, though. You'd best catch him in the morning." The frown on Tummet's rugged countenance caused him to add curiously, "Nothing amiss, I trust?"

"Lord love yer, no sir. I'll find 'im. But if you should meet 'im afore I does, I'd take it kindly if you'd slip 'im the word as I needs to see 'im." Tummet grinned, nodded a farewell to Florian, and crossed to open the door. Going out, he stuck his bullet head back in again, and said, "Urgent-like! 'Night, sir."

"Now, I wonder what that was all about," murmured Cranford, as the door closed.

His dark eyes veiled, Florian said blandly, "I wonder."

Fog had rolled in during the night, and when Cranford left his rooms early the following day his coach travelled through a sepulchral world of damp and drifting vapours. The dismal morning did not restrict commerce, however, and the Jerusalem Coffee House was as crowded and noisy as ever, the warm air heavy with smoke and the smells of coffee and breakfast. Cranford wandered among the tables, searching faces, nodding now and then to an acquaintance, or stopping to exchange a few words with some likely source of information, but failing to either find, or have word of, the man he sought. It was a time-consuming process and the morning was far spent when he left and hailed a chair to carry him down to Lombard Street. The press of coaches, horsemen, sedan chairs, and pedestrians around Lloyd's Coffee House caused him to pay off his chairmen and proceed on foot.

Edging past an argumentative group, he came face-to-face with Sir Gilbert Fowles. The dandy, who preferred to hurl insults from a safe distance, changed colour and moved aside. Cranford moved also, and fronting him said clearly, "Well met, Sir Gilbert. Here is your chance to tell me to my face what you shout from carriage windows or whisper behind my back."

" 'Faith, Cranford," said Fowles, his eyes darting about nervously as heads turned. "What a quarrelsome fellow you are to be sure! I've nothing to say to you. Pray make way."

Once more, as he tried to pass, Cranford stepped in front of him. "I understand you find it highly diverting that I wear a peg-leg. Never be afraid to speak up, dear old dandy. I promise to listen to your sneers respectfully. Before I knock 'em down your throat."

A laugh went up. Livid, Fowles raised his cane. For an instant Cranford thought he was about to be called out, but a burly special constable stepped between them, and suggested genially that the gents "move along. Don't want no trouble here, now do we, melords?"

"Burn it, but we do!" snapped Cranford. "Get out of the way, confound you!"

Others were trying to push past on the narrow flagway, and by the time he had succeeded in eluding the constable and several impatient pedestrians, Fowles had escaped.

"Scaly make-bait!" he muttered.

A vendor roasting chestnuts shouted with a broad grin, "You want me to run and fetch him, guv'nor?"

Cranford laughed. "I doubt you could run fast enough!"

"You faced him down proper, sir," said a chairman who had watched the encounter with interest. "If I was you, though, I'd watch me back with that one!"

It was not the worst advice he'd ever received, thought Cranford, and with a smile to his two admirers, he continued on to Lloyd's.

Inside, he was almost knocked down by a rush of merchants as the bell rang and the announcement of the arrival of a vessel caused near pandemonium.

"Steady on!" he shouted indignantly, flattening himself against a table littered with mugs, tankards, and plates.

"I say, Cranford!" exclaimed an irate voice. "Be so good as to remove your arse from my ale!"

Clapping a hand to his nether regions, Cranford whirled. He encountered a resentful frown that marred features of such classic perfection that their owner would have been London's beau ideal, save for the fact that the splendid midnight blue eyes had a faintly Oriental shape.

"Falcon!" exclaimed Cranford. "What the deuce are you doing here?"

"Whatever my motivation, you may be very glad I'd drunk half my ale," said August Falcon moving his tankard from harm's way.

"I'll not deny that." Cranford slid onto the opposite settle, waved to a passing waiter and ordered coffee and a pork pie.

"Pray join me," said Falcon ironically.

"Deuced good of you to ask," grinned Cranford. "Oh, damme, I forgot. How is your sire? I heard he was thrown."

Falcon, who was extremely fond of his parent, affected nonchalance. "He survives, through no fault of his own. I left him down at Ashleigh, bemoaning his enforced sojourn in the wilderness, and with my sister pampering him disgracefully."

"Well, I'm glad of that. Y'know, August, an he was my sire—"

"Count your blessings he is not! He's incorrigible!"

"—I'd buy a camel and sling the saddle between its humps. Mayhap he could hang on then."

"Farther to fall," said Falcon. "Speaking of which, I caught a glimpse of Furlong in Hyde Park late yesterday. He looked pathetically besotted. Has he fallen victim to the naked cherub at last?"

Cranford hesitated. "You'd best ask him."

"Heaven protect me from the nobly discreet! Will your silly adherence to the Code permit you to tell me if the luscious Benevento is the object of his affections?"

The waiter reappearing at this instant to slam a thick plate and a steaming mug onto the table, Cranford took a swallow of coffee and bit into his pie before replying. "Have you an interest there? Do you mean to call poor Furlong out and put a period to him?"

"If I do," said Falcon grimly, "I'll not ask you to be my second! I've not forgot your last disastrous service to me!"

Cranford's peg-leg had become stuck in the mud when Falcon had fought Gideon Rossiter some months previously, and he said with a chuckle, "Lucky for you that fight went unfinished, else you might have slain a man you now cry friends with."

"I cry friends with no man. Beasts are more civilized and infinitely preferable. Is Rossiter come back to Town yet?"

"Not that I'm aware."

"What about Tio?"

"I think my lord Glendenning has gone up to Bristol or some such place."

Falcon swore softly. "I hear that Furlong had another brush with that fever he brought home from India, and that Bow Street is cross with you for having slaughtered somebody. True?"

"Well, in part, but— Dash it all, August! Here's you shooting questions at me like cannonballs, but when I make a simple enquiry, you're all evasions! What's good for the goose—"

"Do not dare fling maxims at me! What I've suffered from that block, Morris! Besides, I don't recall your asking anything sensible."

"I asked why you were here."

"Just so. *Non*sensical. Your brain should supply the answer. This is the hub of shipping news. Ergo, I am here to obtain news of a ship. Now—"

"You are? Which one?"

"Derek Furlong's East Indiaman. She's considerably overdue and I suspect Owen's worried. I chanced to be in the neighbourhood, so thought I'd look in. Now why the deuce should that throw you into a trance?"

"Shock. To hear you admit a kindly impulse! My heart won't stand it."

Falcon's rare smile glinted. "*Touché!* You have benefitted

from my example, Perry. Continue to study my wit and you may become as well loved as I."

"Heaven forfend! Lacking your skill with sword or pistol, I'd not survive a week! I've often—" Cranford interrupted himself to pound a clenched fist on the table. "Derek Furlong! What a dolt I am! I'd forgot all about the old sea dog! He's the very man to find out for me." He glanced up as Falcon stood. "Leaving, are you?"

"So 'twould appear. I find monologues boring. But by all means continue to entertain yourself. I shall seek out my imitation valet. His conversation, though crude, is at least comprehensible. Oh egad!" Falcon shuddered. "One of my more ardent admirers approaches. I wish you joy of him."

With a graceful wave he blended into the crowd, passing and ignoring the extremely fat individual who came puffing up to occupy the settle he had vacated.

"Give you good day, Perry," wheezed the newcomer. "Poor fellow, how you bear the Mandarin is beyond me."

"Dicky!" Shaking hands, Cranford said, "Be dashed if you've changed a whit since we were both brought down at Prestonpans!"

A waiter hurried over with a tray of eggs, toasted buns, and sliced cold pork.

Richard Tyree thanked him and told him not to forget the ale, then took up knife and fork and attacked the food like a starving man. "They know my habits here," he said indistinctly. "And you're a liar, Perry. I'm three stone heavier, and you know it. Fat and happy, dear boy." A pair of merry hazel eyes scanned Cranford over a forkful of pork. "More than I could say for you. How do you stay so trim?"

"The single life, Dicky. No worries."

"Humph! From what I recall of my bachelor days, the single life was one long worry. But never mind that. What brings you to this den of iniquity?"

"You. I need some information on an alleged passenger aboard an East Indiaman."

"Best go to the Jerusalem—"

"I just came from there. They claim the fellow never sailed, but I have it on excellent authority he boarded at Calcutta and—"

"Not another one!" Tyree put down his knife and exclaimed incredulously, "Rot me! 'Tis a flood!"

"Another—what? Has someone else been enquiring?"

"Blasted covey of 'someones.' There was a naval lieutenant asking the very same questions. About a friend, he said. And a large and unlovely fellow concerned for his master. And not ten minutes ago—" His words were drowned by the clamour of the bell, and a renewed outburst of shouting, and he stood, then climbed onto the seat trying to see the board on which information was being chalked at great speed.

When he sat down again, grunting from his efforts, Cranford leaned closer, and howled, "Why all the frenzy? Is is bad news for you, Dicky?"

"No, praise be. I was hoping 'twas word that the *Lady Aranmore* has made port. She's far overdue, and everyone's out of curl, thinking she's gone down, or been pirated."

Dismayed, Cranford said, "Oh, Jupiter! Isn't she commanded by Derek Furlong?"

"Aye. And if anyone can bring her safe home, that young fella can! Now, I've an appointment in Leadenhall Street when I finish m'breakfast. My coach will be here in a quarter hour. An you'd care to come along, you can tell me of your mislaid friend on the way."

By eleven o'clock the fog had dispersed somewhat, but the morning was chilly, and only a few people strolled about St.

James's Park. Lifting Boadicea from the coach, Zoe entertained few hopes of meeting Miss Benevento today. She allowed Gorton and her beau as long a chat as she dared, then sent Coachman Cecil off, telling him to come back for them in an hour.

Gorton smiled dreamily after the coach, and said, "If you but knew, Miss, how much it means to us to be able to talk sometimes. You are so very kind."

"I wish I could do more." Zoe did not add that when she found the proper moment she fully intended to broach the subject with Lady Julia.

Eager to run, Boadicea was tugging at the lead, and they began to follow one of the footpaths, the dog's little legs flying, and her nose busy. Within five minutes Miss Benevento hurried to join them, her footman following, discreet as ever.

The ladies embraced; Boadicea and the dainty little Petite were entrusted to Gorton and Luigi, and Zoe and her new friend walked on ahead.

Inevitably, their conversation turned to the musicale, and Zoe repeated her compliments on Miss Benevento's poetry reading. "I had such a lovely time," she said. And with a sidelong glance at the beautiful face framed by the fur-lined hood of a long dull-red cloak, she added, "Did . . . you? After Lieutenant Cranford and I had—er, left, I mean?"

A low gurgle of laughter, and the beauty tucked one hand in Zoe's arm and said softly, "What you mean, my dear Zoe— we shall be first-name friends, if you please. What you mean is, how did I like your dashing friend, Captain Sir Owen Furlong? And the answer is, I like him very well. We spent the rest of the day and much of the evening learning about each other. Which was not at all *convenable*, since we had just met. But 'twas most—enjoyable. There! I have confessed. Are you shocked?"

"Oh no! I am excessive pleased! I think him the very nicest gentleman. In point of fact, I had told Pere— Lieutenant

Cranford, that you would make the most delightful couple."

Maria looked briefly startled, then said with a smile, "You have the romantic soul, I see! Ah, but that is to look very far ahead, and me—I find it unwise to look any further ahead than . . . today." She paused briefly, her face pensive, then went on in a resumption of her quick, vital manner, "Now, you shall tell me how you go on in that great gloomy house with your very fierce lady. Have you the happiness, my new friend?"

"Well, Lady Julia is the dearest thing, you know," Zoe answered, for once choosing her words with care. "And—and Lady Buttershaw is not always quite so fierce as she seems. I think. Besides, I am very fortunate to see some of this great city which is—"

"Which is so very great. *Si, si.* And the animals they are a joy, and the ladies are to a fault generous. Yet you do not answer my question. Which means, happiness it does not come to you—no?"

"Well, I—I miss Papa and my home, do you see, but—"

Maria halted and gestured to the servants. "I am fatigued," she said, as they came up. "So Miss Grainger and I, we will sit here and talk for a little while. Be so good as to take the dogs for a nice long walk."

The footman bowed and walked on at once, but Gorton hesitated, slanting an uneasy glance at Zoe.

Maria said reassuringly, "Your mistress will be perfectly safe with me, I promise you."

Zoe nodded, and with obvious reluctance Gorton followed Luigi.

"She is loyal, that one," said Maria, leading the way to a bench.

"Yes, she is, or she would not dare leave us alone. She was told never to let me out of her sight."

"La, la! One might think you were a criminal, and preparing your escape!" They both laughed, and Maria went on:

"Not that I would blame you. I should so very much dislike to be guarded all the time! To say truth, I am not happy either, my Zoe. This London it is a lonely place for one not born to it. Ah, but I see what is in your mind. The gentlemen, they flock around me, you think. This also is truth. But they do not admire me for what I am, only for what I look like. And an admirer of youth and looks, which do not endure, is very different to a true and faithful friend. You are my friend, and I think something is—as my brother would say—cutting up your peace." She took Zoe's hand. "Will you permit that I help?"

Her warm clasp, the kindness in the deep, dark eyes, the understanding smile, touched Zoe's troubled heart. "Oh, how very good you are," she said. "And you are quite right, Maria. I am very worried. Only . . . perhaps I am being silly. Except in the matter of my dear Travis."

"There is but one way to tell a tale. Begin, my dear, at the beginning."

A few minutes later, Zoe asked, "Do you think I am being silly? If you *knew* how guilty I feel, to even suspect that—"

"That this haughty bully of a dowager has put her prying eyes into your most personal correspondence? Pah!" Her own eyes snapping with anger, Maria said, "Like you, I have a brother who is extreme dear to my heart, and far away, alas. If such a one as this Lady Buttershaw had dared intercept a letter bringing news of *him*, I would"—her slender hand formed into a claw—"I would scratch her! Hard!"

The very thought of such a confrontation awed Zoe. She said, "Then you think I am not being foolish and over-imaginative?"

"I think your so-called benefactor she wishes to learn something. And it must be something of great import for her to risk her good name by resorting to behaviour that is so outrageous. If it should become known, she would be as despised as if she had committed a crime!" Maria paused, her brow wrinkling, then murmured dreamily, "You say your Travis he is coming from India. What if he chances to have rendered some great service to—to a Maharajah?"

A kindred spirit! Her eyes glowing, Zoe said, "Like saving the life of his favourite son!"

"Just so. Or his favourite wife. Or even his own life, which he would likely value more highly than either of the others. So he has rewarded your brother with the great Ruby of Ranjipangidad, and your greedy lady has found out, and is determined to have it for herself!"

"Imagine!" breathed Zoe. "Is there such a place as Ranji—whatever 'tis?"

"Who knows?" said Maria with an airy gesture. "But something like that—it could be possible, no? And if it *should* be such a naughty plot, you must be very careful, my little Zoe, and not let your fierce lady know you suspect her wicked designs." She frowned. "Have you spoken of this to Mr. Cranford?"

"Yes. He thinks Lady Buttershaw is short of a sheet."

"Does he so?" Maria laughed merrily. "Which means, I take it, that she is not right in her brain, and with this I agree. Does he advise that you should leave Yerville Hall?"

"No, not now, at least. As he says, the difficulty is that I do not really have any proof. And I cannot very well go rushing off to Aunt Minerva only because I have let my imagination run away with me. Poor Lady Julia would be so hurt."

"Yes, I see that, for she has been kind, poor creature. Perhaps, your fine Lieutenant he is the wise one, and we borrow trouble where there is no cause. But if something should happen to frighten you, Zoe, promise you will come to me. Here—" She fumbled in her muff. "Here is my card, and I will write down my direction . . . There. You will not hesitate? In case of need, you will come? At any hour of the day or night! Promise me this."

Zoe took the card and tucked it into the pocket of her cloak. "Yes, indeed. I promise. And oh, I do thank you so much for being willing to stand by me. But you must stop and think, dear friend. Lady Buttershaw is very powerful among the *ton*. If I were to go to you, I fear 'twould get you into most terrible trouble!"

"Pah!" said Maria, with a snap of her fingers. "This, I do not regard! One word to my brother, and he would mince the meat of her *and* her powerful friends! Besides," she added, with a mischievous twinkle, "we can always call on our beaux, no? Your fine Peregrine, and my dashing Sir Owen. Men, my Zoe, they must be good for something! Ah, here come our people. Is your woman to be trusted?"

"Yes, I believe so."

"Good. Then you must tell her where I live so that in case of need she can bring me a message." She squeezed Zoe's hand and said vehemently, "Be of good cheer, my gentle friend. Now neither of us is all alone in London Town!"

Dusk came a little earlier each night, now that November was almost here, and it was getting dark and the fog swirling in again when Cranford gave his card to Arbour, together with a request that Miss Grainger grant him a brief interview.

The butler bowed, showed him into the library, and went away.

In a very few moments, Zoe came in with a rustle of satin, and her eyes bright with hope. Gorton followed, and sat down just inside the door.

Zoe said eagerly, "Per— Lieutenant Cranford. How nice in you to call."

He bowed, and jerked his head meaningfully, and she led the way to the windowseat, whispering, "Is this very naughty?"

"I rather suspect it is, so we must be quick. Zoe, I am very sorry to disappoint you." Her face fell at once, and he went on, "Pray do not be cast down. Lloyd's was in such an uproar 'twas very hard to make enquiries, and the Jerusalem Coffee House was not much better."

"I quite understand." She smiled bravely. "You were unable to find your friend?"

"Oh, I found him, and I have his promise that he'll send me word the instant he learns anything."

"Do you think he really will? If he has much business on his mind he might not have the time to make enquiries about all the incoming vessels."

"He's busy, 'tis true, but I think he keeps abreast of all arrivals and departures. He has a keen mind and is very knowledgeable. He was able to give me some word that poor Furlong will not like, I'm afraid."

"Not bad news, I hope? He is such a nice gentleman."

"Hmm," he said, fixing her with a stern stare. "You admire him, do you?"

She giggled. "Yes, I do, for I think he is the very best kind of man. And—so does Miss Benevento. Is he a part-owner of some vessel?"

"Eh? Oh—no. But his brother's ship is long overdue. She was delayed and is sailing alone, which is very chancy, you know. I was hoping to be able to take some good news to Furlong, but, unhappily, the *Lady Aranmore* has not yet made port, so— Oh, egad! What did I say?"

Her eyes very wide, Zoe gripped his arm. "The—Lady—*who?*"

"No. The *Lady Aranmore*. Derek Furlong's East Indiaman. Whatever is wrong?"

"Oh, Perry!" she whispered. "Oh—my goodness!"

"Yes. I'm here. What is it? Jupiter! How pale you are become! Are you ill?"

"No! It is—it is—that *name!* I have heard it before! Perry! She is the lady— I mean—I *thought* 'twas a lady— Oh, my! 'Tis the lady they *spoke* of! The men I overheard the night Bo came scratching on my door! They said they were waiting for the *Lady Aranmore!*"

"Did they, though! Are you sure?"

"Yes. Quite sure! What can it mean? Is it important, do you think?"

He said thoughtfully, "I'm not sure. It may be very important indeed!"

Gorton coughed and looked a warning. Cranford rose at once. "I'd best go. Now try not to worry. But I think you are very clever, little Miss Zoe!"

CHAPTER XII

t was close to one o'clock when Cranford paid off the chairmen and walked slowly across the flagway and up the steps of his house. Not finding Furlong at his club, he'd left a note for him, then embarked on a search that had occupied several hours, and left him seething with frustration. Sir Owen had not been at Falcon House that day, or at Rossiter Court, or his house on Bond Street, nor had he called in at Laindon House, the great family mansion of Horatio Glendenning's formidable sire, the Earl of Bowers-Malden. Cranford had taken a hasty meal at Clifton's Chop House, then made the rounds of the clubs and the more popular coffee houses, but without success. Disgruntled, he'd turned for home, deciding that Furlong had very likely taken Miss Benevento to the opera or some such place.

Florian opened the door to his knock. Light streamed from the parlour, the air was warm and smelled of woodsmoke and brandy, and several cloaks hung on the clothes rack.

Relieving him of his cloak and cane, Florian murmured, "Company, sir."

Cranford limped into the parlour. At once, a low-voiced conversation ceased, and three gentlemen turned to regard him unsmilingly.

Owen Furlong stood at the mantel, a glass in one hand and

a frown in his eyes. James Morris sat in the chimney seat nursing a wineglass; and August Falcon sprawled in an armchair, long legs stretched out before him, and a tankard balanced on a pile of books at his side.

Exasperated, Cranford began, "Here you are! If that isn't the—"

"What the devil have you been doing?" interrupted Furlong.

Cranford stiffened, the peremptory tone not improving his temper. He poured himself a glass of wine before responding coolly, "I've been to Leadenhall Street, not that 'tis any of your affair. Falcon knows that. He saw—"

"You didn't tell me that the pretty little lady you've been squiring about Town resides at Yerville Hall!"

"Your pardon, sir." Cranford threw an exaggerated salute. "I'd not realized you required a report on my activities."

"You told me," said Sir Owen, "that you'd come to Town because you were obliged to call on some distant relation."

"Which is precisely what I've been—" The haughty words died away. They were all staring at him as though petrified with astonishment, even Falcon rousing himself sufficiently to sit up straight.

"Do you say—" gasped Sir Owen, incredulously, "that you are related to Miss Grainger?"

"Certainly not." Cranford sat down on the sofa, his chin jutting a warning. "If you must know, Lady Clara Buttershaw's spouse appears to have been second cousin to my late Aunt Eudora."

"The mind boggles at such tangled family threads," drawled Falcon, "But one strives. Would this late Aunt Eudora possibly have been the wife of General Lord Nugent Cranford?"

"My great-uncle. Yes."

Morris exclaimed with undisguised horror, "My poor fellow! You are actually related to that— To Lady Buttershaw?"

"Distantly, and by marriage only, and— Dash it all, Jamie! Now see what you've made me say!"

"Bad form, Cranford." Falcon shook his head reprovingly. "A gentleman does not speak ill of a lady. Especially when she is a relative."

Morris offered sagely, " 'The problems in families are usually relative.' "

Falcon put both hands over his eyes and appeared to be praying.

Fully aware of Falcon's loathing of maxims, Cranford smothered a grin and maintained his air of chill hauteur. "I fancy you will tell me why you've invaded my house, and what gives you the right to question my family background, and my activities. When you can spare the time."

Sir Owen, who had been deep in thought, looked up and countered, "Why were you at Lloyd's Coffee House today?"

There was a set to his jaw and a steeliness in his blue eyes. This was *Captain* Sir Owen Furlong speaking; a far cry from the entranced man who had only last evening been so lost in love. With a quickening pulse, Cranford thought, 'Why? What is it all about?' The unease that had been gnawing at him all day grew stronger, so that he abandoned resentment, and answered, "Miss Grainger has just learned that her brother, who was in the Diplomatic Corps in India, has been very ill and has been sent home. She desired me to try and discover whether he has arrived."

"Why enlist your aid?" demanded Falcon curiously. "I would think her father should have been the one to enquire for his son."

"He did, but could learn nothing. No more could I. But I learned something else, which may be of some interest to you, Owen."

At once eager, Furlong asked, "Is it about Derek? Has he reached port at last?"

"Not that, I'm afraid. And my news may be of little significance. But it seemed to me a rather curious coincidence. I should explain that Miss Grainger is a sort of companion to Lady Julia Yerville. One of her tasks is to see that none of Lady Julia's pets invade the quarters of Lady Buttershaw, who dislikes creatures. A few nights ago, one of the dogs awoke Miss Grainger in the night but went tearing off before she could catch it. She knew Lady Buttershaw would be enraged if the dog was found in that part of the house, so she ran after the animal and had caught it in the lower hall when she heard some guests leaving. Naturally enough, she did not want to be seen in her nightrail. She ducked into a side room and inadvertently overheard a very guarded conversation. It had to do with someone who had evidently violated a trust, or some such thing. And with a lady, whose arrival they were eagerly awaiting so that they could take action. Miss Grainger said it all sounded very grim, and we thought it must have to do with high finance. I'd quite forgot about it until this afternoon, when I chanced to mention the name of your brother's ship to the lady."

Sir Owen said intensely, "The *Lady Aranmore*? I don't see—" His eyes widened. "Oh, egad! Are you saying *she* is the lady those men are waiting for?"

Cranford nodded.

"Be damned!" muttered Furlong.

There was a taut silence. Cranford looked from one stern face to the next. He said, "This is all part of what you're about, is it not? And I am somehow involved. Is Miss Grainger, also?"

Falcon drawled, "Up to her eyebrows, I would guess."

"In which case, gentlemen, I'll have the truth, if you please. Now!"

"I wish we could come at it," muttered Furlong.

"Owen," said Cranford through his teeth, "you put me off once before, because I chance to have a crippled leg. You'll not put me off this time!"

Morris, who had been staring at his boots, asked suddenly, "Why could you not learn anything about Miss Grainger's brother? At Lloyd's, I mean. Surely they could give you some idea of when his ship is due?"

Falcon said irritably, "And what, for mercy's sake, has that to say to the matter at hand?"

"No." Sir Owen lifted a delaying hand. "I wondered the same thing. Why, Perry? They're usually accommodating enough."

"Unhappily, Grainger neglected to notify his family that he was on his way home. They'd not have known a thing about it, save that Mr. Grainger chanced to hear it from a friend, who knew for a fact that Travis had embarked at Calcutta, and should have landed by now. Lacking the name of the vessel, we searched the passenger lists, but he might have vanished into thin air, for all we—"

For the third time he was interrupted as Falcon, his eyes flashing with sudden excitement, demanded, "What was his illness? Not cholera?"

"Why, yes—but how—"

"Oh, damme!" gasped Morris. "You never think . . . ?"

"It *fits*!" Springing from his chair, Falcon said, "A diplomatist, unwell and terrified for his life. Very likely travelling under an assumed name. Just as young Grainger has done!"

Sir Owen said, "Ramsey Talbot said our man is still in Mozambique."

"And how many months did it take that news to reach his ears? Owen, how can you back and fill like a confounded block? Don't you see? We have the answer at last! This

Grainger lad must be your brother's mystery passenger! And his sister is either hand in glove with the Buttershaw dragon, or—"

Cranford leapt up also, and caught Falcon's arm. His face flushed, his eyes deadly, he hissed, "I'll know what you mean by that remark, if you please!"

"They tried to tell you once, you lamebrain," snapped Falcon, tearing free.

Morris contradicted, "Not so. Must be fair, August. We tried *not* to tell him."

Cranford demanded, "Tell me what? And never try to fob me off with your silly fustian about some kind of League and . . ." He caught his breath, and said uneasily, "It *was* so much fustian, was it not?"

Furlong glanced at the others, gave a slight fatalistic shrug, and answered quietly, "Everything we told you before is true, Perry. What we did not tell you is that we *have* learned the identities of some members of the League of Jewelled Men. The Earl of Collington, for instance, and—"

"Gideon Rossiter's *father-in-law*? Owen—you're not serious?"

"Unhappily so. Besides Collington, we've proven Rudolph Bracksby, Lord Hibbard Green, and we suspect General Samuel Underhill, and—"

"And Lady Clara Buttershaw," said Falcon. "There are others; prominent men we know to be members, but who may not be on the ruling committee."

Stunned, Cranford sank back onto the sofa. He made an effort to recollect what they'd told him before; the tale that had so enraged him, and that he'd dismissed as a silly hoax. "But—you said they know who you are," he muttered haltingly. "And Zoe mentioned once that Lady Buttershaw is infatuated with August, and expects him to visit her. Why would she allow him to go there if she knows him for an enemy?"

" 'A little knowledge is a dangerous thing,' " said Morris. "In this instance, the 'little knowledge' is hers."

Falcon nodded. "She knows who *we* are, but I need not tell you the lady is of an arrogance. She does not credit us with suspecting *her* involvement."

"A lady of Quality, involved in high treason . . . ?" Trying to collect his scattered wits, Cranford said, "No. You *must* be mistaken! The woman, unpleasant as she may be, is almost fanatical in her patriotism! Her house is like a museum. She glories in the fact that her family has figured largely in England's history."

Furlong said, "She may have decided that gives her the right to change it."

"And not balk at murder? Or the prospect of another civil war? Surely no lady would willingly involve herself in such madness?"

"Consider Delilah," suggested Morris. "Or Lady Macbeth. Or Queen—"

"If someone doesn't stop him," warned Falcon, "he'll list every scheming female for the last two thousand years!"

Sir Owen smiled. "He's right, though. The ladies are not exempt from the lust for power. No need for us to debate that point. What we must do now is put our information together and see if it gives us a clearer picture. Perry, you can begin by telling us exactly how Miss Grainger comes to be in that house." And unknowingly paraphrasing the words his adored lady had spoken earlier that day, he said, "Begin at the beginning."

Cranford obliged.

Five minutes later, Florian brought in a pot of coffee and, through a brief silence, crept about distributing mugs.

"Phew!" said Morris.

Falcon raised his mug in salute. "I endorse your sentiments for once, my clod. 'Phew,' indeed!"

"Are we all of the same mind, then?" asked Sir Owen.

Cranford said, "I've a question or two, if you please. Among their other nasty habits, you mentioned that your murderous League has schemed to acquire great houses and properties. I take it the choices were not haphazard?"

"By no means," answered Falcon. "They all are strategically situated in the southern counties. Close to a military barracks, an armoury, a harbour, fortress, or some such thing."

"All of which will be attacked or perhaps sabotaged when the League is ready to strike," said Sir Owen. "If you weigh the element of surprise 'gainst inefficiency and complacency, the result is likely to be disastrous."

Cranford nodded thoughtfully. "Next—you spoke of tokens, I think. Jewelled figures that the six leaders use for identification. Why is that necessary? Surely they know their fellow conspirators?"

"Doubtful," said Morris. " 'Tis high treason, dear boy. Their lives depend on absolute secrecy. Were only one of them discovered and put to the question"—he drew a finger across his throat—"an ugly end for the lot!"

"So they wear masks at their meetings," Falcon put in, "and identify each other by the little jewelled figures. Though their leader, of course, knows who they all are."

"We believe each man also answers to a number," added Morris. "And the head of their nasty club, whom they call the Squire, sometimes signs notes with the letter S. Which could stand for 'Squire.' " ·

"Or for half a hundred other names," said Falcon blightingly.

Cranford said, "So for all their grandiose plans, they cannot even have trust in each other. If such a desperate group should feel threatened . . ."

"They'd stop at nothing to protect their dirty skins," said Sir Owen. "Understandably. But if Ramsey Talbot is right, they have entered into a treasonable agreement with certain gentlemen of France, one of whom just may be Marshal Jean-Jacques Barthélemy."

Appalled, Cranford gasped, "The devil you say! Acting for France? Are you sure of that?"

"We're sure of none of it," Sir Owen admitted worriedly. "But Ross thinks, and we agree, that Barthélemy is pursuing his own interests."

"All we're *sure* of," said Falcon, "is that several years ago while Johnny Armitage was in Suez, he chanced to see the mighty Marshal hob-nobbing with Lady Buttershaw and her sister. We believe that because Armitage stumbled upon that meeting, the League sentenced him to death. And damn near succeeded in destroying him."

Sir Owen nodded and said gravely, "We could be wrong. It may be purest coincidence, but now, with the secret Agreement having come to light, it all seems to add up. Each side retained a signed copy of that infamous document, one of which was stolen. If we can only lay our hands on it, we'll have the proof we need to send the lot of 'em to the Tower!"

Morris looked sombre and muttered, "Which the League means to prevent at all costs."

Falcon drained his mug and set it aside. "And that is where you would appear to come into the business, Perry."

"I rather doubt that, you know." Cranford pursed his lips. "Too many 'ifs.' *If* the poor fellow trying to bring the stolen Agreement back to England is Travis Grainger. *If* his supposed Last Will and Testament is in fact the Agreement. *If*—I am the man he knew at school to whom the agreement is to be sent in case of his death. *If* his sister was brought to London only so that she could be watched in case Travis tried to contact her. *If*—I was introduced to Zoe Grainger in the hope we would become friends and I would exchange information with her. And there, do you see, your theory falls to pieces. 'Tis purest coincidence that I am in Town at this particular time, and although I did meet Miss Grainger, our first encounter was exceeding unfriendly, and I had no least intention to ever see her again."

"Perhaps not, but *they* intended you to do so," said Falcon. "The investigation of your supposed accident has been smothered, no?"

"My solicitor was told I would be required to testify," answered Cranford. "So far, I've heard nothing more of it."

"Nor will you," said Sir Owen. "I'll warrant Lady Buttershaw has seen to that. They want nothing to interfere with your hopeful courtship of Miss Grainger."

Cranford shook his head. "Which again makes no sense. If they hoped I would become enamoured of the lady, why did Lady Buttershaw try to arrange a match with Fowles, or Smythe, or any of that silly crew?"

"I doubt she did," said Falcon. "She rushed that business, knowing perfectly well that Miss Grainger would draw back from such a repulsive selection, and be more inclined to encourage you."

"As the best of a bad lot," put in Morris with a grin.

"Have a happy Christmas, Jamie," said Cranford indignantly.

The others laughed, and Falcon went on, "It worked, no? I fancy they banked on the fact that her brother having spoken highly of you would be sufficient for her to cry friends, but if you hadn't liked each other at all, they'd have found some other way to keep you hanging about that house."

"So they could keep an eye on your every move," said Morris. "And—hers."

Sir Owen said, "They knew, Perry, that you were the two people young Grainger would most likely turn to. I must own 'twas neatly done."

"But they couldn't have *known* I would be in Town," argued Cranford. "I only came because . . ." He broke off. Falcon was smiling cynically; Morris and Furlong looked grave. "Good God!" he gasped. "You think— *Lord Nugent?* No! You're very wrong! He's a good old boy. But for him, neither my twin nor I would have been able to go to school after our parents died!"

"And he is distantly related to Lady Clara," murmured Falcon.

"No, I tell you!" repeated Cranford hotly. "The man is a general officer, the soul of integrity, and loyal to a fault! I'll not believe he is also a traitor!"

"How typical it is," drawled Falcon, "that we are ready to believe others guilty of a conspiracy, but if our own family honour is questioned, we sing a different song. Eh, Morris?"

Lord Kenneth Morris, a wealthy Cornish peer and the head of his large and widely dispersed family, had recently been found to have strong ties to the League. Although this was not generally known, James Morris, a man of impeccable personal integrity, felt that the honour of his house had been sullied. He smarted under that awareness and, flushing, said with rare anger, "Damme, but you want thrashing, Falcon! If it weren't that I mean to marry your sister—"

"Have done," said Sir Owen sharply. "Every family has dirty dishes, we all know that. The guilt or innocence of Lord Morris and others we suspect must be proven. But not now! You both have promised Gideon to postpone your personal quarrel till this is done."

Morris mumbled an apology.

Falcon shrugged, and said, "Dare I remark that I think we overlook a point? This stolen letter of yours, Cranford. You said the signature was hard to read, and not a name you knew. What did you guess it to be?"

"Rohdean, I think," Cranford answered. "Or something of the sort."

"Rohdean!" His voice harsh with excitement, Sir Owen

asked, "Perry—might it instead have been *Rathdown?*"

Cranford said frowningly, "Why—yes. I suppose it might very well—"

Morris jumped up and howled, "Excelsior!"

"I do believe we have our proof," murmured Falcon.

Exultant, Sir Owen said, "By all the saints, I think you've got it! Perry—we're really not Bedlamites. The thing is that 'tis all falling together at last! You see, Ramsey Talbot told me that the copy of the Agreement was given into the hands of a Major *Rathdown*. Evidently, the Major became ill, and his letter to you was by way of apology for having been obliged to pass the Agreement on to poor Travis Grainger."

Cranford said eagerly, "And Grainger promised to send the Agreement to me, or to his sister, in the event the League was too hot on his heels for him to deliver it to Whitehall! Then Grainger's alleged Last Will and Testament *is* the missing copy of the Agreement!"

"And all we've to do now, is find Grainger and bring him safely to Whitehall," said Morris. "We're half-way home! Keep your wits about you, Perry! And 'ware the Buttershaw!"

Cranford said, "But—Owen, surely they must guess I know."

"They may suspect you know of the existence of the League, yes. As August said before, they don't think we know about Lady Buttershaw, or about the Agreement. Still it will be safer if we're not often seen together. We shall not be able to meet here again. We arrived separately this evening, and with great caution. We'll leave the same way."

Falcon said, "We must contrive a means to get word back and forth. Assuming you're now willing to join us, Perry?"

"With all my heart," Cranford said vehemently. "I must first get Miss Grainger out of that house, but after—"

Sir Owen snapped, "You most certainly must not! 'Tis vital that the lady stay just where she is!"

"The devil with that!" Cranford's eyes sparked with anger. " 'Tis too dangerous! Besides, once she knows—"

"But she must *not* know," interposed Falcon softly.

Cranford stared at him. "You're mad! Do you think that I'd allow her to stay another minute in that damnable house? Much less keep her unaware of the web around her? You must not have considered the risk."

Falcon shrugged. "We are all at risk."

"And we are men. 'Tis the business of a gentleman to protect a lady from danger, not expose her to it!"

"From what I know of the ladies, they are quite capable of protecting themselves."

Cranford said grittily, "I've often remarked, Falcon, that you have an odd sense of honour!"

"If you mean I don't follow your much vaunted Code," said Falcon, bored, "you are very right. I hope I have more sense."

Troubled, Furlong said slowly, "I really doubt Miss Grainger will come to any harm, Perry. And she can be of inestimable assistance in keeping us apprised of what goes on in—"

Cranford put down his glass gently, and started to the door. "Good night, gentlemen."

"Hey!" said Morris. "What d'ye mean?"

Opening the door, Cranford bowed. "I mean our meeting is done. I'll have no part of your fight after all. And before you say what you're thinking, Sir Owen, consider a certain lovely lady of Rome. Would you throw her into such peril?"

"You become 'Sir Owen' again," pointed out Falcon, amused. " 'Ware, Furlong. I do believe Cranford has formed a *tendre* for the little country miss."

"Your beliefs do not interest me," snapped Cranford, his face red. "Be so good as to—"

Furlong interposed, low-voiced. "Our *country* is endangered, man! I appreciate your anxieties, but—I'll wager that if it were put to Miss Grainger—"

Cranford's suggestion as to what Sir Owen could do with his wager was, to say the least of it, not very polite.

The clocks in Lady Julia's workroom ticked busily. They hung on the walls, were gathered on display shelves or on chests, and two were tall enough to stand on the floor.

On this brisk October morning, Zoe knelt fending Cromwell off while holding securely to the back of Caesar's neck as she groomed him. Of all the animals, the big tabby was most resistant to being brushed, whereas his dog, the springer spaniel, loved such indulgences.

"I am indeed worried about my brother," Zoe admitted in answer to an enquiry from Lady Julia. "Travis was never of a frail constitution, but he does tend to take cold easily. 'All brains and no brawn' my papa used to say. Oh, *do* stop, Cromwell! I was so disappointed that Mr. Cranford had no news for me."

Bending over her workbench, magnifying glass to her eye, Lady Julia murmured, "Then I pray he will have better tidings today, my dear. 'Tis very good of the young man to make such an effort for you. When he did not call yesterday morning, I had thought perhaps you'd tired of him."

"He of me, more likely," said Zoe, rather ruefully. "He has been so good to take me about. He is a handsome gentleman, and I am very sure there must be other ladies would be pleased of his attentions."

"Ah, but you are so bright and merry." Lady Julia lifted her head to smile at her youthful companion. "I fancy you have picked up his spirits. I do not care for gossip, but—well, one hears things, you know, and I believe he was very downcast when his lady love abandoned him."

Zoe's hand on Caesar's neck tightened, and the tabby uttered an indignant growl. "Oh," she said, brushing more busily than before. "I'd not known he was betrothed."

"I cannot say if it had gone to that length. But he had been courting her for several months, and, if my informant is correct, with every indication that his suit was favoured. The lady is lovely, and an older and very wealthy gentleman appeared on the scene, whereupon she apparently decided that poor Mr. Cranford's amputation revolted her, and she could no longer bear with him."

"How monstrous unkind!" exclaimed Zoe indignantly. "I hope she did not allow her feelings to be widely known!"

"She did, alas. Both publicly, and to the young man directly, so I understand. Which was unwise, because he is very well liked." Meeting Zoe's outraged eyes, her ladyship nodded. "I share your reaction, my dear. Unhappily, I know—too well—how it feels to be so humiliated."

"*She* is the one should feel humiliated! And she must be the greatest fool to throw over such a kind and gallant young gentleman only for— Oh—*Caesar*!"

Her hold had relaxed, and with a lithe twist and an annoyed swipe at her hand, the tabby escaped. Cromwell, eager for his turn, leapt in and seized the brush, then lunged off, shaking it ferociously.

Lady Julia was amused, but Zoe stood, and ordering her skirts, scolded, "Foolish creature! How can I brush you if you eat the brush?"

One of the wall clocks began to toll the hour, and Zoe went over to listen. It was a handsome specimen, having a small marine painting above the dial, and a handsome oak case embellished with flowers and leaves of inlaid woods. "How pretty it is," she said.

Lady Julia turned at once, her eyes brightening. " 'Tis one of the newer pieces. I ordered it from Holland a few years ago." She left the bench, and asked, "Are you interested in clocks, my dear? As you know, 'tis quite a passion of mine. It runs in the family, I suspect. My great-grandfather was obsessed with mechanical devices of every kind, and during his travels about the world assembled a remarkable collection, which is housed at our country seat."

"Sundial Abbey." Zoe laughed. "How apropos. Did your great-grandpapa name the estate, my lady?"

"No, 'tis much more ancient. But he passed on his interests. My grandfather liked to build clocks, and taught me a great deal of the art—for it is an art, I promise you. I must show you the clock that was presented to my father by King Louis of France." She led the way to the large and ornate clock upon the parlour mantelpiece. The broad base was gilded and inset with exquisite miniatures; above, two gold cherubs supported the central column whereon was a large painting of two lovers walking in a misty garden, arms entwined. "There is no dial, but do you see the movement?" asked Lady Julia. " 'Tis here, above the pediment."

"The two horizontal bands. How clever! And I have always admired the case clock in your withdrawing room. Is it very old, ma'am?"

"Not as one measures time. Another play on words! How bad of me. 'Twas made by Mr. Tompion, who is known as the father of English watchmaking. They are calling them grandfather clocks now, you know."

"Yes, I've heard that. Did the gentleman invent clocks, ma'am?"

Her ladyship laughed merrily. "No, indeed, child. The earliest mechanical clocks were used in European churches in the thirteenth century, but they did not know of the pendulum then, and their clocks were very poor timekeepers, 'tis said. Often an hour or more behind the time. Only think how late everyone must have been! Speaking of which, I must not keep on or you will be here forever, and I fancy you have plans for this day, yes?"

Zoe blushed. "Well, I did hope Mr. Cranford might call. But he is not here yet. Will you show me what you are working on?"

"With pleasure!"

They went back into the work room, and her ladyship sat down at the bench once more. A beautifully enameled pocket watch case lay open and empty. On a black cloth were spread many little toothed wheels and springs, and tiny deeply grooved columns which Lady Julia said were called pinions. Watching, awed, as her ladyship took up one of the wheels with a delicate pair of pincers and fitted it carefully into place, Zoe murmured, "Oh, but you are so skilled! What incredibly precise work. And what a lovely case."

"And quite valuable," said Lady Julia, "for 'twas made by Mr. Pluvier over a hundred years—"

Viking, who had been watching Cromwell chew on the brush, threw up his head and barked shatteringly.

Lady Julia said, "I suspect someone has called. Run along, child, 'tis likely your gallant."

"But I have not finished the cats! Are you sure—"

"You can finish later. Come to me when you return, and you shall see the little watch all put back together and running merrily."

Pleased by Gorton's advice that Lieutenant Cranford did indeed wait below-stairs, Zoe changed quickly into a Watteau gown of soft pink taffeta that she had been eager to wear. Gorton draped a charming pink and white woollen shawl about her shoulders, and she hurried downstairs.

Cranford had been cornered in the morning room, and it became clear that Lady Buttershaw had no intention of allowing him to escape. She was hospitality at its finest, and was all apologies for having been obliged to neglect him. The health and occupations of General Lord Nugent Cranford were enquired after with many flattering asides as to that retired gentleman's brilliance. Cranford, who rarely saw his great-uncle, had little to impart, but his answers were exclaimed over as though the information they contained was of earth-shaking importance. Of equal fascination were the activities of his *charming* twin, Piers, and his *delightful* sister, Dimity, Lady Farrar, who was, Cranford said with a proud smile, "determined to make me an uncle again." This confidence sent Lady Buttershaw into transports. Sir Anthony and his lady must, of course, be praying for a son, since they already had "a *precious* little daughter." *Dear* Cousin Peregrine must let her ladyship know the *instant* the babe arrived, so that she might send something *very special* to welcome the newborn.

"I do so *adore* little ones," she said sadly, and added with a sigh, "Would I had been blessed with some of my own."

Zoe, who had heard her referring to the children who played in the square as "destructive brats who should be confined to their own gardens," stared in astonishment.

Cranford saw her jaw drop and the glazed look come into her eyes and was hard put to it not to laugh out loud. As always, her emotions were written on her expressive little face for all to see. But if my lady saw that look, he was very sure the fur would fly. He did not want Zoe to be frightened again, and so diverted her ladyship's attention with an account of his small niece's antics.

"Ah," said Lady Buttershaw benignly, "There is naught like family, is there? They bring our greatest joys and deepest sorrows. Take poor Miss Grainger, now. She is most anxious for her brother. Never look so surprised, my pet. Your dear papa has writ to me of Travis and his—ah, rather peculiar behaviour."

Speechless, Zoe stared at her.

Cranford thought, 'Why, you brazen fraud!'

Lady Buttershaw blinked at his expressionless face and said with angelic innocence, "He seems to have vanished somewhere 'twixt Calcutta and Bristol. Such a worry for the sweet child. Perchance you have friends or connections in the shipping business who may be able to help, cousin?"

A stifled gasp came from Zoe.

Cranford said coolly, "It will be my pleasure to be of assistance to you, ma'am."

For a split second her eyes narrowed. Then, she boomed, "Splendid! How do you mean to set about it? If you knew Sir Owen Furlong, 'twould be useful, my dear, for his brother commands an East Indiaman. Might he be the captain you told me of? He could be of great help, I fancy."

From the corner of his eye, he noted that Zoe had become quite pale. He bowed. "You are a fount of—er, wisdom, ma'am. I do know Sir Owen, and will seek him out, certainly." He turned to Zoe. She lifted scared eyes to meet his. He winked surreptitiously, and offered his arm.

"Now?" persisted her ladyship, following them to the front doors.

"Now, I have arranged to take Miss Grainger on a journey," he drawled.

Lady Buttershaw all but sprang before them.

"Along the Thames," he finished sweetly. "I have rented a boat."

"You have?" Her ladyship looked with marked unease at his peg-leg. "Shall you be able to manage, poor boy?"

He gritted his teeth and assured her he would be able to manage.

" 'Twas all I could *manage*," he told Zoe when they were

driving along South Audley Street a few minutes later, "not to strangle the wretched woman! Could you believe the gall of it? She learned of your brother's predicament from *your* letter! Not from anything your father writ to *her*. As if he would do such a thing. She is practically a stranger to him."

"Yes, I know. She is truly dreadful. But—oh Peregrine, I have been so anxious. Have you anything more to tell me of Travis?"

He thought grimly that he had something to tell her, but not of Travis, and not here. And he said, "No, I am sorry to say. But the instant I learn anything, you will know, I promise you."

She stifled a sigh, and said bravely, "I know I have taken a great deal of your time and—and I am so grateful. But you must not feel obliged to take me on the river today."

He smiled. "Although you would like it, of all things."

"Oh, yes!" She clasped her hands and said with her eyes like stars, "It must be the greatest river in the whole world, do you not think? All the people who have travelled along it! The history it has seen!"

He teased, "Like the Vikings, who sailed up it and slew everyone and burned everything in their path!"

"I think you have no romance in your soul," she told him severely.

"Very true. But you have sufficient for both of us, and I'm a good rower, despite what Lady Buttershaw might think."

"I know you are. Travis told me you stroked for—"

"Travis told you a lot of fustian. Now pray do not be tearful and worrying again. He is likely safe and sound and I do not doubt you'll see him very soon. Meanwhile—here we are at Whitehall Stairs, and your royal barge awaits, madame."

That won her to a smile because the "royal barge" was a small rowing boat. But although he had spoken lightly she knew him well enough by now to sense a repressed tension, and she asked, "Why did you decide to take me on the river, Peregrine?"

"Because I have something to say to you, and I don't want you to start jumping up and down."

Her heart gave an odd little leap. She said meekly, "Very well, kind sir."

"Besides," he added, "you look so pretty in that gown, I want all London to see you."

She blushed and did not know what to say, and was glad that he was handing her down from the carriage so that she could bow her head and hide her confusion.

The boatman had thought he was to be hired to row, and was clearly disappointed. Helping Zoe into the boat, Cranford said with a grin, "Be off with you! I do not propose to share my lady with anyone!"

Cheered by the coins that had been slipped into his ready palm, the boatman cast off the line, and Cranford eased the boat deftly out from the stairs and into the stream of boats and barges travelling the busy waterway.

The river sparkled and gurgled under a kindly sun, and Zoe was delighted by it, and by the wider view it offered of the city that lifted its towers and domes and steeples along the banks. Cranford directed her attention to the Privy Garden Stairs, and the new bridge at Westminster which had, he said, been a'building almost ten years and was still not done. The House of Lords and the House of Commons awoke her awed admiration. She inspected each boat that passed by, marvelled at the size and number of the barges, and was amused by the antics of the bargees, several of whom waved and bowed saucily to her.

"They're audacious rogues," Cranford warned. "Do not encourage them!"

She laughed, and trailed her fingers in the water, happily forgetting her anxieties for a little while. Peregrine rowed remarkably well. She studied him covertly. He didn't look like a man trying to forget a broken heart. In fact, she would always enjoy to remember him like this, with the sunlight on his lean face and the blue of the skies reflected in the eyes that could change with such lightning speed from gravity to rage to laughter. She looked away hurriedly as his head started to turn to her, and knew sadly that she had become much too fond of him, and that she was only a country girl who was, perhaps, helping him forget his lost love.

He asked, "Now what are you dreaming of? Some ardent swain in Burford who is heavy-hearted because you are gone?"

She chuckled. "Give me credit for more than one ardent swain, sir."

"Oh, I do. Poor fellows, has their lustre paled, by comparison to your London beaux?"

Her eyes shot to his face, but he was leaning into his oars, his head downbent. She said, "Alas, I think I have none."

"Come now—what of poor old Reggie Smythe, and Purr, and Gil Fowles—heaven forbid you'd choose him!—and—"

"Oh, Lud! With such romances as these I must be glad to return to Burford!"

"Not up to snuff, eh? Perchance you prefer a different type of man. Such as—" He met her eyes and his courage failed him, so that he stammered, "—er, Furlong. You—ah, you like him, I think?"

"Oh, indeed I do! Any lady would." Recalling that moment of enchantment when Sir Owen and Maria had first met, she murmured, " 'Who ever loved that loved not at first sight . . . ?' "

Watching her tender half-smile, Cranford scowled, and said irritably, "You ladies and your poetry!"

"But you must own that the poet can take the words we are too shy to speak, and fashion them so beautifully that no one will dare make them a mockery."

"For example," he said, guiding the boat towards a quiet

area of the bank, " 'Fain would I, but I dare not; I dare, and yet I may not; I may although I care not.' "

She laughed. "Wretched man! Why must you always drive away the spirit of romance?"

For a long moment he looked at her in silence, then he shipped his oars, secured the line to a mooring ring, and said quietly. "Just as well, I think, little Zoe. Come." He climbed out and reached down a hand.

His arm slipped around her as she stepped onto the bank, and her heart thundered. She tried to speak calmly. "Are you going to make me walk home because I dared to speak of romance, Peregrine?"

He did not at once answer. Then he said, "Home to Yerville Hall? No. You are not going back there at all."

She halted, her eyes wide. "What do you mean? Ah, you said you had something to tell me. Is it that you have found Travis after all? Has Papa sent for me? Am I to—"

He put a hand over her lips. "You are to sit down. Here—" He spread his cloak on the grass. "And you are to listen."

large yawl drifted past, her sails flapping in the freshening breeze, and from the city came the clear voices of bells, tolling the hour. Zoe gave no sign of noticing either, but sat very still on the grassy bank, staring blindly at the ever-changing face of the Thames. The hand Cranford held was very cold, and, watching her, he began to chafe it gently. For fear of terrifying her, he had at first given her a considerably expurgated version of the affair, but she had refused to believe he was serious and had laughed at him, so that in order to convince her of her danger, he'd been obliged to broaden his account.

"I know you are frightened," he said, "but you will be quite safe with your aunt—no?"

She did not reply.

He bent forward and peered into her pale face anxiously. "Zoe?"

She murmured, "You hold that t'was all a plot, from start to finish. Lady Buttershaw set out to meet my step-mama only so as to trick Papa into letting me come to Town."

"Yes."

"The gowns *were* made for me. They wanted me there in case my brother wrote to me. But," she frowned in perplexity. "Why not leave me at home? They could have watched me at

Travisford just as well, without going to all this bother."

"I doubt it. In a country place everybody knows everybody else, and strangers stand out like a sore thumb. Besides, they very likely guessed that your brother would not dare go home. If he wrote to you and Mr. Grainger sent his letter on here, it could be more easily intercepted. Also, Travis might feel safe to visit you in Town."

She nodded, and returned her gaze to the water. "Yes. I see. And you were brought to Yerville Hall because they knew my brother planned to send that terrible paper to you for safe keeping. But—" She paused, looking at him again. "The Three Horse Inn? Was that meeting planned also?"

"Purest accident, I fancy. Do you recall how shocked Lady Buttershaw looked when she realized I was the infamous 'doctor?' That was a genuine reaction. One of few. Come now. I'll hire a coach to take us to—"

"No," she interrupted quietly.

Starting up, he frowned and sat down again. "What do you mean—no? Is it because you've not had time to pack your belongings? Never fear, we'll stop on the way to your aunt's house, and buy tooth powder and brushes and the little falderals you ladies need. If you prefer not to go there, I'll take you to the Palfreys. I'm sure my sister would be only too delighted to have your company, and she has the dearest baby girl you will like to— Now why do you shake your head? Have you a loathing for children?"

She smiled faintly but refused to be diverted. "You are very good, Peregrine. But it would not do, you know 'twould not. Assuredly, there would be the most dreadful uproar. You would be held to blame." She raised her hand as he started to protest, and added, "But even if it could be done without a fuss, I must go back to Yerville Hall."

"Great jumping—!" Fuming, he demanded, "Did you hear *nothing* I told you? The woman is demented—and ruthless!

There are things—" He broke off, scowling.

She nodded. "I apprehend that you tried to spare my poor nerves, and that the horrid business is much worse than you have told me. But I will not run away."

He gave a smothered exclamation and jerked his head at the heavens in frustration.

Zoe put a hand on his arm and went on earnestly, "Pray do not be vexed. I *must* be there to warn my brother away in the event he should try to find me, do you see?"

"Be dashed if I do! *I* will warn your brother! Have some sense, girl, these are not play-actors, but unscrupulous fanatics, dedicated to the destruction of our government. And infuriating as it may be at times, I dread to think what they plan to replace it with! As for my reputation—pish! I want you out of that house, I tell you!"

She looked at him worriedly, but again shook her head.

He took her by both hands. "Only see how you tremble, and your little hands are like ice. You're scared to death of Lady Buttershaw!"

"Yes. I am. Loud bullying people always frighten me. But then, I am very easily frightened. And—and not at all brave, like you."

He smiled at her fondly. "You are very brave. But this is nothing for a lady to be involved in."

The smile and the tender voice wrought havoc with her. She stood hurriedly, and argued, "I am already involved. No—please listen, Perry. I *live* in that house. I can help you *and* my brother. I can creep about at night and listen to—"

"Good God! *No!*" Standing also, he snarled furiously, "Miss Romantical Grainger is with us once more! Do you see yourself as some latter-day Jeanne d'Arc? Only look at you! A dainty, timid little flower, setting herself up in opposition to a fire-breathing dragon! Ridiculous! And what am I supposed to do while you engage in your heroical campaign? Lurk about outside and enjoy nervous palpitations? I thank you—no!"

'A dainty, timid little flower?' Zoe Grainger? The same Zoe Grainger her step-mama had named a tree-climbing hoyden? That he should see her in such a light, and be so concerned for her safety, warmed her heart. She felt herself blushing with delight, and said shyly, "But I really will be of use to you all, Perry. Besides—"

He seized her arms and said with fierce intensity, "You will do as you are told, my girl, and go with me. Now! Either to your aunt or to my sister Farrar!"

His hands were bruising her arms, and her heart was beating wildly, but she argued, "I will not! By what right do you dare to order me about, Peregrine Cranford?"

His eyes scorched at her. He pulled her close against his chest. "By this right!" His head swooped down; his lips found and crushed hers.

It was Zoe's first real kiss. She cared not that she could scarcely breathe, that her ribs were cracking, that her heart threatened to beat its way from her body. Briefly submitting to a dizzying excitement, she was brought back to earth with a thump as Cranford jerked back and thrust her from him.

"Oh, Jupiter!" he gasped. "What have I done? I am so sorry! I think I must— I mean— I do apologize, ma'am. But— but—" White and aghast, he drew back his shoulders and said formally, " 'Tis *de rigeur*, ma'am, that I now ask for your hand."

Still dazed, she thought, 'Poor man. He kissed me! In public! In broad daylight! He must think he has fairly trapped himself.' She could not command her voice, and turned away from him, both hands clasped to her heated cheeks, trying to stop trembling and to quiet the frenzied beating of her foolish heart.

A tugboat, nudging a frigate up the river, was hooting its horn repeatedly, and sailors crowding the rail of the frigate shouted and cheered. Guessing this dear proposal to be the cause of their amusement, she half-whispered, "Oh, how horrid!"

Those words seemed to slice through Cranford's heart. Anguished, he gazed at the back she presented to him. The down-bent head, the soft curls clustering under her dainty cap, the trim little figure in its pretty pink gown . . .

Zoe blinked away tears. Did he suppose she wouldn't understand that his hot temper and dear kind heart had conspired to sweep him into that shockingly improper behavior? Did he really think she would demand a proposal of marriage? Her voice was a thread when she said, "As if I would accept such an offer!"

"No. Of course. How could I blame you, when I worded it so very unromantically?" And compounding the felony, he asked, "Would you accept me if I said that I love you?"

'Said it,' thought Zoe, miserably. 'Ah, but if only you meant it, my dearest dear!' And she gulped, "I w-wish you will not—not feel obliged to—go on, sir."

He stood very still, very silent.

Had Zoe looked up and seen the expression in his eyes, so much would have been changed. But she did not look up, and after a moment that was hideous for both of them she managed to say in a voice that shook, "Please—take me back now."

Cranford rallied. "No! Willy-nilly, you come with me, ma'am!"

Looking squarely at him then, she was dismayed by the grim line of his mouth, the hard glitter in his eyes, and she backed away. "Perry! You—you cannot force me!"

"We'll see that."

"No!" She danced back a few more steps. "Have some sense, do! You cannot bundle me into some hired carriage in broad daylight!"

He paced forward, his chin jutting. "Florian and my coach are up on the road."

She looked up the bank and saw the waiting carriage. "But—" she gasped, "but that would be an abduction! You cannot mean it! Perry, we are in the middle of Town!"

"True, and I'll own I do not relish the prospect. But if I must, I can always claim you are my wife and are gone demented."

"No! Please! Be sensible! I have only to scream . . ."

"Yes, and every man within earshot would come running, I've no doubt." Despite the deep ache of his hurt, he managed a smile, and said persuasively, "Zoe, you would hate it, you know you would. There would be a dreadful scene, and—"

Even as he spoke so earnestly, he had been moving closer to her, and now he sprang.

Not for nothing had she climbed and hiked and joined in her brother's sports. She uttered a little squeal and, despite her wide skirts, darted nimbly aside. Cranford was very fast, however, and caught her wrist in a grip of steel.

She whimpered, "Ah! You're hurting me!"

Instinctively, he relaxed his hold.

She wrenched free, ducked as he scowled and his hand shot out again, and then pushed with all her strength.

She suffered a rending pang as he staggered, tripped on the uneven bank and fell heavily. But with a stifled sob, and a renewed chorus of hoots from the river spurring her on, she gathered up her skirts and fled.

She caught a glimpse of Florian jumping from the box of the carriage and running down to help his master. People in carriages were staring in astonishment. Two apprentices halted, and drew back, gaping at her as she ran past. She could have wept with embarrassment and the fear that at any instant Peregrine's coach would overtake her, and she gave a relieved sob when she saw a vacant chair coming towards her.

The chairmen were Irish, and they eyed her askance when she waved them down. Some pedestrians watched her curiously, and the sidelong glances of her prospective bearers informed her that they were looking for her servant. She told them in a low and urgent voice to please hurry as she must get home before she was missed. This appeared to strike a responsive chord in both Hibernian hearts. Their eyes brightened; one made a great show of opening the door and ushering her inside, and the other took up his poles and called cheerfully, "Sure, and 'tis an affair o' the heart!"

She told them to turn up a side street, and only after several minutes passed with no sign of pursuit did she direct them to Yerville Hall. Her hopes to return as unobtrusively as possible were dashed when her bearers sang lustily all the way to Half Moon Street. She managed to attract their attention at that point, and was able to quiet them by calling to them that she did not wish to be caught entering the house. They all but tiptoed the rest of the way.

It was a horrible journey. She was distraught with the fear that Peregrine had again injured himself when he fell: heaven knows, she had never intended he should fall so heavily. She knew also that if she had been recognized by anyone driving by the river she would be quite ruined. The thought of what Lady Buttershaw would say when she heard of the incident made her feel sick with fear, and she began to imagine that the occupants of every passing carriage were staring at the shameless wanton who had shared that passionate and very public embrace.

As they drew nearer to Hyde Park, she struggled to compose herself. She tidied her hair, and considered the manner of her return. If she alighted, alone, and from a sedan chair, there would be no escaping an uproar. She tried to think of a way to avoid such a disaster. When they turned into the square she was surprised to see the front doors of Yerville Hall standing wide. Luckily, she had some cash in her reticule, and she paid off her chairmen before they reached the mansion. They whispered encouragement and smiled at her as fondly as if they'd been assisting at an elopement.

There was a great deal of noise coming from the entrance hall. In considerable apprehension Zoe crept up the steps. The air reeked of burnt feathers. A large lady lay on the floor in a swooning condition. Arbour was using a silver salver to waft fresh air from the open doors. Hackham was placing a cushion under the victim's head, and footmen and maids hovered about, while half a dozen ladies and gentlemen, morning callers, Zoe deduced, were offering loud and conflicting pieces of advice. Zoe was able to slip inside unnoticed just as the butler was so ill-advised as to make the sensible suggestion that an apothecary be sent for.

"I will not have *quacks* in the house," roared Lady Buttershaw.

"But my dear ma'am," protested an elderly and agitated dandy, "if the poor creature has suffered a seizure of the heart . . ."

Zoe said, "She more likely needs to have her stays loosed."

Her words brought an immediate silence and the onlookers stared at her with shocked expressions.

"Vulgar!" decreed Lady Buttershaw. "But the gel may be in the right of it. Arbour! Refrain from flapping about in that stupid fashion. Help Hackham carry Mrs. Fryhampton into the scarlet saloon. You gentlemen must take your naughty eyes away and allow the ladies to deal with things. As they usually do," she added in an undervoice.

Fortunately, Zoe's remedy proved efficacious, the embarrassed victim was conveyed to her coach, the guests were provided with a tasty morsel to gossip over, and Zoe's scandalously solitary return home had gone unnoticed.

Despite that piece of luck, she was close to tears, and felt crushed by her various worries. Hoping to be left to her own devices for the rest of the day, she was told to change her dress quickly and join Lady Julia and her friends for luncheon. It took all her resolution to appear cheerful, when she was sure her heart was breaking, but somehow she contrived not to disgrace herself, and to join in admiring the little watch that was now all put back together, and ticking steadily. When the leisurely meal ended, she was asked to play the harpsichord and sing some country airs for the gathering, and the afternoon was far spent before she could escape.

She went to her bedchamber at last, but had no sooner settled down for a good cry than Gorton came to tell her there were more guests expected for an early supper, and they were all to go on to a concert at the Convent Garden Theatre.

Only yesterday, the prospect of such a treat would have delighted Zoe, but now she would have given a great deal to be left alone with her misery.

Both their ladyships joined the group, which also included Lord and Lady Coombs, Mr. Smythe, Sir Gilbert Fowles, Lord Simmers, and the Honourable Purleigh Shale. Zoe was escorted by the latter gentleman, a fortunate circumstance, since he said very little and although apparently admiring her, seemed pleased when she did not maintain a flow of conversation. What they lacked in gregariousness was more than made up for by Lady Buttershaw, whose voice was never still and who maintained a constant flow of instruction regarding the theatre, its appointments, and its predecessors.

Despite Zoe's intense unhappiness, however, when they entered the fifteen-year-old building its magnificence drove away every emotion but wonderment. From their box she could look down upon a great crowd of people who stood in the pit throughout the performance. They were well dressed, but not well behaved, for it seemed to her that they ignored the music altogether, and spent the evening in hailing friends, and engaging in talk, flirtation and laughter. The three galleries were crowded with more elegantly attired ladies and gentlemen, many of whom were scarcely less rowdy than those in the pit. The glare from the huge ring-shaped chandeliers over the stage, which held as many as three hundred candles, awoke a thousand gleams and glitters from the jewels worn by the ladies, and the cravat pins and rings of the gentlemen. Zoe's attention was caught by an especially brilliant necklace in a box across the theatre, almost opposite to her own. She was surprised when the lady bowed slightly, and her heart gave a spasmodic lurch when she recognized Maria Benevento, with Sir Owen Furlong beside her, impressive in full-dress uniform.

Zoe glanced swiftly at her companions. Like Lord Coombs, the Honourable Purleigh had indulged himself at table, and they both kept nodding off to sleep. Lady Buttershaw and Lady Coombs were appraising the throng through their lorgnette fans, and providing a running critique of the attire and reputation of the various leaders of the *ton* who were present, much to the delectation of Sir Gilbert and Mr. Smythe. Lady Julia was in deep conversation with Lord Sommers. Hiding behind her fan, Zoe managed furtively to beckon to Maria, who gazed at her for a moment, then nodded. From that moment Zoe scarcely noticed the efforts of the musicians, which indeed could scarcely be heard above the din. Maria would come to her, she was sure, but if they were to speak she must find a way to escape the box.

When the first half of the program ended, her problem was solved. Lady Buttershaw and Lady Coombs went off with Mr. Smythe and Sir Gilbert to visit friends. Simultaneously, Zoe saw Maria and Sir Owen leave their box. Lord Sommers took Lady Julia out "for a breath of air," and Zoe was left with the Honourable Purleigh, who was snoring softly, and Lord Coombs, who was snoring loudly.

A moment later, Maria slipped into the box. "My poor sweet," she whispered, her amused gaze on the male occupants. "What enlivening companions!"

Zoe sprang up and took her hand eagerly. "Thank you, thank you! I prayed you would manage to come!"

"Your prayers were answered, my dear. Sir Owen stands guard outside and will warn us if your ladies return. But we must be quick, for should the Buttershaw find me here, there will be a fuss and she will raise her great voice, which you will not at all like. Tell me why you are so agitated."

"It is for Lieutenant Cranford," Zoe whispered, with one eye on the sleepers. "Have you seen him since this morning? He fell, did you know?"

"I knew, but I did not know *you* knew of it. Were you perhaps together at the time? Or did you chance to witness the—er, incident?"

"Yes. Well, that is—" Zoe burst out distractedly, "Oh, Maria! 'Tis my fault that he fell, and I have felt so wretched and been so anxious for him."

"Nonsense! How could it be your fault?"

"We quarrelled, and—and I was angry, and— Oh dear, oh dear! I—I *pushed* him!"

Maria's eyes opened very wide. "*You* did? My gentle Zoe! But how is this? I had understood he fell while walking along the riverbank."

"Yes. He had taken me out in a boat. And—and—oh, I dare not take the time now to tell you the whole, but—he . . . *kissed* me!"

Maria's eyes danced. She asked roguishly, "Where?"

"Full on—on the lips!"

"So I would expect if he knew what he was about. I meant—surely, he did not perform this wickedness in the boat?"

"No. 'Twas on the bank, where *everyone* could see. And the sailors and the—the bargees were laughing and shouting at us, and—Oh! 'Twas *dreadful!*"

Vastly titillated, Maria said, "Shocking! If ever I heard of such a thing! He must have been mad!"

"Well, he was. What I mean is, he was exceeding cross, and lost his temper, and seized me like any—any cave man!" Zoe sighed wistfully.

"Hmm. Why was he so cross with you?"

The Honourable Purleigh snorted and moved slightly, and Zoe answered hurriedly, "Because I would not do—something he wanted me to do."

"Oooh!" breathed Maria. "This Peregrine Cranford, he is not the man I thought him! A gentleman would not behave in such a way. And if he did, would feel honour bound to offer for the lady's hand."

"Yes. Well, he did offer. And that's when I pushed him down the bank."

"Because he—offered for your hand?" Maria blinked. "I can see that you were insulted because he kissed you. But surely, in offering for you he made things right."

"He did not mean it," sighed Zoe. "He was very kind to offer, because, as he said, it was *de rigeur*. I refused, of course, and he asked if I would accept him if he said he—loved me."

"But how charming! You did exactly right to push him, my brave one! Me, I should have struck him! With my shoe! You must see him no more! Never!"

"Oh. I mean—no. Of course not. Only . . ."

A glance at the woebegone little face made Maria's lips twitch. She prompted, "Yes, my Zoe?"

"He fell so hard. I have been fairly beside myself with anxiety. Has Sir Owen mentioned it at all? I pray he was not injured again?"

"No, no. He is of steel, that one. I fancy his pride was hurt, for Sir Owen tells me he is rather—ah, I have not the word . . . um—" She scowled darkly.

With a wan smile Zoe supplied, "Surly?"

"*Si!* That is the one! But—"

There came a flapping of the curtains at the rear. Zoe gasped, and Maria said, "Ah, that will be my faithful Owen. I must go. I will meet you in the park on Monday. Now never fret, my little friend. Your lieutenant he will soon recover his good humour, and likely be calling to take you to church tomorrow."

Mr. Peregrine Cranford did not call to escort Miss Zoe Grainger to church, however, and she joined the retinue that braved a dark and grey morning to accompany Lady Julia to early service at the Parish Church of St. James' off Piccadilly. Zoe had never worshipped in so large a sanctuary. Despite a steady downpour, the fashions worn by the members of the congregation were of prime interest to many of those present, but if Zoe's attention wandered from the sermon, it focused not on fashion but on the splendidly carved pelican above the altar, the exquisite marble font, and the organ case, all of which, Lady Julia imparted later, were carved by that genius Mr. Grinling Gibbons.

When they emerged, the skies were even darker, and the rain unrelenting. A quiet day was spent at Yerville Hall. After luncheon Zoe tried without much success to write a letter to her father, until she was summoned by Lady Julia to read St. Paul's Epistle to the Ephesians, and then to talk to her of Travisford.

Several of Lady Buttershaw's friends came to dine, among them Viscount Eaglund and the Honourable Purleigh Shale. Zoe liked the viscount, but his son's sudden bursts of loud laughter combined with Lady Buttershaw's harsh voice to give her the headache, and she was very glad when they all went off somewhere and she was able to escape to her bedchamber. She prepared for bed, then sent Gorton away and sat down to finish her letter.

It was a forlorn endeavour. Her page faded into a picture of Peregrine gazing down at her with such gentle sympathy; the white gleam of his smile when he'd been overcome by mirth; the molten glare that had been levelled at her when he'd become enraged and swept her into his arms. The memory of his kiss made her heart ache with longing, but then would come despair because he had been trying to protect her, in return for which she had brought him unspeakable humiliation. As brief as had been their acquaintance, she knew him well enough to be aware of his fierce pride. If he ever looked at her again it must only be with, at the very least, dislike. To envision his blue eyes regarding her in such a way brought grief so painful that she could scarcely endure it. But she could envision also her beloved brother, hunted and alone and ill. He would not go near Travisford if he thought his presence would endanger those he loved. But he might try to get a message to her, and if he did and discovered where she was, he would find some way to see her. He might even appear at the front door one day! She shivered. No, she could not have acted in any other way . . .

She awoke abruptly. She had fallen asleep at her little desk, and her neck was stiffly uncomfortable. But something had disturbed her. Perhaps one of the animals had escaped again. She carried the candle to the mantelpiece and peered at the clock. Almost twenty minutes past two. Blowing out the candle she took off her slippers, tiptoed to the door and rested her ear against the panel. Almost at once, she heard a woman laugh softly, and the murmur of a man's deep voice. A voice she had heard before but could not at once identify. It might be perfectly innocent, of course; perhaps Lady Buttershaw had come back with more friends to engage in nothing more sinister than a game of cards or one of the historical discussions that she so loved to dominate. Zoe heard the rustle of satin; the soft click of high heels. The sounds faded; they must be going downstairs. If only she could see who it was, or hear what they were talking about! She edged the door open a crack.

Her bedchamber was situated at the rear or north side of the mansion, with guest suites separating her from Lady Buttershaw's quarters to the left, and Lady Julia's apartments to the right. Opposite was the open well over the entrance hall, and to the right of the well the Long Gallery stretched all the way to Lady Julia's domain.

Zoe eased the door wider. It was very dark except where the outside flambeaux cast a glow through the windows of the Long Gallery. The guests might be standing on the steps waiting for their carriage. An efficient spy would go bravely to the gallery and open one of the windows so as to hear them talking. An efficient spy would not stand here shivering, for fear of being caught. And she had promised Peregrine she could be useful.

She gathered her courage and slipped into the silent corridor, her bare feet making no sound as she ran past the well. The air was sweetened by a whiff of scent; a spicy, alluring fragrance of the type gentlemen loved, and that had probably come from Paris and cost as much as Cook at Travisford spent on a week's groceries for the entire household . . .

Thank heavens, she had reached the window undetected! Mercifully, the catch released easily, and she began to open the casement. She gave a gasp of fright as it let out a shrill squeak. In her overwrought state the sound was ear-splitting, but luckily the lady downstairs was laughing, and the squeak appeared to have gone unnoticed.

Zoe pressed a hand to her jolting heart and leaned out. There were just two of them, standing on the steps in the glow of the flambeaux. The lady's hood concealed her features, but she did not trouble to guard her voice now, and Zoe heard her say in French, ". . . strange bedfellows, indeed! I hope I may be far away when she learns of it."

The man said in the same language, "She will be enraged. So, I think, will many others."

"And you among them, eh, my friend?"

A pause, then he answered slowly, " 'Tis far from our original intent. I sometimes think you do not welcome this new alliance any more than I."

There came the rumble of distant wheels and the lamps of a carriage bobbed along the deserted street.

The lady said, as if on a sigh, "We all have our loyalties, do we not? One does what one must do. Almost the trap it is ready to close. All will be over very quickly, I think, and—"

"And the Squire will launch his—"

"What are you about, may I ask?"

That harsh autocratic voice sent Zoe's heart leaping up behind her front teeth and for an instant she was as if frozen with terror. Wheeling around, her knees were so weak she had to lean back against the window for support.

Lady Buttershaw came marching along the corridor, holding a lamp high.

Zoe felt sick. She tried to answer, but her tongue seemed nailed to the roof of her mouth. And then she heard Lady Julia say, "I thought I heard something."

Dazzled perhaps by the light from her lamp, Lady Buttershaw was addressing her sister, who approached from the other end of the corridor. Zoe was overcome by relief. She had not been seen after all! 'But I will be at any second!' she realized. She looked about in desperation, but this time there was no convenient sideboard to shield her. A large chest between the next two windows was at least ten feet distant, and even if she managed to run so far without the movement being noticed, should either lady bring a lamp into the gallery she would certainly be seen!

Her fingers, wet with perspiration, touched the draperies beside her. Heavy draperies; tied back with silken ropes. If she untied one, it would be remarked. But she was quite small. Perhaps . . . She knelt and dove under the bottom half of the drapery, gathering her dressing gown tight, and trying to make herself as inconspicuous as possible.

"Of course you heard something," said Lady Buttershaw tartly. "My guests are departing."

"Do your guests cause that curtain to click on its rod?"

Peeping out of the narrow space between the drapery and the wall, Zoe saw the light brightening. To her horror it shone on the wet imprint of a small hand below the window-sill. She thought, 'I am going to be sick . . . !'

Large feet were advancing. Lady Buttershaw boomed. "Only look at this!" Zoe's eyes began to blur and she waited with growing faintness to be discovered.

A bony hand shot out.

Zoe's heart seemed to stop beating.

"Confound it," snarled Lady Buttershaw. "That fool of a butler has left the casement unlocked! Small wonder the drapery was rattling. There is an icy blast coming in here! Damme, *why* is it so curst difficult to find reliable servants nowadays? We might all have been murdered in our beds!"

The casement was pulled shut and the lock slammed down.

Lady Julia said, "I scarce think that likely, Clara, since this window is upstairs and so close to the flambeaux. Still, you are right. Arbour must be taken to task."

"He *shall* be! I'll ring for the bird brain this very instant! He deserves to be rousted out of his bed!"

"No doubt, but not at this present, if you please. I want to have a word with you about Jean . . ."

The sisters walked away, their voices and the lamplight fading.

It seemed an eternity before a door closed.

Zoe tottered back to her room, fell onto the bed and wept. This spy business was intended for stronger spirits than hers! She had never been so frightened in her life! At least, when she had been almost caught before, she'd been holding Boadicea, and had a perfectly logical reason for being downstairs. If she had been found this time, whatever reason could she have given for lurking about under the drapery? What would Lady Buttershaw have done to her? Her only hope must have been that Lady Julia would not allow her throat to have been cut on the spot!

She blew her nose and thought disgustedly, 'Oh, *why* do I have to be such a coward?' But coward or no, she had learned *something*, so perhaps even a cowardly spy was better than no spy at all!

CHAPTER XIV

hile not as fashionable as White's, or Brookse's, or the Cocoa Tree, the Madrigal suited Sir Owen Furlong. It was conveniently near to his little house in Bond Street, the rooms were very clean, the play not too steep, and the food excellent. If the cream of the Top Ten Thousand disdained it, some of London's leading writers, wits, and artists did not, and it was beginning to acquire a reputation for fine dining and stimulating conversation.

Furlong had spent the morning at East India House in a fruitless attempt to see Lord Hayes or Lieutenant Skye. He returned to the Madrigal at noon, to find Cranford waiting for him in a quiet ante room, his expression such that Furlong chose his words with care.

Ignoring an enquiry as to whether he'd seen Morris today, Cranford growled that it was not necessary to "tittup about" and that if Sir Owen thought the bruise on his temple was colourful, he should blasted well see the one on his hip. "More to the point," he went on before his friend could respond, "have you seen *her?*"

Without evasion Furlong answered, "Today? No. Miss Benevento intended to walk with her this morning, I believe. Though in this beast of a wind, I doubt—"

"Oh, that won't stop Miss Zoe," snorted Cranford bitterly. "The silly chit has not the sense to keep out of the rain, yet thinks herself capable of playing Heroic Spy for us and outwitting the Buttershaw! Damme, but I *could* not make her understand she must leave that accursed house!"

Furlong said gently, "I am very sure she did not mean—"

"Have done! I let a slip of a girl best me. No need to wrap it in clean linen. Half London witnessed the fiasco, I dare swear, for which I've no one to blame but myself." Cranford glared at the window until Furlong wondered the glass did not crack, then declared with a sort of rough desperation, "I wanted no part of her from the start! You'll recollect that."

"Oh, yes, indeed. You said she was a—er, repulsive screecher, as I—"

"The devil I did! As if I—" He checked. It seemed to Furlong that he winced, and his voice broke. "Well, and I was a fool," he continued huskily. "But . . . Oh, dash it all, Owen! Why must females be so . . . so . . ."

"So—female?" Touched by the despair in his friend's face, Furlong said, "Heaven knows, Perry. I do not. Never have been able to understand the pretty creatures."

Cranford sighed, and Furlong said, "I think you have become—"

Morris flung the door open, exclaiming, "Run you to earth at last, Owen! You'll not believe what—" Catching sight of Cranford, he halted, and gasped, "Perry! My poor fellow!" He grinned broadly. "Are you much hurt?"

"Why should I be hurt?" said Cranford, glaring at him.

"Heard a lady tried to push you into the Thames and that you took a proper header." Morris chuckled. "Bertie Crisp said—"

Cranford, who cried friends with the popular young marquis, growled, "I might have known 'twould be that corkbrained thimble-wit! I collect Bertie was rowing with the

Thames watermen again, and could not wait to spread his gossip all over Town!"

"Well, of course." Unaware of Furlong's frantic gestures, Morris blundered on merrily, "Whatever would you expect? You old rascal! If anyone had told me you were the kind to cavort with some pretty wench in the clear light of day, I'd—"

He recoiled with a gasp as Cranford sprang up to seize him by the cravat and snarl into his shocked face, "She is not a *wench*, damn your eyes!"

Morris tried to free himself, and stammered, "I'm—ah, very sorry. But—but I thought—"

"You haven't thought in years!" Cranford released him with a jerk, picked up his cane, and limped to the door. "Make mock of me if it entertains you. But, I warn you, leave the lady out of it!"

"No—Perry, wait! I don't even know who—"

Cranford wrenched the door open and said savagely, "I begin to think August Falcon is right about you, Morris! Be damned if I don't!" The door slammed behind him.

"Jove!" said Morris glumly. "I properly put m'foot in m'mouth, didn't I?"

"Both feet," confirmed Furlong.

"Then, I take it the lady in question was Miss Grainger. Has Perry lost his wits? He's no rake! And even a rake would know better than to kiss a lady in public."

"True," said Furlong. "I rather suspect he became exasperated. He's not the most placid fellow I ever met, and—well, he was trying to persuade her to go away from Yerville Hall, only she has it in her mind that she can be of help to us by staying there. Which," he added thoughtfully, "she can indeed."

"Dashed plucky of her," said Morris. "But 'twould be a chancy business. Small wonder Perry don't want her to—"

The door opened. Cranford put his head around it and said

shamefacedly, "My apologies, Jamie. My curst stupid temper. The truth is, I'm furious with myself—not with you. May I please be forgiven?"

Morris was the last man to hold a grudge; hands were wrung, backs pounded, apologies accepted, and wine ordered. They gathered comfortably around the hearth, and Cranford told these two good friends exactly what had transpired on the riverbank. He did not spare himself, and when he finished, Morris said kindly, "Poor fellow. I am so sorry. Gad, but we have troubles with our *affaires de coeur!* Even if she should decide she wanted to, Falcon won't let his sister marry *me;* he don't have the sense to know where *his* heart lies; and your lady has refused *you!* Furlong's the only one whose romance prospers, dashed if he ain't!"

Sir Owen grinned. "Ah, but perhaps 'tis just that I've not yet flown my colours. You may be very sure I don't mean to rush the lady."

"I didn't rush Miss Zoe," said Cranford indignantly. "I've known her for two weeks! I doubt my parents met more than once, and that well chaperoned, before they stood at the altar together!"

"Different nowadays, dear boy," Morris pointed out. "Ladies like to be pursued. I fancy Miss Grainger thought you didn't mean it."

"Didn't *mean* it?" spluttered Cranford. "Why the deuce would I—"

"She's likely heard the talk," explained Morris reasonably. "Everyone knows you were mad for the Laxton. And then to kiss Miss Grainger out of doors and in a public place!" He pursed his lips. "Not respectful, Perry. I'll wager she thought it wasn't marriage you had in mind."

Cranford rose out of his chair with a roar of wrath.

Furlong, who had fought laughter through this exchange, intervened hurriedly. "No, no! Come down out of the boughs,

Perry! Jamie's as tactful as any crocodile, but he may have a point, you know. And we've other matters to consider."

Cranford glowered at him, then drove a hand through his hair and sat down again, muttering, "Lord! What a fool I am! You're right, of course. The important thing is that the lady be protected from her sweet self. I did not call on her yesterday. Want her to have time to forgive me. But I daren't leave it much longer!" A hunted look came into his eyes. "When I think of the little soul in that great grim house, with that awful woman . . . !"

Furlong said, "We can check on her through Miss Benevento, praise heaven. And Tummet is watching the house. If we—"

A knock at the door interrupted him, and Florian came in to give Cranford a letter. "It was brought round from Sir Owen's house on Bond Street, sir," he said in his mellow voice. "I thought it might be important."

Cranford thanked him, and as he bowed and left them, handed the letter to Furlong. "Looks like your brother's awful scrawl."

Furlong broke the seal, read eagerly for a few seconds, then exclaimed, "Damn that fool! Derek sent this to Town by special messenger, and Gideon's new man has let it sit for two days! The *Lady Aranmore* is safe anchored in Bristol Harbour, I thank God!"

"Hooray!" cried Morris leaping up in his excitement.

Cranford stood also and asked anxiously, "Does he mention young Grainger—or whatever he's calling himself?"

Furlong read on, and answered, "Yes, by George! Here it is! 'Mr. *Grant*, the mystery passenger I told you of, has—' (Oh, Gad!) 'has disappeared!' " Morris gave a groan, Cranford swore, and Furlong read on, " 'I saw him rolling on . . .' (somebody's) 'neck?' (Confound Derek! That can't be right! Why did he never learn how to form his letters properly?) 'I saw him . . .' (Ah!) '*strolling* on the *quarter-deck* the night before we expected to make port. We were delayed for thirty-six hours by a heavy fog that obliged us to ride at anchor outside the harbour. During that time, Mr. Grant disappeared. As you know he had offered . . .' (no!) '*suffered* a severe illness and was not fully recovered. I fear he must have become faint and fallen overboard. Now I am further delayed by a great many' (something) 'idiots demanding to know what happened to the poor fellow.'" Sir Owen paused and glanced at Cranford's stern face. "He may have decided to swim for it, you know, fearing what might await him when they docked."

"True." Cranford threw on his cloak. "But it would be a taxing swim for a sick man. Does Derek say anything more?"

Furlong ran his eyes swiftly down the page. "Not about Grainger—or Grant."

Morris said gloomily, "Likely he was knifed and tossed overboard."

Watching Cranford limp to the door, Furlong called, "Do you go to warn Miss Grainger?"

"Of course."

"Then carry a pistol with you. And keep in mind that Tummet will be in the Square garden. He's a good man in a brawl."

Cranford scarcely heard him. All he could think of was that he must get to Zoe. He prayed she would not refuse to see him.

It rained steadily throughout the night, but although Zoe was awake, she scarcely heard it. Her mind was so full of conjectures and anxieties that sleep was out of the question, and not until the early morning did she doze off at last. Gorton brought in her breakfast at eight o'clock and drew back the window curtains on a blustery grey morning. The rain had stopped, but the sky was leaden, and a stiff wind snatched leaves from the trees and chased them into a colourful Autumn scamper across the sodden lawn.

Gorton looked surprised when Zoe told her that she meant to take Cromwell to the park today, but she said nothing. Zoe found covert glances coming her way, and realized she must look as heavy-eyed as she felt. She exerted herself to be cheerful, and evidently succeeded, as Gorton was soon chatting easily.

There was, she said, a great to-do. Lady Buttershaw had left a note for her maid commanding that Mr. Arbour wait upon her at ten o'clock, precisely. "The time," said Gorton, lowering her voice and looking solemn, "was *underlined* and followed by two exclamation points. A sure sign that my lady was vexed. And poor Mr. Arbour like to suffer a nervous spasm, wondering whatever he's done to offend."

Zoe felt a twinge of guilt. If the butler lost his situation, it would be her fault, but how to remedy the matter she could not think. For the moment her most urgent need was to find Maria and relay to Sir Owen (or Peregrine) the conversation she'd heard last night.

Coachman Cecil suggested politely that Miss Zoe might consider taking the dog for his walk along the Thames today. After the heavy rains, the park, he said, would likely be "a mucky set-out." He adored Zoe, and when she proved adamant he voiced no more objections. Once they reached the park, however, it was very clear that his warning had been justified. Most of the pathways had become long puddles, and the grassy areas more closely resembled a bog. There were no strollers to be seen, and no sign of Maria's neat coach. Zoe alighted at the corner of Great George Street, and she and Gorton walked as far as Horse Guards Parade, but the wind was biting. Cromwell investigated railings and areaway steps with his usual verve, but Zoe saw that Gorton was shivering and clutching her thin cloak tightly about her. Seething with frustration, she realized there was nothing for it but to turn back. She kept a hopeful eye on the traffic, but to no avail. At the corner, a frigid blast met them, and she was almost as pleased as Gorton when Coachman Cecil came up and guided the team into the kennel beside them.

On the return journey, Zoe continued to scan the passing traffic, but when they approached Yerville Hall she had to admit it was hopeless, and her heart sank.

Gorton, who had been watching her in growing anxiety, said, "Ay do hope your letter has not brought bad news, ma'am?"

"Letter?" Zoe asked sharply, "What letter?"

"Whay, the one what come for you Saturday. Ay saw you reading it at your desk, and Ay thought—"

"That was a letter *I* was writing!" Agitated, Zoe said, "Elsie, are you very sure there was a letter brought for me?"

Beginning to be frightened, Gorton nodded, "Yes, Miss Zoe. Ay chanced to be fetching your kid shoes with the red ribbons—they were so muddied after you went in the boat with Mr. Cranford that Ay had left them in the kitchen to dry. The underfootman carried in the second post, and he put it on the table for a minute because Chef had cut up some stale cake and we was all give a bit. And the scullery maid—a proper widgeon she is—knocked the post over. So we all helped pick it up, and Ay saw it distinct. Your name it said, not no mistaking!"

"Did you chance to see how much had been paid? Was it more than a penny?"

"It was marked plain, Miss. One penny."

That meant London. Who in Town would be writing to her? It couldn't be Travis—no, surely it could not! She asked, "What like was the writing?"

"Oh, very fine, Miss. And a flourish to the letter *Z*, as I never— Oh, Miss! Whatever is it? Did not you get your letter?"

'A flourish to the letter Z . . .' Travis had always written her name with that teasing deviation from his beautiful copperplate. Then he was *home*! He was in Town, and had written to her, and his letter had been withheld. She felt dazed, and heard herself telling Gorton that she was all right.

"That you're not, Miss," said Gorton anxiously. "So white as any sheet is what you are. If 'tis because of your letter, Ay shall go direct to Mr. Arbour, and ask him for—"

"No! You must not! Here we are, thank heaven! Perchance Lady Buttershaw had not time to sort the mail, and now my letter is waiting upstairs."

The house was gloomy and dark, and resounded with the voice of Lady Buttershaw, who surged across the entrance hall in full cry, surrounded by her little crowd of sycophants.

Upon catching sight of Zoe, she bellowed redundantly, "So there you are! 'Tis a good thing you are come home. The streets are more unsafe daily! *Hourly!* You will do well to keep indoors for the rest of the day!"

As if to emphasize her remarks, she flung the hood of her cloak over her head with a dramatic sweep. Unhappily, her vigour dislodged her wig, which settled down over her eyes, blinding her. When the pandemonium died down she seemed to have forgotten her own advice, and the small and vociferous party went out into the unsafe streets with no evidence of trepidation.

Zoe proceeded up the stairs, and Gorton murmured, "You could have asked her la'ship about your letter, Miss."

Zoe shook her head, and all but ran to her bedchamber. There was a folded paper on the mantelpiece. With a sigh of relief, she flew to take it up, but her heart sank. It was a note from Lady Julia's footman, Whipley, to the effect that her ladyship was gone out with friends and would not need Miss

Grainger until this evening. Exasperated, Zoe tossed the note aside and paced restlessly to the window.

She was only dimly aware of the lowering clouds, or how the wind whipped the branches of the trees about, for her thoughts were turned inward. Any lingering doubts she may have held were gone now. Peregrine was absolutely right. There really *was* a League of Jewelled Men; they really *were* hunting her beloved brother. And, incredible as it seemed, Lady Buttershaw *was* a member of the League! She had opened and read Papa's letter, and now she had kept another letter, which had almost certainly been written by Travis.

Gorton, who had made a quick search of the bed, the chest of drawers, and the little secretary in the corner, said worriedly that the letter was not to be found.

"Of course 'tis not," said Zoe. "I am not meant to have it."

Gorton gripped her hands together and said she could not believe that. "Whay ever would may lady keep your letters from you, Miss Zoe? Her la'ship is not kind, if Aye dare remark it, but she was properly bred up and is Quality. She would not do anything so low!"

An implacable anger was burning in Zoe's heart. "She is gone out. And Lady Julia is out as well." She looked steadily at her nervous abigail. "I mean to have my letter, Elsie."

"Well, er, yes, of course, Miss. When may lady comes home—"

"Now," said Zoe, starting to the door.

With a yelp of alarm, Gorton flew to stand before it. "But Hackman cannot give it to you, Miss! Not even if he wanted, which he don't if Ay know *him*! And Lady Buttershaw's woman is so sour as any lemon and wouldn't lift a hand to help, not if you begged her!"

"I do not mean to beg anybody. Or to ask anybody. 'Tis my letter! I will have it!" There was stark horror on Gorton's paling countenance and Zoe added earnestly, "Elsie, there is something very wicked going on in this house. I cannot tell you all of it. I can only say that my dear brother's very life may depend on my reading that letter, and—I mean to do so!"

"Oh, *Miss*," wailed Gorton. "How *can* you?"

"Does her ladyship lock the door to her room?"

"No, of course not! But—"

"Then what is to prevent me from going down there and walking in?"

"Oh . . . *Miss*! Oh, my dear departed granny! Oh, help!"

Zoe reached for the door handle.

Really frightened, Gorton caught her arm and cried imploringly, "Do *not*, Miss Zoe! They won't allow it! Hackham will stop you. Or Whipley or—or one of the lackeys. Miss— you *dare* not! *Nobody* goes to Lady Buttershaw's apartments 'less they're summoned. *Nobody!*"

Zoe was afraid also, but she said, "I know, but I must! From what I have seen of Hackham and Whipley, they're not the kind to tend to their duties when there's a chance of avoiding them. With both their ladyships gone out, they're likely down in the kitchen this very minute, badgering Chef to open a bottle and slice some cake for them! Will there be other maids, Elsie? What of her dresser?"

"Lady Buttershaw sent her to Sundial Abbey to fetch some winter cloaks. She'll be away another day, at least. But—but her *woman*, Miss! Such a prune-faced creature is Truscott, and has never said a kind word to me in all the years I've worked here."

In her agitation, Gorton had neglected to employ her careful accent, and Zoe said, "You really are worried for my sake. Thank you, dear Elsie. Please, won't you help me? If you could just go down to Lady Buttershaw's suite and knock on the door and ask Truscott—"

Gorton gave a little shriek and shrank away. "Oh, *lor'*! Oh, I couldn't! Not *never*, Miss! Oh, I'd—I'd swoon away afore I even *got* to the door. Never been near it, I hasn't!"

She looked ready to swoon at the very thought of taking such a terrible step. Zoe, who well knew the power of fear, said gently, "No, I understand. Then do you think you could instead keep watch and come and tell me at once if Truscott goes out? You could do that for me, couldn't you?"

Trembling, but very conscious of the fact that this pretty young lady had been most kind to her and to Cecil, Gorton nodded convulsively and made her shaken way down the stairs to keep watch.

Thus it was that only a quarter of an hour later, Zoe was advised the coast was clear. Her pulses quickened as she slipped into the corridor. It was chilly and dim, and she walked along rapidly. Unlike Lady Julia's wing, there were no doors blocking off Lady Buttershaw's apartments. Probably, thought Zoe, because the woman inspired such terror in the staff that they would not dare come near her domain.

Only when she passed the last of the guest suites did it occur to her that she had no idea which of the remaining doors opened into my lady's study, or bedchamber, where she thought it most likely that the missing letter might be found.

The first door seemed to loom up and tower over her. She bit her lip nervously, raised a hand and knocked. Silence. She knocked again, then opened the door. She looked into a room that made her blink. It was evidently reserved for my lady's toilette and was rather astonishingly garish. The walls were hung with a silk print of purple and gold fans, the velvet draperies at the windows were scarlet, two white chests were gilt trimmed. There was a chaise longue covered in deep pink velvet, and in the centre of the room stood a large hip bath, a fine cheval-glass beside it. "My goodness!" murmured Zoe, and hurried across the corridor.

On this side she discovered a room that had the air of an audience chamber; certainly not the type of chamber she sought. The next two doors opened into a green saloon that was almost a shrine. The air had a musty smell, the walls were hung with ancient tapestries, family portraits, and historical memorabilia. There were stands containing armoured figures; many weapons of bygone centuries hung in racks or were mounted in glass cases. And the whole was so reminiscent of Lady Buttershaw, that Zoe shivered and closed the door hurriedly, her nerves tightening because this desperate expedition was taking so much time.

She recrossed the corridor, and stepped into a large and luxurious bedchamber. Once more, the decor seemed voluptuous and out of character: the curtains on the enormous canopied bed were of naughtily sheer purple silk with gold tassels, and the window draperies were a rich purple velvet. A large portrait hung on the wall beside the bed. She gave it a cursory glance. The gentleman was not above thirty, she judged, and despite an air of pride and cynicism, was extraordinarily handsome, with finely chiselled features and hair of jet black. The eyes were deep-set and thickly lashed but of a slightly alien shape, like none she had ever seen. Hurrying to the dressing table, she had a brief thought that he was the last type of man she would have expected Lord Buttershaw to be, and then forgot about him. There were no letters on the dressing table, nor did the three chests of drawers yield anything of interest. With a nervous moan, she sped back into the corridor.

A parlour came next, over-furnished and over-heated, with a well-banked fire burning under a ponderous chimney-piece despite the absence of the owner. One swift glance convinced her to move on. And, at last, she entered a spacious combination book room and study. Her hands were by now damp and her heartbeat erratic. She ran to the large and beautifully wrought desk before the windows. There were several letters lying there, but the one she sought seemed to leap at her.

"Thank heaven!" she whispered, and snatched it up.

Travis' writing was a little less neat than usual, but he had been ill, which would explain that. She moved to the windows and read the cramped and crossed lines eagerly:

My *dearest sister*,

By the grace of God I am back in England, but under circumstances that forbid me to present myself to my father. I must tell you that I was sent home following a long illness. En route, I came into possession of a document of great significance. It is an extreme treasonable Agreement, Zoe, between several highly born British aristocrats, and some powerful gentlemen of France, led by Marshal Jean-Jacques Barthélemy, of whom I am very sure you have heard.

I am sworn to deliver this paper to the Horse Guards. However, you may guess that heads will roll should I succeed, and several attempts have been made to stop me. I have been obliged to hide myself, but I fear I may be discovered at any time. If I attempt to get to Travisford or to Whitehall, I am very sure to be intercepted. I hired a fellow who seems to be honest, and sent him down to try and speak with you at home. He was chased off by my father's new bride, but luckily met dear old Bleckert, who told him where you are now staying. (I shall be interested to know why you are no longer in residence at Travisford!)

It is a piece of luck for me that you are in Town, however, where I can visit you, hopefully with less chance of putting you in danger. There are many men I could ask for the help I very badly need, but this plot appears so widespread that I dare not confide in anyone save you, dear Zoe, or Peregrine Cranford, whose integrity I would trust with my life.

I mean to rest here for a day or two. Then, if all goes

well, I shall call on you. In the event this is not suitable, know that I am staying at the little inn Mama told us of. Do you recall? The place with the waiter who was so amusing. Oh, and I am at present using the name of the music master you fell in love with when you were ten . . . I feel sure you cannot have forgot *him*!

My deepest apologies for greeting you with such trying news. Pray discuss it with *no one*. You cannot guess how I long to see you, little sister. And I see that I have been too wrapped up in myself to enquire as to your health. I trust it is good and that you will forgive

Your loving brother,
Travis

Zoe stared down at the paper in her hands, her eyes wide and unblinking. They knew now that he was in England. But, thank heaven, his name and whereabouts could be known only to herself, and so— She must not stay here! She started to the door with the letter, then paused. If she took it, Lady Buttershaw might guess she had dared to come and appropriate it, and she would be warned. No. It was better to leave it here. The important thing was that now she knew where to reach Travis. She must do so at once!

The corridor seemed darker than ever, and a few downstairs candles had been lit, throwing a soft glow on the walls. Running lightly towards her room, she heard a man say, "I allus thought th' old crow was touched in the upper works, but I didn't think she was that far took! She could give him twenty year, at least."

Zoe stopped abruptly. It must be two of the footmen! They were coming up the stairs, and she was too far from her own room to reach it before they would turn at the first landing! Once again, she must hide. To her left was the big musty room with all the historical paraphernalia. The two men might logically be going in there. Desperate, she plunged into the room on her right, and knew she would be safe for the moment. They certainly would not come into Lady Buttershaw's bedchamber.

A voice she recognized as that of Hackham, her ladyship's personal footman, sneered, "Lots of rich old hags buys themselves pretty boys, mate."

"Aye, but not *that* pretty boy! She's gone off her tibby, proper. Unless you're bamming me."

It sounded as if they had stopped just outside! Zoe's heart convulsed as the door latch lifted. 'Dear God!' she thought, panicked. 'They *are* coming in here!'

She was so frightened that she turned completely around, searching for a refuge. Her wide paniers would prevent her from climbing into one of the three large presses, or slipping under the bed. Then she saw another door at the side of the room. A dressing room, perchance, or the abigail's room. Running to it, her heart in her mouth, she heard Hackham say threateningly, "I'll prove it, all right. But—you *ever* tell I let you in here, it'll be the worse for you, my cove!"

The door started to open. Zoe rushed through the inner door, and had time only to draw it partially closed.

She was in a small dark room.

And several people sat there, watching her!

Her heart stood still. As from a great distance she heard the two footmen laughing softly but hilariously. In this room nobody spoke. Hardly able to breathe, she reached out to steady herself against a chest, only to discern another face nodding at her from atop it. A featureless face. She thought, 'Thank goodness! They are only wigs on head stands!' The relief was so intense that she had a sudden need to laugh . . . To shriek with laughter . . . Or to burst into tears. Her knees gave out under her and she sank down, pressing both hands over her mouth, lest hysteria overcome her.

Through the slightly open door she caught a glimpse of the

other man. Whipley. Lady Julia's personal footman. Hackham was telling him not to make so much noise.

Whipley gulped, "I never woulda believed it! Right by her bed, too! Can't you just see the old bag, lying there, eating her heart out for the 'breed'? And him not worth a decent English-man wiping his boots on! Cor! Can't help laughing, can yer? If ever I see such a sorry set-to!"

Hackham said, "Well, you've seen one now. And that's sixpence you owe me!"

"It was worth it, mate! Come on down to my room, and I'll pay up!"

"Careful! You moved that eiderdown. Tidy it up, quick! She's got eyes like a cat, and if she ever thought I'd been in here—Gawd help us all!"

A rustle was followed by some whispering and the cautious opening of the outer door.

They were gone.

As soon as her rubbery knees would support her, Zoe followed. She could hear the housekeeper's voice as she passed the stairs, and her blood ran cold as a familiar bellow assailed her ears. Lady Buttershaw had returned! She flew along the corridor to her room, horrified to realize how narrow an escape she'd had.

Her bedroom door opened and Gorton's head peeped out. Zoe rushed to her, and suddenly was in her arms, weeping.

"Oh . . . Miss!" quavered Gorton, weeping also. "I were that scared! When Hackham and that horrid Whipley went past I was sure . . . as sure you'd be caught. Oh, Miss! You're so *brave*!"

"Brave!" Zoe groped for her handkerchief and wiped her eyes furiously. "Only see how brave I am! Snivelling and shaking like any leaf, when I should be strong and—and leaving this beastly place!"

Her face a study in distress, Gorton cried, "*Leaving*? You—

you don't never mean for good and all, Miss Zoe? Say you don't!"

"I must." Zoe ran to snatch a warm cloak from the press. "I cannot explain now, Elsie, but at all costs I must keep my brother from . . ."

Her words died away. The letter had come on Saturday, and this was Monday. Travis had written that he would call 'in a day or two'! What if he should come even while she was on her way to him? There was a strong family resemblance. He was sure to be recognized, even if he gave his assumed name. Chilled, she thought, 'Heaven help the dear soul if they ever get their hands on him!' No, she could not leave. But somehow she must warn him.

Gorton asked hopefully, "Has you changed your mind, Miss?"

"Yes." Zoe handed her the cloak. "But I must get a message to my brother. If I wrote a letter, could you take it to— Oh, no. That will not do. Whipley would likely follow you!" She began to pace up and down, wringing her hands, and trying to think. If only Peregrine would come . . . or if she could just get word to Maria . . . Of course! Maria could go to Sir Owen, who would tell Peregrine and all would be well! She said, "Give me my cloak, Elsie, and put on your own. We're going out for a walk!"

Downstairs, a lackey sat on a stool in the alcove by the front doors. He was engrossed in picking at his cuticles, but he sprang up as Zoe hurried across the hall, and bowed respectfully. "Very nasty out there, Miss Grainger," he offered.

It was unprecedented behaviour, and Zoe's strained nerves grew tighter. She said coolly, "Indeed? I feel the need of some fresh air, even so. Be so good as to open the door."

Instead of obeying, he moved to block the way. "The streets is most unsafe," he said, "and her la'ship asked partic'ler that you stay indoors this afternoon. If you please."

"I do not please," said Zoe, trying to look haughty. "Now, stand aside at once!"

"I am indeed sorry, Miss Grainger," said Arbour, coming across the hall at his stately pace, "but Lady Buttershaw left strict orders that you should not venture out. There have been more street riots, you see, and . . ." He shrugged apologetically.

"Are you saying I am *forbidden* to go out for a walk?" demanded Zoe. "Lady Julia said nothing of the kind to me."

Arbour looked pained, and murmured that Lady Yerville would return shortly, and he would be only too glad to abide by her instructions.

Zoe stared at him. He was clearly not a happy man, probably living in dread of being turned off because he had left the casement open last night. It would be more than he dared do to contravene Lady Buttershaw's instructions.

"Perhaps," he suggested, "Miss would care to walk in the back garden?"

"Miss" had no time to waste on back gardens, for already another scheme was forming in her mind. She told Arbour coldly that she would wait until Lady Yerville returned, and went back up the stairs once more.

In her bedchamber, she threw her cloak aside and hurried to the desk.

Gorton said in a failing voice, "They don't mean to let you go out, Miss Zoe! Oh, how dreadful it is! Whatever does it all mean?"

Zoe snatched up a quill pen and pulled out a sheet of writing paper. "Elsie, if I write a note to my brother, is there someone you could pay to deliver it?"

Receiving no answer, she turned in the chair. Gorton, very pale, stood staring at her wide-eyed over hands that were clasped to her mouth. Zoe put down the pen and went to hug the woman. "My poor friend, I know how much I ask of you.

But, I swear, Elsie, *truly* this is a matter of life and death!"

Gorton wet her lips and croaked, "If—if I get caught, Miss . . . I'll be turned off without a character—surely! I—I'll starve!"

It was a grim, and very possible result. Zoe said earnestly, "If you get caught you can always say that you were only obeying me. And—and that it was not your place to refuse my orders. But—oh, Elsie, I promise you faithfully, when I leave this horrid house, I will take you with—" She did not finish the sentence.

From nearby there came a familiar howl.

Gorton gave a squeal of fright.

Zoe felt the blood draining from her cheeks.

Had Lady Buttershaw given orders that Miss Grainger was not to go out because she had questions to ask Miss Grainger? Did my lady mean to demand that she be told where Travis Grainger might be found? And if—as she must—she refused to give that information . . . What would they do to her?

She heard again Peregrine Cranford's dear angry voice '. . . a dainty, timid little flower, setting herself up in opposition to a fire-breathing dragon . . .'

She was not a dainty little flower. And she was a good deal more than timid; she was a rank coward. Her attempt to be a spy had been a nightmare, and she had seemed to spend most of her time shaking in her shoes and ready to faint from fright. The prospect of the terrifying Lady Buttershaw shouting at her, bullying her, perhaps, heaven forbid, beating her, made her eyes grow dim and her breath come in shallow little gasps.

There came a brisk heavy tread in the passage outside. A hand was lifting the latch of the door.

Gorton leapt to her feet and rushed to open the press and fumble among the gowns, whispering, "Oh, gawd! Oh, gawd help us!"

It was a prayer Zoe echoed.

Chapter XV

o doubt you misunderstood," said Cranford, holding open the door that the footman attempted to close. "I wish to see Miss Grainger. Did you give her my card?"

"As I said before, sir," responded the footman, his stiff demeanour reflecting disapproval of such ill-mannered behaviour, "Miss Grainger is—not—at—home."

"Which covers a multitude of sins. Do you mean she is not at home to Mr. Cranford? Or do you mean she is gone out? No, do not try and push me away, else I'll forget my manners!"

He looked quite capable of it, thought the footman. You had to be careful of gents with that particular glitter in their eyes. Smit, was this Cranford cove, and when a gent was smit, there was no telling what he might do. In an attempt to soften the rejection, he lied, "Miss Grainger is gone out, sir."

"I'll wait."

To the footman's great relief, a rescue party in the form of Mr. Arbour and a lackey advanced ponderously across the entrance hall. "I do not expect their ladyships until very late tonight, Mr. Cranford," said the butler. "However, an you would care to leave a message . . . ?"

Cranford looked grimly from one to the other. Realizing that Zoe might not wish to receive him, he had scrawled a hurried "Miss Grainger—I have some news for you!" on the back of his calling card. He'd been left to cool his heels on the doorstep until the footman had returned to deny Miss Grainger and make it clear that he was expected to leave at once. He knew that however much Zoe might despise him, she would be eager to learn if his "news" concerned Travis. The unlikeliness of her having refused to see him took on an ominous significance. He was sure that both these fellows were lying, but he could not very well demand to be allowed to wait until "very late tonight." He therefore declared an intention to return in the morning, and walked out into the rain.

Crossing the street, he stood with his back to the enclosed gardens and looked up at the mansion. Undoubtedly, he was being watched, and without turning his head, he said softly, "Tummet . . . ? Are you about?"

A rustle of leaves and Tummet's growl, "Abaht to take root, Mr. Cranford! Is the cats-a'purring?"

"I collect that refers to rats stirring, rather than felines purring, in which case I fear they may be. Tell me quickly. Did any of the ladies leave the house today?"

"Both the lady nobs done. Yussir."

"Was Miss Grainger with them? Be quite sure, now."

"That she were not! Lay me life to it, I would, mate. The two la'ships went out a hour or so back. One come home."

"Came home? Which one? When?"

"The one what's mad fer me guv'nor. Lady Buttershaw. 'Bout ten minutes ago."

Cranford's jaw set. "In that case, I want you to go at once and find something for me."

"Can't do that, mate. Me orders is to keep watch, and—"

"I am countermanding your orders. Besides, if I know you, Tummet, you'll be able to do what I ask with no difficulty, and be back here in jig time."

The man whom August Falcon referred to as his "pseudo valet" had known many occupations in his eventful life, and few things had the power to surprise him, but when he learned what he was expected to produce, he said an alarmed, "Strike a perishin' light! You never mean it, Lieutenant, mate! You couldn't never—"

"Probably not. But you could. Now I'll tell you where to put it until we're ready. Oh, *do* stop arguing, man, and pay heed!"

A lackey flung open the door to Zoe's bedchamber, and Lady Buttershaw stamped in, reticule on her wrist and her eyes narrowed.

Zoe stood, and waited with wobbly knees, and her breath fluttering.

"I am informed that you were annoyed because I thought it best that you not go out," bellowed her ladyship. "So you sit and sulk, do you? And are pale besides! Pretty behaviour! I will tell you that pallor and pouts are most unattractive qualities in a maiden. You may be grateful I had the foresight to desire you to remain at home. My friends and I encountered ruffians loitering, and the weather is inclement besides. How have you occupied yourself in my absence?"

Zoe tried to speak and had to cough to regain her voice. "I was writing a letter to my papa, ma'am."

The beady dark eyes darted to the little desk and the clean sheet of paper lying there. "You have no news to convey, I take it," said her ladyship dryly. "I have something for you, however. Can you guess what it is, I wonder?"

"I—er, no, my lady," croaked Zoe.

With the manner of a conjuror pulling a rabbit from a hat,

Lady Buttershaw drew what appeared to be Travis' letter from her reticule and waved it aloft.

Zoe tried to look excited. "Is it from my papa, ma'am?"

" 'Tis not his writing. I have a keen eye for handwriting and would most certainly have recognized it. And since 'tis improper for a gel to receive letters from Unknowns, I think—I really think I must demand to know what it contains."

Staring at her, Zoe was so astounded by such barefaced hypocrisy that she was temporarily incapable of responding.

"Ah, but you are speechless with delight." The thin smile that seldom reached her ladyship's eyes spread across her teeth. "You may open it, but I require to know at once from whom it is come."

Zoe yearned to scratch the bony hand that thrust the letter at her. It was indeed Travis' letter, very neatly re-sealed. " 'Tis from my brother, ma'am," she said, and thought, 'As you know very well, you wicked creature!'

"But how charming. Filial loyalty is always to be applauded. Very well. Enjoy it, my dear gel." And with a stern admonition to Gorton that Miss Grainger's gown looked as if she had worn it while grooming the horses, Lady Buttershaw marched to the door. Gorton ran to open it, and she was gone, calling stridently for Hackham.

Zoe sank weakly onto the bed.

Gorton flew to kneel beside her. "She *give* it you, Miss!"

"Yes." Zoe broke the seal and her eyes travelled the page, half expecting it to be a re-worded forgery. But nothing was changed. She'd been so sure the woman would have insisted on knowing where Travis stayed, and why he had been so mysterious in giving his direction. Instead, not one quesiton had been asked.

Scanning her face anxiously, Gorton asked, "What is it, Miss? Has it been altered?"

"No. And I cannot understand why I was not made to explain . . ." Zoe closed her eyes as the answer came. "Oh, how can I be so dense?"

"That you're not, Miss! But I am. May I ask—what your brother has done?"

Zoe smiled at her fondly. "My faithful Elsie. He has done nothing wrong. But he has brought a—a certain letter back from India. 'Tis a letter Lady Buttershaw wants very badly. I think she would stop at nothing to get it."

Her eyes round with dismay, Gorton whispered, "No one dare go 'gainst her! If your brother writ down his direction, she's likely got that letter already!"

"He told me where he stays, yes. But in a sort of code we made up as children. I was sure Lady Buttershaw would try to force it from me. I should have known better! She has no need to know where he is now. He says in this letter that he will call on me here. All she has to do—is wait."

"Oh—*Lor*'! Then—then you still want to try and send him that note?"

Zoe nodded. "He is ill. I must help him. Elsie—*please*—if I give you the note, can you get Cecil to deliver it?"

Gorton hid her face against Zoe's knee and trembled. Stroking her shoulder, Zoe said, "As soon as I can be sure my brother has my note, we will run away to my aunt in Richmond. She is a very kind lady. I know she will take me in. Elsie, I *promise*, when I leave, you will go with me!"

Gorton blinked up at her tearfully. "C-Cecil, too?"

Surely, thought Zoe, Peregrine, or Sir Owen, or perhaps Maria, would help her to keep her word. She said firmly, "Cecil, too!"

Struggling with the straps around his leg, Cranford swore blisteringly. He had returned home to find his rooms empty and no sign of Florian, nor the note he would usually leave if he'd gone off somewhere. "Just when I most need him," he muttered, pulling the straps tighter.

He'd sent the house messenger boy off to the Madrigal, with a note for Sir Owen, but there had been no response as yet. He stood and tested the foot and was heartened to find he'd evidently adjusted it properly, for it felt quite secure. It had better be!

By the time he'd checked his pistol and slung on his sword-belt, the boy returned with word that Sir Owen had not been at the Madrigal. He'd even asked for him at White's, "But he wasn't there, neither." And, yes, he did know Mr. August Falcon. "Everybody knows *him*," he said, with the suggestion of a sneer that vanished when Cranford's cold stare turned his way. "He was riding along the Strand," he vouchsafed hurriedly, "with Mr. Fowles."

Cranford stiffened. Fowles? Why the deuce would August Falcon consort with that vicious slug? He said, "Do you mean Sir Gilbert Fowles?"

The messenger boy looked dubious. "Dunno," he said with a sniff. "The one with all the teeth, what's got his own chair, and changes the side panels and the chairmen's coats to match whatever he's wearing. Proper high-stepper, he is."

Cranford grunted, and tossed him a coin. He would wait here no longer. Nor did he propose to waste more time in scouring the Town to find his friends. He wrote a brief note to Florian, then donned cloak and tricorne and went out into the fading and wet afternoon.

Zoe sat down at her dressing table, folded her hands in her lap, and made a strong effort to compose herself. It seemed an age since Elsie had left with Travis' letter and the bribe, a florin, which would likely seem a fortune to the fireboy. He was just a scrap of a lad, Gorton had told her, but she had once saved him from a beating, and out of gratitude he sometimes risked carrying a message to her beloved.

Their whole dependence was on the boy being able to smuggle Zoe's letter to the coachman, and impress on him that the letter must be taken *at once* to Mr. Andreeni at the Inn of the Silver Cat on King William Street. Gorton had said that if her Cecil couldn't slip away himself, he'd likely entrust the letter to a link boy he knew, and with that Zoe had to be content.

It had been her intention to send her brother to Peregrine, and not until she was already writing the letter had she realized that she had not the least notion of where he lived. He had mentioned the street once, but all she could recall was that it had something to do with chickens. Sir Owen Furlong was her next choice. Peregrine had mentioned that Sir Owen had loaned his house to friends, and was at present staying at his club, but—which club? Again thwarted, she had to discard Sir Owen.

Relations, or old family friends, might be watched. There was Maria Benevento, of course. Dear Maria had offered to help, and represented the ideal solution. No one would suspect Travis to be acquainted with her, and she could at once apply to Sir Owen for help. It seemed wrong to involve her in such a dangerous enterprise, but, unable to come up with an alternative, Zoe had overcome her scruples. She had written warning her brother that under no circumstances was he to come to Yerville Hall, but instead he must go to Miss Benevento at once, as the lady was a good friend and was, furthermore, acquainted with Peregrine Cranford.

She stood and paced about restlessly. She had done all she could. Now she could only wait and pray that Travis would receive her message in time. Pausing she looked once more at the clock on the mantelpiece. Only twenty minutes past three? It seemed as if it must be at least six o'clock! She whirled around when the door opened.

Gorton hurried in with a tray. "You never had any lunch, Miss," she said.

There was no need to ask how her mission had prospered; her face was alight with triumph. Running to her, Zoe whispered, "Cecil has my letter safe?"

"Better than that, Miss. The link boy set off half an hour since. Your brother is likely reading that letter this very minute!"

Suddenly, Zoe was very tired. Closing her eyes, she breathed, "Thank God! Oh, thank God!"

"Amen to that, Miss," said Gorton devoutly. "Now, you just eat up some of this nice cold meat and fruit Ay have brought you. Ay fancied you'd rather have lemonade than milk. Are you hungry, Miss?"

"I am ravenous!" declared Zoe, and devoted herself to the sliced beef and crusty buttered bread, while Gorton bustled about, gathering washing for the laundry maid. "If Ay dare ask, Miss," she said, "what do you mean to do now?"

Zoe looked up with the bright sparkle restored to her eyes. "I must wait until I am certain my brother has my letter. And then, dear Elsie, tonight, with luck, we shall be off to Richmond-on-Thames! We must drink to our success! Or we would," she amended, "if you had a glass!"

Gorton brought the water glass from the bedside table, and they poured half the lemonade into it and toasted each other merrily. Returning to her belated luncheon, Zoe exclaimed, "Oh, if you knew how relieved I feel! My brother is home at last, and Mr. Cranford must be pleased with me when he finds out Travis is safe at Miss Benevento's house."

Gorton finished her lemonade and asked curiously, "Is that where you sent him, then?"

"Yes. The lady has been such a good friend to me, Elsie. So kind. And so beautiful, do not you think?"

"Oh, I do." Gorton smothered a yawn, and apologized. "One of the two loveliest ladies in all London Town. Though I never thought I'd say that of two foreigners, Miss Zoe, least of all, a Frenchy."

"Do you mean Miss Katrina Falcon? I hear she is judged the leading Toast, but I'd understood she has only some Chinese ancestry."

"That's right, Miss. And a very nice lady, in spite of what people say." Gorton giggled. "Lady Buttershaw, you know, is mad for her brother."

"Yes, I know. But you are mistaken, Elsie. Miss Benevento is Italian, not French."

"Is that a fact? So that's why her name is different. I fancied 'twas just that gentlemen's names change when they inherit titles, you know. Do you suppose 'twas a second marriage, then? They must have the same parent on one side, surely, for my Cecil says that Miss Benevento looks very much like her brother."

"Ah, I remember she said she was most fond of her brother. How came Cecil to meet him? Elsie . . . ?"

Gorton pulled back her head and blinked rapidly. "Oh, dear! I am sorry, Miss. Cannot seem to keep my eyes open. I 'spect 'tis all the . . . excitement."

"Yes, but you must not fall asleep now! Tell me about Miss Benevento's brother."

"Well, I've heard of him, of course. Everybody has. But I've never seen him. My Cecil did whilst he was in the Low Countries, and says that for all he's a Frenchy, he's a brave man and a credit to his country. I'm s'prised he would've gone . . . so high if he's . . . half"—her head nodded—"half-Italian."

Chill little fingers were creeping down Zoe's spine. "Elsie?"

Gorton snored softly.

Zoe stood, and shook her. "Wake up! Who is he? Tell me his name."

"What?" Gorton blinked at her drowsily. "Oh—you mean the Marshal."

"The . . . *Marshal?*" whispered Zoe.

"Mmm . . . He's got two first names . . . them Frenchies is so strange . . . Marshal Jean-Jacques . . ."

"Barthélemy?" gasped Zoe.

Gorton mumbled something, bowed forward on the table cushioning her head in her arms, and fell fast asleep.

Watching her with eyes dilated with horror, Zoe knew that she would be unable to awaken her. They must, she thought numbly, have put something in the lemonade. Elsie had finished her glass, whereas she herself had only taken one mouthful.

With a faint sob, she flew to the door. The latch lifted, but though she pulled with all her strength, the door would not move an inch. She beat against it foolishly and unavailingly, and shouted, then screamed demands that she be let out at once. And at last, slowly, wretchedly, she sank to her knees, leaning against the door and facing the hideous truth. Maria Benevento was Maria Barthélemy, sister to the great French soldier Travis had discovered to be aligning himself with the League of Jewelled Men. From the very start, the friendship between beautiful sophisticated Maria and countrified Zoe Grainger had been a ruse, designed only to lure her into betraying her brother.

Huddled against the door, tears of guilt and rage streaked down her cheeks.

There was no one to help her undo the terrible thing she had done.

Poor Gorton was in a drugged sleep.

She was locked in and quite helpless.

And she had sent the brother she adored . . . to almost certain . . . death . . .

A thunderclap woke her. For a moment she was bewildered and could not think where she was. Then everything rushed back, and she realized that she must have swallowed enough of the lemonade to cause her to doze off. It had likely been a brief doze, because the room was not much darker than it had been before. Lightning flashed blindingly, and rain was beating furiously against the windows.

The windows! What a dunce she was! Kneeling here, snivelling, when she might be knotting sheets together so as to climb down. They'd likely not felt it necessary to keep watch, believing her to be sound asleep.

Clambering to her feet, she flew across the room and threw the casement open.

From outside there came an explosive, "Deuce take it!"

And she was staring down into the drenched but indignant features of Peregrine Cranford.

The upper half of the window was designed purely for the admission of daylight and was immovable, and only the lower section could be opened. The casement was small, but Zoe leaned out, and as he stepped closer threw her arms about his neck and hugged him, laughing and crying and babbling of her joy and relief.

Grinning broadly, Cranford gasped, "Let go, you wild woman, else you'll have me off the ladder!"

The ladder! Dashing away tears, and sniffing, she peered downward. "Oh! My heavens! Perry—how ever could you climb up a ladder?"

"By wearing that stupid artificial foot, and 'tis blasted uncomfortable, I can tell you! 'Twas only by the greatest luck that I saw Gorton moving about in your room, else I'd have had the deuce of a time finding you. And then what must you do but dashed near guillotine me when you flung the casement open!" Despite the scold, his eyes were tender, and he asked then, "Am I to take it that you are pleased to see me? I was half-inclined to force my way in the front door, but they said you were not at home, so I thought I'd best make sure before—"

"Oh, if you knew! But— You *don't* know!" She put a hand to her head distractedly. "Perry! I am locked in, and poor Gorton has been drugged, and there is so *much* to tell you, and— Oh, how I *prayed* you would come for me!"

The tenderness in his eyes was replaced with a very different expression. "Why, that wicked old beldam! I *thought* 'twas something of the sort! Come along then, my brave tree climber. Out with you! Oh, gad! The casement's not very wide. I'm going to disgrace you again. Take off those paniers."

"Yes. No! Perry, I had thought the same, but I see now 'tis hopeless. Even without my skirts I could not climb through. Besides—" She flinched and waited out a crashing peal of thunder. "Besides, there is no time. Someone downstairs may see the ladder at any second. I must tell you this very quickly. I heard some of them talking last night. About some kind of change of plans, and—and strange bedfellows, and that 'she' would be very angry, and—oh yes, that the Squire was *ready*!"

"By Gad, but you've done wonderfully! You can tell me the rest after I get you out. What—"

"No! You must go now! Travis is—"

"I go nowhere without you, my girl! We'll get to your brother in—"

"Oh, stop! Do stop! You *must* listen! He managed to get a letter to me. Lady Buttershaw kept it, but I was able to find it. Travis writ that he would call here. *Here*, Perry! They would not let me go out, so—"

Cranford swore grittily.

Zoe went on, "—so my poor Gorton smuggled a note to

him, and I told him to go to Maria! I didn't know where you lived, you see, and—"

"Well, then, all's right and tight. Miss Benevento will send for Owen, and—"

Her hand across his lips cut the words off. She said, "Maria Benevento has another name, Perry. She is Maria Barthélemy. And my brother writ that Marshal Jean-Jacques Barthélemy has allied himself with the League!"

For a stunned moment he perched on the ladder staring at her blankly while the rain soaked his hair and sent little rivulets winding down his face. "So 'tis truth," he whispered. "Barthélemy! Lord help us!"

"I pray He will! But Travis may have gone to Maria already. They may be—be questioning him at this very moment!"

"He has the Agreement, then?"

"Yes. And he will trust Maria, you see, because I said . . . like a perfect fool, I said she was a faithful friend! You must go to him! At once! Perry, I *beg* you. Go!"

His jaw set. "And leave you here? Be damned if I will! That stewed prune of a butler will open the front door quick enough with my pistol under his fat paunch!" He started an awkward descent of the ladder. "I'll have you out of there in jig time, and—"

Zoe reached out and grabbed his hair. He gave an indignant yelp, and she said fiercely, "And if anything happens to you, my brother is as good as doomed, and I shall never forgive you, Peregrine Cranford! *Never!* If you go quickly, you can come back for me. They think I am fast asleep, and will likely do nothing to me for a—a long while yet. Don't let them win, Perry! Don't let that—that wicked Maria laugh and gloat because I am silly and gullible and she so easily deceived me! Once you are away you can send your man to me, or summon the Watch, or *somebody*! Only—*please*—oh, please do go!"

For a wrenching few seconds he gazed into her pale, tear-streaked face. She was right, of course. Her brother and the Agreement must be protected at all costs. But what a terrible cost! To abandon the dear brave girl here, alone and helpless . . . ! To leave this gentle creature who held his only hope for happiness. Her hand released his hair, and caressed his cold cheek. He reached up and seized it and pressed a kiss into the palm. Then, without a word, he began the slow and painful descent to the shadowy garden.

The most dangerous moment came when he took down the ladder he had hauled here from the side of the house. He dared not leave it propped under Zoe's window to warn the occupants that someone might have spoken with their prisoner, nor dared he let it bang against the wall but had to guide it cautiously. Candles and lamps had been lit inside the mansion now, sending bright beams shining into the dusk. Even as he lowered the ladder to the ground he saw a lackey lighting a branch of candles in the withdrawing room, only a few feet from him.

The wind got under the ladder and it was torn from his hand to fall with a crash across the terrace and send a large potted plant toppling. Cursing bitterly, Cranford ducked as the lackey jerked around. The casement above his head flew open and he held his breath.

The lackey called, "One of the terrace urns has blowed over!"

A woman's voice shouted indignantly, "Well, close the window, you fool, and go and see to it!"

The casement was slammed shut.

Between a limp and a run Cranford made for the alley wall at the east side of the house. The ladder would have been a great help here. The wall was high and topped with broken glass. The rope ladder Tummet had left for him was still behind the bush where he'd hidden it, but this was the hard part. Much as he'd longed to be the one to climb up to Zoe's rescue, he was aware of his limitations, and had fully intended to keep watch while Tummet did all the climbing. Only there had been no sign of the man, so he'd had no choice. It had been dashed tricky climbing over, but he'd managed somehow, without getting thoroughly sliced by the glass. With luck, the return journey would go as well. He crouched low as lightning flashed garishly, then twirled the ladder over his head, tossed it up, and heard the hooks ring home on the top. Above the clamour of the storm he heard a man's voice. So the lackey had come out. He must be quick. Three years back, he would have been over this wall in a trice. Only it was not three years back. It was now, and just to move from rung to rung was a desperate struggle. He was the only man who could send help to Travis Grainger—the only man who could get his beloved lady out of that loathsome house! Whatever happened, he must not fail!

He was almost to the top when he heard voices close by. A man grumbled, ". . . say she's been took sick, so I got to take the dratted beasts out in the dratted rain, and I'll have to wipe orf their dratted feet when—"

A deep bark and a shout.

Abandoning caution, Cranford grabbed for the top of the wall. He swore as glass drove into his palm, then scrunched under his boot. Egged on by a cacophany of barks, he jumped down into the alley. He told himself dizzily that his landing could have been worse, but for several seconds he sprawled there, trying to catch his breath, and hearing the clamouring of the dogs and the shouts of the men. A cat yowled as he struggled to his knees, and one of the men voiced a very unkind assessment of both dogs and cats.

A woman shouted, "What's to do out there?"

In a very different tone, the man answered, "Just the dogs chasing a cat, ma'am. Only playing, belike."

A door slammed, and thunder bellowed again.

The dogs were still barking frenziedly.

It was no time, Cranford decided, to lounge about. He dragged himself up and limped along the alley, praying that Tummet had by now returned to his post. It was unlike the man to have let him down. Only something really important would have lured him away.

He peered cautiously around the corner of the house. The square was deserted. Flambeaux were already lit outside several mansions and flickered as the wind moaned along the street, driving the rain under porches and pediments and almost extinguishing the flames. It was very cold, and Cranford shivered as he walked farther up the square, then crossed the road to the central gardens. His hand throbbed, and in the glare of lightning he saw that his palm was bloody. He wrapped his handkerchief around the cut absently. With every second his fear for Zoe intensified. If Tummet didn't come, he might *have* to leave her, at least until he could get word to Furlong, or Morris, or *someone*! To judge from this square one might think him the only man left in London Town! Where in the *devil*—

"That you, Lieutenant C?"

He gave a gasp of relief. "Yes, it's me! Damn your eyes, Tummet! Where have you been?"

"Got took up, sir. Fer loitering, they said. Lucky fer me, we run into a little war dahn near Spring Gardens, and I was set free. Rescued from the clutches of law'n order by the common man, I was. Cor! From the look of the common men wot come to me rescue, they just broke outta the Fleet Prison! But—" Tummet stopped abruptly, and peered at Cranford in the wavering light from a nearby flambeau. "Crumbs, but you're a mess, guv'nor! You never tried to climb over that there wall yerself? Might'a knowed you'd fall! But I gotta admit as you're a plucked 'un, if—"

"I *did* climb over! I'll admit I made mice feet of the return, but I saw and spoke with Miss Grainger."

Tummet was all admiration as he listened to a brief sketch of what had happened in his absence, but when he was ordered to rush a warning to Furlong, he protested vigorously. *"I'll* get inside Yerville 'all, Lieutenant, mate. *You* go and find Sir Owen! That 'and o' yourn looks nasty, and—no disrespeck, but if there's more climbing to be done, I can—"

"Manage better than me? Very true. But there won't be a chair or a hackney to be had in this storm. Whichever of us goes after Furlong may very well have to run all the way to the Madrigal, or wherever he has got to. And nowadays I'm not a fast runner."

"No, and if you goes in there orl by yerself, mate, you'll 'ave abaht as much chance as you'd 'ave of plucking a flea's eyebrows! Unless— You got a good plan to get the lady out?"

"I'll contrive something. Whatever happens, I'll not leave her."

"But—"

"Oh, have done with your 'buts'! Find Sir Owen! Fast! He knows where Miss Benevento lives. Then send me some reinforcements, if you can. On the double, man! *Go!"*

Tummet groaned, but responding to the note of command in Cranford's voice, he went sprinting off into the dark.

Left alone, Cranford drew his cloak tighter around him and glanced about. If he were to go and beat on the doors of some of these mansions, would he be given help? He tried to picture the reaction of Lady Buttershaw's neighbours when told that the *grande dame* of Society was part of a treasonable plot; that a maidservant lay drugged in her house; and that a young lady was held prisoner. He gave a cynical snort. They'd have him put under strong restraint, is what they would do! But to try and break into Yerville Hall alone would be a chancy undertaking. The mansion, he knew, fairly swarmed with servants, and although it was doubtful that one of them had a single kindly thought for her ladyship, they feared her, and in any kind of uproar would obey her.

He fought the raging need to go and pound on that confounded door and then force his way inside at gunpoint. He must exercise self-control for once, he told himself sternly; be more like Piers and use his head instead of letting passion rule him. It would not help the girl he loved if he was knocked down. His best hope was to get inside somehow and carry her off by subterfuge. He was racking his brain for a workable scheme when he became aware that something other than rain was being carried on the wind. The thunderclaps were farther apart now, but he could hear shouts, and a grumbling roar, as of many distant voices upraised in anger. Tummet had said a mob had freed him from the constable near Spring Gardens. From the sound of things, there was another disturbance closer at hand.

He brightened. Here, then, was his subterfuge!

He limped across the road and up the front steps of Yerville Hall. Pounding on the door, he heard a carriage clatter up the street, and he began to shout wildly for help.

The horses slowed. From the corner of his eye he saw carriage lamps. "Help!" he howled. "Murder!"

There came a startled exclamation behind him, then the front door swung open and against the sudden flood of light stood Arbour, staring at him in astonishment.

"Help!" raved Cranford at the top of his lungs. "They've taken her! Call the Watch!" He hurled himself at the butler, who retreated hastily.

"Be dashed if it ain't poor Cranford," drawled a faintly amused and very much disliked voice from the carriage.

'Fowles!' he thought grimly. 'The last swine I'd have wished to see!'

Arbour stammered, "Sir, you're hurt! Wh-what on earth—"

"I demand to know the meaning for all this uproar!" Lady Buttershaw marched across the entrance hall, her eyes glittering with anger.

"They've taken her!" Cranford gabbled, staggering towards her. "You must . . . get help!"

Recoiling, she gasped, "Good heavens! You're all blood!"

"So he is." Gilbert Fowles sauntered in and scanned Cranford's artistically swaying form through his quizzing glass. "Who has been taken, my poor block? Or are you drunk?"

"Miss—Miss Grainger," gasped Cranford, restraining an impassioned urge to strangle him. "The mob . . . dragged us from my coach and we were separated. Arbour! Never stand there like a . . . confounded statue! Run for a Constable! Quick!"

Lady Buttershaw barked, "Arbour, you will at once see to it that all the servants go down to the kitchens. And *remain* there!"

Only too glad to escape, the butler hurried off, calling to footmen and lackeys.

"What's all this?"

To Cranford's enormous relief, Lord Eaglund came inside, but before he could respond, Lady Buttershaw bellowed, "Poor Cranford has been hurt by those miserable rioters. I fear his brain has become disordered. He thinks Miss Grainger was in his carriage, whereas she is upstairs, asleep in her bed."

The viscount looked in bewilderment from her ladyship to Cranford's soaked, muddy and bloodied self.

About to declare himself, Cranford checked as Mr. Rudolph Bracksby arrived on the scene. For all his hearty manner and good looks, the powerfully built gentleman had always impressed Cranford as exerting himself to please only those who could be of use to him. It was not hard to believe that he was, as Furlong had said, a member of the League. And if Lord Eaglund cried friends with him . . .

"She *was* with me," he howled shrilly. "She slipped out to join me." They all stared at him, and he improvised in desperation, "We were eloping!"

"NONSENSE!" roared Lady Buttershaw.

" 'Faith, but I wonder the poor girl would want you," sneered Fowles. "She must be desperate, indeed."

"Why do you *stand* here?" Cranford dodged around her ladyship and made for the stair hall. "I'll *prove* she is not in her room!"

"I say! No—my poor fellow—" Aghast, the viscount started forward.

Arbour and Fowles both ran towards Cranford at the same instant, and the three men collided.

"Idiot!" snarled Fowles, pushing the butler aside.

"Do not *dare* go up there, Cousin!" Accustomed to instant obedience Lady Buttershaw elbowed her way between the men and marched to the foot of the stairs, her great skirts hindering Lord Eaglund as he attempted to pass her. When it dawned on her that she was being defied, she screeched an outraged, "*Hackham!* Stop Mr. Cranford! He has gone mad!"

Hackham appeared on the upper landing. He started down, eyeing the "madman" warily. Cranford reached out to him and appeared to collapse. Instinctively, Hackham grabbed him. Not for nothing had Cranford excelled in sports. Hackham found himself holding what he later described as a steel spring. Cranford straightened and his left fist came up from his knees and landed solidly on the footman's jaw. Lady Buttershaw shrieked and sprang aside with remarkable agility and a glimpse of frilly scarlet drawers as Hackham descended the stairs involuntarily and rapidly. Hard on her heels, Bracksby did not fare so well, and was flattened by the flying footman.

Cranford had a fair idea of the location of Zoe's room and he limped to it with all possible speed. The key was in the lock. Logical enough, he thought, as he turned it and swung the door open.

A strong grip closed on his shoulder, and he was jerked around. Fowles' vindictive face was behind the fist that flew at him. He ducked. Zoe gave a startled cry, and Fowles swore as he missed and his knuckles made a crashing assault on the door. Cranford landed a solid right to the mid-section and, as Fowles doubled up, had the satisfaction of seeing him acquire the look of an expiring trout. Eaglund and Bracksby were almost upon him. Everyone seemed to be shouting at once. With one arm around Zoe's shoulders, he wrenched the pistol from his pocket and held it steady.

The shouting and all movement ceased.

"Thank you," said Cranford politely. "That's better. Now if you will all be so very good as to go back down the stairs . . ."

"But my dear boy," said Eaglund in his gentle way, "you really must try to be sensible. You can see that Miss Grainger really is here, just as her ladyship said."

"And locked in," said Cranford.

Zoe cried, "You don't know what has happened, Lord Eaglund. My brother—"

"Back!" snapped Cranford, moving forward, his arm still about Zoe's shoulders. "You waste your breath, m'dear. They're all in it."

The viscount retreated a few steps.

Straightening up, but leaning against the wall, Fowles panted, "You have only one shot . . . dear old Perry."

Peregrine glanced at him. "Are you willing to take it, dear old Gil?"

"Good heavens, Cousin Peregrine! Whatever are you about?" Lady Julia had hurried up unnoticed, and now stepped directly in front of him. "Put that weapon down at once!"

With an exultant shout, Fowles reached around her to snatch for the pistol.

Terrified lest he crown his career by shooting a lady, Cranford managed to wrench the weapon aside. It went off deafeningly. The recoil was agonizing; the pistol fell from his grasp and he clutched his wrist painfully.

Lady Julia rounded on Fowles and her small white hand cracked across his face. In a voice Zoe had never heard before, she hissed, "You clumsy blockhead! You might have killed me!"

Fowles muttered something, and drove a powerful right jab at Cranford that sent him to his knees.

Sight and sound blurred. He knew he was moving, but an indeterminate time later was bemused to find himself sitting on a chair in the blue ante-chamber that he remembered as being adjacent to the downstairs withdrawing room. He blinked in an effort to clear his head. The viscount was no longer among them. Lady Buttershaw was shaking Zoe, who looked tearful and very frightened. There was a livid mark on her pale face, and at the sight, rage seared through him. Starting up, he snarled, "Which of you miserable traitors *dared* to strike her?"

Fowles, who had been standing behind his chair, slammed him down again and Zoe half-sobbed, "Don't hurt him! Oh, pray do not!"

"The devil with that," growled Cranford, turning on Fowles furiously. "Is this the carrion who hurt *you?*" He looked straight into the muzzle of a pistol and said with disgust, "It takes a brave man to abuse a lady and strike an unarmed man."

"But I have wanted to strike you for so long, my dear old schoolmate. You cannot think how galling it was to hear everyone rave of your athletic prowess. Of course," Fowles purred, "those days are over for you . . . eh?"

Lady Julia sat on a gold sofa and said quietly, "Clara, for heaven's sake bind up his hand. 'Tis gruesome."

None too gently, Lady Buttershaw unwound the handkerchief. Cranford gritted his teeth. Unmoved, she said, " 'Tis an ugly wound, and he has brought some of our wall with him."

"Glass?" Interested, Fowles said, "No—don't remove it, dear Lady Clara. It might prove—useful . . ."

Zoe gave a smothered cry, and started towards Cranford. Bracksby stretched out his arm to keep her back. She pleaded, "I beg you—let me help him."

Bracksby frowned. "Do you know, Gilbert, sometimes you really are an unpleasant creature." He turned to Zoe. "But he has a point, my dear. If you have any fondness for Perry Cranford, you would be well advised to answer her ladyship's question—now."

Cranford suspected that by this time Owen would have charged to Travis Grainger's rescue, but it would be as well not to let them suspect that. He shouted, "Zoe! They won't—"

Fowles clamped a hand over his mouth and said lightly, "Our war hero is going to tell you with proper gallantry that we mean to put a period to your brother. But that's not certain, you know. On the other hand, if you refuse to help us . . ." He glanced over his shoulder, "Rudi, come and hold his arm."

Distracted, Zoe cried, "How can you be so cruel? Lady Julia, I cannot believe you would—"

"Fight for an ideal?" Lady Julia said, "Ah, but I would, child. The Yervilles have always been ready to lay down their lives when this beloved land was at risk. And she is at risk now. Given away to a German prince who cares not a button for her—or all the centuries of tradition that—"

Cranford tore free from Fowles' clasp and said, "That you are ready to sell to a *French* despot, eh?"

Fowles' grip bit into his shoulder.

Lady Buttershaw swung up a vase and advanced on him, her face red and contorted with fury.

Fowles flung up a hand, warding her off. "What's this?"

Bracksby said, "Pay him no mind. Come now, Miss Grainger. We believe we are doing what is best for England, but we none of us like this sort of ugly business. We'd intended to wait for your brother to—"

"If there has been any dealing with France," snapped Fowles, "I'll have no—"

"Do not be so shatter-brained as to listen to Cranford!" trumpeted Lady Buttershaw. "You know very well our only arrangement with France is for munitions. Tell him, Julia."

Lady Yerville looked at her for a moment. "Can you really be such a fool?"

The vase fell from her sister's hand. Her eyes goggling, Lady Buttershaw gasped, "*What* did you *dare* to call me?"

"I called you what you are."

Lady Julia stood. The gentle invalid had vanished, replaced by a hard-eyed implacable woman.

Staring at her, stunned, Cranford had the brief sensation that nobody in the room was breathing; that they all were in a state of shock.

Still in that cold and remorseless voice, Lady Julia said, "For most of my life you have bullied and browbeaten me, Clara. It was of small importance and in your way I knew you were fond of me, so for the most part I overlooked your nonsense. I even allowed you to believe you were chosen to join the League before me, though that was far from the case."

Fowles stood as though turned to stone.

Equally immovable, Lady Buttershaw stared at her sister in utter disbelief.

"I have surprised you, I see." Lady Julia's smile was faint and chilling. "I sought for years for a way to avenge myself on the shallow and cruel society that destroyed me and the man I worshipped. You liked to believe that Percy Gatesford jilted me because I was burned. Not so. His father, aided by our ignoble monarch, forced him to throw me over!" Her pale cheeks flushed, and the big blue eyes glittered with almost maniacal hatred. "His royal majesty dared—*dared* to tell Percy the continuance of his line was more important . . . more *important* than his love for me . . . !" She took a deep breath and in a hushed silence leaned back and said in a gentle voice that was more appalling than her hissing fury, "He must pay, do you see? And in this only, Clara, I go my own way—the Squire's way—and will brook no interference from you, or—anyone!"

Cranford thought, 'We're dead in her eyes. She won't let Zoe or me live after that damning confession!' And he said, "So you mean to give England to a power-mad lunatic like—" His words were choked off as Bracksby seized the wrist of his injured hand.

"We mean to have the Agreement that was stolen," said Lady Julia, smiling at Zoe. "I really cannot wait any longer, child. Where is your brother?"

Zoe saw Cranford's face twist with pain, and it was more than she could bear. In desperation, she pleaded, "Stop! Please stop! I sent him to Maria Benevento!"

"Barthélemy?" whispered Fowles, patently horrified.

Lady Julia laughed. "But how delightful. Do you see, Clara, how well our plans have served us? Now pray be so good as to call up my coach. Maria may need our aid."

Heartsick, Zoe sank onto the sofa.

As if in a daze, Lady Buttershaw nodded and walked to the door. Even as she reached for the latch, it lifted, and Hackham, looking bruised and dishevelled, appeared. He threw a venomous glance at Cranford, and announced, "Mr. Falcon has called, ma'am."

She slammed the door in his face, whipped around and

looked back into the grim room, her eyes dilating. "Julia! I'll not have August harmed!"

"Use some sense, Clara," said her sister, impatiently. "This is no time to indulge your infatuation for that worthless half-breed!"

Lady Buttershaw's jaw jutted. "Julia . . . I *warn* you . . . !"

Lady Julia stood. "Oh, very well. But you must get rid of him quickly." She glanced at Bracksby and he at once pulled Zoe to her feet.

Freed, Cranford leapt forward, but Lady Julia was close beside the girl. A small dagger glittered in her hand.

She said softly, "Make one sound, *dear* cousin, and this child will pay dearly."

Zoe whispered, "Perry—she would not!"

But in Lady Julia's pale eyes was the glow of fanaticism and, helpless, he knew that she would.

CHAPTER XVI

ut how delightful!" Falcon had followed Hackham part of the way along the corridor, and for Lady Buttershaw all other considerations faded into insignificance. She hastened to intercept him, hand outstretched, and eyes aglow. He bowed and pressed a kiss upon her fingers. Shivering visibly, she simpered, "Such a *frightful* night, and you so gallant as to brave the elements to call upon me. *Dear* August! Come. You cannot yet have dined. We shall have a cozy dinner, tête-à-tête, in my private parlour." She added with a provocative glance that appalled him, "Upstairs."

"Tête-à-tête?" His brows lifting, he halted and drawled lazily, "Have I mistaken the matter, then? I'd understood Cranford to say I was to meet him here and that Miss Grainger would join—"

"Silly boy!" Her laugh shrilled out, and she took his arm and leaned as close to him as her wide paniers would allow. "But they have gone, my dear. Mr. Cranford escorted Miss Grainger to dine at Lord Coombs' house."

Obstinately halted outside the withdrawing room, he bent his head perilously near to her cheek, and breathed, "You sly minx! I think you are a conspirator."

She was breathlessly still.

Over her shoulder his eyes darted around what he could see of the withdrawing room. Empty. But she had come along this way, and he was sure that the voices he'd heard had been in one of these rooms.

"A . . . conspirator . . . ?" she echoed with considerably less than her customary resonance.

"With Cupid, wicked one." He allowed his lips to brush her cheek. "Own it, Clara. Your romantic soul has persuaded that you allow them a moment alone together . . ."

The unprecedented use of her given name, the touch of his lips sent her heart galloping. Her eyelids drooped and, ecstatic, she swayed to him.

"I'll wager," breathed Falcon very softly, "they are—" He halted, jerked back, his eyes widening, and roared an explosive sneeze.

Lady Buttershaw watched in alarm as another sneeze followed the first.

Moaning, Falcon groped for his handkerchief and moved away from her, dabbing at his eyes.

A small ginger and white cat wound between his ankles.

"Get it . . . away," he cried hysterically. "Why bust they always cub after be?"

Snarling with frustration, Lady Buttershaw made a grab for Charlemagne. As though sensing the violence of her intentions, the little cat sprang sideways.

No mean actor, Falcon's voice rose in a horrified howl, and he staggered back. "Get it away!"

In hot pursuit of the cat, Lady Buttershaw essayed another snatch.

Falcon reeled against the ante-room door and wrenched it open.

White as death, a pretty girl he guessed to be Zoe Grainger stood by a sofa. Lady Julia was at her side, an arm about her and the other hand holding a dagger. Just as white, and obviously terrified, Cranford stood as if frozen.

Zoe thought numbly, ' 'Tis the gentleman in the portrait . . .'

Charlemagne, eluding Lady Buttershaw and scared by her bellowed demands that Falcon not go "in there," shot after him as he reeled inside, racked by uproarious sneezes.

Cranford seized the moment and hurled himself at Bracksby. The two men crashed into the sofa, which went over backwards, throwing Zoe to the floor and sending her ladyship into a violent collision with Sir Gilbert Fowles.

"Your *damnable* pets, Julia!" trumpeted Lady Buttershaw, plunging into the chaotic room.

Cranford rolled clear, got to his feet and helped Zoe stand.

The scared Charlemagne leapt into her arms.

Bracksby wrenched out his sword and turned on Falcon, who retreated, sneezing helplessly.

Cranford limped to Falcon's aid.

Fowles tore a small pistol from his coat pocket.

In that same split second, Zoe heard a sound she recognized. She thought fleetingly, 'I'm sorry, Charley,' and tossed the cat at Fowles even as he aimed the pistol at Cranford's back.

With a yowl, and the feline instinct for self-preservation, Charlemagne hooked his claws into Fowles' shoulder.

Fowles also yowled and made a strong effort to beat away the unwanted hanger-on.

There came a thudding rattle. A large black and white shape hurtled vengefully at the villainous human who appeared to have upset his cat. Quite impervious to anything that stood in his path Viking did not deviate from it and Rudolph Bracksby gave a startled shout as he was staggered and fell to his knees.

Fowles screamed, and disappeared under Viking's attack.

Cranford reached for the fallen pistol, but behind him, Bracksby, moving with smooth agility, was already regaining his feet, sword in his hand and murder in his eyes.

Zoe snatched up a small marble statue of St. George and brought it crashing down on his head. "I cannot like violence," she said. "But you are a very nasty man."

Cranford laughed breathlessly, and held out his arm. "And you, little one, are a true heroine! You have saved the day!"

Lady Julia was trying to pull Viking off Fowles.

Fingers crooked, Lady Buttershaw started towards Cranford.

"No, really, my dear Clara," gasped Falcon between sneezes. "Your nature is . . . too generous for such . . . vulgarity."

She halted and stared at him, rather pathetically irresolute.

Morris came in, supporting a drooping Elsie Gorton, and holding a pistol jammed against Hackham's spine.

"Rats," he complained. "I see I've missed a good brawl. I found this poor lady crawling down the stairs, so—"

"Oh, thank heaven!" cried Zoe, running to her.

Kneeling beside the moaning Fowles, holding her torn gown closed, Lady Julia turned such a malevolent glare on Cranford that he instinctively stepped back a pace.

"Fool!" she said balefully. "Do you fancy you've won? Run to the Horse Guards with your tales! I am very sure that Maria already has our copy of the Agreement. Without it, who will believe you?" Her gaze took in Falcon and Morris. She added with a smile that chilled Cranford's blood, " 'Tis past time, I think, for us to administer—*châtiment quatre*. And this time, with finality!"

There was an instant of taut silence.

Wiping his eyes, Falcon drawled, "Which confirms you as a traitor to your country, madam."

"Only losers are traitors," she riposted. "And, I promise you, we will *not* lose!"

Suddenly, unexpectedly, and with incredible volume, Lady Buttershaw lapsed into screaming hysterics.

It was the last straw for Morris. He sprinted for the door, the rest of them following hurriedly.

The entrance hall was empty except for a white-faced Arbour, who backed away from the victorious little group.

Cranford said urgently, "We must find Owen. With that damnable Agreement in our hands, we'll have our proof!"

Luigi, whose name was actually Louis, straightened from searching the garments of Mr. Travis Grainger and handed his mistress a large flat packet. He said in French, "It proclaims itself to be the Last Will and Testament of a Monsieur T. Grant. But it is, I think, that which you seek, mademoiselle."

The lady Zoe knew as Maria Benevento took the packet, still watching the unconscious man who lay on the sofa in her cosy parlour. Also speaking French, she said, "He looks very bad. I trust you did not hit him too hard, Louis?"

"It is that he has been ill, mademoiselle. He will live. But in case he regains consciousness, he is securely bound, I assure you."

She nodded, and tore open the packet. A glance was enough. "Yes. Then we are done here. Hurry to the stables and order up my coach." She quailed as a brilliant lightning flash was followed at once by a great peal of thunder. "Ah, but this horrid storm, it comes back. If you see Greta on the way, tell her to make haste. One might suppose I had sent her to Edinburgh instead of to collect my necklace from the jeweller!"

"Mayhap the repairs are not completed, mademoiselle."

"They were to have been completed yesterday!" she said,

in one of her rare but fiery displays of anger. "If they have failed, they will hear from me, I promise you! And I shall have the repairs made in Paris. I would be gone from this city as quickly as it is possible."

He glanced at her obliquely as he left. She looked tired, and her eyes were haunted. This had been, he thought, not a happy time for his beautiful lady.

Left alone, Maria went in search of Petite's little coat. "This beast of an English climate," she murmured to her small pet as it trotted after her. "How glad I will be to escape it." She took up the coat, and then stood for some moments gazing down at it sadly, and seeing instead a proudly held head, a pair of smiling blue eyes.

Petite abandoned hope of a walk, curled up on the bed, and within a minute was fast asleep.

Sighing, Maria returned to the withdrawing room and went at once to the sofa. Despite the sunken cheeks and the pallor of illness, this young man's resemblance to Zoe was marked. He lay so still that for a panicked moment she thought he had died, and she was relieved to find that he was still breathing steadily. She took up the packet as thunder pealed again, and started to pull out the papers it contained.

A hand came over her shoulder and twitched the packet from her grasp.

With a shocked cry she whirled around.

Owen Furlong watched her gravely, raindrops scattering from his cloak as he flung it back and slipped the agreement into his coat pocket.

She whispered, "Owen . . . !" and thought that she never had seen such sadness in a man's eyes.

He bowed slightly, "Mademoiselle Maria Barthélemy, I believe."

"Maria Benevento Barthélemy," she corrected, her chin lifting proudly.

Keeping his eyes on her, Furlong walked quickly to the sofa and leaned down to feel Grainger's cheek.

"He's alive," she said. "A blow on the head; nothing serious. I could not let my Zoe's brother be harmed."

His smile was faint. He said as if very weary, "Do you know, I would not believe it. When Tummet came, I—I nigh strangled him for daring to . . ." He could not finish the sentence, but he regained control quickly, and managed to ask, "Was it for France, my dear? Or for your brother?"

"Both. Owen, Owen! My darling, do not let this come between us."

"Will it? Did you ever care a jot for me, lovely one? Or was I just a convenient source of information?"

"Ah, how can you say such things? From the moment we met—" She stretched out both hands imploringly. "I love you! Come with me!"

He stepped away from her touch. "And give up my country?"

"Your country is doomed. These people— Owen, there is such power at work here. Such ruthless power. Your government will fall, and—"

He said quietly, "I will fight with my last breath to prevent that, Maria."

She gave a muffled little cry and covered her face with her hands. And she was so lovely, so ineffably beloved. His eyes blurred with tears, and he seized her and crushed her against him. And with all his heart, all his future in the balance, cried brokenly, "My love, my precious love! Stay here and marry me. I'll see that you are not named in connection with this ugly business." He kissed the silken dark hair so tightly pressed under his cheek, and murmured with passionate intensity, "Only let me spend the rest of my life caring for you; cherishing you. 'Twould make me the proudest man in the world, Maria. 'Tis very soon, I know, but . . . I have never truly loved before. Surely, you know it. I have no need to tell you how I adore you." He tilted her chin upward, and saw tears gleaming on her cheeks. "Beloved, you are weeping too . . ."

"Yes." She groped blindly for her muff and pulled out a handkerchief. Dabbing it at her eyes, she said, "I weep because . . . I love you, my fine brave English gentleman. And I wish— with all my heart that I could accept your—most impetuous— offer, but—" The handkerchief fell, and she stood straight, a small pocket pistol pointed steadily at him. "But—I cannot," she said sadly. "All my life my brother has cared for and shielded me. I love him . . . too much to betray him. Dearest Owen, you hold his life in your hands. You must give me back the Agreement."

For a moment he stood in silence, gazing at her. Then he said with quiet but infinite despair, "No, my love. I will see to it that you have ample time to get away, but your brother's ambitions are a threat to all I am sworn to defend." He turned to the door. "I must get some help for Grainger, and—"

"Stop!" Her voice shrill, she cried. "Owen—for the love of God, do not make me—"

With his hand on the latch, he turned for one last yearning gaze at her. "I shall always remember," he said wistfully, "how very beautiful—"

The pistol shot cut off his words.

Half-blinded with tears, Maria watched in anguish his shocked look of disbelief as he was slammed back against the door. He took a stumbling step towards her, then crumpled and fell. She hurled the pistol away, and ran to kneel beside him and pull frenziedly at his cloak. A small crimson stain already marked the shoulder of his coat. He opened his eyes and whispered her name. Weeping, she tore out his handkerchief, formed it into a pad, and thrust it under his coat. "I aimed for . . . your arm," she sobbed.

He smiled wanly, and his white lips whispered, "I . . .

love . . ." He sighed, his eyes closed, and he lay still.

Maria's tears splashed his quiet face as she bent to kiss him and smooth back the thick, powdered hair. She retrieved the Agreement from his coat then, and, standing, took up a cushion and knelt again to put it tenderly beneath his head.

It was thus that his friends found him, ten minutes after Maria had gone.

Two afternoons later, Lady Buttershaw said sternly, "I will tell you, Julia, that it does not befit your station in life to be such a watering pot!"

Lady Julia Yerville leant back on the sofa in the ground-floor withdrawing room, and raised a handkerchief to her eyes. Her frail hand trembled as she wiped away a tear. She said in her gentle voice, "I—I know, Clara. But I was so fond of—of the dear child. I cannot credit—" Her voice was suspended.

Lord Hayes exchanged a grim glance with Lieutenant Joel Skye, who sat beside him.

Standing before the blazing fire, Rudolph Bracksby put in sharply, "Is this really necessary, gentlemen? We have told you how Cranford attempted to elope with Miss Grainger, who was in Lady Buttershaw's care at the time. And of the violence he and his friends"—he threw a contemptuous look at Cranford, Falcon, and Morris, who stood near Hayes—"visited upon us when we attempted to restrain him."

Skye said, "These gentlemen have also told us their version of the affair, sir, which—"

"Which is a lot of poppycock," roared Lady Buttershaw at full volume. "I do not scruple to tell you, my lord, that the gel is a lying little baggage who was seen cavorting—*in public*—with that lecherous young rake"—she stabbed a finger at Cranford—"in the *full light of day!* As for this fanciful nonsense about some kind of treasonable secret society scheming to top-ple the government—I am appalled, my lord! APPALLED I say, that *anyone* would dare use the name Yerville in connec-tion with such a plot! Down through the centuries the Yer-villes have stood for, fought for, and died for all that was de-cent and fine and honourable about this nation! Our very *name* is a by-word for integrity! I did all in my power to remove that ungrateful gel from an unhappy home. In return she abused our hospitality, deceived my poor sister, who is all too willing to believe the best of everybody, and brought shame and *degradation* upon this house! How you could—"

Lady Julia held up her frail hand, silencing what promised to be a lengthy monologue. Looking with great sad eyes at Zoe, she pleaded, "Why, dear child? Why must you treat me so un-kindly, after all we have—" She broke off.

Falcon, leaning back against a table, was clapping his hands. "Jolly well done, m'dear," he said mockingly. "You missed a great career in the theatre!"

For just an instant Lady Julia's martyred gentleness slipped.

Watching her keenly, Lord Hayes thought, 'Good Lord!' He said, "In view of the seriousness of the charges, and the fact that similar charges have been made before this, I fear we have no choice but to refer the matter to—"

"You may refer the matter to his gracious Majesty, for all we care," roared Lady Buttershaw, her face dangerously red. "But I will be *damned*, my lord, if I will allow you to upset my sister further. In case it has escaped you, sir, Lady Julia Yerville is an *invalid*! I will say without equivocation that any man who could look upon her pitiful frailty and suspect her capable of engaging in treason and violence has a seriously disordered in-tellect and should be put under strong restraint! Now—be so good as to take yourself and your unpleasant acquaintances from my house, sir! AT—ONCE!"

"You know," drawled Falcon as they all returned to the

waiting coaches, "you have to admire the woman, if only for her colossal gall."

Mopping his brow, Morris said unsteadily, "You admire her because she admires you. For myself, being a mere mortal man, she scares me to death!"

Cranford handed Zoe into the coach. "She won that round, certainly. I wonder if we have made any headway at all."

As he sat beside her, Zoe said, "How could they doubt us? After all that my brother was able to tell them, besides what we said. And when I think of poor Sir Owen . . ." She shook her head regretfully.

Climbing in and taking the opposite seat, Falcon said, "Poor Sir Owen made mice feet of the business by allowing sentiment to blind him to reality."

Indignant, Zoe exclaimed, "How can you be so unkind? He *loved* her! And he lies there, breaking his poor heart and blaming himself—"

"As he should. No man with half a brain, m'dear lady, would allow himself to become so attached to someone that he could be reduced to such a pitiable condition."

Morris seated himself next to Falcon and said with a grin, "What he's really saying, Miss Zoe, is 'If you can't find the right button, sew up the buttonhole!' "

"Oh—*Egad!*" snarled Falcon.

Cranford smiled, and patted Zoe's hand as the coach began to move off. "Never fret, ma'am. Had the ball hit an inch to the right, 'twould have pierced the lung and we'd be burying him. But luckily, the lady is a poor shot."

Zoe sighed. "Or a very good one."

"Either way," said Morris, "Owen's pluck to the backbone. He'll make a recover."

"*He* may," said Falcon. "The question is—will we? Without that da—er, without that Agreement, I doubt the great

East India Company director believed a word we said."

Morris snorted, "If you were to ask my opinion—"

"Extreme unlikely," said Falcon.

"—the mighty director," Morris persisted, "couldn't direct a starving flea to a fat dog!"

There was laughter at this, but Cranford said, "That may be so, but d'you know, Jamie, I think Skye believed us."

"Oh, splendid!" drawled Falcon. "Exactly what we need. The backing of a young naval subaltern. Mercy, but the Squire must be shaking in his shoes!"

Zoe said loyally, "You may mock, Mr. Falcon, but I agree with Peregrine. And it seemed to me that Lord Hayes did not regard us with disgust, either."

Cranford thanked her for her support, and asked with proper nonchalance if he was to be permitted to escort her back to Richmond.

She blushed and said shyly that he was very kind but it was not really necessary, since Gorton and Cecil Coachman awaited her at the Inn of the Silver Cat.

"As you wish," said Cranford, and concentrated on the passing scene.

Morris opened his mouth, met Falcon's ironic stare, and closed it again.

The following day Gideon Rossiter returned to Town. He was a tall, lean young man with thick, curling brown hair and a pair of intelligent grey eyes. He had been distracted with worry because of his enforced absence from Town, and was aghast when his friends apprised him of the latest developments in their battle against the League. He went at once to the Madrigal to visit Furlong. He had himself spent a year of misery in hospitals after being severely wounded in the War of the Austrian Succession, and he seated himself beside the sickbed and looked down at the drawn face on the pillows with understanding and compassion.

"How do you go on, my poor fellow?"

Still very weak, Furlong turned his head away. "I properly—let you down, Gideon. That—that damnable Agreement was in my hand! Did you know? With it, we could have borken the League! And I—I allowed it to be—"

"I'd scarce call getting a hole blown through you 'allowing'—"

Sir Owen interrupted wretchedly, "I don't know what they've told you. I collect they tried to spare my feelings. The truth is—"

"Now, Owen, do have some sense," said Rossiter with a smile. "Can you picture Falcon trying to spare anyone's feelings?"

"I can guess that . . . he must hold me in—deepest contempt."

Rossiter said gently, "I think August has not yet known what love is. Or the power of it." Meeting Furlong's haggard eyes, he added, "I have, you see. So I've a fair notion of what you're going through. Did they tell you she had put a pillow under your head, and tried to apply a bandage?"

Not trusting himself to speak, Furlong managed a slight nod.

Rossiter said, "Perhaps you should consider that 'twas a very sad case of your simply being on opposite sides. Two people, neither of them evil, bound by ties that were impossible to break. From what I've heard, I rather suspect this has been almost as hard on the lady, as on you."

Furlong moved his hand feebly, and Rossiter took it in a firm, cool grip.

"Gideon," said Furlong, his voice shredding, "you're such a—a blasted good friend. I am—so *sorry!*"

"That will not do, sir!" Rossiter drew back, man-like, from all this soul-bearing. "Did you know that little Miss Grainger overheard a woman declare that the Squire is ready to strike? Or that the fragile Lady Julia Yerville has warned us of *châtiment quatre*? Hurry up and get well, dear old boy, we need you! I believe that our fourth chastisement may very well pull us into a fight to the finish!"

The room at the Horse Guards was cold and quiet. Waiting, Lord Hayes glanced over interlocked fingers at the men seated around the table. In addition to himself and his aide, some of the most powerful gentlemen in government had gathered here. An admiral, his usually agreeable features reflecting irritation; a thickset, craggy-faced general; a gravely dignified cabinet minister; a highly regarded diplomatist; a prominent member of the House of Lords; and a bushy-browed and quarrelsome-looking member of Parliament.

Hayes prodded, "Well, gentlemen? You've heard it all."

"Aye, and we've heard it all before," said Admiral Anson, frowning. "Or I have, at least. Six months ago young Gideon Rossiter was filling my ears with the same tale, more or less."

"And did you believe any of it, sir?" asked Hayes.

The admiral hesitated. "At the risk of sounding gullible, I must admit I was concerned. The trouble is, they've nothing to back their allegations. And one does not make unfounded charges 'gainst a belted earl, a fabulously wealthy baron, a highly regarded landed gentleman. Least of all, 'gainst a gentle, long-suffering *invalid* lady, who is admired and respected throughout the *ton*, and her sister, who—well, God help us all! Of course, had they anything more than conjecture and some odd coincidences . . ."

The Honourable Mr. Willis-Formby, a frown on his lofty

brow, said thoughtfully, "They've the sworn testimony of some very-well-born young fellows."

"Almost every one of whom has something smoky in his background," argued General Early, glowering at the cabinet minister, whom he privately considered to be an intellectual do-nothing.

Sir Jones Holmesby's well-modulated voice was raised. "And one of whom, with nothing in the least smoky in his background, has an astonishing faculty of memory, and from all I can gather was damn near murdered for his efforts to bring a treasonable document all the way from Calcutta."

Lord Hayes leaned forward. "I agree. I also was sceptical at first, I'll own. But there cannot be all this smoke without a flicker of flame *somewhere*, gentlemen. Dare we ignore these warnings?"

"We certainly cannot deny that London's streets are becoming ever more violent," observed Lord Tiberville, whose nervous tic and high-pitched fretful voice belied a fine mind. "Street riots are practically a daily occurrence, and the public is unprecedentedly hostile to any figure of rank or authority."

"Being stirred up," barked Henry Church, Esquire, thumping a fat fist on the table. "Egged on! Blasted revolutionaries!"

"Which is exactly what Rossiter and his people claim." Hayes nodded to his nephew and the lieutenant stood.

"Gentlemen, at Lord Hayes' request, one of London's most venerable journalists is here." Skye saw storm clouds on several faces and went on hurriedly, "A man who has his pulse on the Metropolis, if anyone does." He went to the door and ushered in the "venerable journalist."

Sir Jonas Holmesby smiled faintly.

"Oh," grunted the Member of Parliament, mollified. "How do, Talbot?"

Ramsey Talbot bowed. "My lords . . . gentlemen."

A little flushed, Lord Tiberville said dryly, "Give you good day, Ramsey. Hayes says you've your finger on London's pulse. I thought I had. Be glad to hear your views."

Ramsey Talbot glanced around the group and laid his tricorne on the table. Not taking the seat Skye offered, he said sardonically, "D'ye know, I doubt that, my lord. But I'll give 'em to you, anyhow."

He spoke for fifteen minutes.

When the door closed behind him, there was a short silence.

"Zounds . . . ," muttered Admiral Anson. "I'd not realized it had gone that far."

Sir Jonas mopped his pale brow and said solemnly, "Hayes is right, gentlemen. We must act!"

They were, at last, in agreement, and there ensued a debate upon when, where, and how the action should take place. An hour later they were again agreed, if not quite unanimously.

November had arrived. The holiday season was fast approaching, and many members of the cabinet and the Horse Guards were already deep in festive plans. But action would be taken. After Christmas.

Having reached this decision they filed out well pleased with themselves, as evidenced by a burst of talk and cheerful laughter.

Admiral Anson, Lord Hayes, and Skye remained.

They looked at each other in silence.

The admiral shook his head.

The lieutenant, his dark eyes glittering wrath, swore under his breath.

Lord Hayes said softly, "My poor England . . . how does she ever survive?"

Chapter XVII

he wind was frigid, and occasional drops of sleet drove at Cranford's face as he rode towards London Bridge. It was stupid to be going down to Richmond again. Already the turnpike keepers at the toll gates were beginning to greet him like an old friend. It was a long ride, and were it not for the fact that he meant to be on hand in case Rossiter needed him, he'd take a room somewhere and stay down there. "And for what?" he thought gloomily. To hover about for hours on the lane leading to Lady Minerva Peckingham's estate, hoping to catch a glimpse of the sweet little face he missed so terribly? Stupid! But then, he seemed unusually adept at stupidity. He had, for example, imagined himself to be in love with Loretta Laxton, who had proven to be fickle and without kindness. And yet he could not look back on their brief *affaire de coeur* and fail to be grateful to the lady. She had, as his twin had tried to warn him, used him to advance herself socially, but whatever her reasons, for a little while she had made him happy. And, to be fair, his affection for her had been scarcely less shallow, to a large part built on pride that so admired a beauty would glance his way. Certainly, he had experienced not one iota of the deep hallowed devotion that is real love. A gentle, outrageous, unaffected, incredibly valiant country girl had brought him that wondrous joy, when she'd crept unbidden into his heart and made it her own.

He sighed heavily. But no more than Loretta did Zoe want him. His proposal had, in fact, embarrassed her. The memory made him wince, and he thought bitterly, 'Small wonder, you sorry fool,' and once more acknowledged that it was the height of stupidity to try again; to risk the deeper and final hurt.

He'd been stupid these past four days, to no avail. He never seemed to be there when Zoe drove out, but he was determined to persist, and to improve upon his first and so horribly clumsy proposal. This time, he would be smoothly assured; in full possession of himself. No halting, awkward words, none of that unmanning inward terror. Poised and debonair—as August might be at such a moment. He had several scenarios ready for use in the unlikely event he should encounter her. In the first, he would say airily that he'd just come down to discover how her brother went on—and pray she didn't simply tell him and drive on. In the second, he would be astounded, and say he'd been visiting friends and had not dreamt Lady Peckingham dwelt nearby. That one was a touch chancy, because she might ask him to name the friends . . . The third scheme called for his bringing a great bouquet of roses, dropping to one knee beside her coach, and telling her how much he adored . . . worshipped . . . loved her with all his heart. He sighed. Which was perfectly true. He'd actually bought the great bouquet of roses once, and they'd been dashed costly, because the season was done. They'd also been very cumbersome across his saddle bow, and had evoked some rude comments from stray children and a couple of impertinent yokels. He had scratched himself on the thorns, and on being splattered with the mud thrown up by a passing carriage it had dawned on him that if he knelt in the road, not only would Zoe not even be able to see him, but he'd likely get covered with mud and look a proper figure of fun as her coach rolled on past him. The fourth scenario made his throat close up with fright whenever he tried to rehearse it. So all he'd done thus far was to skulk about like a lovesick idiot and prepare himself for another rejection. It would be final, for in that dreadful event he must respect her decision, and abandon hope.

He was quite aware that the logical and most simple course would be to drive straight to Lady Peckingham's door and request to see her niece. But to be turned away from the front door seemed to him so horribly cold; a decision considered without setting eyes on him, and delivered through some disinterested household minion. Heaven knows, she'd made it plain that she didn't want him. On the ladder he'd thought for a moment . . . But she'd been somewhat hysterical and overcome with gratitude at that moment, because he'd come to help her. After the various uproars were over, she'd seemed to avoid his eyes, and when she did meet them, would look quickly away, as if even the sight of him offended. As Loretta had been offended . . . The thought made him cringe, but he forced himself to face it. Loretta could not be thought of in the same breath as his sparkling little Zoe, but . . . he must accept that a man with one foot was not the most spectacular matrimonial prospect . . .

On the other hand, he could still ride, and he rode well, thank goodness, and looked not too dreadful on horseback. In fact, Mitten had said— But Mitten was his sister, of course, and prejudiced. Morris wasn't prejudiced—was he? And Morris had said Zoe watched him when he wasn't looking at her. He brightened, and glancing at the big carriage that rolled past taking up much too much of the roadway, saw her.

His jaw dropped. *Zoe? Back in Town? What the devil . . . ?*

"Hey!" he yelled, reining around so abruptly that a following rider was almost unhorsed.

He spurred his mount to reckless speed, creating havoc in the morning traffic crowding London Bridge. "Hey!" he shouted again, ignoring the flood of uncomplimentary remarks that followed his thundering gallop.

Two dragoons rode ahead of the carriage. Drawing level, he saw that it carried the Horse Guards insignia on the panels, and glancing inside, saw joy—unmistakable joy—brighten a pair of beloved but rather shadowed green eyes.

"Hey!" he shouted for the third time.

The guard on the box glanced down at him indifferently. "What?"

"Where the deuce are you taking this lady?"

"Horse Guards."

"Why? What for?"

"Dunno."

"Is she under arrest?"

The guard's eyes narrowed. "No bread and butter o'yourn, mate. Get along."

"Get along, be damned!"

"Then get squashed," jeered the guard.

Cranford reined back in the nick of time and narrowly missed being run down, as a troop of dragoons clattered their juggernaut-like path through the vehicles.

Zoe's face was pressed against the window.

He took off his tricorne and waved it at her, and followed the carriage to Whitehall.

He was denied admission at the gate until he announced brusquely that he was Lieutenant Peregrine Cranford, late of the Fourteenth Light Dragoons, and nephew to General Lord Nugent Cranford, and that he had urgent business with "the occupant of that carriage."

His peg-leg was duly noted. His air of authority indisputable. His credentials acceptable. He was admitted.

Once inside the bustling corridors, his task began again, but at length he traced Zoe to a room fronting on Whitehall. The sergeant outside the door to General Underhill's office looked at him admiringly, but regretted that the general was interrogating a prisoner, and—

"The hell he is!" Cranford shoved him away, and was inside.

Looking very scared, small, and solitary, Zoe sat facing a slightly built general officer of late middle age, who stood leaning back against his desk while addressing her in a quiet but decidedly menacing fashion. He stood straight as Cranford burst in.

A major with a square resolute face and powerful shoulders was seated at a smaller side desk. He sprang up demanding wrathfully, "Who the devil are you, sir? And how dare you—"

Ignoring him, Cranford snapped, "I am Lieutenant Peregrine Cranford, General, formerly commanding an artillery battery attached to the Fourteenth Light Dragoons at Prestonpans. I am betrothed to this lady, and I demand to know why—"

Zoe stood, watching him as though he wore shining armour and carried the cross of Saint George.

The sergeant rushed in and seized Cranford by one arm. "Begging the general's pardon!"

"I should curst well think so," said Underhill. "Put him out!"

"I'll be back," shouted Cranford, struggling. "With my uncle, General Lord Nugent Cranford, and Lord Hayes of the East India Company! And"—he added, clinging to the door frame as the sergeant tried to drag him out—"the Earl of Bowers-Malden, who—"

"Wait!" General Underhill was smiling. "Let be, Sergeant. You may go."

Breathing hard, the sergeant closed the door behind him.

Zoe flew to stand beside Cranford and slip a cold little hand into his.

"In that case, your uncle and 'Frosty' Hayes being good

friends of mine, I must make allowances. Especially," Under-hill added, sitting down behind his desk, and nodding to the major who was evidently his aide, "especially since I'll own I've a soft spot in my heart for young lovers. Otherwise"—he waved a pen at Cranford and finished with a touch of steel—"I'd have you clapped into the stockade, young fella!"

"Since I am not on active service, General, I think that would be unlawful," said Cranford boldly. "As is this seizure of Miss Grainger. I presume you issued an order for her arrest?"

Underhill laid down his pen very gently. "Do not take that tone with me, Lieutenant! The young lady was good enough to come here to testify as—"

"I had no choice," interrupted Zoe. "Your horrid soldiers frightened my aunt half to death, and forced me—"

"Now, now, Miss," soothed the major. "You mustn't tell fibs, you know. Nobody forced you to do anything."

Cranford snapped, "Then she is free to go! I thank you!"

"You are high-handed," said the general, an angry glitter coming into his eyes. "But I suppose that fighting spirit won you your medals, eh?"

Zoe said wonderingly, "Why, Perry! I did not know—"

He seized her arm. "Very likely, sir. By your leave." With a short bow, he led Zoe to the door, saying clearly, "I must get word to the earl, before he roars in here. He was sending for his solicitors when I left."

As the door slammed behind them, the two officers looked at each other.

The general said grittily, "Damn and blast that confounded young pest!"

In the corridor, the sergeant came to attention. "Good day, sir!"

Cranford glanced at him and caught the suggestion of a grin. "Carry on, Sergeant," he said with a wink, and hurried Zoe out.

He wasted no time on talk, but called up a chair, instructed the bearers to go to the Bedford, and rode alongside. When they arrived at the coffee house, he entrusted his mare to a stableboy, and took Zoe into the dining room. Not until they were seated at a secluded table, and he'd ordered up a light luncheon did his pent-up anger explode. "Now pray tell me," he demanded, "how on earth it came about that those pompous military blockheads were permitted to make off with you, alone and unchaperoned. Have your aunt and your brother gone off to Brazil, perchance?"

"No, Perry, but—"

"Devil take it, Zoe! An I'm not about to keep an eye on you, you're no sooner out of one boiling cauldron than you've popped into another!"

"Oh, yes, Perry. But—"

"What the deuce did that old curmudgeon of a general want from you?"

"He wanted me to sign my original statement about that horrid accident."

"Did he, by Jove!"

"Yes. And I was also to swear that there was no truth in what you said about the League of Jewelled Men, and that their ladyships had nothing to do with any of it."

He growled, "Silly block! How could they have nothing to do with it, if it didn't exist in the first place?"

"Exactly so." She leaned across the table, and said fervently, "But never mind all that. Oh, Perry! How brave you are! I have worried so about your poor hand. Is it healing well?"

"As good as new," he said. In point of fact, he had spent an extremely unpleasant hour in the surgery of an irascible doctor named James Knight, who Furlong insisted was one of the finest men in London. He was probably correct, because although Dr. Knight had grumbled that by all rights Cranford would never be able to move his fingers again, that unhappy condition had not materialized, and his hand, although still bandaged, was healing rapidly. He shouldn't have made light of the injury, he thought belatedly. A fellow with more experience in *affaires de coeur* would have nobly hinted at the misery he'd endured, and won her sympathy. So much for being smooth and poised! He was just no good at this romance business, and would probably never summon the fortitude to put any of his scenarios to the test.

With the colour restored to her satiny smooth cheeks Zoe seemed to him the embodiment of youth and springtime. She was gazing at him in such a way that he had to remind himself that such a glowing look was inspired by gratitude, and he tried not to hear the small voice that named him a wooden-head for not taking advantage of it.

The waiter returned with succulent slices of cold ham, bread still warm from the oven, two cheeses, fruits, and little iced cakes. Zoe ate heartily, with none of the coy restraint expected of a maiden. He thought, 'She'll be a plump little married lady, like Mama, with happy children gathered about her,' and the picture gave him such a pang that he had to devote himself to his food and not look at her.

When her hunger was somewhat appeased, she told him that Travis had been asleep in his bed when the soldiers came at seven o'clock this morning, and that poor Lady Peckingham had been terrified when informed that her niece was required in Town on a matter involving High Treason. "I told Gorton to send Cecil to find you," she said shyly. "I hope 'twas not an imposition, but Travis is far from well, and would only make himself worse if he had to stand up to another military interrogation. And I could not appeal to poor Sir Owen. How does he go on?"

He thought, 'So I was third choice . . .' Furlong was not making quite such a good recovery as they had hoped, which his doctor said was due to the effects of the earlier bout of fever he had suffered. Cranford had his own ideas on the subject, but he assured Zoe that Sir Owen was going along nicely.

"Thank goodness! Peregrine, I owe you so much, and truly I am grateful. However may I thank you for once again coming to my rescue?"

Gratitude again! He said curtly, "By not feeling that thanks are required. Now, to be more sensible, we must decide what is to be done. I cannot feel you are properly protected with your aunt. I mean to take you to The Palfreys to stay with my sister. Farrar, my brother-in-law is a grand fellow, and—"

"Yes. You have told me about him. But—surely it would not be quite . . . proper? I mean, we are not really . . . what you told General Underhill."

He had said they were betrothed. He thought, 'Now is the moment!'

Zoe looked up at him, her cheeks even more pink, and murmured, "Indeed, I was surprised you would say—such a thing."

"Oh. Well—er, 'twas all I could think to say to justify my presence there. I apologize if I caused you to be embarrassed. I did not mean—"

"No. No, I know you did not."

She was avoiding his eyes again. Lord, why could he not be smooth-tongued and romantical for her, instead of making a proper mare's nest of it? His voice sounded harsh when he said, "Then you will come?"

For a moment she did not answer, then she said quietly, "If you think it wise. But I must send word to my aunt, and Travis. They will be very worried."

"I'll do that. Are you ready? I'll hire a coach and we can leave for Romsey at once."

"Romsey! But—that's miles and miles! We could not reach there tonight, surely? It—it would not be proper."

"No," he admitted with a sigh. " 'Fraid you're right, and

I'm a dunce. Nothing for it, then. I'll take you down to Richmond, and perhaps your aunt will let me— Gad! What a lame-brain! The Rossiters are back in Town! You can stay with Gideon and his wife! At least for tonight. We can make more permanent arrangements tomorrow."

"A bridal couple? Are you sure . . . ?"

"Lord, yes. They've known each other forever. Childhood sweethearts, you know. Not as if they'd just recently . . ." Her innocent gaze rested on him wonderingly. He felt himself colouring up, and stammered, "er, f-fallen . . . in love. I can—er, take you there now. At once!"

"Oh," said Zoe.

She looked rather downcast. He said, "Unless there was something else you would like to do?"

"I had hoped," she said wistfully, "to go down by the river again."

His heart gave such a leap that he wondered she did not see it. In view of what had happened the last time they had been by the river, he thought it a decidedly promising sign. But he must not build on it too much. He paid their shot, and, leaving his mare in the stables, hired a hackney coach.

At the Savoy Stairs he handed Zoe down and offered his arm. The afternoon had become even more chill, and the wind was bitter as they strolled along the bank. The sleet had stopped at least, but it was, he knew, a terrible time to approach her again. He should wait for a bright Spring day, when her life had become less troubled; or at least until her brother was recovered. Come to think of it, he had no least right to speak to her without first obtaining Travis Grainger's permission. Travis Grainger! Gad! Who'd ever have thought—

Zoe asked gently, "Why do you smile, Peregrine? You have been so quiet. Are you angry with me for running you into so much trouble?"

"Angry!" He drew her to a halt. How anxious she looked.

How sweet and altogether adorable. He loved her so much that if she said no this time, he really would not be able to go on living. He croaked, "Might we . . . stop? Just for a minute. I mean—"

"Of course. Is it your leg? Oh, dear! A lady is not supposed to speak of such—er, articles, is she?"

"No, but you're not a lady. Oh, God! What I mean is—Don't be cross! Please do not! What I mean to say is—is that you're just a country—er, you're not—you don't—" Without a trace of smooth poise, he gabbled, "I mean—you're just like my mother!" And wished he had hurled himself to a watery grave.

Zoe looked at him. She was like . . . his *mother?* It was certainly better than being a "diversion." Especially if he held his mama in deep affection. But scarcely a romantic declaration. Probably, she had embarrassed him by suggesting they come down to the river; to the riverbank that must always be so very dear to her heart. And then she had confirmed her lack of proper behaviour by speaking of his—limb, and embarrassed him still more. In an attempt to put him at his ease, she gazed out at the river. If only she had just a little of Maria's easy charm. Lovely Maria, who had betrayed her, and so brutally shot down poor Sir Owen. The river traffic was as busy as ever. The water looked grey and cold today. Some ducks were swimming about, and she murmured absently, "I wonder if their feet get cold."

Furtively mopping his brow, Cranford gulped, "Whose?"

"The ducks."

He glanced at them. If their feet weren't cold, his certainly were. Was. She was probably cold, too. And what was the use? It was hopeless. *He* was hopeless. Despairing, he said miserably, "We'd best go. The wind is too cold for you."

She said, "Yes," and feeling twenty years older, started to turn back.

"*No!*"

Shocked by his shout, she looked up at him.

"No," he said again. "Do not look at me, Zoe. I m-mean Miss Grainger. Look at—look at . . . the ducks. That—er, scrawny fellow trailing along there, do you see?"

Bewildered, she said, "Why, yes, but—"

"No. Don't turn your head." His hands were wet. He felt a little sick. But watching the curve of the smooth cheek against her hood, he leaned closer and said, "When—when I d-dared to offer for you, you— Morris said . . . he said you didn't believe I meant it."

Zoe began to tremble. She faltered, "Well, I knew . . . you only thought of me as a—diversion, so—"

"As a—*what*? No—don't look at me!"

"A—diversion, Lady Julia said. To take your mind off— your beautiful lady."

"My beautiful . . . ? Who on earth— Oh! Do you mean Miss *Laxton*?"

She said helplessly, "I did not mind. Really. I know I'm not pretty. And—and I have . . . silly romantic notions, and—no Town polish, and—" Despite herself tears were beading on her lashes, and her voice broke. She gulped, "And I say things . . . ladies should not—"

"And because of that, you doubted my sincerity."

She nodded.

Cranford took a deep breath. It was, he thought, The Right Time! And, heartened, he dared Scheme Four.

Leaning very close to that smooth cheek, he said softly, "Little Zoe, my sweet country maid, my lovely and kind and courageous innocent . . .

> *"Doubt thou the stars are fire;*
> *Doubt that the sun doth move;*
> *Doubt truth to be a liar;*
> *But never doubt I love."*

Zoe turned her head then, her eyes swimming with tears, yet bright with a joy that dazzled him. "Oh, *Perry!* How very . . . *beautiful!* And you said *I* was romantical!"

Cupping her face between his hands, he felt suddenly as poised and self-assured as a dozen August Falcons. He said tenderly, "I'll never have two feet, my darling, and you'll have to endure hearing me thump about on this silly wooden peg. But I can offer you a nice home, and the comforts—if not the elegancies of life. And my heart. Dearest, *dearest* Zoe. Won't you please at least consider this 'horrid doctor' who loves you so very—"

"Oh, Perry!" she sobbed, reaching out her arms. "I thought you didn't want me!"

There was only one answer to that . . .

A passing tug hooted repeatedly.

Shouts and whistles came from two ocean-going barges.

Outraged faces stared down from the windows of passing carriages.

The ducks with their cold feet paddled on, undisturbed.

And Peregrine Cranford, his lips pressed to those of the country maiden he adored, banished all her doubts. Forever.